Annihilation

Hailing from Sioux Falls, South Dakota, Megan DeVos is twenty-six years old and works as a Registered Nurse in the operating room. Her debut *Anarchy* series amassed over 30 million reads on Wattpad, winning the Watty Award in 2014.

THE ANARCHY SERIES

Anarchy
Loyalty
Revolution
Annihilation

MEGAN DEVOS

ORION

First published in Great Britain in 2018 by Orion Books,
an imprint of The Orion Publishing Group Ltd
Carmelite House, 50 Victoria Embankment
London EC4Y 0DZ

An Hachette UK Company

1 3 5 7 9 10 8 6 4 2

A CIP catalogue record for this book is
available from the British Library.

ISBN 978 1 4091 8390 7

Typeset by Input Data Services Ltd, Somerset

Printed and bound in Great Britain by Clays Ltd, Elcograf S.p.A.

www.orionbooks.co.uk

For my mother, who never got
to read this but still believed
in me all the same.

One: Peril

Grace

A deafening *bang* ripped through the air the moment my finger put pressure on the trigger, launching a bullet from the chamber of my gun. Everything seemed to freeze around me as I stood locked in place, somehow still standing despite being torn to shreds on the inside.

It was surely impossible, but in that moment, I could have sworn I saw the bullet as it sliced smoothly through the air. My eyes stayed fixed on it, riveted and horrified all at once, as the distance between it and the gun increased more and more. A strange buzzing sounded in my ears, blocking out everything but that odd, muffled noise that crept its way into my brain, as the bullet met an obstacle.

The sound I should have heard was the bullet making contact with a human chest. It should have sounded heavy, wet, painful. There should have been a ripping of flesh, a gush of blood, maybe a crack or two of bone.

The muffled sound only grew louder, threatening to suffocate me and press me down into the dirt.

Though my ears couldn't hear it, my eyes could see it. I stood captivated in the worst way as I watched the bullet rip through his shirt, his skin, his muscle. It hit in the most lethal place, directly over his heart, before making its way through the heart itself. A shiver ran through my body as blood immediately filled the hole, soaking his shirt and dripping to the ground as he plummeted to his knees, face paling more and more by the second.

Blank, lifeless eyes seemed to lock on to my own as his body hovered for a moment, caught between the balance of standing and falling down. My stomach churned as I watched, unable to look away even though I so desperately wanted to. That tiny fraction of time ended as his body fell forward, landing with a solid thump in the dirt. Dust rose from the ground to mix with the smoke already obscuring the air, adding an ominous haze so reminiscent of the terrible act I'd just committed.

His chest didn't move as he lay face down on the ground; the blood was pooling so quickly around him that I already knew it was too late to go back.

I knew what I'd done.

Just like that, Jonah was dead.

I sucked in a harsh breath, inhaling smoke and dirt alike, but I was still unable to move. My muscles stayed firm, locked into place. Every beat of my heart felt like it was pumping knives through my veins, then working their way through my skin, piercing wherever they could reach until I was a bloody, battered mess.

I couldn't tear my eyes away from where Jonah had landed. The deep red of the blood seemed to burn into my brain, and the stark contrast of his quickly paling body only made it seem more drastic. I couldn't see his face, but I didn't need to; the last, silently pleading look he'd given me followed by the flat, lifeless one as he fell would be cemented into my memory forever, never to be forgotten.

Another image suddenly shoved its way through my mind. It was that of decaying bodies, some dismembered and some rotten, piled in a corner like rags. It was that of hands severed from their limbs, with spikes spearing through them to pin them to the walls. It was that of threatening words scrawled on the walls in the blood of those bodies that haunted me. Before my eyes, Jonah's body morphed into one of them, my mind tormenting me and playing tricks as payment for what I'd done.

I'd killed my own brother.

Still, I was unable to move, though I felt a prominent shake set into my body. My hands quivered in front of me, unable to lower the gun or even move my arms. Still, I could hear nothing, though I knew the world around me must have been filled with chaotic noise. I could see nothing but the oppressive haze and the blood surrounding Jonah's lifeless body, not that I could rip my eyes away. I felt bile creeping up my throat as my body rebelled against me, but I couldn't even manage to lean over and expel it.

I could feel my mind shutting down, desperate to spare me from realising what I'd done. My hands were shaking so badly now I thought I might actually drop my gun, and my legs felt like they might collapse at any moment. Air ripped so harshly through my lungs that it was painful, and my heart was either beating wildly or not at all.

I couldn't even tell.

Just when I was about to lose all hope and give in to the crushing agony threatening to overtake me, I saw a figure appear out of the cloud of dust and smoke. A familiar hand closed around mine as he took my gun from me. His long fingers intertwined with mine as he tugged on my arm, wasting no time in taking me away from the evidence of what I'd done.

The heat of his touch seemed to snap me out of everything, and the sound came crashing down so quickly it was like someone had lifted a vacuum from around me. My feet stayed rooted in place as all my senses started to function once again, and his grip on my arm jerked my body sideways. His voice reached me as I watched his lips move in complete shock.

Hayden.

'We have to go, Grace.'

His voice was laced with urgency and resolve, and it was clear he was trying to remain as calm as possible for my sake, but his desperation to get us out of there was more than apparent.

'Grace, come on, move,' he urged, tugging on my arm when I continued to stare at him. I couldn't seem to process anything, and my mind felt hazy with either too many thoughts or too few.

Again, I couldn't move even though I could now hear the relentless noise. Gunfire, shouting, fighting, burning, and other noises bombarded me from all directions, their volume magnified times a hundred in comparison to the odd buzzing silence I'd heard moments ago.

'Jesus Christ,' Hayden muttered lowly.

I watched blankly as he stashed our guns behind his back before stooping quickly in front of me. I didn't have time to realise what he was doing before I felt his arms wrap around me, lifting me off my feet. He draped my legs over one of his arms while he threw my arms around his neck, holding me firmly against his chest as he started to run.

He moved quickly, and it was obvious we were still in great danger from the urgency of his actions, but still I couldn't react. Each step he took felt like a jarring blow to my body as the emotional pain manifested into physical. Even though I wasn't hurt, it felt like it as Hayden carried me away.

'Hang on, Grace,' he instructed as calmly as he could.

I managed to tighten my arms slightly, but it wasn't enough to keep my weight from shifting around as he ran as fast as possible. When a high-pitched whistle whizzed just inches above our heads, I realised how real the danger actually was. I sucked in a harsh breath and blinked furiously, clearing my head for the first time since I'd pulled the trigger.

'Put me down,' I gasped.

Hayden let out a sigh of relief that I suspected had nothing to do with carrying me and everything to do with me finally snapping out of my trance. He set me down as quickly and gently as possible. Then, he grabbed my hand and tugged once more, taking off at a sprint as I finally managed to make my limbs cooperate. He whipped a gun from behind his back and handed it to me before taking the other for himself.

Another whizzing bullet narrowly missed us as we tore along the street, which was strewn with more debris and obstacles than before. Horror twisted at my stomach as I realised Hayden and I were fleeing alone.

'Where are—'

'Duck!' Hayden shouted, cutting me off as his hand yanked me to the ground.

He barely managed to throw his body over mine, pressing his chest to my back, as yet another familiar high-pitched whistling sounded above us. Just as before, it was followed almost immediately by a deafening boom as something crashed into the pile of rubble in front of us, springing fire and debris into the air from the explosion.

Apparently the Brutes had more ammunition for their bazooka.

I coughed and sputtered a few times, pawing at my eyes to get the dirt out of them. Hayden recovered more quickly, wasting no time in hauling me back on my feet.

'Come on!' he urged, shooting a fleeting glance over his shoulder.

Again, we started sprinting. The air was even thicker than before, thanks to the fresh disturbance, making it even more difficult to see and breathe. I tugged my shirt up around my nose to filter the air, but my tank top offered little protection. Hayden's grip was tighter than ever on my hand as he led me through the fray, dodging debris and heavy fire with every step. Gunshots echoed around the space and bullets whizzed past us, but the new smoke and dust gave us cover we had desperately needed.

We ran, desperate to know where Kit and Dax had gone but not brave enough to ask and find out. We seemed to run forever. The sounds never went away and the blanketing dust was relentless. I was about to suggest we figure out a new plan when I heard a screeching of tyres on pavement not too far ahead of us.

'There,' Hayden muttered quickly, picking up the pace.

I could hear muffled shouting from behind us as the Brutes and whoever was left of Jonah's crew pursued, but the familiar rumble of an engine was closer, calling me to it through the haze. Finally, I could make out the vague outline of the jeep, though it was impossible to tell who was inside.

'Is it them?' I asked, coughing yet again as I squinted towards the vehicle.

'I don't know,' Hayden admitted gruffly.

Together, we ran and closed the remaining distance between us and the car. I felt like my heart was about to pound out of my chest in anticipation as I tried desperately to identify the driver. For a moment, it had occurred to me that whoever it was might not have been our friends but enemies waiting to kill us.

My fears were placated, however, when I saw Kit behind

the wheel. A huge breath of relief pushed from my lungs as I saw him waiting, urging us on with waves of his hand. But I couldn't see Dax anywhere in the car.

Hayden and I skidded to a halt right outside the door, sending dirt flying beneath our feet. He whipped open the door and practically threw me in before following, leaning forward urgently between the seats to shout instructions at Kit.

'Go, go!' he shouted. 'We have to find Dax!'

'I don't know where he is,' Kit said quickly, stress radiating from his tone.

My stomach dropped like a rock, terrified. Dax couldn't be dead, right? He'd survived this long; it didn't seem possible that he wouldn't make it out now.

'He's got to be out there still,' I said, shaking my head firmly. 'We'll find him.'

Hayden shot me an anxious look over his shoulder and placed his hand on my thigh, squeezing tightly as if clinging to the hope I was right.

'Let's go, we have to look,' Hayden instructed. 'Drive!'

Kit obeyed immediately and slammed his foot down on the pedal, bringing smoke from the tyres as the jeep shot forward. Hayden's shoulder collided roughly with mine before he managed to right himself as Kit whipped the vehicle around.

'You two better be ready to shoot,' Kit muttered darkly, squinting tightly to try and view the road ahead.

I nodded sharply even though he wouldn't see and released the magazine on my gun to check my ammo. I knew only one bullet would be missing. I'd fired once, and that bullet was now firmly buried in Jonah's chest.

Almost immediately, the loud bangs of gunfire sounded around us, and the familiar crunch of metal echoed out as the bullets missed us but ripped through the jeep.

'Dax!' Hayden called, leaning out of the window before firing a shot into the smoke.

Kit honked the horn and called out Dax's name as well. All the noise would only draw more attention to us, but everyone knew it was necessary to try to find our friend.

'Dax!'

Again and again, we called his name. Kit manoeuvred the jeep as quickly as he could around the area, narrowly missing buildings, debris, and missing chunks of road. Again and again, Hayden and I fired into basically nothing. Our targets were hidden from us, just as we were from them, except the people we were firing at weren't driving around in a raucous jeep while shouting.

'*Dax!*'

My voice was laced with fear and frustration, squinting and listening carefully for any sort of reply, but it was almost impossible to hear over the chaos consuming everything around us.

I could feel the fear that we wouldn't find him creeping up, but I forced it down as I reloaded my gun and fired once more. Hayden seemed to be growing increasingly anxious beside me as well, and I noticed him firing his gun more and more often as his fear countered his usual reluctance to kill.

'Where the hell are you?' Hayden muttered impatiently. His knee jumped up and down beside me as his leg bounced nervously. '*Dax, Jesus Christ!*' Hayden roared. He sounded angry with frustration and desperation.

'I don't see him anywhere,' Kit admitted tightly, face contorted in deep concern. He whipped the jeep around for what felt like the hundredth time as yet more bullets whizzed by us.

'We can't leave him,' Hayden snapped angrily.

'I didn't say that—'

'You were about to—'

'No, I—' Kit was cut off by a different voice this time, which sent a wave of careful hope rushing through me.

'Over here!'

'Dax?!' Hayden shouted, rigidly alert as he heard what I did.

'I'm here!'

This time it was more than obvious that we'd all heard him. I sagged with relief immediately as I identified the voice.

Dax.

'I see him!' I shouted, leaning forward suddenly and pointing straight ahead.

He was no more than a shadowy figure, but I could see him standing about twenty feet away, waving his arms while coughing in the smoke and dust. Kit accelerated even more before slamming on the brakes, sending Hayden and I crashing into the seat backs before snapping backward.

'Try not to kill us,' Hayden snapped again, clearly still on edge.

I hardly had time to absorb his words. I watched as Dax moved as quickly as possible, hindered by a heavy limp and a shockingly large amount of blood pouring from somewhere unidentified. He reached the side of the door and fumbled with the handle before Hayden leaned over the seat and threw it open. Dax winced as he climbed inside, pulling the door shut, not even a second before Kit hit the accelerator and whipped away again.

I could feel no relief as I saw Dax's shockingly pale face. There was no hint of his usual smile or lightness; only extreme pain and obvious injury registered there.

'What happened?' Hayden demanded, leaning forward to study him.

I followed the trail of blood with my eyes, raking down his left arm, noting the bloody bandage at the end concealing whatever lay beneath.

Dax didn't reply as he leaned his head back against the headrest and blew out a deep breath, eyes closed tightly. His breath was shaky and uneven, but at least he was breathing. Kit cast a worried glance across the console as he drove, and I was relieved to hear the sounds of gunfire and shouting getting softer and softer as we finally managed to pull away from the chaos.

'Dax!' Hayden hissed, frustrated with his lack of response. Fear and anxiety were clearly written across his face as I glanced at him quickly before refocusing on Dax.

'Bloody Brutes, mate,' Dax muttered, grimacing in pain as the jeep hit a divot in the road.

My eyes returned to the bandage at the end of his arm, and my mind was instantly flooded with the same horrific images from before.

Decaying hands nailed to the wall.

Severed limbs ending in ragged stumps.

Thieves.

Thieves.

Thieves.

I suddenly squeezed my eyes shut as I sucked in a terrified breath. My nightmares and reality were starting to mix before my eyes, and there was nothing I could do to stop it.

'Grace.'

My eyes snapped open at the sound of Hayden's voice. I blinked a few times to find him studying me closely, and I felt the heat of his hand on my leg once more. His thumb rolled over my thigh before he squeezed once, concern written across his face as he watched me beneath lowered brows.

'It's okay,' he mouthed, giving me a slow, reassuring nod. I gave a shaky nod in return and tried to hold it together.

Again, I forced myself to look at Dax and focus on my medical training.

'Dax, what happened?' I asked as calmly as I could.

Again, he didn't reply, but he finally opened his eyes and lifted his head from the seat. With a slightly unsteady hand, he reached to unwind the makeshift bandage from his left arm. I watched, transfixed and horrified, as bloody layer after bloody layer was removed. I was all but convinced I was going to see a rotten stump of an arm by the time he finally removed it.

But instead of the shocking stump I'd been expecting, I saw a battered, bloody hand. His pinkie and ring finger were gone, severed by an obviously sharp weapon, and the middle finger was bleeding badly, but the rest of it was there.

'Jesus Christ . . .' Hayden muttered as he stared, lips parting in shock.

'You're telling me,' Dax muttered bitterly. He paused for a few moments before continuing. 'At least it wasn't my good hand.'

I let out an oddly relieved gasp of a laugh. Dax had lost two fingers and gained a limp, but I could see no other obvious signs of injury or bleeding. If he could already make a joke, I dared hope that it meant he'd be okay.

'You don't need two full hands anyway, mate,' Kit said lightly from the driver's seat, also obviously relieved.

'Just good old Righty,' Dax said, waving it weakly by his side. I groaned as I realised what he meant.

'Dear God, Dax, it's been minutes and you're already making jokes,' I said.

I was surprised by that flicker of amusement, but it didn't last long as the cold, heavy truth of everything we'd just been through crashed back down on me. I collapsed back into the seat and let out the deepest sigh yet, closing my eyes now that I knew Dax probably wasn't going to die.

We might have all survived, but one person had not.

Jonah.

It was only a few seconds before I felt Hayden shift beside me. He looped his arm around my shoulders and hauled me onto his lap. There, in the back of the jeep, I curled into a ball on his lap, hiding my face in his chest as his strong arms held me as closely as he could manage. I felt the warm heat of his lips at my ear and heard the soft whisper of his voice.

'I love you, Bear.'

I could feel my body starting to shake as reality set in all over again. My throat burned and my eyes felt hot, but no tears came. Instinctively, I wrapped my arms around Hayden's chest, hugging him as tightly as I could manage while he held me securely.

'It's okay, you're okay,' he murmured, continuing even though I couldn't manage to respond.

His fingers drifted over my skin wherever he could reach, comforting me and soothing me when I so desperately needed it. Even when Kit hit a bump in the road, Hayden held me still, protecting me in every way he could. My fingers twisted into the now ragged fabric of his shirt, desperate to haul him even closer and revel in the comforting warmth he provided.

'I'm so proud of you, Grace.'

I bit my lower lip as I drew a shuddering breath. I felt tears pricking at my eyes now. His words were hushed and just loud enough for me and only me to hear. He murmured things over and over, never stopping even though I didn't reply. The entire ride back to Blackwing, Hayden held me and whispered, doing his very best to comfort me after what he knew I'd done.

'You're so strong, Bear.'

Every word he spoke wrenched the tears closer and closer to the surface. A single choking sob escaped from my lips before I succumbed to them – they were oddly silent, yet no less painful as they burned me from the inside out. Hayden's grip tightened on me even more when he realised I'd finally given in, and still his gentle words continued.

'I love you so much.'

It was finally over and done with.

I had been strong enough to finally do it, but in that moment, I had never felt weaker.

Two: Masochism

Hayden

I held Grace on my lap. Her arms were wound tightly around my chest as she hugged me, burying herself as far as she could in my arms. My shirt was now dotted with warm, wet tears as she cried silently. Quiet murmuring streamed past my lips in a constant flow, but I wasn't sure she even heard my words in her distraught state. I couldn't blame her; she'd just done potentially the hardest thing she'd ever had to do in her entire life.

I never felt more inadequate at comforting her than at that moment.

'It's all right, love,' I whispered again, lips fumbling at her ear as I cradled her even closer.

My hand ran over whatever part of her I could reach, and I tucked my face in the crook between her shoulder and her neck to shield us from the world as much as possible. I so desperately wanted to get back to camp so I could take her back to our hut; I knew she was holding back, fighting off the complete breakdown surely working up inside of her, and I knew she wouldn't fully let go until we were alone.

She felt so fragile in my arms now, as if every bump of the jeep would shatter her from the inside out. I could practically feel her pain, leaking out through her skin before ripping through mine and settling down to my bones.

The car was silent as Kit raced back to Blackwing. Dax seemed to be focusing on blocking out the pain in his hand. His weak attempt at humour had disappeared moments after I'd pulled Grace into my arms, and he'd closed his eyes to shut out the world. Kit focused on the road, driving as quickly as possible without putting us in danger.

My lips pressed into Grace's temple as I felt the jeep hit rougher terrain, meaning we were finally creeping into the trees surrounding camp. We would be home soon, and I could finally take Grace to be alone. Dax let out a quiet hiss from the front seat as Kit hit a tussocky patch. Grace hardly moved as I held her firmly, buffering the roughness of the road. Finally, I felt Kit start to slow the vehicle before stopping it completely and killing the engine.

A sigh of relief pushed past my lips as I sat up and blinked. A rather large group of people had surrounded the jeep, their familiar faces anxious as they waited to see who had returned. I wasn't surprised to see Docc, his face somehow calm and intense all at once. Malin was there too, and she rushed to greet Kit as soon as he exited the jeep. He accepted her hug readily and spent several long moments relaxing into her body.

When Dax made no move to leave the jeep, Docc stepped forward with Leutie on his heels. She looked relieved when she saw we'd all returned, but concern crossed her features as soon as she noticed Dax's reluctance to move and the way Grace was cradled in my lap. She appeared torn over who to greet first and surprised me by pulling open the door to the back from where Grace and I had yet to move.

Leutie's eyes darted to Dax in the front, who was being helped out by Docc, before she spoke.

'Oh my god, is she okay?' she asked, voice filled with fear and concern.

That was an odd question. I knew very well that the answer was no, she was not okay. However, I knew Leutie meant in a physical sense, in which case she was all right aside from a few cuts and bruises.

Grace sniffed against my chest but didn't reply. I suspected she'd fallen back into her sort of trance-like shock from before.

'She did it,' I answered, ignoring her first question.

'Oh, Grace . . .' Leutie said softly, features falling into one of understanding and sadness.

She backed up from the jeep as I inclined my head, gesturing her out of the way. Slowly, carefully, I shifted both our weight until I placed my feet on the ground and pulled us both out of the jeep. I carried her the way I had before – legs draped over my arm, her arms looped around my neck – and took a few steps forward. Her face was buried in my neck, shielded from the world around us. A quick glance over my shoulder told me Docc was helping Dax into the infirmary and that Kit had separated himself from Malin to assist.

'See if you can help them, Leutie,' I told her. My voice was flat, unable to muster my usually commanding tone.

'Okay,' she replied with a quick nod. She paused awkwardly and opened her mouth before snapping it shut again. Her eyes darted to Grace in my arms, unsure of what to say. 'Grace, I'm here if you want to talk, okay?'

Again, Grace didn't reply as I held her.

'Thanks, Leutie,' I answered for her. She gave a small nod and cast one last sad look at Grace's dejected figure before darting after Docc, Dax, and Kit.

I started walking without a word to anyone else, moving towards our hut as quickly as I could without jostling her. A small wave of relief washed through me when Grace tightened her arms around me, before relaxing once more. She had yet to say much of anything, but that small gesture told me she at least was listening.

'We're going home, Grace,' I whispered to her. Again, she gave a subtle movement by nodding slowly. I felt the need to keep up a string of constant reassurance in her silence. 'We'll be alone soon. Only a little longer,' I murmured.

We passed a few people on the way, all of whom shot confused then sympathetic looks at Grace's huddled figure in my arms. It seemed that even though we hadn't told anyone of our plan, word had spread through Blackwing.

If she didn't already have the respect of everyone in my camp, she did now. She'd made the greatest sacrifice of them all to save everyone, and that was not lost on them. Again, I felt a surge of pride that I could call her mine.

This strong, determined, amazingly selfless woman was mine, just as I was hers.

'I love you, Grace,' I whispered, my throat tight with emotion.

Again, she gave a weak squeeze of her arms around my neck in response. I knew she probably wouldn't speak for a while; having just gone through a major grieving process with Jett, I understood, even if there were some glaringly large differences between the situations. While it was never easy to lose someone, Grace's loss carried an even heavier weight, as she'd been the one to cause it.

Finally, we arrived back at our hut. I moved carefully through the doorframe and shut the door behind me. I set her down gently on our bed. The mattress sagged beneath her weight, and I knelt down in front of her to study her.

Her face looked flat and blank, and her eyes were dry even though I knew she'd cried earlier. They were unfocused and aiming somewhere between us, as if she couldn't manage to look at me. Slightly parted lips blew out slow, even breaths, and the usual natural colour to her skin was all but gone. Slowly, I reached a hand up to run my fingers across her cheek before hitching them under her chin.

'Grace,' I murmured softly, guiding her gaze to me. She blinked once but didn't really do much else. A painful pang struck my heart as I watched her, clearly numb and broken.

'Babe, look at me,' I continued as gently as possible. Her eyes blinked once more before she finally managed to meet my gaze. My thumb drifted slowly across her jaw. 'I know you're hurt and I completely understand that this will take a while to get over, but just know you had to do it. It had to be this way, even if it's hard to see that now. You saved hundreds of people, Grace. Hundreds. And I could not love you any more than I do right now.'

I felt myself getting emotional, and my throat burned slightly as I spoke, but I meant every single word and knew she needed to hear it. She was shutting down, locking herself in her head, and I knew she'd have trouble remembering why this had had to be done in the first place. The last thing I wanted was for her to regret something that everyone knew was for the greater good.

She drew a shaky breath and seemed to feel the intensity of the moment, because the numb, blank look was replaced with a more intent one as she hung on to my every word.

'You don't have to say anything, all right? You were there for me and I'm going to be here for you. Just let me take care of you.'

She gave a small nod as she tugged her lower lip into her mouth. I tried to give her a reassuring smile but it felt sad on my face, so I gave up and let my fingers tickle across her skin as I tucked a loose strand of hair behind her ear. It was only then that I noticed the flecks of blood streaked across her cheeks and the bruise forming on her jaw. She didn't appear to be bleeding any longer, but the legacy of the fight she'd put up were obvious.

'Let's get you cleaned up,' I murmured quietly. Again, she gave a small nod.

I stood from in front of her and grabbed her hand, guiding her to her feet. She allowed me to lead her into the bathroom, where it was just light enough to see what I was doing but dark enough to give the room a calm feeling. Again, I faced her and let my hands fall to her hips; she never took her gaze from my face, watching my every move.

My fingers tucked beneath the hem of her shirt, feeling the warmth of her skin across the backs of my hands as I started to lift it upward.

'Arms up,' I instructed softly.

She obeyed and raised her arms above her head, allowing me to slip the fabric over her body slowly. Every inch of skin that was revealed was damaged in some way, as nearly her entire left side revealed the long, jagged scar she'd sustained ages ago when she broke her rib. Once the shirt was free of her torso, the scar directly over her heart was visible, too.

Without thinking, I ducked my head, pressing my lips lightly over the rough edge in her skin. I let the kiss really sink into her scar before moving lower. Again and again, I pressed my lips to the rough scars and uneven flaws. When my lips reached her hipbone, I pressed one last kiss before standing back up in front of her. Her eyes were closed and a single tear had slipped from her eye, wetting a trail down her cheek. Even now, pain was radiating from her. I wanted her to feel loved, warm, beautiful. I wanted her to feel all the things she so deserved, because I knew she wasn't feeling any of them at that moment.

I sighed once, feeling inadequate and unworthy of her as

my fingers traced around her hips and started to undo her shorts before dropping them to the floor, taking her underwear with them. Still, she didn't open her eyes. She barely shifted her weight to kick away her clothes.

She stood before me now, naked, broken, vulnerable. Again, I felt her pain as if it were ripping through my own body, burning me from the inside out with nothing to stifle the searing agony. I moved quickly to remove my own clothes, casting them aside before regaining my touch on her hips. Slowly, I guided her under the shower, where she finally opened her eyes, though she remained silent.

When I pulled the tab to start the shower, she hardly reacted. Immediately, the cold water poured over us, drenching our skin and lifting some of the dark red blood from Grace's flesh. I raised my hand from her hip to brush it away, sending burgundy-tinged ribbons dripping down her body before they disappeared down the drain. She stood perfectly still, not reacting at all as I moved slowly and carefully, making sure to clean every speck of dirt and blood from her body without hurting her.

The filth from my own body washed away as well, and soon, we were both left clean. The air around us seemed loaded with so many words that weren't being said, weighing down around us heavily with the water from above. I knew the shower was about to run out, but I couldn't manage to pull myself away from her just yet. Her beautiful green eyes were locked on mine as she stood inches away, as she let me pet my fingers gently across her skin. She made no move to touch me or do much of anything, still too numb to act.

When the shower gave a final sputter and stopped altogether, I let out a low sigh and shifted us backward before grabbing two towels. I wrapped mine quickly around my waist before looping hers around her shoulders, shrouding her with it. My hands moved gently over her body, drying her skin as best I could. Once I was satisfied, I linked my hand with hers again and led her back into the room. She let me pull her back near our bed, where I tore myself from her to collect clothes.

Just as before, I repeated the process in reverse as I dressed her. She obeyed my whispered instructions silently, lifting her arms and feet when I needed her to without a word. When we were both dry and dressed as much as was necessary for bed, I let out a sigh of relief. *Finally,* I would be able to hold her like I'd been dying to since everything happened.

'Come on, Bear,' I soothed, taking her hand yet again and guiding her into bed.

I lifted back the covers and let her crawl in before following, sinking in to the mattress with her. She shifted to face me as I drew the covers up around us, cutting us off from the world. I could feel the heat from her body, the physical pain she exuded, and the blank numbness she was suffering.

I looped my arm around her back and tugged her into my chest, slipping my other arm beneath her head to cradle her closer. Her hands rested lightly on my chest as her eyes went out of focus again. Slowly, I leaned forward and pressed a kiss to her temple, lingering for a few moments.

'Do you remember what you told me?' I whispered.

A small wave of relief washed through me when her eyes flitted to mine, seeing me again. I caught the hint of confusion in her gaze, so I continued.

'When Jett died . . . Do you remember what you said?' I explained quietly. She watched me silently, waiting for me to continue. I took a deep breath.

'You said that you have to feel it so you can deal with

what happens before you move on,' I continued. Her eyes flitted back and forth between mine, suddenly engaged again. 'It hurts, but that's okay, because it won't hurt like that forever.'

Her face tightened as she swallowed once, jaw quivering slightly.

'And I know it's not the same. It's not even close to the same. But I know it will be okay eventually, and for right now when it's not, you have me.'

A silent tear slipped from her eye and streaked sideways until it disappeared into her hairline. I shifted even closer to her.

Another small wave of relief ran through me as she finally moved on her own, linking her arms around my neck as she hugged herself to me. Automatically, my arms tightened around her. I felt the warm heat of her tears at my neck as she finally let herself cry again, and I could feel the shake to her body with every breath she managed to take in.

'It's all right, Grace,' I murmured into her ear. My hand smoothed down her back once more. 'Just let it out. It's just me.'

It was as if my words had obliterated the invisible wall between her and her emotions, because as soon as she heard them, a choking sob ripped through the air as her entire body convulsed. My eyes squeezed shut and I tightened my grip on her, relieved she'd finally broken down completely. She had to hit the darkest, most painful pit of despair before she could start to climb out, something I knew from experience.

It was something I'd only got through because of her.

The gasping of her sobs echoed through the air, settling onto my skin and sinking down to my bones. Her entire body was shaking now no matter what she did, and her tears soaked my neck even more. All the while, I held her, trailed my hand down her back, murmured things to her. As much as I wanted to take this pain away from her, I knew I couldn't; she had to feel it to heal, and she was definitely feeling.

I lost track of how many times I told her I loved her, how strong she was, how proud I was. She had yet to speak since arriving home, but it didn't matter. As long as she heard me, that was enough. My grip on her never loosened as she clung to me, and it seemed like years later when she finally relaxed enough to pull back to our original position.

Her eyes were red and puffy, offsetting the green of her irises to make them seem like they were glowing.

'I wish I could have done it for you,' I whispered.

She shook her head and closed her eyes for a moment before looking at me again. She seemed to melt into me even more.

'I wish I could feel this for you. Take that away for you.'

Again, she shook her head. Her brows were low over her eyes, still beautiful even now.

'I wish I could,' I repeated, voice almost silent.

She let out a deep sigh and surprised me by bringing her hand to my face, tickling her fingers along my jaw before entrenching them in my hair. I was even more surprised when she pressed her lips to mine, holding them as if letting the pressure of our kiss breathe life into her again. Afterwards, I felt my stomach flutter and my heart thump heavily, just as it did the very first time I'd kissed her.

'I love you, Hayden,' she whispered.

Her eyes held mine as she bit into her lower lip again, fighting off tears that threatened to return. She gave a small nod as if to reiterate her point.

Finally, she had broken her silence. I sagged with relief.

'God, I love you, Grace,' I replied earnestly. 'So much that it hurts.'

'I know how you feel,' she answered. Her hand lingered on my jaw where she'd placed it moments ago.

'I think you're hurting because of something else,' I said as lightly as I could.

'I am, but trust me, I know how you feel,' she reassured me. 'That's how I feel all the time – like I love you so much that it hurts.'

I squeezed my arm around her, desperate to draw her closer.

'Masochists, aren't we,' I murmured, allowing my lips to quirk up on one side. The attempt at a smile felt odd on my face. She paused a few seconds, dropping my gaze for a moment before reconnecting it. Again, a small half-smile almost managed to reach her eyes.

'We are,' she agreed quietly. 'The best kind of masochists.'

Three: Mitigate

Hayden

Five days passed before I saw Grace smile for real.

Five days of holding her, comforting her, reassuring her the best I could.

Five days for her to heal enough to free her mind for a few fleeting moments.

It happened one morning when we were lying in bed, lazing about longer than we should have because I was unable to pull myself from her. Her back was pressed to my chest and her head rested on my arm as I curled around her. We were both awake, enveloped in a comfortable silence. I felt the soft tips of her fingers as they trailed over my fore-arm again and again, running gently over the surface to raise tiny goosebumps on my skin.

She still carried such an obvious weight on her shoulders, and her thoughts were constantly swarming with memories of what she'd had to do, but she was healing, and that was all I could hope for.

'Hey,' she murmured softly to me. I was pleased to see her eyes looked clear for the first time in days, as if she were finally able to fully focus on me.

'Hiiii,' I replied with a soft smile.

'I've been thinking,' she started slowly.

'Oh no,' I joked lightly, hoping to draw a smile from her.

I was rewarded when I saw the corners of her lips quirk up slightly, though it wasn't the full-blown, breathtaking smile I craved seeing.

'I think today's the day,' she said seriously.

I instantly knew what she meant. In the five days since I'd carried her back to our hut, she had yet to leave it. What little food she'd managed to eat had been delivered to us, though I hadn't been able to coax much into her. Dark circles had formed under her eyes and her face seemed slightly more angular than usual. She hardly moved from the bed, but when she did, her body was obviously weak from lack of energy.

'You think so?' I asked hopefully. I hated seeing her this way even if I understood it.

'Yeah,' she said, nodding. 'I think it's time I get some fresh air, don't you?'

'Definitely couldn't hurt,' I agreed, trying not to appear too eager. 'Fresh air, some food . . .'

'Smooth,' she said. This time her smile was real as she grinned at me; I was thrilled to see it finally reach her eyes, which beamed at me from a few inches away.

Her first real smile in over five days, as beautiful as ever.

I returned it and shrugged.

'You know I'm right,' I told her gently. My thumb trailed lightly over her hip, which seemed to protrude more than usual. She looked too thin and it worried me.

'I know,' she agreed quietly. 'How about we eat something and visit Dax?'

I felt a wave of relief at her words; this would be a big step for her, and I was pleased she felt strong enough to take it. Aside from a few minutes here and there, usually to check on Dax, I hadn't left her side since we got back. Everything else could wait.

'That sounds great.'

She shot me another small smile and a determined nod. My fingers gently squeezed her side one last time.

After getting properly dressed, Grace and I were on our way to the mess hall. Upon arrival, I felt every single person turn to look at us. It was like a flashback of when she'd first arrived and everyone had stared at her everywhere we went, only now, instead of malice and mistrust, they looked at her with admiration and awe. I felt a surge of pride all over again.

Grace looked around at everyone, easily noticing their stares. I could tell she felt somewhat awkward with all the attention, so I slipped my hand in hers and tugged lightly, directing her towards where Maisie was serving food.

'Come on,' I murmured softly.

She obeyed and let me lead her away. Everyone must have realised they'd been staring, because their gazes fell and they resumed their previous activities. A familiar quiet chatter started up again in the room. Maisie, who had slowly been healing from her own loss, managed a real smile at us both when we approached.

'Hayden,' she said with a nod to me before turning to Grace. I nodded back.

'Grace,' she continued, warmly. 'I heard what you had to do. And I know you had a lot of reasons and Jett was probably only one of them but . . . thank you for what you did. Your sacrifice is not lost on me.'

I saw her eyes glisten slightly as a few tears gathered, though she managed to blink them away. I was torn between gratitude to Maisie for her kind words and resentment for bringing it up so soon after Grace had finally managed to leave our hut.

Grace cleared her throat and gave a curt nod. 'Of course.'

She seemed unable to say more, but Maisie understood. She cast her another warm smile before handing her a plate of food. She handed me mine as well, which I noticed had significantly less on it than Grace's; it appeared I wasn't the only one to notice her diminishing weight. I murmured a quiet 'thanks' to Maisie before ushering Grace to a table, hand still linked in hers until we had to sit down across from each other.

Grace picked up a fork and poked at her food, pushing it around on her plate slowly. Her gaze was trained downward and a while passed before she seemed to feel me watching her. She cast me a guilty look and sheepish grin before taking a bite, as if reading my mind. I grinned in satisfaction when she took another bite and finally started to eat my own.

We ate in comfortable silence for a while and she had about a third of her plate cleared before she paused to speak.

'How does everyone know?' she asked softly, keeping her voice down as she glanced around at everyone. 'They all seem to know . . .'

'Kit made the announcement when we got back,' I told her. 'And Docc told some people what we were going to do before we even left. Word travels fast, especially something like that . . .'

I shrugged. Her expression was difficult to read.

'Are you okay with them knowing?' I asked.

'I guess so,' she replied. 'I don't know. Aren't they going to think less of me? That I'm some . . . I don't know, heartless monster or something?'

'Grace, no,' I said instantly, shaking my head. This was something I suspected she'd been worrying about for a while, especially after Shaw's comment from before: *Maybe you're more like him than I thought*. 'I promise you no one thinks that. They know how difficult it was and they respect you for that. Plus, they know what you did probably saved a lot of people's lives. Trust me when I tell you, what you've done and what it all means is not lost on them.'

She sniffed once and nodded before pushing her food around on her plate some more, not taking a bite.

'Do you trust me?' I pressed, ducking my head to try to get her to look at me. Her eyes flitted up to meet mine.

'Of course I do,' she replied easily.

'And do you believe what I said?' I asked gently, raising an eyebrow. She was quiet for a while as she studied my face intently.

'Yes,' she finally said.

'Good,' I said simply, nodding. 'Now will you please eat?'

'Okay, okay,' she said with a small grin, obliging me by taking another bite.

I took the last bite of my food and waited patiently as Grace continued to eat, watching her endearingly. Every so often something distracted her, so I'd nudge her hand gently with my own and let my eyes dart to her plate. She'd grin guiltily and take another bite. This went on for a while, but she only managed a little over half her plate before she pushed it away from her.

'I can't eat any more,' she said, shaking her head and leaning back from the table. 'I'm full.'

'Are you really?' I asked sceptically, raising a brow at her.

'Yes, promise,' she said earnestly. 'Stuffed.'

I let out a small sigh and nodded. She held out her fork to me, offering me the rest silently. I hated to admit that I was still hungry, and with our dwindling supplies, the last thing I wanted to do was waste food, so I finished off her plate in just a few mouthfuls. She smiled in satisfaction before we stood to return our plates.

'Shall we go and see Dax?' she asked. Her tone sounded the lightest it had in days, which brought a smile to my lips.

'We shall.'

We both waved goodbye to Maisie, where again the eyes of all those present became fixed on us. Grace did her best to ignore them, and soon we were outside and on our way to the infirmary. It was cloudy and humid today, quickly bringing an uncomfortable, sticky feeling to my skin. A soft wind trickled through camp and lifted the hair off my neck, providing some relief.

Soon, we had arrived at the infirmary.

Her mood seemed to sober instantly as she entered the dark building. It was still humid inside, but less so than the stiflingly oppressive outdoors.

I saw Kit, Leutie, and Malin gathered around the bed that could only belong to Dax. Docc, I noticed, was sitting at his desk on the other side of the room, where Shaw's bed had been moved to give Dax some space. Shaw appeared to be asleep and was still very bruised and battered from what I'd done to him.

When Dax's visitors noticed us, they parted to let us by the side. Dax was sitting up in bed, left hand wrapped in a neat white bandage and right ankle bound in a thick wrap. A few cuts and bruises littered his skin, but he was very much awake and alert judging by the wide grin on his face.

'Finally come to see me, have you?' he said lightly, grinning at Grace. This was the third time I'd seen him since we'd arrived but Grace's first.

'Been a bit preoccupied,' she said with a small smile and shake of her head. 'See you're healing up all right.'

'Yeah, I'll survive,' he said with an unconcerned shrug. 'Docc over there stitched me up pretty good.'

'What happened to you?' she asked curiously.

'Bloody Brutes tried to cut my hand off. Guess they wanted to add one to their collection. Some huge guy was holding me down, but I managed to break away – not quickly enough to avoid the knife, but enough to keep most of my hand. They're a pretty twisted lot, I tell ya.'

'Jesus,' I muttered. My eyes darted immediately to Grace, where I saw her swallow harshly. She was already having nightmares about that place and I hoped this wouldn't make it worse.

'Twisted my leg in the process, but Docc says it's just a sprain and should be better soon,' Dax concluded with a shrug.

'So you're all right?' Grace asked, cautiously hopeful.

'Oh yeah, you're not getting rid of me that easily,' Dax said with a wide grin.

Everyone laughed. It was then that I noticed Leutie standing on one side of his bed with her hand resting on the mattress. Kit and Malin stood on the other, shoulder to shoulder. Malin appeared more serious than usual, which reminded me she'd lost her father the night we'd lost Jett.

'I'm glad,' Grace said with a soft grin. I reached out instinctively to grab her and, once more, squeezed gently. She turned to look at me and cast me a small, slightly sad smile.

'How are you doing?' Leutie asked. Grace let out a heavy sigh and shrugged non-committally.

'All right, I guess,' she answered honestly. All eyes were on her.

'Do you want to talk?' Leutie questioned kindly.

'Oh, um,' Grace blinked as if she hadn't thought about it. 'No, that's okay . . .'

'You should,' I told her gently. 'Maybe you need someone other than me.'

She turned to me quickly, frowning. As much as I wanted to be the one to fix her, it could help to have someone who'd actually known her brother for most of their life talk with her. I would sacrifice my selfish desire to be that person for her if it meant she'd heal faster.

'Really,' I told her, nodding to reiterate my point.

'All right,' she said slowly, as if unsure I really meant it.

I squeezed her hand once more and kissed her cheek. 'Go on, then.'

'Aww,' Dax said sarcastically, grinning widely at us all the same.

'You have no room to talk anymore,' I said quickly, pointing at him.

Dax opened his mouth to reply before snapping it shut again. A sly grin spread across his face. 'All right, fair point.'

'Ready, Grace?' Leutie asked her calmly.

'Mmhmm,' she hummed, nodding.

'I'll come and see you later,' Leutie murmured to Dax. He nodded and gave her the most genuine smile I'd seen from him in a long time.

'See you in a bit,' Grace murmured to me before squeezing my hand one last time and pulling away. I nodded.

Grace and Leutie were just about to leave when Malin spoke.

'Do you, um, do you mind if I tag along? I don't want to intrude but it'd be nice . . . just to talk, you know?'

My eyes immediately flitted to Kit, who looked slightly confused and guilty all at once. Malin seemed to be avoiding his gaze as she pleaded silently with Grace and Leutie.

'Sure, of course you can,' Grace said kindly. She, too, looked puzzled, but brushed it off quickly. My stomach twisted uneasily at the thought of them talking, but I waved it away.

'Girl talk, how fun,' Dax quipped, earning a nervous chuckle from Kit. Apparently he, too, had something to worry about.

'Great,' Kit said sarcastically, a slight smirk clear in his features.

I let out a small laugh and pulled up a chair, sitting down beside Dax.

'Well, since they're leaving . . .' I trailed off, grinning. 'Let's see what's left of your hand.'

'You want to see the bloody stump?' Dax pressed proudly. 'It's pretty gruesome, I'll warn you.'

I chuckled. 'I think I can handle it.'

Dax shot me a sceptical look before beginning to unwind the bandage covering his hand. I tried to ignore the uneasiness in the pit of my stomach. I wanted Grace to heal, so if this could help, all the better. She needed a support system beyond me in case something should happen to me someday, and I was glad she'd found somewhere to start building that.

Grace

It felt odd to be separated from Hayden after spending so much time alone with him. I'd have been lying to myself if I said I wasn't a little nervous. I felt so fragile and weak, as if I'd been broken in half by what I'd done, and I was afraid I'd crumble back into bits without him and his constant reassurance. I knew, however, that it was impractical to be with him at all hours of the day and that I needed to learn to heal on my own as well.

Leutie, Malin, and I made our way towards the edge of camp, wandering aimlessly until we stumbled across two benches. Trees bordered us on one side while huts filled in the other. I sat down on one, leaving the other for Leutie and Malin to share. It felt foreign to be with a group of girls for once rather than surrounded by guys, which was how I spent a vast majority of my time.

'So,' I said somewhat awkwardly. Malin fidgeted with the hem of her shorts for a second and stared into the dirt, while Leutie cast me a soft smile.

'How are you?' Leutie asked kindly.

'Fine,' I replied, hardly pausing to think.

She shot me a doubtful look. 'Really?'

I sighed. 'No, not really. Better, though.'

'I'm sure Hayden's told you but . . . you did the right thing,' Leutie reassured me, nodding sincerely. 'I can say as someone who lived in Greystone up until very recently, you absolutely did the right thing.'

'Did I?' I asked tightly, grimacing as I glanced at her. 'I keep thinking that there's never enough reason to kill your own brother. Like I've committed some darkly evil sin or something.'

'Oh no, Grace, please don't think that,' Leutie pleaded gently. She rose off her bench to join me. Her hand reached to grasp mine. It was odd to see her small hand in mine when I was so used to Hayden's much larger one. 'Things were awful when he was around. People were dying, starving . . . even those living were miserable. There was no reasoning with him. Shaw was one of his best friends and he tried, but even then Jonah didn't listen. And you saw how Shaw flipped on him . . . There was no other option, Grace. Trust me.'

I let out a deep sigh. These things were reassuring to hear, but I knew I would never have peace over my actions; I just had to accept them and try to move on, because the redemption I so desperately wanted would never come.

'Okay,' I breathed out slowly. 'Can we talk about something else? I feel like it's all I've thought about since it happened and I just want to try and move on.'

'Of course,' Leutie agreed. Her hand squeezed mine once more before releasing it. 'Anything come to mind?'

I glanced across the space to Malin. She'd asked to come along so clearly there was something on her mind, but she hadn't volunteered to speak. Her fingers continued to pick at her shorts and her eyes seemed unfocused on the ground. Maybe she wasn't ready to speak.

'I've got something,' I said suddenly, feeling a flash of amusement. 'How's Dax doing?'

The corner of my lips quirked into a self-satisfied smile when I saw a blush creep up Leutie's cheeks. Her lips tugged into a grin that she couldn't manage to subdue.

'He's fine,' she said sheepishly.

'Oh, come on,' I chided, nudging her with my shoulder. Malin let out a soft chuckle from across the space. 'I saw that kiss.'

'Stop, Grace,' she whined happily, covering her face with her hands. Her cheeks were redder than ever as I grinned at her.

'That was the first one, right?' I questioned, thoroughly enjoying being out of the line of questioning for once.

'Yes,' she admitted. She peeked out from behind her hands at me and flashed me another guilty grin.

'I think he really likes her, Grace,' Malin said gently,

smiling at Leutie. 'Haven't seen him really even talk to a girl since . . .'

She trailed off and frowned. It never really occurred to me before, but Malin had probably been friends with Violetta. She'd lost her too, not only Dax. It was so weird to think about their lives a few years ago: Dax had been with Violetta, Hayden had been, somewhat, with Malin. They'd all had lives and relationships before I'd come along, and it was strange to think how different things were now. I shook my head, refocusing on the conversation.

'Do you like him, Leutie?' I asked, grin returning to my face.

'I don't know, do we have to discuss this?' she asked exasperatedly, finally dropping her hands from her face.

'Yes,' both Malin and I said at the same time. I shot her a conspiratorial grin.

'Ugh. I do, all right? He's really funny and nice and . . . sweet, I don't know, can we stop now?' She fidgeted with her fingers and refused to look at Malin and me, both of us grinning widely in satisfaction.

'He's a *really* good guy, Leutie,' I told her sincerely. Finally, she managed to look me in the eye.

'Yeah?' she asked hopefully.

I nodded slowly and raised my brow. 'Yeah.'

She let out a deep sigh and allowed herself an indulgent smile, avoiding my gaze once more.

'You're both lucky,' Malin said wistfully. I suspected this was the reason she'd wanted to talk.

'What do you mean?' I asked cautiously. Her legs were crossed at the ankles and she leaned forward on the bench, holding herself up with her hands on either side of her thighs.

'I'm really sorry . . . I don't want to dump all my problems on you guys but . . . Kit . . .' she trailed off and pursed her lips. I'd always suspected Malin wanted more from Kit but had hoped I'd been wrong. Malin took a deep breath and started again.

'I don't know if you guys know but . . . my father was killed the last time Greystone attacked.'

'I heard about that,' I said, feeling suddenly guilty for not acknowledging it sooner. 'I'm really sorry, Malin.'

'That's awful,' Leutie murmured sincerely. She looked on the edge of tears. Leutie had always been kind and sensitive, taking on others' problems as her own. It was one aspect where I'd wished I was more like her. To be so kind and caring with everyone was something I did not have.

'Thank you,' Malin said softly. 'We weren't particularly close or anything but he was still my dad, you know?'

I suddenly felt the loss of my own father, who I had been very close to. I shook my head, attempting to clear away the feelings.

'I know,' I agreed quietly.

'Anyway,' Malin said, continuing. 'Kit was so great for a few days after that but now he just . . . I don't know. He just kind of shuts down whenever I try to bring anything up and it sucks because I need him. And whenever I try to talk about what we are or how he feels, he just completely closes off and refuses to talk about it. I just don't know what to do.'

I suddenly felt terribly sad for Malin. It was very obvious that she had strong feelings for Kit, maybe even loved him, and that it hurt her a lot when it wasn't reciprocated. I tried to imagine being in her situation or going through the things I had without Hayden.

'I'm so sorry,' I said again, shaking my head slowly. 'Has he ever talked about that stuff? Feelings and whatnot?'

'No,' she said dejectedly. 'And at first that was fine because we just started out as a physical thing, you know? But then I started to get feelings for him, so I guess that's my fault . . .'

'It's not your fault,' Leutie said quickly. Again, she got up and moved back to Malin's side. It was as if she was drawn to whoever needed her comforting touch. 'You can't help who you fall for.'

'Do you think he has feelings for you?' I grimaced as I realised how harsh that sounded. I tried to soften it as I continued. 'What I mean is . . . he's kind of . . . serious, isn't he? Stoic? He hardly seems like the type to express his emotions. Maybe he does feel them and just doesn't know how to show you?'

'That's what I used to tell myself, but I just feel like he doesn't,' Malin admitted sadly. She gave a dejected shrug. 'And I didn't really notice how unattached he was until I saw you and Hayden . . .'

She trailed off and I felt my stomach twist uneasily. She must have seen it on my face because she continued.

'I don't mean to make it weird or anything. Yeah, there's a little history between Hayden and I, but honestly . . . it's nothing at all compared to what you two have. He's never looked at anyone the way he looks at you.'

Suddenly the uneasiness in my stomach was gone and I was left simply feeling bad for Malin again. It was so clear she just wanted Kit to love her the way Hayden loved me, and I felt myself getting angry with Kit for putting her through this. Malin had never done a single thing wrong to me, and even though she might have made me slightly uncomfortable before because of her history with Hayden, that was all but gone now as she revealed this vulnerable side to me.

'I think I just got lucky,' I admitted truthfully. I still found it hard to believe that someone like Hayden loved someone like me so much.

'I don't think so,' Malin said. She shook her head and gave me a perceptive look. 'I think you guys were meant to find each other.'

I couldn't seem to find the appropriate response to her words, so I just smiled. Malin seemed to sense my loss of words, so she spoke again.

'Anyway. I really am happy for you guys. It gives me some hope, you know? Like, of course, I'm insanely jealous of what you have, but I'm happy for you. I just wish I had that with Kit.'

'You know what I think you should do?' I said suddenly, sitting up and leaning towards her. Her heartbreaking story had made me more eager to help her.

'What's that?'

'Give him an ultimatum. Tell him he either grows a pair and admits his feelings or end it altogether. It's not fair of him to toy around with you like this. If he likes you, he needs to tell you and stop being such a child about it. If he doesn't, well . . . at least you'll know and you can move on.'

My voice was passionate. I suddenly felt so grateful to have Hayden as I thought about all he'd done for me throughout our relationship, especially the last week. He'd never once complained or pushed me further than I was ready for. He'd stuck by my side through everything, healing and fixing me the way no one ever had before.

At that moment, I felt like sprinting away from everyone and running straight to him, but I held back.

'You're right,' Malin said. I blinked and remembered what I'd said as I nodded encouragingly. 'Yeah, that's exactly what I need to do.'

'Yeah!' I said sharply, excited and energised.

'Um, yeah!' Leutie said, joining in a few moments too late. I let out a light chuckle and sprang to my feet.

'I'm really sorry but I just remembered something,' I lied distractedly. My need to run to Hayden was overpowering. 'Good luck and let him have it, all right? Don't let him walk all over you. Let me know how it goes.'

'I will, thanks Grace,' Malin said sincerely, flashing me an empowered grin.

'I've got to go, but I'll see you guys later. This was . . . nice,' I concluded honestly. As odd as it was to have such a classic girl talk, I had to admit I had enjoyed it. 'See you.'

I waved once at each of them before turning sharply and walking back towards our hut. My pace was quick and determined, increasing in speed with every step. The conversation about Malin's struggles and Leutie's blossoming relationship had ignited something in me. Of course I already knew how incredible Hayden was, but to see such a sharp contrast to how things could have turned out made me feel even more adoration and gratitude for him.

I needed to see him, and I needed it to happen as soon as possible.

I was about halfway to our hut when I started jogging, desperately hoping he'd be there. I'd left him at the infirmary, but that had been a while ago. A few people turned to stare at me as I ran by, but the intensity of my feelings pushed me on.

Finally, our hut came into view as I closed on the last few yards. Without pausing, I pushed my way through the door, slamming it shut behind me as I moved inside. A huge sigh of relief pushed past my lips as I saw Hayden spin sharply, reacting to my sudden, unexpected entrance. Soon I was just a few feet away from him. His brows lowered in confusion and concern flitted across his face as he opened his mouth to speak.

'Grace, wh—'

He was cut off, however, when my lips landed firmly on his. I roped my arms around his neck and hauled him down to me. He didn't react at first, surprised by my sudden arrival, but after a few moments he recovered and returned my kiss. He lingered for a few seconds before he pulled back.

'Grace—'

I shook my head sharply and cut him off again. This time, he didn't try to fight it as he let his hands rise to either side of my face, cradling my cheeks as I kissed him. My body seemed to ignite on the spot as I deepened the kiss, letting my tongue slip along his lower lip while my body pressed to his. He sensed my urgency, because he returned the action and let one of his hands trail down the side of my body, landing on my bum to haul me firmly against him.

With all the relentless emotions rolling through me and wreaking havoc on my body, there was one thing I desperately wanted.

I didn't want to talk.

I didn't want to cuddle.

I just wanted him.

Four: Burn

Grace

It was like I was on fire and the only thing that could stop me from incinerating on the spot was Hayden's lips, Hayden's hands, Hayden's body.

I needed them all, and I needed them everywhere.

If he was confused by my sudden assault, he'd waved it away, because the heat of his hands burned through the suddenly irritating clothes I wore as they smoothed down my body. His fingers curved into wherever they passed over: my ribs, my hips, my bum. The pressure he put down on me drove me further into his arms, and I deepened the kiss as my fingers entrenched themselves in his hair.

A rumbling groan slipped from his lips as I felt his tongue delve smoothly into my mouth. His hands, which had fallen to my backside, tugged more firmly to press me into his front, where I could already feel him growing harder and harder by the second. Heat was already starting to burn through me so strongly that I was fairly certain I was going to explode.

Hayden kissed me deeply as I ripped my hands from his hair, trailing them down his sides before I gripped the hem of his shirt. I tugged it upward, revealing his toned, flat stomach, and over his head. His green eyes met mine, wild and burning. I dragged my own shirt over my head, breathing quicker than I should have been.

I didn't give Hayden the chance to hesitate or speak again, as I launched myself back into his arms. His mouth met mine, kissing me deeply. The way he touched me now was in such a sharp contrast to how he'd been all week; there was nothing gentle about the way his hips ground into mine, the firm grip in which he held my jaw, or even his kiss as the needy desperation I was feeling seemed to flood through him as well.

My hands smoothed down the sides of his bare torso, feeling every uneven ridge in his skin from the scars and muscles beneath. When I reached the waistband of his shorts, my fingers wasted no time in digging beneath. I was about to tug them downward when his hands dropped from my face, then hooked under my thighs and lifted me off the ground.

A hot gasp left my lips in surprise as my mouth tore from his. I wrapped my legs tightly around his waist as he moved backward to the edge of the desk. My weight now supported, his hands ran roughly up my sides, sending a searing wave of heat through me. He paused just long enough to send a dark, lustful gaze trailing up my body.

That look was enough to make me lose all self-control. My legs tightened around his waist as I drew his body in, craving the contact between our cores.

'Jesus, Grace,' he muttered against my mouth, voice deep and raspy as he spoke.

I could hardly find words to respond as his hands slid up either side of my thighs, pressing firmly into my skin to sear down to the bone. My back arched involuntarily as his fingers slipped beneath the band of my pants, tugging hard enough to pull them free along with my underwear. I felt his hand drift upward to undo the catch on my bra. In a matter of seconds, he had me completely naked for him.

My breath was already uneven and shallow as he tore his lips from mine to trail heated kisses down the side of my neck. My hands moved of their own accord, roving from his hair to his shoulders to his sides. I felt wet heat on my skin as Hayden ducked lower, shifting down my chest, where he placed a single kiss over the scar above my heart before continuing on the path. My head tilted back and a low moan slipped past my lips as I felt his mouth close around my nipple, wetting the skin with his tongue as it swirled around it.

I saw him drop to his knees in front of me, a hand on each of my thighs as his fingers kneaded gently into my skin. I caught the ghost of a smirk on his face before he ducked forward and ran his tongue up my centre, causing the world to black out as my eyes closed once more in pleasure. My bare chest caved in and out quickly as I struggled to control my breathing, but the way Hayden's tongue dragged devilishly slow up my core made it nearly impossible.

A deep groan rumbled from Hayden's chest as his hands smoothed up my legs, as if he was enjoying himself just as much as I was. The sound of it sent a vibration through my centre that reverberated through my entire body, drawing yet another moan that I tried and failed to stifle. The pressure he put on my thighs was strong enough to hold me still as his tongue circled expertly around my sensitive bundle of nerves.

Again and again, his tongue moved to quickly push me towards my end. I could feel the pressure that had already built up, waiting to be released with every swipe and twirl of his tongue. Each time the tip of his tongue circled around me, he'd follow it by putting down pressure with the flat of it, making it difficult for him to hold me still as my body thrashed uncontrollably. Just when I thought I couldn't handle any more, I felt the relief I'd been craving as my release finally hit. My back arched even more as my head tilted backward, eyes closed and lips parted, as I felt my orgasm rip through me. Hayden didn't stop his actions until I was gasping for air, body going limp on the desk as I started to come down.

He pressed one final kiss into my hip before trailing them back up my body, savouring each and every bit of my skin that he passed over until he got to my neck. I reached up to wind my arms around his neck to haul him forward, bringing my lips to his. He kissed me firmly and let his hands trail up my sides once more, pulling me closer to his body.

When my now very sensitive centre met his, I could feel how hard and ready he was through his shorts. With all my strength, I managed to shove my still buzzing body off the edge of the desk. My legs almost gave out beneath me as I landed on the ground, but my grip on Hayden held me up. He seemed surprised when I stood but continued to kiss me until my hands landed on his chest, shoving him backward strongly enough to break our kiss.

His eyes were wild and blazing as he blinked at me, almost as breathless as I was. I pushed him backward again until the backs of his legs collided with the chair to his desk. My body followed his until I stood in front of him, where I leaned up to press a kiss to the base of his throat. I tucked the band of his shorts under my fingers, tickling the skin and soft hairs that trailed down from his stomach. I could hear his rattled breathing above me as I kissed his chest this time, tugging down on his layers slowly.

'Grace . . .' he murmured in that same deep, gravelly tone from before.

I pressed one last kiss into his skin before letting my eyes dart up to meet his; he was watching me intently, brows pulled low over his burning green eyes. His face was flushed, lips slightly swollen, and there was an obvious desperation in his eyes.

Burning for me, just as I burned for him.

That was all it took for me to tug down the layers firmly, freeing him from his clothes as he kicked them hastily away. I shoved at his chest one last time to push him down into the chair before dropping quickly to my knees in front of him. Just as he'd done to me, I pushed my hands up his thighs until I reached his hips. I gave him one last blazing look before my eyes dropped down his body to where I could see how clearly ready for me he was. A flash of smug pride ripped through me as I realised I had done that to him.

Without further hesitation, I ducked forward, pressing a few kisses up his thigh before I let my tongue drag up the length of his shaft. A low, rumbling groan ripped from his chest at the contact, encouraging me further. My hands trailed up and down his thighs as my tongue smoothed up the silky skin again, circling the tip a few times before I let my lips close around it. Hayden was already restless beneath me as I felt his hips shift uncontrollably.

I ducked forward again, drawing as much of him into my mouth as I could, though he was far too big to completely fit. Again and again, I bobbed forward, hollowing out my cheeks to draw as many chill-inducing sounds out of Hayden as I possibly could. Each time my mouth enveloped more of him, his hips would shift and his breath would catch as if holding off coming undone for me. One of my hands left his thigh to wrap around his length, moving in time with my mouth to take care of as much of him as possible.

His hands tangled in my hair, desperate to hold on to something as I continued to move over him. I could feel his body tensing up and hear his breath getting faster and faster, so I knew I was almost there. Encouraged, I took him deep into my mouth until I felt him press at the back of my throat. He was practically shaking as I smoothed my tongue up his entire length, certain I was about to finish him when I felt his hands free from my hair to grip under my arms.

He tugged me upward to my knees, before leaning forward and kissing me roughly. I kissed him back, completely wound up again after recovering from my first orgasm. Before I knew what was happening, he lifted me off the ground and twisted me around, placing me on his lap while he remained sitting in the chair. He held me by my hips, positioning me so I could feel him pressing at my entrance.

'You good, baby?' he murmured into my neck as his lips sponged over the skin heatedly.

'God, yes,' I gasped, leaning back into him and tilting my head to the side.

That was all he needed before he pushed into me, stretching me fully and causing my mouth to fall open in a silent, satisfied moan. My head tilted back to land on his shoulder as his lips continued to move over my neck, wetting the skin as he let his tongue dart out here and there. I felt his arms snake around my sides from behind me, and I gasped when his hands landed on my breasts to knead them gently a few times before trailing down my sides. My own hands rose to mirror his, intertwining our fingers as he let them fall to my waist to guide my actions.

With Hayden's help, my hips rose enough to draw him almost completely out of me before falling back down, earning gasping moans from each of us. It had been so long since we'd been together that I'd almost forgotten what it felt like.

Only Hayden could make me feel the way I did, be it emotionally or physically.

When Hayden tugged one of his hands free from mine to let it slip between my legs, I almost came undone on the spot. The calloused pads of his fingers pressed down on my clit, which was still tingling from what he'd already done to me. He drew circle after circle over me in perfect rhythm with the way his hips shifted beneath me. My breathing grew even more erratic as my heart thumped in my chest, pumping blood through my veins so fast I could almost hear it.

With one arm free and desperate for more contact with Hayden, I reached behind me to loop my hand behind his neck, drawing him forward enough so I could press my lips to his. His lips parted to let his tongue delve into my mouth. The combination of the way he moved inside me, his fingers over my nerves, and his lips on mine caused a thick haze to roll over my body, clouding my mind and making my blood boil in my veins.

I could feel my muscles start to tense and my back arch even more as my inevitable end drew nearer. Our bodies were slick with sweat as we continued to move, and I could feel the pace quicken as Hayden's hands guided my hips faster and faster over him. Each time he pushed into me felt like it was chipping away at my control, which was all but lost at this point.

Just when I thought I was about to succumb to the pressure building inside me, I was practically thrown off Hayden's lap. I landed so briefly on my feet that I hardly had time to realise what was going on before he spun me around and tugged me back down so I faced him. My legs gripped either side of his waist as he guided me quickly back down onto him, bringing a renewed stretch that caused both of our mouths to drop open again.

My eyes struggled to stay open as I moved over him, drawing him in and out before swirling my hips around to let him move inside of me. Again, Hayden snaked a hand between us to press down on my clit once more.

'Oh my god,' I gasped as my head tilted back.

I felt heat at my throat as Hayden took advantage and trailed his tongue up my skin. Even though I was on top, Hayden very clearly controlled the pace as his hips moved beneath us and the firm grip of his hand guided my hips. My body was practically jelly at this point, and all it took was a few deep movements and circles of my clit for my second orgasm to rocket through me. My body convulsed, wrapping my arms tightly around Hayden's neck to press my chest into his. He continued his actions, working me through my orgasm as he felt my muscles tighten around him.

'Come on, Hayden,' I gasped, as my hips swivelled around his one last time, drawing a lone groan from his lips as I felt his body tense.

'Grace,' he moaned breathlessly, stiffening briefly as he came.

He collapsed backward in the chair, drawing my body with his as he pulled himself from me. His arms looped loosely around my waist, both of us panting and covered in sweat. Happiness and love for him pumped through me.

'I love you,' he murmured quietly, voice still soft and low.

I felt the heat of a kiss press into my shoulder, which brought a satisfied smile to my lips. His face was flushed and practically glowing as he looked at me. He was so incredibly beautiful that I couldn't resist ducking forward to kiss him one last time.

'I love you, Herc.'

He lingered for a few seconds before pulling back. The separation was brief, however, as he pressed several pecks onto my lips over and over again, only stopping when my smile got too wide to allow him to kiss me.

'I missed that,' Hayden admitted. His breath finally returned to normal as he studied me, soft smile still on his face.

'Me, too,' I answered honestly.

'Not sure what I did to deserve that, but I'll take it,' he said with a lopsided smirk.

'Maybe I just love you,' I said with raised brows and a playful grin.

'Hmm,' he said doubtfully. 'If you say so.'

I giggled and reluctantly climbed off him, offering my hand to pull him up. He accepted and stood, hovering just a few inches away as he gazed down at me.

'Shower?'

'Yes,' I answered.

He smiled and grabbed my hand, leading me into the bathroom. Since we were both already naked, Hayden wasted no time in tugging me beneath the shower and pulling the handle to start the water. As always, it was cold and sent me crashing involuntarily into Hayden's chest. He chuckled and let his hands fall to my waist as he looked down at me endearingly.

Our shower was quick since this time there was no blood or mud to clean off, hindered only by Hayden repeatedly shaking his head vigorously to send water flying out in all directions. I shrieked in laughter as he held my hips still and shook his head, pelting me with the water droplets while he cackled in amusement. I shoved weakly at his chest, too happy to care as I half-heartedly tried to fight him off. Finally, we both managed to clean ourselves off just as the water ran out.

After drying off and getting dressed in the bare minimum, I found myself being tugged into bed by Hayden. I had no idea what time it was, although it was still light outside, but I couldn't have cared less as I settled under the blankets with him. He faced me and pulled on my hips until I draped a leg loosely over his, tangling us together. His arm draped over my hip and mine folded up near his chest. It was my favourite way to lie with him.

'You want to know what brought that on?' I asked, locking eyes with him.

'Do tell,' he said with a small, self-amused smile.

'I was talking with Leutie and Malin and I just . . . I just realised how grateful I am to have you. You're everything I need and so much more. I don't know how I got so lucky,' I admitted honestly.

'I'm the lucky one,' he said, raising a brow briefly.

'No, really,' I said, shaking my head adamantly. 'After everything we've been through and everything I've done . . . I could never have got through it without you.'

'You're strong, Grace,' he murmured. 'You would have.'

'No,' I rebuffed. 'I wouldn't have. I needed you to make it through that and I couldn't be more grateful to you for loving me the way you do. Just . . . thank you.'

'You don't need to thank me for that,' he murmured softly, finding my gaze once more.

'Yes, I do.'

He shook his head slowly, building the intensity between us as if I didn't understand what he was trying to say.

'You are everything to me, Grace. Absolutely everything.'

My lips parted as I drew in a silent gasp. My heart thudded at his words, blown away because of how accurately they reflected my own feelings.

'You don't have to thank me for loving you. The way you

love me is more than enough,' he continued when I couldn't find the words. 'Do you understand?'

'Yes,' I said, suddenly breathless.

'Good,' he murmured quietly.

If there was one thing I was absolutely certain of, it was that I would never be able to explain exactly how deep my love for him went. The mere thought that he felt the same was enough to make me happy for the rest of my life, no matter what obstacles we would face. As far as I was concerned, it would be okay, because we would face them together, linked by a love so intense and heart-wrenching that even we couldn't fully comprehend it.

Five: Orchestrate

Grace

The first thing I noticed when I woke in the morning was that my body felt cooler than usual. Subconsciously, I shifted around beneath the covers, feeling for the familiar comforting heat that I'd grown so used to having when I slept. Soft sheets slipped past my fingers, all cool to the touch as the other body I searched for remained out of reach.

A few feet away from the bed, spread out on the rough wooden floor in the push-up position, was Hayden. He didn't seem to notice I'd woken, because I watched with a slightly open jaw as he lowered his body weight, flexing the muscles visible in his bare back before pushing himself up again. He did it again and again, each time luring me into more and more of a daze as I watched his beautiful body move. Finally, after pushing himself up one last time with tantalisingly toned arms, he seemed to notice me. He pushed himself to rest on his heels, shoving slightly sweaty hair out of his face to flash me a wide grin.

'Good morning, beautiful,' he said easily. His hands rested on his hips and he breathed slightly heavier than usual thanks to his physical exertion; I didn't miss the thin sheen of sweat that covered his skin, highlighting the natural tan, the firm muscles rippling down his chest and abs, and black ink stained into the surface.

I could practically feel myself drooling.

'Back at you,' I replied. He clearly caught my tone and smirked, satisfied with his effect on me. I shook my head to try to focus. 'You're up early.'

He shrugged non-committally. 'We have a lot to do today, but I didn't want to wake you. You seemed tired.'

He smirked again and did a poor job of hiding his pride because we both knew he was the reason I was so tired.

'Shut up,' I laughed.

He grinned, bringing out the dimple in his cheek, before he crawled forward on all fours, towards the edge of the bed. His lips drew ever closer before stopping to hover an inch from my own, pulling me forward like a magnet. He held a kiss for a few lingering moments before he drew back and stood up, stretching his long, lean body and rolling his shoulders.

'That's enough lazing about,' he said with another breath-taking grin. 'Up you get.'

'All right, all right,' I grumbled with a playful roll of my eyes. Hayden's light mood was helping keep my mind off darker subjects that still lurked beneath the surface of my mind, and I was grateful for it.

Hayden nodded in satisfaction before grabbing a towel to wipe the sweat off his body, apparently in no mood for a shower. I took the opportunity to get dressed and ready for the day. After about fifteen minutes, we were both prepared and heading out the door.

'So what's the plan for today, then? Since we have *so* much to do,' I said with a sideways glance in his direction.

'We have to talk to everyone, pretty much. Shaw, Docc, Dax, Kit, maybe Barrow . . .' he trailed off, frowning in thought.

It had felt like things were over after I'd finally managed

to kill Jonah, but nothing had really been settled. We still had no idea what would happen with Greystone, and there was still the ever-looming threat of the Brutes in the city. Barrow, on the other hand, now confused me more than ever. He'd hated me from day one but had miraculously saved my life when Greystone had attacked, which meant I had virtually no idea where he stood or what was even going on with him.

'I should try and talk to Malin as well,' I added as I remembered our conversation from yesterday. I'd departed rather quickly and wondered if she'd had the chance to talk with Kit or not.

'What, why?' Hayden asked sharper than he probably intended.

'It's nothing, just girl stuff,' I said vaguely, watching closely for his reaction.

'Girl stuff,' he repeated with a frown. 'Like . . .?'

This time I actually let out a small laugh. I knew what he suspected we were talking about, because while I knew he had history with Malin, he was not aware that I knew as he had never told me himself. It obviously bothered him every time I talked to her and while I found it funnier and funnier, I decided to put him out of his misery.

'Not that it has anything to do with our conversation but . . . I know.'

His eyes widened involuntarily and he shot me a slightly panicked look before he controlled his features once more and tried to look casual.

'What do you mean?' he said unconvincingly.

'I know you guys were together,' I told him coolly.

Again, his eyes widened as they darted towards me. He led me to a small, secluded area between two buildings. I turned to face him, keeping my features unreadable. I shouldn't have, but it was kind of fun to see him sweat over such a trivial thing.

'You . . . you do?' he asked, frowning in confusion. My brows rose as I shot him an amused smile.

'Yes.'

'How?' he pressed.

I noticed his fingers fidgeting with the hem of his shirt. In all the time I'd known him, I hardly ever saw any hint of nerves, but it was there now. Raids, fighting, even killing didn't affect him this way, but bringing up past relationships made him nervous.

'Malin accidentally said something ages ago, way back that night when the war sort of started,' I told him.

'You've known that long and never said anything?' Hayden asked, gaping at me. 'That was months ago.'

I shrugged. 'It didn't really matter, honestly. You're not my first, but you didn't ask me about it so why would I ask you?'

'I didn't ask you because I don't want to hear about that,' he said, visibly cringing. 'I don't want to think of you with someone else . . .' He looked as though the thought made him sick.

'It's never been like it is with you, I promise.'

'I know,' he said more calmly. 'I've never felt anything I feel with you before. None of it . . . you're the only one.'

I was pleased he'd said such a thing because it was exactly how I felt.

'I love you,' I murmured softly, stepping closer so only a few inches remained between us as I looked up at him.

'And I love you,' he returned, mirroring my tone. I felt the warm heat of his hands on my hips. He gave a small shake of his head and flashed a slightly disbelieving smile. '*God*, I love you.'

'What matters is right now, yeah?' I coaxed.

'Yeah,' he agreed.

'Right, so, you can stop being so weird whenever I talk to Malin because your "secret" wasn't much of a secret in the first place,' I said with a cocky grin.

'All right, all right,' he muttered.

'Good,' I said happily.

The word barely managed to slip past my lips before his pressed to my own, holding me against his body with his hands on my hips and lower back. My hands closed around the soft fabric of his shirt, tugging him down to me as he let his tongue snake across mine once. He filled the gaps between my lips with his lower lip one last time before pulling back. I watched as his eyes glanced around guiltily, but it seemed no one had bothered looking between the two buildings to catch our private moment. Not that it mattered now that we were officially known to be together, but it was nice to have some privacy.

'Let's go,' he murmured quietly. 'Lots to do, remember?'

I walked happily beside him, closer than was probably necessary, as we made the rest of our journey to the infirmary.

It was still fairly early and I had been expecting the patients, mainly Dax and Shaw, to be asleep, but I was obviously mistaken when tense, irritable voices drifted through the air. Dax's voice was easily recognisable even though it was abnormally angry.

'. . . Say it one more time, mate, and you'll be stuck in that bed for another month,' Dax spat venomously.

Hayden and I shot confused glances at each other before hurrying to Dax. He sat up haughtily in bed, glaring daggers across the room at Shaw, who appeared to be doing his best to appear cool and unbothered but was failing judging by the way his hands had closed into fists around the blankets around him. Docc, I noticed, sat at his desk with his face in his hands as if he'd given up in defeat and exasperation.

'It's not my fault if you're insecure about yourself. You wouldn't be so pissed off if you didn't think I was right,' Shaw shot back smoothly. Only the bulging vein in his forehead gave away his irritation.

'What the hell is going on?' Hayden interrupted firmly.

All at once, Dax and Shaw's heads jerked to look at Hayden in surprise as if they hadn't realised we'd arrived. Even Docc sat up rather quickly before relaxing in obvious relief that someone else had come to intervene.

'Thank god,' Docc muttered tiredly. I frowned and suspected this bickering had been going on for quite some time.

'Nothing,' Shaw said with a casual shrug. He winced as he moved, and his hand darted to his rib, which was obviously still healing from Hayden's assault.

'Nothing,' Dax grumbled after shooting another glare in Shaw's direction. The bandage on his left hand looked pristine and white, as if freshly changed.

Hayden raised a questioning brow at Docc when it became obvious neither Dax nor Shaw was going to explain.

'We've had two very big personalities in a very small space for a while,' Docc said with a sigh. 'They've been going at it for hours now.'

'What about?' I asked.

'Everything.' Docc shook his head as he spoke and looked slightly bewildered.

'Men,' I muttered under my breath as Dax and Shaw took turns glaring at each other. Hayden was the only one who heard but ignored my comment.

'All right, well, we have some things to discuss so you're going to need to put that on hold,' Hayden said firmly.

'Or stop altogether,' Docc said optimistically. Shaw let out a derisive snort while Dax crossed his arms indignantly across his chest. Docc let out a defeated sigh. 'What is it, Hayden?'

'We need to talk about what we do next,' he said. 'But we should get Kit first.'

'I'll go,' Docc volunteered quickly. It was obvious he was eager to get some space from Dax and Shaw. 'Be back in a moment.'

He rose quickly and moved past us to fetch Kit, leaving Hayden, Dax, Shaw, and I alone. As soon as the door to the infirmary shut, Dax spoke quickly.

'I mean it, you sack of shit, keep your mouth shut,' Dax growled.

'Just ignore me if you think I'm so wrong. All I said is your girl is going to be comforting me soon when she gets bored with you,' Shaw said nonchalantly.

I felt my mouth drop open as the true source of the argument emerged. That was what they were fighting about? Leutie?

'You guys are ridiculous,' I muttered.

'Hayden, please hit him again for me. Do us all a favour,' Dax said, rubbing his forehead with his fingers as if greatly stressed.

'Shaw, how about you just shut the hell up about girls in general, yeah? Keep in mind we're still the ones keeping you alive,' Hayden said sharply.

'For now,' Shaw muttered. 'Won't be injured forever. I'll be healed up soon enough.'

'Yeah, well, we can see to that, too, can't we?' Hayden threatened. Shaw glared at him, silently admitting that Hayden was right. 'That's what I thought. Just shut up if you know what's good for you.'

'Hey, guys,' Kit said, interrupting everyone's quarrelling by entering the infirmary with Docc. He looked tired and even more serious than usual, which only made me more curious about he and Malin.

'Hey,' Hayden greeted quickly. 'All right, now that everyone's here . . . we need to talk.'

'About what?' Dax questioned. He looked like he was trying very hard to focus on the conversation and forget whatever had been going on before.

'Everything. Greystone, the Brutes, Blackwing. First of all . . . what do we do with Greystone now?'

'Well, you killed Jonah, so you're off to a pretty menacing start,' Shaw said bluntly. My stomach clenched at the mention of what I'd done. I didn't want to think about it, but our conversation made that pretty much impossible.

'How many are left in Greystone now? Hundred and fifty? Two hundred?' Kit mused, brushing the backs of his fingers along his jaw in thought.

'Give or take, yeah,' I agreed. 'Maybe less after that last fight in the city . . . It was hard to tell who was Greystone and who were Brutes, honestly.'

'So what do we do with them?' Kit continued.

Everyone frowned in silence as they tried to come up with a logical solution.

'We could all go over there? Force them to talk with us and try to work something out? Without their leader and with so few of them left, I doubt they'll put up much of a fight. Wasn't that the whole point of killing Jonah?' Dax theorised.

'Yes,' I admitted. That had been our rationale, so to change our plan now wouldn't make much sense.

'So we send people over to negotiate some sort of surrender?' Hayden said. The words sounded odd for our situation, but I supposed that was technically what was going on.

'I think that's the best solution. Like Dax said, they can't exactly do anything other than whatever you say. And our friend Shaw here can help convince them, can't you Shaw?' Docc said calmly. He shot a pointed look in Shaw's direction, who only scowled. 'You wanted Jonah to be stopped and he's been stopped. A common enemy makes us allies, even if that enemy is gone.'

Everyone was quiet as they waited for Shaw's response. I didn't trust Shaw as far as I could throw him, and it was abundantly clear that the feeling was mutual on all accounts, but he was an obvious asset that we had to use for the greater good, even if we hated it.

'We are all on the same side even if some of us can't get along,' Docc continued steadily. Dax gave a heavy sigh, but he didn't say anything else.

'All right, that's settled,' Hayden concluded when no one objected. 'We'll take a trip to Greystone and tell them the war is over. They don't even think of attacking us and we won't attack them. We don't have to work together, we just don't have to kill each other.'

'That sounds good,' I said, speaking for the first time in a while. 'What about the Brutes? They're getting bolder every time we run into them.'

'I was hoping we could just ignore them and they'd go away,' Dax said unhappily.

'Fat chance,' Shaw said with a scoff. Dax opened his mouth to retort before Hayden cut him off.

'We knew there was a good chance we'd have to step in,' Hayden said. 'I think we need to start up the surveillance again. Learn as much as we can to see if there's a way to stop them before they get brave enough to come all the way out to Blackwing.'

'When do we start?' Dax asked. Hayden frowned at him, eyes darting to his injured hand and leg.

'You're not going anywhere for a while,' Hayden told him. 'But soon. I say we take care of Greystone as soon as possible before we worry about the Brutes.'

'What about tomorrow? We'll want to go during the day so they don't think it's a raid and try to do something dangerous,' I said.

'Good thinking,' Docc said with a solemn nod. 'Hayden, you should talk with Maisie about the food situation. I believe it's got quite dire.'

Hayden let out a frustrated sigh before nodding. 'Yeah, all right. We may have to go on a raid to see if we can find something.'

'So much going on . . . Greystone, Brutes, food shortages . . .' Dax started. 'And I'm stuck in bed. Murder me.'

'Gladly,' Shaw muttered, just loud enough to hear across the room. For once, Dax managed to ignore him.

'You'll be able to start rehabbing that leg soon, don't you worry. Then you just have to retrain your hand to work with half the fingers it had before,' Docc said reassuringly. 'You'll do just fine.'

'Helps to have some motivation, eh Dax?' Hayden said smoothly. I caught the hint of amusement in his tone and knew he was referring to Leutie.

'Shut up, Hayden,' Dax grumbled as he flipped him off with his good hand. I was surprised to hear Hayden let out a small chuckle after the heavy conversation we'd just had.

It felt good to begin making plans and taking action once more, but the pile of things on our plate was daunting, and I didn't relish the idea of taking them all on at once. We had no choice, however. With so much to live for, I'd do anything to carry on.

'All right, if we leave, can you promise not to kill each other?' Hayden said with a pointed glance at Dax and Shaw.

'No,' they both muttered at the same time.

Hayden rolled his eyes and turned away before calling a 'goodbye' to Docc and Dax before retreating towards the door. Kit did the same, and I turned to follow as well.

'Bye, guys. Heal up, Dax. We need you,' I said with a smile. Finally, I was rewarded with a smile of his own after his unnaturally bad mood.

'I know you do,' he said with a confident shrug. 'I'll be back to bugging you in no time.'

'Can't wait,' I said sincerely. I gave a small wave and jogged to catch up with Hayden and Kit, who were just exiting the building.

As much as a pain in the ass as he was, Dax lightened the mood considerably. I hoped he'd heal up soon so things could go back to normal with our group. That, and I was pretty sure he was going to drive Docc insane if he stayed in the infirmary much longer.

'I've got to get back to something, but I'll see you guys tomorrow for the trip to Greystone, yeah?' Kit said quickly. He glanced distractedly over his shoulder and barely listened to our replies before he started retreating.

'Yeah, all right, see you,' Hayden said, barely noting Kit's hurried behaviour. Now I was almost certain something was up with him and Malin, and I knew I wouldn't be able to talk to her just yet like I'd hoped.

He had barely gone when another person arrived to take his place. When I saw his face, my immediate reaction was distaste. I felt my features pull into a frown before I remembered what had happened the last time I'd seen him.

'Barrow,' I greeted evenly, staring into the grey-green eyes that were focused on mine.

'Grace,' he said in an equally even tone.

Hayden moved to stand closer to me, edging my shoulder back with his own as he moved subtly between Barrow and me. It appeared he still did not fully trust Barrow even after he'd saved both of our lives. It became apparent that Barrow was now free to roam camp again, because he was alone and free, after he had been tied up for so long.

'What do you want?' Hayden spat. Barrow's eyes darted to Hayden's quickly before returning to mine.

'I need to speak with you,' he said to me, ignoring Hayden's question.

'You can speak to us. You're not going anywhere alone with her,' Hayden interrupted.

'Fine,' Barrow said with a shrug. 'This is awkward for us all, but I need to apologise to you.'

My mouth dropped open in surprise. That had not been at all what I'd been expecting. 'Okay . . .'

'In light of recent events, I see now that you are not a danger to us.'

'Are you serious?' Hayden scoffed derisively. Barrow ignored him and continued.

'I shouldn't have treated you the way I did or harmed you. I'm sure you can understand that I've known these boys and the people of this camp since it started. I'm very protective of everyone here, so I couldn't just accept an outsider coming in and threatening that. I'm still not fond of you because I don't care for your attitude, but I hate anyone who'd attack us more than I hate you. It's clear now that you're on our side.'

'Yeah, no shit she is,' Hayden grumbled. 'She had to kill her own brother for you to see that? Jesus Christ.'

Hayden seemed to be more upset by this than I was. I couldn't fully blame Barrow for acting the way he did at first. I certainly understood the need to protect those I loved. Hayden, Dax, and Kit were almost like sons to Barrow, so it was easy to see his line of reasoning, even if he had taken things way too far.

'It's all right,' I said with a sigh. 'I was never a danger to you, but at least you can see that now.'

'I do, and again I'm sorry. Just know it came from a good place,' he continued. His features remained stiff and it was clearly difficult for him to speak to me civilly at all, much less apologise, but I recognised the strength such a thing took, and I respected that.

'I know,' I said honestly.

'Just saying, Barrow, you better not even look at her wrong from now on,' Hayden said threateningly.

'I get the message, trust me,' Barrow said, raising his hands in surrender. His eyes focused on Hayden for a while. He appeared deep in thought as Hayden stared back, a slightly confused expression on his face.

'Quite the man you've turned into,' Barrow said thoughtfully. There was no sarcasm or malice in his voice, merely a slight sense of awe and even endearment. 'I remember when you were just a boy.'

Hayden didn't appcar to know what to say, because he stared back at Barrow in mild confusion.

'Hmm,' Barrow hummed, nodding to himself as if remembering something. 'Well. Now that that's done, I'll be off. Getting back into the rounds and such.'

'Yeah, you do that,' Hayden said flatly.

'Until next time,' Barrow said with a small duck of his head. I gave a curt nod in return as I watched him shift around us to continue on his way. We were both silent until Barrow was far enough away that he wouldn't hear.

'That was weird,' I admitted. Hayden and I stood shoulder

to shoulder, watching Barrow's figure grow smaller and smaller until he turned around a corner and disappeared completely.

'Yeah,' Hayden agreed distractedly. 'That's more like the old Barrow. The one that wasn't crazy with hatred for you.'

'I think he'll always hate me a little,' I said with a small, smug grin.

'He'll have to deal with it,' Hayden said before throwing his arm casually around my shoulder.

I felt oddly happy about how things had gone today, even if our decisions were only clearing away one storm to make room for another. It was a never-ending cycle, like clouds gathering at the base of a towering mountain.

'Yes, he certainly will.'

Six: Usurpation

Grace

The jeep rumbled loudly as Hayden drove it towards Greystone. Usually we'd walk such a short distance, but since we didn't know what exactly it was that we were walking into, we decided driving would be safer. I sat in the backseat, as always, with Kit filling the front seat.

Our usual raiding crew was smaller today, and noticeably quieter thanks to Dax's absence. He had grumbled loudly when we left him, claiming he could still come along even though we all knew he couldn't. He was healing, but he still had a long way to go before he would be ready to take on raids again. The only thing that comforted him after our departure was Leutie's arrival to keep him company in the infirmary.

A knot had formed in the pit of my stomach and was growing tighter by the second as we drew closer and closer to my former home. Last time I'd been there, I'd gone alone and left with Leutie. Even then, it had felt foreign to me, like the place I'd grown up was no longer there. I was nervous for how it would feel now, after everything that had happened. Jonah's blank face filled my mind as the image that was permanently burned into my brain assaulted me; I saw the shock, saw the expression wiped from his face, saw him fall to his knees.

Saw him die.

'Grace.'

I blinked once and refocused my eyes on the mirror, where Hayden was studying me closely. His voice was low and deep as he spoke, meant to pull me from the thoughts he could apparently read on my face. I cleared my throat and took a deep breath, gathering myself once more.

'Yeah?'

He studied me for a few more moments and cast me a concerned frown before speaking again.

'Should we just pull up, or what do you think?'

I shrugged and thought. 'I guess so. I don't know if they'll put up a fight or anything, but I suppose we'll see.'

My gun sat beside me on the seat, loaded and ready, though I hoped we wouldn't have to use it. It was hard to say what would be going on in Greystone now that their leader, Jonah, was dead. Were there others who were ready to step up and fill his position? Were there those who opposed him and had now taken power? Was there even anyone left strong enough to take control?

A loud 'click' sounded from the front seat as Kit readied his weapon. Greystone wasn't that far away and I could already see its edges as we approached. Adrenaline started to pump through my system and I sat up a little straighter, leaning forward between the seats to get a better view. Hayden glanced at me over his shoulder and shot me a small, close-lipped smile, reassuring me silently.

Only about three hundred feet remained between our vehicle and Greystone, yet no one seemed to be firing at us. Every second that ticked by, I waited in anticipation for the first round of bullets, but we were now a hundred feet away and there was still nothing.

Fifty feet.

Ten.

Hayden manoeuvred the jeep through the buildings on the outskirts of the camp, and still we met no defence. Nerves ticked at my stomach, almost more unsettled by the lack of activity than if they had fired on us immediately. Everyone was silent, as if afraid that speaking would alert them to our presence, even though the jeep was far from quiet.

The camp looked completely deserted. When usually there would have been people roaming around and going about their duties, now there was no one.

A frown crossed my face as Hayden drove closer to the centre of Greystone. Each building that we passed was familiar to me, though there was an obvious air of neglect around the place, as if no one had moved through this area of camp in a while. The shacks people lived in, which were pretty grim and barren to begin with, now looked positively decrepit and unkempt. It was as if all life had disappeared from Greystone.

'Does it look . . . different?' Kit asked, breaking the silence as he frowned out of his window. His gun was ready in his hands even though it didn't appear he'd need it.

'Yes,' I replied. 'Very different.'

Hayden didn't say anything but glanced in the mirror once more, reconnecting our gaze for a split second before refocusing on the road. I didn't dare voice my thoughts, but that didn't stop them from flooding through my mind.

Was there even anyone left after Jonah's destructive reign?

Minutes passed by in awed silence as we all searched for signs of life. I was about to give up hope that we would find anyone when a quick flash of movement caught my attention. My head snapped towards the motion, but whatever it was had already disappeared.

'I saw something,' I announced, searching urgently for the source again.

'Where?' Hayden asked quickly, slowing the vehicle.

'Back there, towards the middle,' I said.

Hayden resumed driving. I quickly realised that we were heading towards the direct centre of camp, where my old house was, as well as my father's old office.

'Everyone stay alert,' Hayden murmured. I readjusted my grip on my gun and raised it. Kit did the same in the front seat.

Even here, in the heart of camp where it was usually the best kept, things looked as if they hadn't been attended to in months. My eyes raked over the crumbling building, the wild weeds, and the overwhelming lack of life as Hayden drove. Frustration and trepidation grew stronger inside me when I didn't catch any further movement.

'This is pointless,' I grumbled, irritated. I wasn't sure what I expected to find at Greystone, but it wasn't this.

'What do you—'

Hayden's voice was suddenly cut off when he had to slam on the brakes. The jeep screeched to a halt, skidding in the dirt and sliding a few feet before it jerked to a stop just in time to avoid directly hitting a woman who had appeared in front of it. She stood firm with what looked like a makeshift spear in her hands, glaring through the windshield at us. I tried to adjust to the shock of her sudden appearance. I'd hardly got a good look at her when several more people appeared, surrounding our vehicle with their own variations of spears.

'Shit,' Hayden muttered tensely. His hand slipped to grab his gun, which had been stowed beside him, while Kit and I stealthily aimed our own at the people surrounding us.

'What do we do?' I whispered, barely moving my lips.

It seemed that we were in a silent contest with the people outside to see who dared break first. A quick glance around told me there were about fifteen surrounding the car and a few more lingering in the back. We were outnumbered, but we had guns and a vehicle, while all they seemed to have were rudimentary spears.

'Stop the car,' the woman directly in front of us demanded.

Hayden's hand twitched, reluctant to obey this woman. He scowled, and I could tell he didn't like not having the power.

'Stop it or we'll kill you,' the woman continued.

She was tall and lean, but muscled and clearly very powerful. I guessed her to be about thirty years old, and I was surprised that I didn't recognise her at all. Usually when we ran into people from Greystone, I either knew them or at least vaguely recognised them.

With an audible growl, Hayden turned off the ignition.

'Do you know her?' Hayden murmured, directing his question at me.

'No,' I admitted.

'Great,' he muttered.

Silence fell over us again as the woman surveyed us, taking her time to study each of us in turn before finally letting her gaze settle on me. A flash of recognition crossed her face when she saw me.

'Grace Cook,' she said firmly, holding my gaze. I tried my best not to react as I stared back at her, staying quiet. 'Would you mind stepping out of the car?'

'No,' Hayden said sharply, cutting off my chance to reply.

As uneasy as the woman's stare made me, I didn't feel fear. She was intense and strong, but for some reason, I did not feel threatened by her powerful gaze.

'It's okay, Hayden,' I whispered, reaching forward to let my hand land briefly on his shoulder.

'Grace, no—'

'We won't hurt you if you don't hurt us. You have my word.'

The woman's voice cut off Hayden's protest. Despite every bit of training I'd ever had, I strangely believed her.

I moved to surreptitiously slip my gun behind my back before reaching for the handle. I opened the door with a soft 'click' but was barely outside when Hayden apparently decided he couldn't let me go alone, because he copied me and exited the vehicle as well. As soon as we were both out, he moved to stand slightly in front of me while still giving me a clear view of the woman who had spoken.

'Who are you?' I asked sharply, keeping my stance tense and ready to spring to action in case she went back on her word. Again, she studied me for a few moments with an intense stare before she spoke.

'A friend to you.'

'I need a bit more information than that, I'm afraid,' I said firmly. I thought I saw a flicker of amusement in her eyes.

'You're just like I heard you were,' she murmured. 'I'm Marie. These are my friends.'

She gestured around her as she lowered her spear and set it on its end in the dirt. Her action caused a ripple effect as everyone that had surrounded us did the same.

'And who are you, Marie, exactly?' I pressed, taking a step forward to stand next to Hayden. He shot me a tense glance but allowed me to stand at his side. Kit had opened his door and stepped out as well.

'We're what's left of Greystone.'

My eyes widened and lips parted slightly in surprise as I glanced around. There couldn't be more than thirty people gathered here. Surely that couldn't be all that was left?

'This is it?' I asked incredulously.

'There are about twenty more in a secure building, but they're mostly young or elderly.'

'You're in charge?' I assumed. Judging by the fact that she was the only one speaking, it wasn't hard to guess.

'I am. After Shaw disappeared, I took over the force trying to overthrow Jonah, but it seems you've done that for us.'

My stomach gave an uncomfortable twist at the mention of what I'd done, but I brushed it off. If this woman was telling the truth, we really were on the same side. I decided not to mention the fact that Shaw was still alive.

'What about the rest of Jonah's people?' Hayden demanded, speaking for me.

'Very few survived the war. Those that did decided they'd rather live on our side than face us.'

A light snicker came from somewhere to my left, bringing a sardonically twisted grin to Marie's lips.

'Well, most of them. We had to do away with a few.'

I frowned, unsure of whether I believed her or not. These people could be all that remained of Jonah's force, but I had the nagging suspicion that we'd already be dead if they were. I'd seen the piles and piles of bodies that had accumulated from attacks on Blackwing alone and knew we were only one of Jonah's targets, so it wasn't difficult to believe he'd lost most of his force.

'What do you want?' I asked, refocusing on Marie.

'You're the ones who came to us, my dear,' she said coolly. 'I should be asking you the same question.'

'We came to see what was going on over here. You say there are about fifty of you left?'

'Give or take a few,' Marie answered.

I felt a sudden wave of nausea roll through me. Fifty

remaining of a camp that once held over six hundred. The devastating loss was almost impossible to comprehend.

'Jesus,' Hayden muttered.

It was a bittersweet feeling that these people were strangers to me now, passed over in my previous life here. It was clear by looking at them that they would not have been those I interacted with much. They were younger teenagers, or middle-aged men and women, some who looked to be about my father's age or older; they were hardly the types to have gone on raids before, which were the ones I interacted with the most.

I passed over a face before I did a double take as I finally recognised someone. The last time I'd seen him, he'd been in a crumpled heap on the ground, crying in pain and fear as he clutched at his slashed ankles. He sat in what looked like a makeshift wheelchair now, crippled by the way my knives had slashed his Achilles tendons so long ago. He watched me with hints of awe and fear in his face, still so young-looking at maybe sixteen.

The boy I'd spared the night I'd taken Leutie to Blackwing.

The boy I'd threatened to kill if he ever crossed me.

The boy that owed me his life.

Nell.

His eyes widened as he saw me recognise him, and I focused on keeping my features blank and unreadable as I turned back to Marie. I didn't know if they knew I was the one to do that to him, but I wasn't keen to make our connection known if he had indeed kept his word. I didn't know how this situation would turn out, and the potential for needing someone on the side of what was left of Greystone was still very real.

'So, as we were saying,' Marie continued, interrupting my momentary distraction. 'What is it that you want?'

I paused, glancing at Hayden for guidance. He was better at this sort of thing than I was, but Marie appeared to have some sort of strange respect for me and I wanted to use that to my advantage.

'We want to end this all for good. Jonah's gone, the war is over. You keep to your camp and we'll keep to ours. You and I both know we outnumber you greatly now and if you try anything, it won't work in your favour.'

Marie gave a serene nod and tapped her finger on the shaft of her spear as she thought.

'There is no need for thinly veiled threats, Grace. We have no intention of attacking Blackwing ever again.'

'Well . . . good,' I finished lamely, but I held my ground.

'Indeed. We have enough to worry about with getting our camp back together and other issues. Rest assured that no one from Greystone will set foot anywhere near Blackwing.'

Again, I oddly believed her. It was blatantly clear that their numbers had dwindled so far that they were in danger of dying out. Their capabilities of continuing to wage a war they had all fought against in the first place were pretty much non-existent.

'Do I have your word in return?' she asked calmly.

I glanced to Hayden again. He dipped his head to bring his lips to my ear, hiding his mouth behind my face. 'Do you trust her?' he murmured. I took a deep breath and thought, drawing on every bit of experience I had. Slowly, I nodded and held his gaze. He gave a small, curt nod of approval. I pursed my lips and turned to focus on Marie yet again.

'You have my word. We officially have a truce. But just know that if you break it, it won't be pretty,' I said, unable to resist. Again, a small flash of amusement crossed her face.

'Excellent. You'll be leaving, then?' Marie said pointedly.

'Yes, we will,' I replied. My eyes darted back over to Nell, who hadn't said a word but was watching me very intently. It was as if he knew that even though we'd struck this deal between Blackwing and Greystone, his debt was not paid; he still owed me his life.

Marie gave a nod and shot me a small smile as I started to turn. I stopped.

'One more thing,' I said quickly. Marie raised a brow as she waited for me to continue. I was suddenly very aware of everyone's eyes on me as I spoke. 'I need to go to my dad's old office.'

I had been expecting her to protest, but she didn't. She simply ducked her head and gave an understanding look. 'Of course. You know the way.'

I nodded sharply and took off, causing Hayden and Kit to jump to action behind me. Marie fell into step behind us as one of her crew followed, but the rest of them stayed behind without a word. Despite the truce we'd just agreed to, my body was still on edge as nerves and adrenaline pumped through me.

Celt's office wasn't far, and I could already see its door as I approached. Without hesitating, I closed the remaining distance and pushed open the door. There was enough light outside to filter through the grimy windows, illuminating the small space. Just like the last time I'd been here, I was hit almost immediately with the familiar smell of my father: stale tea, gunpowder, and old paper.

Pain and sadness welled inside of me at the memories that came rushing back, but I pushed them down as I strode purposefully towards his desk. I was surprised to see it relatively unchanged from how I remembered it, especially considering the fact that Jonah had probably used the space after my father had died. Hayden, Kit, Marie, and her companion waited tensely in the doorway, giving off a somewhat awkward air as if they weren't sure how to behave around each other just yet.

My eyes landed on the reason for my coming here. Just as I remembered, the silver frame stood atop his desk. It still held the one photo that remained of my entire family. We were all there – my mother, father, brother, me – and we were all alive. It struck me suddenly that I was the only family member left, which cemented my decision. Before I could change my mind, I reached forward to grab the frame, clutching it to my chest without studying it too closely.

I would take it with me to have as a reminder of them. If I had it my way, I would never set foot in this place again. I had to finally say goodbye to them, separate myself from my former life, and move on. They were gone, and I didn't want to think about my losses any more than I had to, but I didn't have to forget them completely.

'Okay,' I said smoothly, moving quickly to rejoin everyone.

I could feel Hayden's eyes on me, but I didn't want to talk about it just yet. I wanted to take my photo with no questions asked. He opened his mouth to speak before clamping it shut again, as if sensing my mood.

'Let's go,' he said calmly.

Things got quiet as we walked back to our jeep, which I was somewhat surprised to see untouched. Part of me had expected some sort of ambush, as if our truce had only been a false pretence, but nothing happened. Hayden, Kit, and I piled back into the jeep while those who remained of Greystone watched us peacefully. I glanced around one last time and tried to decide if I should say something. Marie was watching me with a difficult-to-read expression.

'Goodbye, Grace. Hopefully I don't see you again,' she said calmly.

'And you, Marie,' I returned honestly.

Hayden started the engine and shifted it into gear, preparing to leave.

'Oh, and Grace,' she continued, stepping forward slightly to pause his actions.

'Yeah?'

'I think your father would be proud of you,' she said sincerely, giving an approving nod. I swallowed and nodded, pleased by her words.

'Thank you.'

With that, Hayden pulled away. No one from Greystone made any attempt to stop us, and the looks on the faces I could see appeared to be relief. I felt cautiously optimistic for the first time in a long while. Our pile of issues was still sky-high, but this was, hopefully, one less thing we would have to worry about.

I let out a contented sigh as I leaned back in my seat, catching Hayden's gaze in the rearview mirror once more. It was impossible to miss the hint of pride in his expression. I mirrored him, letting a soft grin tug at my lips. It seemed, for once, things were looking up.

Seven: Indisposed

Grace

It had been a few days since we'd returned from Greystone, and there had been virtually no action, which was more than welcome. Things were settling into a normal routine again, which felt oddly ironic because I'd got used to the constant stress of dealing with some issue. The only thing keeping me from fully relaxing was the looming threat of the Brutes. I knew we'd have to make another surveillance trip soon, because it had been far too long since our last one and we had relatively no information on what the situation was with them. We had already decided sitting by in blissful ignorance was too dangerous; we had to at least keep an eye on them.

It had been yesterday when we'd held a small meeting with Kit, Docc, and Dax, who had finally been allowed to leave Docc's constant supervision in the infirmary. Leutie had taken over the job of taking care of him, something he both resented and basked in. I suspected that as much as he wanted to be independent and back to his old self, he greatly enjoyed the attention from Leutie. Each time I saw them, their grins seemed a bit wider, faces a bit happier. It was interesting to see them seemingly growing closer, because unlike Hayden and I, they didn't have to hide it. They could be openly happy with each other and no one batted an eye anymore.

Everyone had agreed that we needed to make another surveillance run on the Brutes, so Hayden, Kit, and I planned to go within the next few days. I felt nervous because of how the last one had turned out, but I hoped such a situation wouldn't arise again. The last time, we'd had to watch an innocent girl be dragged down into the depths of the Armoury, which had caused quite the fight between Hayden, Dax, and I. This time, I hoped it would go smoother.

I was starting to feel overly warm and could feel sweat pricking at my forehead, so I slowly shifted the blanket covering us down. A few moments passed and I realised it hadn't really helped, because a sleeping Hayden behind me was the main source of heat. I frowned, realising that something was off. He was always warm, of course, but now he was too warm.

I shifted slowly, careful not to disturb him, until I'd twisted completely in his grasp to face him. A quiet breath of surprise slipped between my lips when I saw the sheen of sweat covering his face, causing a few strands of his dark hair to cling to his skin. His breathing seemed a little faster than normal, and his usually tan face seemed paler than usual. Gently, I raised my arm and pressed the back of my hand to his forehead. Immediately, I could tell he was burning up with some sort of fever.

'Hayden,' I murmured gently, running my hand down his damp face.

His features twitched at the sound, but he didn't wake.

'Hayden, wake up,' I continued, a little louder this time. My hand fell to his chest, where I felt his heart pounding faster than usual. A quiet groan rumbled from his chest as I shook him gently.

'Hayden,' I said one last time.

His eyes squeezed more tightly shut before opening

slowly, blinking a few times as he adjusted to the light. Again, a groan sounded from his throat as he turned his face to bury it in the pillow.

'Morning,' he mumbled, words stifled by the pillow and the rasp in his voice.

'Do you feel okay?' I asked in concern. I could see the hair at the base of his neck sticking to his skin, which was also slick with sweat.

'Mmhmm, 'm fine,' he rumbled.

'Are you sure? You're burning up,' I told him. My hand pressed to what I could reach of his forehead again before he turned to look at me through bleary eyes.

'Why's it so bright?' he asked, ignoring my statement and blinking a few more times in confusion.

'You slept in later than normal,' I told him distractedly. 'Did you hear me? I think you have a fever.'

'No, I'm fine, Grace,' he muttered slowly, giving a feeble shake of his head.

I was far from convinced when I looked at him closer. He could hardly keep his eyes open, but when he did, they were rimmed with red and slightly bloodshot. The pale tint to his face made his usually angular features appear flat, and the sweat seemed to only gather more and more by the second. Judging by the way he tried to tug the blanket back up and pull me closer, he felt cold even though he was very clearly hotter than usual.

'You're not,' I said with a determined shake of my head. 'I'm going to go and get Docc.'

'Oh, come on,' he griped weakly. His arms tightened around me as he hauled me closer to his chest. 'Just stay with me, I'll be fine.'

My hands landed on his chest in protest, halting his attempts to cuddle into me. He frowned.

'I'll be right back,' I told him gently.

My hand ran down his chest once before I wiggled out of his grasp and climbed out of bed. As soon as I was separated from him, the relief of cool air took the place of his overwhelming body heat, reaffirming my suspicions. I moved quickly to throw on some more appropriate clothes and a pair of shoes before heading towards the door.

'Grace,' he called groggily.

I ducked my head back inside. 'Yeah?'

'I love you.'

I grinned. Even in his sick state when I'd only be gone a few minutes, he felt the need to fulfil our promise.

'I love you, Hayden,' I returned easily. His eyes closed sleepily as a contented smile fell upon his lips. 'Stay put.'

He gave another nod and tugged the blanket up around his shoulder, snuggling further into bed. This time, I exited without delay. My feet moved quickly, eager to get to Docc and bring him back to check on Hayden. It was only when I was outside and moving through camp that I realised just how late it was; people were milling around outside, and the way the sun beamed down on us told me it was at least noon, if not later.

A few people said 'hello' to me as I passed, which I returned distractedly. A group I passed were digging in the ground around some feeble plants, attempting to coax them to mature into something edible. A few looked like they were doing well, but for the most part, we were struggling to produce anything substantial.

'Grace!'

Malin rose from where she was crouched in the dirt next to Perdita. It appeared they were working on some plants as well. My head had turned towards the sound of my name but I hadn't stopped. Malin caught up to me, matching my quick pace.

'Do you have a second?' she asked, her tone bright.

'I'm sorry, Malin, but not really,' I said hurriedly.

'Is everything okay?' she asked, noting my rush. Concern flashed across her face as her eyes narrowed.

'I think Hayden's sick. I'm heading to get Docc,' I told her.

'Oh no,' she murmured, frowning. 'Well, I'll just be quick then – I think I'm going to talk to Kit today.'

I really did want to talk to her about her situation and help in any way I could, but I didn't have time to dedicate to it now.

'That's good,' I said sincerely. 'How do you think it'll go?'

'I'm not sure,' she admitted. 'He's been off and on the last few days and I just can't take the whole not knowing thing anymore, you know?'

'Yeah, I understand. Well just keep in mind what I said before, yeah? Don't let him out of it without a solid answer. Good or bad, it'll be better to know.'

'You're right,' she agreed with a determined nod. 'Thanks Grace. I'll let you know how it goes?'

'Please do,' I replied, glancing at her and nodding to reaffirm my point. 'Good luck!'

'Thanks,' she said with a grin. We were at the door of the infirmary now, so she gave me a small wave before peeling off back in the direction we'd come.

It was cooler inside, as it always was, as I entered. Things seemed quiet now that Dax had been allowed to go back to his own hut, leaving Shaw as the only long-term patient. As always, I found Docc seated at his desk, where he was sorting through some vials of medicine.

'Grace, what brings you in?' he asked calmly, flashing me a peaceful look.

'It's Hayden,' I replied. 'I think he's sick. Can you come and see him?'

'Of course,' he answered smoothly, rising from his desk. 'Let me get Frank to watch Shaw and I'll be right there, okay?'

'Okay.'

I nodded once and turned around, heading quickly back home. I had to resist breaking into a jog in my haste to get back to Hayden. This time, no one tried to speak to me, and I was quickly moving through the door again. I was relieved to see him still curled in bed, even though he clung to the blankets despite the warmth.

Quietly, I moved to the other side of the room, where he always kept a few bottles of water. I grabbed one and sat on the edge of the bed, placing my hand on his blanket-covered shoulder to wake him once more.

'Hayden,' I murmured.

He was difficult to wake, and it took a few repetitions of his name and a few not-so-gentle shakes of his shoulder to rouse him.

'Hey,' he finally said as he blinked up at me. His hand reached for me to try to pull me under the cover with him, but I resisted as I twisted the lid off the water.

'Here, drink this,' I instructed gently, holding it out to him. 'Docc's on his way.'

'You didn't need to do that,' he grumbled with a reproachful look. He propped himself up on his elbows and accepted the bottle before taking a long drink.

'I did, I'm pretty sure you've got a fever,' I informed him.

'I'm fine,' he rebutted stubbornly.

'You're covered in sweat,' I pointed out. Hayden shrugged

and gave me an unconcerned look. I gave him a pointed look and tapped the water bottle, silently instructing him to drink more. Again, he rolled his eyes, but obliged me by taking another sip.

'Maybe it's just hot in here,' he argued.

'I'm not sweating,' I said coolly, arching a brow at him. 'And you slept until noon.'

'Maybe I'm just tired,' he rebuffed in the same tone as before.

'Hayden,' I said flatly. 'You're sick, accept it.'

'I don't get sick.'

'Why do I get the feeling that you've just always been in denial when it's happened before?'

'Don't know, but I don't get sick,' he replied obstinately. I just rolled my eyes at him instead of replying while I coaxed more water into him. I was saved from arguing further by a soft knock at the door.

'Come in,' I called.

Docc's slow footsteps approached, as he stood at the foot of the bed, small bag in hand.

'Hello, Hayden. Feeling under the weather, are we?' he asked calmly.

'I'm fine,' Hayden muttered belligerently.

'Hmm,' Docc hummed. He moved to the other side of the bed and set down his bag before he started rummaging through it. I wasn't surprised to see him pull out a thermometer, which he held out to Hayden.

'Temperature, please,' he instructed. Hayden cast me a glare as if I were putting him through all this for nothing but reluctantly accepted the thermometer and placed it under his tongue. He could glare at me all he wanted, but I knew he was sick and I was going to do something about it.

A few quiet moments passed as we waited. Docc glanced around our hut pensively while I watched Hayden, who stared directly ahead. His jaw was clenched tightly, and the way he held himself up made the muscles in his chest stand out beneath the damp skin. Finally, the thermometer beeped. Hayden removed it immediately and handed it back to Docc, who read the number.

'Grace is right, you do indeed have a fever,' Docc said, unsurprised.

I resisted the urge to say 'I told you so'. Hayden avoided looking at me now that he knew I had been right.

'How's your head feeling? Stuffy at all?' Docc continued.

'Not stuffy,' Hayden replied. 'Kind of dizzy I guess.'

He looked reluctant to admit it, but now that his fever was confirmed, it seemed he'd given up his charade of feeling fine. Docc nodded.

'Do you feel warm or cold?'

'Cold.'

Docc asked about other symptoms, but it seemed Hayden didn't have many other complaints. After a while, Docc let out a quiet sigh and concluded his questioning.

'Well, it sounds to me like you've just got some sort of bug that causes a fever. I'd give you some medication but I'm afraid we've run out of anything that'll bring it down, so you might just have to sweat this one out.'

'We don't have anything?' I asked in alarm. While a fever wasn't the worst-case scenario, it made me nervous to think we didn't have any medications at all.

'I'm afraid not,' Docc answered with a frown. 'Odds are, his fever will break sometime today or tomorrow.'

'Yeah but what if it doesn't? What if it gets worse?' I questioned, anxiety rising.

'Grace, it won't,' Hayden reassured me. My eyes darted

quickly to him before refocusing on Docc in concern. I raised an eyebrow in question.

'It's not likely, but if a fever gets too high, it can cause permanent damage to the body. Though, like I said, most fevers break on their own.'

My stomach churned anxiously. It would be one thing to wait and see if Hayden got better on his own if we had medications readily available should he not, but hoping for it to break without any sort of backup plan made me very, very nervous.

'We could go on a raid,' I suggested. 'See if we can find something that'll bring down a fever—'

'No,' Hayden said sharply, cutting me off.

'Well, obviously you wouldn't go—'

'No, Grace,' Hayden repeated, shaking his head. 'You're not going without me.'

'I'm afraid you can't go anywhere, son,' Docc interjected calmly.

'Even more reason why she's not going,' Hayden argued stubbornly. 'If I don't go, you don't go.'

'Hayden, come on,' I pleaded. 'What if you need medication and we don't have it?'

'I won't need it. You heard Docc, most of the time it just breaks on its own. I really don't feel that bad, anyway,' he said with a shrug. I had a hard time believing him when his face grew paler by the second and the sweat continued to prick at his skin. It seemed holding himself up was tiring.

'Yeah, *most* of the time,' I muttered unhappily. 'I'd rather not take the risk.'

'How about a compromise?' Docc suggested. Hayden immediately shook his head while I waited for him to continue. 'If Hayden's fever hasn't broken by this time tomorrow, Grace will go on a raid for the necessary medication.'

'Deal,' I said quickly, cutting off Hayden's protests I knew would come. As much as I didn't want to wait, it was better than not going at all.

'You're overreacting,' Hayden grumbled, shooting me a weak glare.

I shrugged, unconcerned. 'You'd do it for me, wouldn't you?'

Hayden clenched his jaw and let out a defeated sigh. 'Yes.'

'All right, so that's settled. Anything you can do for him, Docc?' I asked, redirecting my gaze from an unhappy Hayden to a patiently waiting Docc.

'I'm afraid not. Just keep drinking, son, and try not to use too many blankets no matter how cold you feel. You don't want to overheat.'

Hayden gave a small nod and relaxed back into his previous position, giving up trying to hold himself up. A flash of concern washed through me again, and I moved to gently push his hair out of his face.

'Thanks, Docc,' I said sincerely.

'Of course.'

His voice was smooth and calm, and after a small duck of his head, he left the hut. It felt so odd to see Hayden so weak and vulnerable; it must feel uncomfortable for him to be in such a position.

'You don't have to be so tough all the time, you know,' I told him gently. My fingers repeated their motions of raking gently through his hair, combing the damp strands back from his pale face as I sat beside him.

'I can't help it,' he murmured softly.

His eyes were closed as he rolled to lie on his side, facing me where I was perched on the edge of the bed. His hand snaked out from beneath the blanket to land on my knee, squeezing once. Heat seared through my skin where he touched me both from the contact and the elevated temperature of his body.

'Just let me take care of you,' I coaxed. 'You need to rest.'

A heavy sigh pushed from between his slightly parted lips, and his hand squeezed my knee again.

'All right, Bear.'

I ducked forward to press a light kiss to his forehead. His breathing was already evening out, as if the short conversations with Docc and I had tired him again. Gently, I pulled his hand from my knee before rising and moving to the bathroom. I wet a small washcloth before bringing it back into the room.

He didn't react at all as I dragged the damp rag across his forehead, wiping away the sweat. After I'd cleaned his face, I folded the rag up and placed it as evenly on his forehead as his position would allow to cool him down. His breathing had slowed even more now, telling me he'd fallen asleep again.

I felt unusually helpless as the day passed very slowly. He'd wake up every now and then and talk to me a little bit before drifting off again, just as feverish and sweaty as ever. It was only when my stomach started to rumble incessantly that I finally admitted defeat and decided to leave to get some food. He hardly stirred when I woke him to tell him, waving me off and declining my offer to bring him anything.

I practically ran to the mess hall, reluctant to leave him alone. Maisie expressed her concerns when I told her about Hayden. She didn't let me leave without a small jug of soup and a few of the vegetables they'd managed to grow, instructing me to feed him even if he hated it. When I returned, I found him exactly as I'd left him: burrowed deeply beneath his blankets, sweaty and pale, and asleep.

I managed to get him to eat about half of the soup

before he refused, and he stayed awake for about an hour after that. It had grown dark now, and even after an entire day of me caring for him, he still denied being sick.

'Do you want to shower? Sometimes that helps,' I suggested lightly.

'Yeah, that's a good idea,' he agreed, surprising me. I'd been expecting resistance. He'd been cranky after being 'babied' all day, as he'd so lovingly put it.

'Okay,' I said with a satisfied grin.

I stood from where I'd been perched the vast majority of the day on the side of the bed, stretching to the left and right before ducking to pull down his covers. I offered him my hand to help him out, but he ignored it with a disgruntled look and climbed out on his own.

'I'm not dying, Grace,' he muttered grouchily.

'Don't joke about that,' I said seriously, frowning. I knew he wasn't dying, but that didn't stop me from fearing the irrational.

'Sorry,' he said with a sigh.

'It's okay,' I said lightly.

I took his hand and led him into the bathroom, where we both stripped down and stepped into the shower. Hayden had only been wearing a pair of shorts to begin with, so it didn't take long. As always, the water was cold as Hayden pulled the lever and caused it to pelt down on us. Instinctively, I stepped closer to feel his overwhelming body heat. I was surprised when I felt his hands land on my hips, rolling his thumbs over my skin lightly. Our eyes connected as I tilted my head back to look up at him, noticing he looked the most awake he had all day.

'Thank you for taking care of me,' he murmured softly, voice sincere and honest.

'You don't have to thank me,' I told him with a soft smile.

'I do. Thank you,' he repeated.

'You're welcome. Are you feeling any better? Be honest.' I arched a brow at him as if daring him to lie.

'I don't know,' he admitted reluctantly. 'The shower feels nice, but I still feel like shit.'

A frown automatically creased my features. 'I'm sorry, Herc.'

I saw the small glint that sparked in his eye and the twitch of his lips. 'It's all right.'

Instinctively, I leaned up on my toes to bring my lips to his, but as soon as he realised what I was doing, he darted out of the way.

'What are you doing?' he asked quickly, eyes shifting from happy to incredulous in about a half a second.

'Um . . . I was going to kiss you . . .' I muttered somewhat awkwardly, frowning in confusion.

'I'm sick,' he said flatly, pointing at himself. 'I don't want to get you sick, what if I'm contagious?'

I rolled my eyes and let out a small chuckle. 'I think that ship has probably sailed, don't you?'

'We shouldn't tempt fate,' Hayden said, shaking his head and giving me a mock-scolding look with a hint of amusement.

'Oh, really?' I asked lightly, grinning at him. He gave a solemn nod.

'Really.'

'That's a shame,' I said, half joking and half serious.

'I'm very heartbroken,' he replied in an overly serious tone.

'Me, too,' I laughed, grinning up at him. The water continued to pelt down on us.

'Wait, I've got an idea,' Hayden said, watching me. His

hand then left my hip to press over his mouth, the back of it to his lips and the palm facing me.

'Okay, now kiss me,' he instructed, voice muffled by his hand over his lips. His green eyes twinkled with a hint of mischievousness.

I gave a small snort of laughter as I realised what he meant. It was with a happy grin and indulgent shake of my head that I leaned up on my tiptoes to press my lips into his palm, directly where his lips lurked beneath.

'It's not quite the same, I'm afraid,' I told him.

'It's not, but we must make sacrifices,' he continued in his feigned serious tone.

'I think you're getting a bit delirious. Time to get you back to bed.'

As if on cue, the water ran out of the shower. I moved to grab us each a towel to dry off. We dressed quickly in the minimum required clothing. Already, I could see the exertion of taking the shower and simply standing for a few minutes had worn him out, because the sweat was already returning to his skin and his breathing seemed laboured.

'I mean it, back to bed,' I instructed gently.

'You coming with this time?' he asked, hanging up his towel and moving towards the bed.

I hesitated. The last thing I wanted to do was overheat him when we were trying to break his fever. Hayden noted my resistance.

'Please?' His green eyes widened as his brows rose, pouting out his lower lip and folding his hands in front of him in a pleading gesture. I let out a light laugh and shook my head, unable to resist him.

'Fine, but if you get too hot, I'm banishing you to the other side of the bed.'

'Deal,' Hayden said with a shrug.

He crawled into bed, collapsing almost immediately into the pillow as he pulled up the covers. I copied him and was greeted instantly by his arms winding around my waist to haul me against him. I could already feel how warm his body was and knew his fever had not improved. He'd slept all day, yet it was still clear he was exhausted from the sickness.

'Sleep, Hayden,' I murmured, ducking my head to press a kiss into his arm that was circled around me.

'Yes ma'am,' he whispered, breath pushing softly across my neck.

Just like that, he was asleep. I hoped he'd feel better in the morning. I fell asleep surprisingly quickly, apparently tired out from a long day of doing nothing. My sleep was often interrupted, however, from the stifling heat of his body. More than once, I had to pull away, though it never lasted long because his arms would somehow find me and bring me back to him. After many restless hours and very little sleep for me, the sun was finally starting to creep up in the sky.

I managed to make it until maybe eight or nine before I turned to examine Hayden. Almost immediately, it was very apparent that he was only getting worse. His skin was starkly pale and sweat had gathered even more than it had the day before. Quick, uneven breaths panted between his lips, and his heart hammered wildly in his chest even in sleep. Fear started to flood through me, imaging the worst-case scenarios in my head.

I brought my hands to cradle his face, feeling the heat exuding from his skin and the damp texture brought on by sweat. 'Wake up, Hayden.'

His eyes flickered a few times before he opened them, pupils blown wide in the semi-darkness.

'You're worse,' I told him with a frown.

'No,' he groaned, giving a small shake of his head before clamping his eyes shut once more.

'You are,' I insisted, rolling my thumbs along his cheeks. 'I'm going today.'

'Grace, no,' Hayden begged weakly. His voice was scratchy and impossibly low, thick with sleep and sickness as he pleaded with me.

'I'm sorry, Hayden. You need medicine and I'm going to get it for you, okay?'

A tight groan rumbled from his chest in protest, but he couldn't even manage to open his eyes again. I felt a painful pang in my heart as I observed his obvious discomfort.

'I'll be back before you know it, all right?' I leaned forward to press a kiss to his damp forehead. 'I love you.'

All he did was give a weak nod, which only cemented my decision. If he didn't have the energy to try to stop me from going, it really must have been getting bad. Quickly, I climbed from beneath the covers and got dressed. I had my shoes on and was heading to the door when, again, Hayden's voice stopped me.

'Grace,' he said hoarsely. I turned to look back at him to see he'd managed to twist around enough to look at me, leaning over the covers that were tangled around him.

'Yeah?'

'I love you. Be careful.'

My lips pulled into a smile. I nodded in determination.

'I will.'

Eight: Imperative

Grace

I moved determinedly through camp, advancing quickly towards one of the huts near ours. I knew I couldn't go completely alone on a raid, and with Hayden sick and Dax still recovering, that only left one person. A sharp knock sounded on his door as I tapped it a few times, bouncing up and down on the balls of my feet impatiently. I heard a muffled grumbling from inside before the door swung aggressively open.

'What?' Kit snapped sharply, dark eyes narrowed as he looked down at me. I blinked in surprise at his harsh reaction.

'Hey, um,' I started, frowning as his gaze did not soften. 'Hayden's sick and we don't have any meds to treat him so I was hoping you'd go with me to find some.'

Kit's jaw tightened and I thought I saw a flash of anger behind his eyes before he let out a humourless ghost of a laugh.

'Perfect,' he muttered sarcastically. 'If it was anyone other than Hayden, I'd tell you to shove off.'

My jaw dropped open in surprise at his angry, stony tone. What had I done to him?

'Okay . . .' I said slowly, eyeing him in confusion. 'Let's go then.'

Kit gave a gruff grumble that I couldn't decipher before joining me, apparently suitably dressed in what he was already wearing. I turned and headed directly towards the raid building, Kit following a few steps behind. The man on guard gave us each a respectful nod as we entered and grabbed our weapons, loading extra rounds and a few other basic supplies into a backpack before heading to the garage.

It wasn't until we had loaded ourselves into the jeep and were driving past the meagre excuse for a garden that I remembered Malin approaching me from it yesterday. Apparently their conversation hadn't gone too well. It all suddenly made a lot of sense as I cast a sideways glance at Kit, who was driving. He glared straight ahead, hands gripped evenly on either side of the wheel so tightly his knuckles turned white. I was suddenly surprised he'd agreed to come along at all.

'Are you all right?' I asked, unable to bear the slightly awkward, angry tension any longer.

'Yep, just fine,' he snapped. The muscle in his cheek twitched, and the thick scar on his neck caught my eye.

I didn't press him further. It was beyond obvious he was lying, and if it had been Hayden or Dax, I wouldn't have let them get away that easy, but Kit was slightly different. I didn't share the same easy friendship with him that I did with Dax. He reminded me a lot of people from Greystone, except he didn't have the same pointless ruthlessness that a lot of them did.

I stayed silent after that and glanced out the window, watching as the shattered ruins of the city rose before us. We hadn't even discussed where we were going, but we both knew it had to be the city. Greystone was all but ruined, so I knew they wouldn't have what we needed. I let out a deep breath to try to relax, silently praying that we'd find the proper medications overlooked somewhere.

We were about halfway between Blackwing and the city when Kit spoke again, surprising me.

'You know, you really didn't have to butt in,' he grumbled tightly. I blinked and turned to look at him again.

'What?'

'Nothing,' he muttered bitterly.

'All right . . .'

I gave him a sceptical look that he did not see and returned my attention out of the window. Every bump in the road we hit felt like it was jarring my bones as nervous tension crept up, anxious to get what we needed and get back to Hayden.

'It's not your business,' Kit continued, as if he hadn't just brushed me off. I didn't say anything in reply and waited. Sure enough, he continued. 'What the hell did you even say to her, huh?'

'You mean Malin?' I asked cautiously, confirming my suspicions.

'Of course, Malin. Who else?' Kit snapped harshly, throwing an irritated look in my direction before refocusing on the road.

'See your talk didn't go well . . .' I murmured, grimacing.

'No shit,' he said flatly. I frowned, trying to keep my irritation down.

'What happened?' I questioned.

'Not that it's your business, but since you've already involved yourself . . . She fucking ended it.'

My mouth dropped open, surprised even though I suspected it from the way he was acting. I felt a little less irritated when I considered what he was maybe feeling.

'Yeah but . . . why?' I asked evenly.

'I don't know, you're the one who put all those thoughts in her head.'

'Did she ask you what you wanted out of it?'

'Yes,' he admitted gruffly.

'And what did you say?'

His jaw clenched tighter for a second and I saw the muscles flex in his arm as his grip on the steering wheel constricted. I almost expected him not to answer when he spoke.

'I said I didn't want anything.' His voice was dark and heavy, as if reluctant to say the words. I frowned.

'Did you mean that? That you don't want anything with her?' My voice was light and careful as I spoke, cautious not to set him off so I could hear his true feelings.

'Yeah,' he said, rather unconvincingly. He let out a deep sigh and shrugged, pushing his hand through his hair momentarily.

'No. I don't know,' he finally admitted, frowning. I felt, of all things, a smile threaten to pull at my lips.

'This is just my opinion but . . . judging by how you're acting, I'd say you messed that up big time.'

Kit let out a dissatisfied scoff, shaking his head. We were nearly to the city now and I knew our conversation had to be cut off so we could focus on the raid, but I hoped to ease his mind a bit.

'Okay, I'm just going to ask you since you're being so stubborn. Just answer, don't think, okay?'

'Shoot,' he muttered, rolling his eyes.

'Do you love Malin?'

I felt myself holding my breath as I waited for his answer. Despite my instructions, I saw the internal battle waging in his mind written clearly across his face. Long seconds ticked by before he finally answered.

'Yes.'

He seemed almost annoyed to admit it, but at least he'd confessed it. My smile broke through this time.

'Then you have to tell her, you idiot,' I said, shaking my head. 'She broke up with you because she thinks you don't.'

'She never cared before, why would she care now?' he muttered, frowning.

'Because she loves you,' I said simply, shrugging as if it were obvious.

'I don't know why,' he said with a sigh.

'I don't either, but she does, so,' I said, a hint of amusement in my tone. I was pleased when I saw him give a ghost of a chuckle.

'Made quite a mess, didn't I?' he asked.

'A bit, yeah, but she'll take you back. Just don't be such an idiot. Tell her.'

Kit bit down on his lower lip and dragged his teeth over the surface before releasing it and letting out a deep breath. 'Yeah, you're right.'

'I know,' I said cockily, grinning at him.

'Easy,' he said flatly, arching a sarcastic brow at me. It was as if he had a limit for amusement, and he'd already reached it with that tiny amount.

Again, I grinned. I was pleased Kit had finally admitted his feelings and felt happy for Malin that he would, hopefully, stick to his word and make up for it. The happy feeling started to dissipate, however, when the crumbling walls of the city appeared on either side of us as we entered its limits. Hayden's face flashed through my mind and I could practically feel the overwhelming heat radiating off his body as I refocused, determined to succeed. I shoved down the anxious tension I felt and tried not to think about what would happen if we failed, because the thought of something happening to Hayden made me want to throw up on the spot.

'I think we should try some of the general stores or

pharmacies first,' I said quietly, lowering my voice as I always did in the city. It was instinctual.

'Yeah, all right,' Kit agreed, nodding.

He slowed the vehicle to manoeuvre a little easier, driving to avoid bits of debris in the road and missing chunks of concrete. My eyes scanned constantly, searching for any sign of movement that would give away an enemy. Adrenaline seared through me, putting me even more on edge as I leaned forward, gun loaded and ready. We'd driven a few blocks into the city when we came across the first store. The doors were broken off the hinges and practically every piece of glass in the window frames had been shattered, but I didn't object when Kit slowed the jeep to a halt.

'First stop?' he asked, cocking a brow.

'Yeah,' I said, nodding. My eyes were riveted on the building, still searching for signs of life, but I saw none.

As quickly and quietly as I could, I opened the door and climbed out of the jeep. Kit turned off the engine and did the same, following me as I moved towards the door. As always, I raised my gun and swept it around, squinting into the darkness of the building as I approached. Glass crunched beneath my boots and a soft breeze picked up the wisps of hair that had fallen from my ponytail, though the rest of the area was silent. I blinked a few times to let my eyes adjust to the darkness as I crept further inside.

After scanning the entirety of the store, I relaxed a bit. Thick layers of dust had settled over everything and an undeniable air of neglect existed here. I turned back to look at Kit, who had his gun raised as well, and nodded.

'Clear,' I whispered, still keeping my voice down.

Neither of us lowered our guns much, however, before we started moving through the aisles. My eyes raked the shelves, pleading with the universe to find *something* we could use to bring Hayden's fever down, but everything was bare. I couldn't even find a basic cold medication. I forced a frustrated sigh between my lips as I moved down the aisle one last time, hoping I'd missed something the first time, but the results were the same.

'Anything?' Kit called quietly from the other side of the store where he'd been searching.

'Nothing,' I admitted in frustration.

'Same here,' he muttered. 'Let's get out of here. On to the next one.'

I nodded and swallowed my disappointment as I followed him back to the jeep. We climbed in, and the engine roared back to life as he started it and took off. Again, I studied the streets, looking for Brutes or other threats, but I didn't see any. We were still pretty far from the heart of the city, which was where most of the Brute action took place.

Another building, vcry similar to the first we'd stopped at, came into sight after driving a bit further. Kit and I repeated our actions, searching the store thoroughly but coming up empty. I felt foolish that I'd been optimistic enough to think we'd find something as rare as medication in the heavily ravaged city.

We stopped at twelve more buildings, each of which had the same disappointing result. After the last one turned up nothing useful, we retreated to the jeep for what felt like the hundredth time. A heavy *slap* sounded as my hand landed on the dash, frustration getting the better of me as I hunched forward and rested my head in my hands. Hayden was probably getting sicker and sicker while Kit and I crept around the city, coming up empty-handed time and time again.

'There's nothing here,' I said angrily, words muffled by my hands. 'Everything's gone.'

'Yeah,' Kit agreed. My head snapped to the side to throw

him a glare, irrationally angry he'd agreed with me.

'You're supposed to say, "No, Grace, we'll find something!"' I told him bitterly, returning my face to my hands and letting out a defeated sigh.

'Do you want me to lie to you or do you want the truth?' Kit asked, irritation leaking into his own voice. I knew Hayden was like a brother to him and that this was stressing him out as well.

'Neither,' I mumbled unhappily.

Kit let out a frustrated huff but didn't press me, letting me sulk in my frustration.

'There is one more place,' he said slowly, voice dangerously low.

My stomach clenched. Grisly images of severed hands tacked to walls, rotting limbs hopelessly tangled together, and words written in blood immediately bombarded my mind, making my anxiety rise and my heart clench. I could practically feel the cold, rotting flesh on my skin as I felt a shiver run down my spine.

'The Armoury.'

My voice was hollow and flat as I spoke. I'd reached this conclusion about ten stops ago but had desperately clung to the hope we'd find something in the city. After so many stops, it was quickly becoming clear that we'd have no other option; if we wanted to save Hayden, we had to go into the place that had haunted me since the day I set foot in there.

'Yes,' Kit said solemnly. 'I was hoping we wouldn't have to but . . . it's not looking good, Grace.'

'I know,' I admitted. I sat back up and cast him a wary glance. 'I was thinking the same.'

We were both quiet for a second as we pondered our dilemma. It would be nearly impossible to get in, get what we needed, and get out without being noticed. We'd got lucky last time when they'd all been mysteriously gone, but I somehow doubted that would happen again.

'What are the odds he gets better on his own and doesn't even need medicine?' Kit asked seriously, turning to study me.

I sighed, frowning. 'I don't know. A few years ago in Greystone, there was this fever going around that knocked out about thirty people . . . Everyone was perfectly healthy before and we all thought that too – that it'd break and go away – but it didn't.'

'Is this the same?' Kit asked, brows furrowed low.

'I don't know, but do you really want to take that chance?' I asked, raising a brow. 'I don't.'

Kit didn't respond as he mulled over my words, thoughts racing. My mind was already made up, and I suspected I'd decided a while ago. It didn't matter if there was a chance Hayden would get better on his own. I was not willing to risk him dying simply because I was afraid of the one place that could have what we needed to save him.

'You don't have to come with, but I'm going,' I told Kit firmly, gathering my strength.

'We could check some other places first, maybe?' Kit suggested, half-heartedly at best. I shook my head instantly.

'It's already been hours. We don't have time for that,' I argued. 'Like I said, I'm going but you don't have to. Maybe it'll be better if it's just me. Easier to sneak in and all.'

'Yeah right,' Kit scoffed. 'Hayden would kill me if I let you go in there alone.'

A sad smile pulled at my lips because I knew he was right.

'He might kill me for going at all,' I said with a humourless laugh.

'You might have a point,' Kit said, nodding. 'But I think we both know that we're going.'

I took a deep breath and felt a rush of appreciation for Kit. 'Yes, we're going. Let's not waste any more time, yeah?'

'You got it.'

With that, Kit started up the jeep and immediately drove off. Even though my mind was whirling with the terrifying images I'd been haunted by for so long, I forced myself to focus on my lookout as we drove. Just as before, I scanned for Brutes or other enemies, gun raised and ready to fire.

I was jittery, but I tried to focus on Hayden to give me the strength I needed. Last time, I'd needed him to keep me anchored down, to bring me back to calm after seeing such horror. This time, he wouldn't be here to do that, and it was more imperative than ever that we got through it.

Far too quickly, Kit had arrived near the entrance to the Armoury. We were about two blocks away from the building that held the door, and Kit found a decent place to park the jeep so it would be fairly well hidden. He killed the engine and glanced at me expectantly. I gave a curt nod, more to myself than to him, and climbed out of the jeep before I could second-guess my actions.

Nauseous wave after nauseous wave rolled through me, sending my stomach heaving with every step I took. My feet carried me to the edge of the alley we'd parked in before I paused and leaned around the edge to look down the street. I was just about to suggest we wait to see the guard we'd observed weeks ago when a flash of movement caught my eye. I retreated as far back as I could while still keeping my eyes fixed on the motions.

Kit pressed flat against the wall beside me as I watched the lone Brute that had appeared. A large gun was secured in his hand as he started to walk in the opposite direction to us, glancing from side to side as he patrolled the entrance. When he turned the corner, he disappeared from sight for a few moments before reappearing on the other side, completing his round and returning back inside.

'We should go now,' I breathed, retreating to copy Kit and press myself into the wall. 'They just did a round so that'll hopefully give us an hour before the next one.'

'I agree,' Kit whispered, nodding. He gave me a serious and determined look. 'I've got your back.'

'You, too,' I replied, flashing a forced smile that exuded nothing but anxiety.

I drew a deep, somewhat shaky breath and refocused. My muscles felt tight and my heart was hammering a hundred miles per hour, but I was ready. This had to be done.

For Hayden.

'Let's go,' I muttered.

With that, I pushed myself off the wall and rounded the corner, moving quickly and stealthily as I advanced towards the opening to the garage shop where the entrance was located. Kit followed silently behind me. My eyes scanned every direction, keeping lookout for any Brutes that may have been outside, but we encountered none. The door to the garage shop was slightly ajar, and after a quick peek into the dark building, we moved inside.

I recognised the space instantly and saw the couch Hayden and I had hidden behind. It had been a close call when the pair of Brutes had appeared, but they hadn't seen us and we'd managed to escape. I hoped we'd be that lucky this time.

Kit darted behind me, making sure no one was in the room with us, before we dashed to the back of the building where the door that led to the steps was. Nerves tugged at my stomach as I leaned against the wall and peered down the dark stairwell, trying and failing to see into the pitch-black area. Muffled sounds could be heard as they drifted through the air, though it was difficult to tell what exactly it was. They seemed to be growing fainter, meaning whatever it was must have been moving away from us.

Again, Kit appeared beside me as he waited for me to make a decision. I noticed my hands were shaking slightly in front of me when the end of my gun wavered. I blew out a frustrated breath, annoyed with my body for rebelling against my mind. After listening for a few more seconds, I ticked my gun towards the entrance, indicating it was time to go.

Hayden's face swam through my mind as I took my first step into the dark, dingy stairwell. I saw him laughing, smiling, watching me in adoration. I saw his face turn pale and sweaty, muffled beneath the blankets. Seeing him change in my mind from happy and healthy to obviously sick gave me the strength I needed to keep stepping down the stairs, disappearing into oppressive darkness more and more with each step.

It wasn't long before the air started to smell musty and the light was all but extinguished. Just as before, the stairs felt like they went on forever. Pressured thumps of my heart pushed blood vigorously through my veins, and I forced my breathing to slow down. I was thankful for my training that made me naturally quiet, because I was already busy enough calming the struggle in my mind to have to worry about my body making noises as I moved.

I almost tripped when my foot finally landed on flat ground and heard Kit stumble similarly behind me before he caught himself. It was so dark that it was literally impossible to see my hand in front of my face, much less any incoming enemies. The only good news was that we would be equally difficult to see. I stretched my arm out blindly as I walked forward, jumping slightly when it collided with the cold, damp wall. I remembered how last time we'd been here there had only been one way to go from the bottom of the stairs, so I took a few tentative steps and met no resistance.

'This way,' I whispered as quietly as I could.

Kit murmured a quiet reply and followed as I started to move down the corridor. With one hand on the wall to guide me and another on my gun, I moved as quickly as I dared without making any noise. We walked for what felt like hours but was probably only minutes. The muffled noises we'd heard before grew louder and louder with each step, making it blatantly apparent we would not be so lucky as to find the Armoury empty this time.

Raucous and unruly shouting could be heard, the tones almost all deep and gruff as I listened. A chill shot down my spine as we drew closer, and goosebumps pricked at my arms when I made out a few rough phrases.

'. . . kill the little shit like a rat in the gutter.'

'Bloody smells in here.'

'. . . not enough *women* . . .'

My stomach heaved at the last one, reminding me of what I'd overheard the time we'd barely escaped this place. It wasn't difficult to understand what they wanted. A large group of mostly men would no doubt be eager for more women, and I suspected their reasons were of the insidious kind. A shaky, nervous breath ripped from my lungs as I pushed on, squinting into the darkness as a faint glow was finally visible up ahead.

If it had felt like it had taken forever for the light to appear, it seemed to take only half a second before we were feet away from the doorway we'd discovered last time. Kit and I pressed ourselves into the wall, listening closely as the crude voices continued to pour out of the opening. I tried not to zero in on any specifically, having heard more than enough already.

Slowly, I stepped closer to the door, gun raised and gripped tightly in my hand. Every inch I advanced brought a rotting, putrid scent to my nose that I recognised all too well. My mind was instantly bombarded with more horrific images of pale, rotten skin and ghostly grey limbs separated from their bodies. It was like my nightmares were coming to life and surrounding me already, and I hadn't even stepped foot through the doorway.

Kit's touch on my shoulder returned me to the moment, and I realised I had stopped moving. I couldn't quite make out his features, but I got enough of an impression that I knew I had to carry on, shifting closer and closer until I was right at the edge. My ears pricked for sounds of a guard or someone else right on the other side of the doorway, but all I heard where the rough voices from deeper within the cavern.

As surreptitiously as I could, I leaned around the edge to peer into the Armoury. My mouth dropped open in shock as I saw the same room as before with one glaring difference. Now, instead of being completely abandoned, it was swarming with Brutes. More than I could dream of counting milled about inside, some sharpening knives, some moving supplies around, some just sitting around talking to each other. Men of all ages could be seen, and I had to look very closely to find any women. The ones that I did see were far from feminine and were tougher-looking than any I'd ever seen.

'What is it?' Kit breathed, his voice barely audible from behind me.

'They're everywhere,' I replied. My heart was pounding so hard it felt like it was trying to work up my throat to escape my chest.

I could only see a small portion of the gigantic room, so surely even more lurked in the darker spaces beyond the reach of the light here. My eyes stayed firmly away from the far right of the room, where I knew what had haunted me probably remained. The stench wafting from inside the cavern was enough evidence of the destruction that lay inside; I didn't need to see the decaying bodies to know they were there.

The more I glanced around, the more I tried to focus on the contents of the Armoury rather than the people. Just as before, it was stacked and loaded with boxes and boxes of supplies, some just a few yards inside the door. My eyes darted to the nearest person, who was about twenty or thirty feet away with their back to the entrance. No one seemed to bother keeping watch on the door, confident in their vast numbers.

My heart flipped as the person turned to grab something, and I jerked back around the corner, squeezing my eyes shut and praying silently they hadn't seen me. It took every bit of concentration I had to still the nervous jitters in my legs. When no one arrived to catch us after a few moments, I let out a quiet breath of relief. Leaning back over, I saw that the person had resumed their work and was once again with his back to us.

'We have to go, quickly. There are only a few people over here and they're not looking,' I instructed as quietly as I could to Kit.

He nodded and I leaned over the edge of the doorway again. Nothing had changed, so I took a deep breath, stooping low and keeping my gun ready, before darting inside and sprinting a few feet before throwing myself silently behind a pile of boxes. I glanced back at Kit, visible by only a dim light reflected in his eyes, and nodded. He took a quick look around and copied me, sprinting towards me and landing almost silently on the ground next to me.

From where we had landed, we couldn't see anything, which was dangerous. I already felt like I was going to throw up with nerves, but I shoved them down as I grabbed a box and pulled it towards me, wasting no time in opening it and searching through its contents. I was disappointed to see it held things like rope and zip-ties instead of something that could help Hayden. I shoved it aside and grabbed another, Kit doing the same behind me.

Every second that passed felt like a ticking time bomb until we were inevitably caught, and I cringed at every single sound we made even if it was no more than a whisper. I opened box after box only to find things we hadn't come for. Apparently Kit was having the same issue, because I saw his hands clench momentarily into frustrated fists when he opened yet another box full of canned food.

'It's not over here,' he huffed quietly, frowning around. 'They were sorted last time, remember?'

'Shit, that's right,' I murmured, pushing the wisps of hair back from my face.

'They were over there,' he said. He pointed at a different group of boxes about thirty feet away, where several Brutes lingered just on the other side of the pile.

'Great,' I muttered. 'Ready?'

'As I'll ever be,' he said with an almost sarcastic shake of his head.

Again, I crept towards the edge of the boxes to peer around them cautiously. The people standing next to the cartons we were aiming for stood facing each other, meaning some had a very good chance of seeing us. They were distracted, however, by an argument going on between them. I could feel precious time slipping away with every second we wasted, so when the one who had the best chance of seeing us ducked to tie his shoe, I bolted.

My feet carried me as quickly as I could, not even daring to look around to see if I'd been spotted. It was difficult to run hunched over, but I managed to make it to the right spot without anyone raising any alarm. Kit landed milliseconds after I did, apparently having followed me instead of waiting this time. I was about to reach for a box when a sudden voice made my blood run cold.

'What was that?'

Shit.

'What?'

'Over there, I saw something.' This voice, the first voice, belonged to a man.

'Shove off, wanker, don't try to change the subject,' growled a different man.

My heart all but stopped as I heard footsteps approaching. Their arguing continued.

'I'm not, I'm telling you. I saw something,' said the first man, his voice growing louder as he neared.

'We've got to go,' I whispered tensely. 'Grab a box and run.'

I had no idea if these boxes contained what we needed or not, but I hoped Kit's memory was correct. The footsteps were right on the other side of the boxes now, and I could practically smell the stench of body odour drifting off the men as they drew ever closer.

I reached for a box as Kit did, trying to get a good grip on my weapon before preparing to sprint away.

But it was too late.

'Looks like we've got ourselves a couple of thieves.'

I glanced up, petrified as I saw the dirty, scarred faces of the two men looking down at Kit and me as we crouched down.

'A pretty thief,' the second commented.

'It'll be a shame to lose those hands. Maybe she'll make use of them first,' said the first, a sick sneer spreading across his face.

'Don't need those when we have what's between her legs.'

I was unable to think, move, or even breathe as my nightmare loomed in front of me, more real than ever as I gaped at them. They leaned forward, reaching for me. Two pairs of sweaty hands gripped my arms and started to drag me upward when a deafening bang ripped through the air.

I was instantly splattered with hot, sticky liquid as the air filled with the bitter, metallic scent of blood. My jaw fell open in shock as I saw the first man's head snap backward, a gaping, ragged hole ripped straight through his forehead. The second man swore in surprise and turned to glare in shock at Kit, whose gun was aimed at him. He barely opened his mouth to say something when a second bang echoed in the cavern, blasting an identical hole in his own face. He had hardly dropped to the ground when Kit's free hand yanked me to my feet. Somehow, we each managed to hang on to our boxes, our guns temporarily stowed at our waists.

'Run!' he shouted, briefly tugging me towards the door we'd entered.

His word snapped me back to action, and my body took over as I started sprinting. Kit's gunshots and the Brutes' loud voices had drawn the attention of practically every single human in the space. A fleeting glance over my shoulder almost tripped me up as I saw Brutes running after us, some with weapons and some empty-handed. Snarling yells and horrific words were hurled at us as we fled, a few yards ahead of them as they gave chase.

Clutching the box tightly under my arm, I sprinted after

Kit. The hallway quickly became pitch-black again and I couldn't see at all where I was going, bumping into the wall a few times as my body tried to run in a straight line. Every few feet we ran, a deafening bang would echo through the small space and a bright blaze of light would temporarily illuminate it, giving brief, terrifying flashes of the horror pursuing us.

I didn't dare turn around to fire for fear of tripping. I pushed myself as hard as I ever had to keep pace with Kit, who blazed forward. The barbaric sounds and gruesome calls of the Brutes echoed around us, invading my senses from all sides. It was impossible to tell if they were gaining on us or not, but I tried to focus on escaping.

I felt like we'd sprinted for ages, and I was beginning to fear we'd never reach the stairs when Kit stumbled in front of me, swearing loudly before scrambling to his feet and starting to climb. I copied him, glancing once over my shoulder just as someone fired his gun. The temporary flash illuminated the man's grungy, bloodthirsty face, and I felt the *whoosh* of the bullet as it barely missed me and lodged itself into the wood of the steps beside me.

'Go, go!' I shouted at Kit, urging him on.

Finally, there was light visible as we neared the top of the stairs. Fear, anxiety, and a thousand other emotions ripped through me as I pushed myself on, nearly falling down when a figure appeared at the top. Before I could even look and see who it was, I raised my gun and fired, dropping the shadow to the ground. We sprinted the last few steps and leaped over the body, which a quick glance told me was a Brute.

Kit and I sprinted recklessly through the garage, shoving aside anything in our way as we desperately clutched our boxes and weapons. We were just about to the door when the Brutes reached the top of the stairs and started to spill out. I knew once they were out of the narrow corridor, they would be much faster. My legs pumped even harder, propelling me forward.

Now that we were out of the narrow hallway, Kit and I ran side by side, turning to fire randomly into the crowd as often as we dared. The rubble of the street flashed by as we hurtled outside, heading down the cracked pavement towards where the jeep was hidden. We were only maybe ten yards ahead of the Brutes and would have to move impossibly quickly to make it out alive.

'Keys, Kit!' I shouted, breathless and winded from all the sprinting.

'Got them!'

Kit had to stash his gun hastily in his jeans in order to pull the keys free, but I heard them jingling as we ran. I turned again and fired over my shoulder, not even bothering to aim or see if I'd hit anyone. Every time I turned around, there seemed to be more and more Brutes, and they were gaining on us.

'*Shit*,' I hissed.

I was running so quickly that I almost flew past the small opening the jeep was enclosed in, catching it only because of Kit veering suddenly to the side. My body felt like it might shatter as I heard Kit start the engine and throw it into reverse, slamming on the brakes to cause us to shoot backwards quickly. The jeep had barely backed out into the streets when the Brutes caught up to us, starting to surround the vehicle.

'Go, go, go!' I yelled, urging Kit on as I practically bounced in the seat.

Kit obliged and slammed on the gas, bolting the jeep forward. I felt a few rough bumps as the jeep flattened a few Brutes, the cracking of their bones audible even over the roaring crowd. Guns and other weapons echoed through the air as they fired at us, but we were already speeding away, leaving them behind in the dust. I turned around anxiously, gripping the seat deathly tight as I watched their figures grow smaller and smaller.

Somehow, some way, we had made it out alive.

Now, we just had to make it back to Blackwing and hope Hayden would as well.

Nine: Contingent

Grace

The engine of the jeep roared as Kit sped away from the destruction of the Brutes behind us. My heart still hammered wildly in my chest and sweat trickled down the sides of my face as I leaned back against the seat, eyes closing and breath pushing slowly in relief. The moment of relief was short-lived, however, as I realised a very major problem still existed.

I opened my eyes and glanced down at my lap to see the box I'd somehow managed to carry as I fled. I was terrified that it did not contain what we needed to help Hayden. I retrieved Kit's box from the backseat, where he'd tossed it roughly in his haste to climb into the vehicle. Two boxes, fairly large in size but not large enough to calm my nerves, now sat in my lap.

'You going to check them or what?' Kit asked, glancing sideways at me with a tight expression.

I blew out a deep breath and placed jittery hands on top of the first one.

'What if it doesn't have what we need?' I asked, stalling.

'We won't know if you don't open it, now will we?' Kit asked, voice torn between impatience and understanding.

I drew my lip between my teeth as I closed my eyes, steadying myself for a moment before I moved to tear open the first one. My fingers seemed reluctant to cooperate, and I fumbled more than I should have before I finally pried open the first flap. I could practically hear my stomach twisting nervously as I peered into the box.

Immediately, a breath whooshed out of my lungs when I saw it contained medical supplies. Quickly, I shifted around the contents, speedily examining the items to look for what I wanted: an antipyretic. I picked up bandages, sutures, antibiotics, vitamins, but nothing to bring down a fever. I started to grow frantic, shoving packets aside as I desperately searched for more, but there was nothing.

'Shit,' I muttered, giving up and slamming the flaps closed again. I anxiously pushed a few strands of hair behind my ear and shoved the first box to the backseat. While we could use the supplies, they weren't what I desperately hoped for. All my hopes now lay within the second box.

Moving as quickly as I could and struggling more than I should have, I finally managed to rip open the second box. My stomach plummeted when I saw the contents looked very similar to the first.

No, no, no.

I grabbed items and flung them out of the box, checking hastily before confirming they weren't right. Kit swore in surprise when a box of bandages almost hit him in the face. I huffed in frustration as the box became emptier and emptier. I had all but given up hope when my hands closed around one of the last items. My eyes darted to the label quickly, already resigned to failure, and I nearly tossed it away before I did a double take and refocused on it.

Antipyretic.

'Oh my god,' I breathed, collapsing back into my seat as I clutched the bottle close to my chest. 'Yes, yes, *yes*.'

'Did we get it?' Kit asked sharply, noting my reaction.

'We got it,' I sighed with relief.

'Thank god,' Kit muttered. He, too, relaxed a bit as he drove. 'Would have been a real shitstorm for nothing if we hadn't.'

'I'll say,' I agreed. I clutched the bottle of pills tightly in my other hand, hanging onto it for dear life.

I felt exhausted on every level: mentally, physically, emotionally.

After a few more moments I was relieved to see the familiar trees that surrounded Blackwing coming into view. A tumult of emotions was already rolling through me, terrified that we'd come back to something worse. I saw Hayden's face in my mind, pale and sweaty and ill, and desperately hoped he hadn't got worse while we were gone. It had been hours, and evening was fast approaching. Plenty of time for things to take a turn for the better or worse.

I perched on the edge of my seat, prepared to bolt from the car the moment it stopped. My knee bounced up and down anxiously, holding back from telling Kit to hurry more than he already was.

Finally, mercifully, our hut came into view. Kit slammed on the brakes right outside, though I'd opened my door before we'd come to a complete stop. I hurried inside, not bothering to look if Kit followed or not. I tried not to think of the possibilities and held my breath, terribly nervous to see Hayden's current state.

The first thing I noticed was how hot it was inside. It seemed dark, too, even though it was still early evening. It took a moment for my eyes to adjust after being outside, but I saw he was there, exactly where I'd left him, buried beneath a heaping pile of blankets. Sweat poured down his shockingly pale face, and quick, panting breaths escaped his dry, ghostly pale lips. Hair stuck to whatever bit of his skin it reached. He was even worse than before.

I sat on the edge of the bed and reached to place a hand on his shoulder, which was damp and searing hot. Fear crept through me that he'd got this bad in a matter of hours.

'Hayden,' I said gently, shaking him slightly. He did not react. 'Hayden, wake up,' I repeated more firmly.

Again, he did not move. I shook him more forcefully before running my hand along his side.

'Hayden!' I called, loudly enough to draw a stifled groan from him.

A flicker of relief managed to break through the nervous tension I felt, but it was quickly extinguished when he hardly managed to open his eyes. He didn't seem to really register that I was there, because his eyes shut quickly as if already drifting off again.

'Hayden, you need to take this,' I instructed gently yet firmly. I opened the bottle and tipped a few pills into my hand, reaching to grab the water that sat next to the bed. He said nothing, asleep once more.

'Hey,' I said, giving him yet another gentle shake. His eyes opened again in surprise.

'Bear,' he rumbled, voice deep and scratchy.

'Hey, Herc,' I said with a soft smile. My hand moved automatically to pet his hair back from his face. His green eyes appeared darker than usual in contrast to the paleness of his face.

'Bear, don't go,' he pleaded. His eyes squeezed closed for a moment before he managed to reopen them. 'I'll be fine, you don't need to go.'

Confusion washed through me as I frowned, searching his face. He must have been even worse than he looked if he didn't remember me leaving.

'I already went,' I told him. 'I'm back now. You don't remember?'

He frowned, blinking a few times in confusion.

'Don't go,' he repeated, shaking his head. It was as if my words were in another language or something.

'I'm back, Hayden,' I said slowly. My hand continued to smooth back his hair.

'Please don't go,' he murmured. A hand snaked out from beneath the blankets to reach for me, landing on my knee. He squeezed it weakly.

'I won't go anywhere,' I promised. I hated to see him this way. 'You need to take these though, okay?'

'What is it?' he murmured, eyes drifting shut again.

'No, don't go back to sleep,' I said quickly, voice somewhat frantic. 'Here, open up. They'll bring your fever down.'

Hayden frowned, as if he wasn't following.

'Just trust me,' I pleaded, holding them out.

'Okay,' he assented.

His hand left my knee to clumsily pick up the pills, popping them into his mouth before he allowed me to tilt the water bottle to his lips. He took a long drink before pushing it meekly away.

'Okay, now you can sleep,' I told him softly. He was already melting back into his pillow, eyes drifting closed once more.

'Sleep with me,' he requested groggily.

'Soon,' I promised. I wanted to make sure he actually got better before I crawled into bed with him.

'Soon,' he repeated, giving a small shake of his head as he pulled up the blankets. It seemed he'd acquired those off the couch as well, against Docc's instructions. I planned to remove a few as soon as he was asleep.

It only took a few seconds for him to doze off again, leaving me to sit and stare. It hardly felt real to see him like this, and now that I'd got him to take the medicine, the strange rush of adrenaline I'd felt was fading. All I wanted to do was crawl into bed with him and feel his arms around me, but I couldn't. He had to start to recover before I could consider anything of the sort.

Slowly, I rose from the edge of the bed, though I doubted the disturbance would wake him. I probably could have jumped on the other side and he wouldn't have moved. Still, I was cautious not to move too much as I peeled back some of the blankets, gathering them in my arms before moving to deposit them on the couch. Then, I moved to the bathroom to wet a rag, which I carried back into the main room. Sitting on the edge of the bed once more, I gently ran the rag over his face to wipe away the sweat that had settled on his skin.

Pleased with my work, I sat back to examine him a bit closer. His breathing was still too fast and he was pale, but at least he wasn't drenched in sweat and buried beneath too many blankets. I couldn't help but lean forward to press a light kiss onto his temple.

It scared me to see him in such a way. Not only was he physically weak, but he didn't seem to really know what was going on. I knew that only really bad fevers had such an effect on the mind, and I desperately hoped the medications would start to kick in soon. The hours would surely be like agony to wait for them to pass, but I had no intention of ever leaving his side. I noticed his hand still lay peeking out of the blanket, so I reached for it to grasp with my own. Slowly, I ducked down to press a light kiss to his knuckles that he would not feel as he slept.

'How is he?'

I jumped and bolted upright at the sound of Kit's voice. I

turned to see him standing in the doorway, leaning against the frame. It was impossible to tell how long he'd been there.

'He's not good,' I said honestly. 'But he took the meds so I guess now we just wait and see.'

Kit didn't say anything but gave a pensive nod. His arms were crossed loosely across his chest.

'How long have you been standing there?' I asked, not really caring.

'Long enough,' Kit said with a light shrug. 'You really love him, huh?'

Kit appeared to be deep in thought and I suspected he had someone else on his mind.

'I really love him,' I answered easily.

Again, Kit was quiet. His gaze had fallen to the floor as he pondered whatever was going through his mind.

'Speaking of . . .' I prompted, trailing off expectantly. I was surprised to see a slight quirk of his lips as he smiled softly.

'Yeah, speaking of. I've got to go find Malin.'

'Just be honest. Maybe get over yourself, a bit,' I said lightly with a grin.

'Yeah, yeah,' Kit muttered, waving me away playfully. 'See you, Grace.'

'See you,' I replied. He turned to head out before I stalled by calling him back. 'Hey, Kit!'

He turned to glance back at me. 'Yeah?'

'Thanks for coming with me today. I wouldn't have made it alone,' I said honestly.

'It's nothing,' he said dismissively. 'Anything for that guy.'

He tipped his head towards Hayden, who was sound asleep, before continuing.

'Take care of him, yeah?'

'I will,' I promised, meaning it with everything I had.

Kit nodded again and ducked out, closing the door behind him. I sighed and turned back to Hayden, who I was pleased to see breathing a little easier now. My hand pressed lightly to his forehead, where his skin was still burning hot. Impatience flared inside me and I tried to force it down; the medicine would take a while to kick in, and I just had to trust that it would work.

Time passed very slowly when I had nothing to do but observe Hayden. The sun slipped from the sky as the darkness of night cascaded over us, bringing with it the welcoming cooler air. While it had been swelteringly hot before, it now felt pleasantly cool in our hut. That, combined with the fewer blankets, meant Hayden wasn't sweating as much as before. Every half hour or so, I'd press my hand to his forehead, feeling the difference and trying not to grow even more impatient with the slow changes.

It wasn't until about three hours later that I actually noticed him cooling down. By four hours, his breathing had started to slow to a more normal pace. After five hours, some of the colour started to return to his face, though there was no denying he still looked peaky. I was relieved, however, that he appeared to be getting better as the hours ticked by.

My body began to grow stiff from lack of movement, but I tried to ignore it. I shifted in my position, twisting and stretching here and there, but I never left his side. His hand remained claimed in mine, and I entangled my fingers with his over and over again, noting every speck of skin and fine line on his hand. I almost had every single detail memorised when he issued a soft groan, jerking my attention back to his face.

He was lying on his side, facing me. I watched as he groaned again and turned to bury his face momentarily in his pillow before turning back to me and opening his eyes slowly. It was dark out now, but I'd lit a few candles to cast the hut in a soft glow. Though difficult to tell in the lighting, I thought his face looked like he'd regained even more colour.

'Hey,' he greeted hoarsely.

'Hey,' I replied softly. My hand still held his, and he gave a light squeeze of my palm.

'What time is it?' he asked. He sounded confused, but not in the delirious way he had before.

'Late. You slept all day,' I answered. 'How do you feel?'

'Like shit,' he grumbled. 'But a lot better than before.'

Again, I felt a wave of relief. He sounded more like his old self, even if he was exhausted and groggy.

'Do you remember earlier?'

He frowned, confused. 'Earlier? What did I say?'

'It was right after I came back but you thought I hadn't left yet. You didn't want me to go.'

Hayden's eyes widened before his brows pulled low. He shook his head. 'I don't remember any of that.'

'You were pretty out of it,' I told him, pursing my lips.

'Apparently,' Hayden muttered. 'This is so embarrassing.'

I let out a soft laugh. 'Why?'

'Because I'm sick and apparently saying things I don't even remember,' he said adamantly.

'You didn't say anything embarrassing,' I assured him, squeezing his hand again.

'Right,' he scoffed sceptically. I was pleased to see a ghost of a smile pulling at his lips.

'You didn't! You're very sweet when you're sick,' I told him. My own smile widened.

'Aren't I always?'

'Erm,' I said, pretending to grimace. His brows raised

before I shook my head and laughed. 'You're always pretty good.'

'Mmhmm,' he hummed, before he grew serious again. 'So I take it you got medicine?'

'We did.'

'We?' he asked, raising a brow.

'Kit went with me,' I told him.

'Oh, that's good.'

'Mmhmm,' I replied, ducking my head in agreement. My eyes studied him a few moments longer. 'You do look a lot better.'

'Where'd you get it?' Hayden asked, ignoring my observation.

'You sound like you feel better, too,' I continued, hoping to distract him from his question. He would not be happy about it and I wanted to avoid telling him if I could.

'Grace.'

'Do you want anything? Food or water?'

'Grace.'

'Because I'm sure I could find you some food if you're hungry—'

'Grace!'

I snapped my mouth shut and looked at him guiltily. He was watching me suspiciously, clearly not biting at my attempt for distraction.

'Where did you get it?' His eyes were narrowed sternly as he waited for my answer. I sighed.

'Well . . . we tried looking everywhere first. We went to every place we could think of and even a few new places, but there wasn't anything so . . .'

Hayden seemed to be growing tense as he listened. 'So . . .?' he pressed.

'So we went to the Armoury.'

'You *what?!*'

I grimaced at his harsh tone, expecting such a reaction.

'We had no other choice, Hayden. It was the only place left to look,' I said truthfully.

'You went to the *Armoury*?!' he seethed, glaring at me.

'Yes, and it's a damn good thing we did, because you were so much worse when we got back,' I argued stubbornly, holding his tight gaze.

'Grace, you shouldn't have done that,' Hayden said, shaking his head. 'It's dangerous.'

'We made it back,' I rebutted.

'Yeah, you're lucky,' he muttered angrily. 'What happened? How did you get in and out of there with the medicine?'

I bit down on my lower lip, stalling again. Hayden regarded me disapprovingly. He raised an eyebrow, willing me to continue.

'We, um . . . well we made it all the way in there just fine. They don't have anyone guarding the door or anything so we got through to this first pile of boxes but they didn't have what we needed so we moved to this other area but . . .'

'But?' he prompted impatiently.

'But they saw us and caught us while we tried to hide,' I said quickly, as if he might not hear what I said. A flash of emotions crossed Hayden's face before his brows lowered even more, intensifying his gaze.

'They caught you?'

'Yeah, well kind of,' I said. 'Two of the Brutes came over and started talking but – but Kit shot them before they could do anything, so we just grabbed a box each and ran for it.'

Hayden was silent, alternating between jaw clenching

tightly and relaxing as if he was feeling several different emotions at once.

'They chased us all the way up to the street, but we got in the jeep and managed to get away before they caught us. We got lucky that the right medicine was in one of those boxes because we didn't have time to check before we ran.'

'Oh my god, Grace,' Hayden breathed, shaking his head. 'Are you okay?'

'I'm fine,' I replied, holding his gaze. Hayden shifted forward so he was closer to me and placed both of his hands on my thighs.

'No, really,' he persisted, shaking his head. 'Was it . . . like last time?'

I felt a slightly painful pang in my heart as the memories of that horrific place came rushing back.

'I didn't see it all,' I said. I didn't need to be more specific for him to understand: I hadn't seen the rotting pile of bodies. Not this time.

'Are you sure you're okay?' he pressed, voice loaded more with concern than anger now.

'Yes, I think so,' I said honestly. I'd done what I had to in order to save him.

I felt a wave of relief crash over me as he hauled me forward into his lap. I wound my arms around his neck, scooting closer as I let myself melt into him.

'You shouldn't have done that, Grace,' he murmured. My heart gave a warm, heavy thud.

'I had to,' I insisted.

'You could have got hurt,' he continued.

'I know, but it's okay, Hayden. It all turned out okay.'

I felt Hayden sigh as he hugged me. My eyes drifted shut as I let the warmth of his touch envelop me, soothing me and washing away the stress I'd been under all day. It was just what I needed after everything, and though he was still sick, he was clearly well on his way to recovery. I had accomplished what I needed to and nothing he could say would make me regret my decision to go.

'You shouldn't have gone there but . . . thank you for what you did for me. I love you, Grace.'

'I'd do anything for you,' I admitted honestly. 'And I love you.'

There was no place I'd rather have been than in his lap, curled against his chest with his arms around me. There was no better way to distract me from the horrors I'd faced, and there was no better way to comfort me than the way he did. Even though I was trying to heal him, he returned the favour without even trying.

With Hayden, I was home.

Ten: Dubiety

Hayden

It was the middle of the night when I was shaken from my sleep, disturbed by the murmured words and sudden jerks of Grace's body against my own. I lay on my back with her curled into my side and head on my shoulder, her leg hitched around mine and arm draped around my torso.

I realised that, for the third night in a row, she was having a nightmare.

Gently, I bent my arm so I could run my fingers down her scalp, shifting enough so I could get a better look at her face, which was contorted in fear.

'Grace,' I murmured. 'Wake up, love.'

As always, she did not respond to my first attempts. It seemed that with every passing nightmare, it was harder and harder to shake her out of them. A frightened whisper slipped past her lips that I could not decipher as her grip tightened on me even more.

'Grace, it's okay,' I continued, voice gentle yet firm. 'You need to wake up.'

My other hand rose to shake her more firmly, trying to pull her from the depths of sleep.

'No . . .'

Her voice was weak and fearful as she mumbled something I couldn't hear.

'Please wake up, Grace,' I begged. Each nightmare she endured weighed heavily on my heart. I felt helpless that I couldn't stop this from happening, and guilty because I knew it was her recent trip to the Armoury that was the cause – the trip she'd gone on to save me.

'Please, love,' I repeated.

Finally, she sucked in a sharp breath that told me she'd woken up, eyes wide and bewildered as she glanced around in fear before she realised where she was. I hated that I'd come to know exactly how things would go whenever this happened.

'You're okay,' I murmured gently, rubbing my hand up and down her arm.

She let out a deep sigh and raised a hand to rub over her forehead.

'Again?' she questioned, embarrassment and frustration leaking into her voice.

'I'm sorry, Grace,' I said sincerely. Before, her nightmares had been relatively few and far between, but I was to blame for this sharp increase in frequency.

She shifted and brought her arm to my chest before resting her chin on it, frowning at me as I glanced down at her. 'Don't be sorry. It's not your fault.'

'I feel like it is,' I muttered guiltily. 'It's because you went back to the Armoury, isn't it?'

Grace's silence confirmed what I already knew. Her green eyes studied me closely, reluctant to admit the truth.

'We've been over this,' she said with slight exasperation. 'You would have done the same for me. You're better now and I'm glad I went. I'd do it all over again, nightmares or no nightmares.'

I frowned at her, believing her but still unsatisfied with my ability to do anything.

'I'm serious,' she continued when I didn't reply.

She gave an earnest nod before scooting towards me, pausing an inch or two away from my lips. I still felt guilty, but it didn't stop my hand from snaking upward to hook under her ear and pull her forward. My lips connected with hers in a gentle kiss, lingering for a few moments before I reluctantly released her. She settled back into me, laying her head on my shoulder once more. I felt the tips of her fingers trace gently over my side as she hugged me loosely.

'Goodnight, Hayden,' she murmured sleepily, apparently uninterested in discussing her nightmare any further.

'Goodnight, Grace.'

As I held her tight and prepared to drift off to sleep again, I wanted to believe she would be okay. I knew she was strong, so incredibly strong, but I had a sinking feeling that these nightmares wouldn't go away anytime soon. Worse, I had an odd sense of foreboding as if there was more to what was causing them, like a mere raindrop preceding a torrential downpour.

Dax

I squeezed my eyes shut momentarily, fighting off the bright sun that had started to creep over the horizon. I felt the heat of Leutie's arm pressing into mine as she sat beside me, leaning close for warmth as we sat at the top of the tower in the crisp morning sunlight. We'd only been up there an hour or so and I was already having trouble focusing. I checked my hand, which had healed enough to just need a light bandage over the butchered fingers.

'It's pretty up here,' Leutie observed. I turned my gaze to her face to see her studying the view with a placid expression. 'All the trees and stuff.'

The trees and greenery was something I'd grown up with, so I took it for granted. Leutie, who had grown up in the harsh and starkly bland camp of Greystone, took great joy in such observations.

'It is, huh?' I agreed, unable to take my eyes off her face. As if she felt me watching her, she turned and sent me a soft grin.

I felt drawn to her and didn't bother resisting as I leaned forward, closing the distance between us to press a kiss to her lips that she accepted. The pressure remained for a few moments, indelible and meaningful, before she kissed me back, making me feel things I hadn't sensed in a very long time. When I went to touch her face, I had barely applied any pressure to her soft skin before I was brutally reminded of the ugly remnant of my hand.

Immediately, I dropped my touch and drew back, sucking in a breath before letting it out in a disappointed, slightly embarrassed sigh. I felt inadequate, as if I were missing more than just a few fingers.

A look of confusion flitted across her features when I broke the kiss, but it didn't take long for her to trace my emotions as her eyes darted to my hand.

'Oh, Dax,' she murmured, scolding me gently. She reached forward to take my hand in her own. 'I told you that you don't need to worry about this.'

I couldn't seem to look at her as I studied my hand, flexing my fingers a few times. She had indeed told me over and over again that it didn't bother her in the slightest, and to her credit, she'd never once done or said anything that would make me not believe her, but I couldn't shake the feeling. Ever since the first time I'd kissed her, impulsively and unexpected even to myself, she'd been by my side. I got to know her more and more each day, and every day I discovered things about her that drew me into her even more.

'I know,' I replied. 'But I—'

'Shh,' she said, cutting me off with a shake of her head. 'Don't waste a thought on it.'

As if to further emphasise her point, she lifted my hand and brought it to her lips, kissing the back of it gently. She placed it on the side of her face, exactly where I'd barely touched her before retreating. She cast one last meaningful glance at me before she leaned forward again, bringing her lips to hover near mine. Again, I was unable to resist as I leaned forward, kissing her while my hand pulled her closer to me. Her lips parted easily for mine, and she let out a soft gasp when my tongue smoothed against hers.

It was things like that that told me how innocent she was. I never pushed her to do anything and our kisses were often sweet and simple, but there were times when the heat would grow and the touches would become more desperate.

Times like now, when her fingers kneaded my skin in her desire to pull me closer. Times like now, when I felt her breath growing more uneven as my lips moved over hers. Times like now, when all I wanted to do was pull her into my lap and feel her body against mine.

Taking a chance, I broke the kiss to trail my lips across her cheek, to her ear, and finally down her neck. My lips parted over her throat, sucking lightly to draw a soft, satisfied moan. She pulled me closer and her head tipped to the side, in encouragement. I felt more and more eager to continue and had just let my teeth nip at her throat when a sudden *bang* sounded off in the distance.

Immediately, we both sprang apart, slightly wild and bewildered-looking as our eyes darted around guiltily.

'What was that?' she asked, her voice breathless as her hands fidgeted in her lap, newly freed after quickly withdrawing them from around my neck.

'Gun,' I replied.

I scanned the horizon, squinting against the bright light of the sun. I looked towards Greystone and the city, expecting to see an approaching group, but I saw nothing. I had nearly given up trying to see where the sound had come from before my eyes snapped back to something I'd overlooked.

'There,' I breathed, pointing so Leutie could see. She leaned forward slightly and studied where I indicated.

'What is it?' she asked, frowning.

'I don't know,' I murmured.

Reluctantly, I stood from where I'd been sitting next to her to stoop behind one of the guns with a scope. Pressing my eye to the opening, I quickly found the source of movement.

'Three people,' I replied. 'Could be Brutes.'

'Oh, no,' Leutie said, fear obvious in her voice. 'Why would they be out of the city?'

'I don't know,' I repeated, trepidation creeping up.

I continued to watch as the people moved closer, more details emerging as moments passed. I saw two men and one woman, and they were moving faster than people would normally on foot. Upon closer inspection, I saw that bicycles were bringing them closer to Blackwing. I frowned, confused when I saw no obvious weaponry. Their clothes, too, were strange – they were too clean.

'I don't think they're Brutes,' I continued, thinking out loud as I continued to look through the scope.

'Who, then?'

I felt my brows pull low as I studied them, details growing clearer with every second as they got closer. I waited with bated breath until finally, the details of their faces were visible. I sucked a quiet gasp between my lips as I recognised one of the men heading straight for Blackwing. It was a face I hadn't seen for a while but knew nonetheless.

It was hard to forget any of the leaders of any of the camps, and this one was no different.

'Renley,' I told Leutie.

'Who's Renley?'

'He's the leader of Whetland. Or one of them, at least.'

I was torn. The usual protocol was to take out any approaching enemies, but we hardly ever interacted with Whetland at all. I could have sworn I saw Renley's eyes darting up to the tower as he rode, as if looking straight at me. I became convinced when he gave a nod and reached for something in his pocket. My body tensed and my finger reached for the trigger, poised to fire if he pulled out some sort of weapon.

Finally, as if in slow motion, I saw him draw the object from his pocket. My body sagged with relief as I let out the breath I hadn't known I was holding when I saw he'd pulled out a swatch of white cloth, a makeshift sign of surrender, which he waved in front of him.

'We have to find Hayden,' I said, jumping back from the gun and grabbing Leutie's hand to yank her out of her sitting position. She appeared surprised but recovered quickly, keeping hold of my hand as we bounded down the stairs.

As soon as we reached the bottom, I broke out in a sprint, still tugging Leutie along as she tried to keep up. We had to move quickly, because I had to alert Hayden before Renley and the others from Whetland reached Blackwing. They were probably less than five minutes away.

Finally, we reached his hut. With complete disregard, I burst through the door, causing it to nearly swing off its hinges. My eyes darted around before locking on the flash of movement that came when Hayden bolted upright in bed, surprised by my sudden entrance. Grace followed, looking slightly sleepy yet alert as her wide eyes landed on me.

'Hey—'

'Dax, what the hell—'

'Look, I'm sorry, but we have a situation,' I said hurriedly. Both of them appeared to be decently dressed and like they'd just woken up so I didn't think I'd interrupted anything, but I made sure to keep my eyes focused on Hayden just in case.

Hayden shot a concerned look at Grace and I noticed his eyes flick down her body, as if making sure she was completely covered, before turning back to me.

'What do you mean? What's going on?' he asked, climbing out of bed quickly. He moved to throw a shirt over his bare torso, leaving the athletic shorts he already wore before tugging on his tennis shoes.

'We were on tower duty and we heard a gun go off, then I saw some people coming from Whetland. Renley's with them.'

'They're coming right now?' Hayden asked hurriedly. He looked around distractedly before grabbing what looked like a pair of shorts off the floor. Without a word, he tossed them to Grace. I averted my eyes again, feeling slightly awkward as apparently she dressed under the covers. Leutie had yet to say a word but still stood beside me with her hand in mine.

'Yeah, on bicycles. He had this little surrender flag thing so I didn't shoot, but I don't know, it could be a trick or something so I just came to get you.'

'What the hell,' Grace muttered, crawling out of bed and rushing to the desk. She pulled two guns from the drawer and handed one to Hayden, slipping on her boots quickly.

'Let's go,' Hayden commanded now that he and Grace were both ready. I nodded sharply and turned to leave with them right behind. Once outside, we all broke into a jog again as we headed to the edge of camp.

'Dax, have you got a gun?' Hayden asked as we ran.

'Yeah,' I replied. I dropped Leutie's hand and reached behind me to pull the gun I carried from my waistband.

'Good,' Hayden muttered gravely.

When we reached the edge of camp, everyone came to a stop and readied their weapons. We hardly had time to catch our breath before I heard the telltale rustling of leaves out of sight beyond the treeline. Leutie stepped closer to me, hiding slightly behind my shoulder as she squeezed my arm with her delicate hands.

'You should go back, Leutie,' I murmured, glancing anxiously over my shoulder to meet her light blue gaze.

'No, I'll stay,' she said softly, determination in her eyes. I felt a reluctant pang of fear in my heart and felt my anxiety rise even more, but I didn't push her further.

That was all the discussion we managed because the sound grew louder. Branches and leaves moved before the first bike broke through the brush, carrying Renley. He didn't appear the least bit surprised to see us waiting, and it was only a few seconds before the other two appeared behind him. All of them skidded to a stop and dismounted, taking a few steps before stopping about ten feet away from us.

Grace, Hayden, and I all had our guns raised, aimed directly at their chests, but again, they showed no weapons.

'Renley,' Hayden greeted firmly, keeping his voice flat and even.

'Hayden, right?' Renley replied, surveying him closely.

Hayden didn't reply, though his silence confirmed his identity. 'What do you want?'

My eyes darted suspiciously to the two people on either side of Renley. One was a girl of maybe sixteen, though she looked strong and certainly unafraid. The other was a woman, roughly the same age as Renley at twenty-five or -six. Renley stood out clearly between them, tall and strong. His dark hair was cut rather short and the start of a beard decorated his face.

'We don't mean any harm,' Renley said calmly. 'There's no need for the weapons.'

'We'll decide that,' Hayden said sharply. Renley didn't reply but instead gestured to the older woman on his left.

'This is Ari,' he said. He then gestured to the girl on his right. 'And this is Kenna.'

No one on our end replied, though no one looked surprised.

'You're Grace, correct?' Renley continued, addressing her now. To my surprise, he then looked to me. 'And you're either Kit or Dax. I'm sorry, that's as specific as I can be. I don't know you, apologies.'

He addressed Leutie last, causing her to grip the fabric of my shirt behind my back. She so desperately wanted to be brave with this sort of thing, but it was not her strong suit.

'How about you tell us what you want before we get all friendly?' Hayden demanded, voice tight with tension.

'Fair enough,' Renley said with a shrug. 'Well, first of all, I know you know it's strange for us to be here at all. We like to keep to ourselves, but unfortunately recent events have made that difficult.'

'Such as?' Grace prodded.

'I'm sure you're aware of the growing problem with the

Brutes in the city. They've been venturing further and further out, and unfortunately, it seems we've become a favourite target of theirs.' He let his eyes drag over each of us, studying us calmly before he carried on. 'Imagine how detrimental this is to us, seeing as we have very little in the way of weaponry.'

'Imagine,' Hayden repeated flatly. 'What's your point, Renley?'

'I have a proposition for you,' Renley said.

Everyone waited anxiously.

'I'm assuming that since the Brutes are branching out more and since Greystone seems to have dropped off the map, you lot are struggling as well, yes?' This time it was the woman, Ari, who spoke. She, too, was calm as she studied us.

I glanced to Hayden, curious what he would divulge to these people. His jaw clenched angrily and he let out a reluctant huff. 'Yes.'

'I figured as much,' Ari continued, nodding. 'What is it you need?'

'Food,' Hayden answered. 'Our crops won't grow because of the trees and there's only so much hunting we can do.'

'And what we need is protection. The ability to protect ourselves and, if necessary, physical backup,' Renley said.

'Let me guess, you want to trade,' Hayden remarked harshly. I knew Hayden wouldn't like that idea. He was very independent and had always resented the idea of relying on others to survive, even though how we lived now was potentially more dangerous as we relied on raids and spotty crops at best.

'Indeed,' Renley said, nodding. 'In exchange for a few guns and ammunition, we promise to supply you with enough crops to sustain your people.'

Leutie sucked in a breath behind me, and I had to admit

that sounded like a pretty good deal. Our quickly dwindling supply of food was made apparent this morning when all we'd had to eat was an egg, split between Leutie and I. I glanced at Hayden again to see him lock eyes with Grace, communicating with her silently in a way I couldn't quite decipher.

'How do we know you won't use those guns against us?' Hayden asked, raising a brow.

'For what purpose? You have nothing else we need,' Renley said simply. 'No offence.'

Hayden looked offended anyway as a scowl crossed his features. 'How will we get our food if we agree to this?'

'You'll have to pick it up,' Renley admitted. 'I'm afraid we have very few vehicles as most have been damaged or stolen by the Brutes.'

'Of course,' Hayden muttered bitterly. 'What about this backup thing? Backup for what?'

'I'm not sure at the moment, but should the Brutes launch some sort of massive attack against us, we'll need support.'

Hayden frowned and turned to Grace again. I was reluctant to get involved in another situation that could lead to another war, especially considering we'd just finished up fighting one.

'You should know,' Renley said, interrupting our thoughts, 'we killed two Brutes on the way here. Looked as if they were heading for Blackwing.'

It shouldn't have been shocking if they were already attacking Whetland, but it wasn't great news to hear that the Brutes were potentially venturing out to Blackwing as well.

'You'll need food to keep your camp healthy and strong. Just a thought.'

'Give us a minute,' Hayden requested sharply.

Renley nodded and waved a hand in acceptance. Hayden

cast him a cautious look before taking Grace's arm and steering her backward, ticking his head to me to indicate I should follow. I took Leutie with me as we gathered about twenty feet away, ducked together in a small circle.

'What do you think?' Hayden asked, focusing mainly on Grace and me.

'I think we need to do it,' Grace said quickly, casting a glance over her shoulder at Renley, Ari, and Kenna. 'He's right, we're going to need food soon and we have a few weapons to spare, don't we?'

'I don't like relying on other people,' Hayden said anxiously. 'And we have no idea if we can trust them.'

'They've only raided a few times though, right? And they're never really successful? I hardly think they're the type to intentionally start something.'

'That's true . . .' Hayden admitted. He chewed on his lower lip as his gaze dropped down in thought.

'And if what they said about the Brutes is also true . . .' Grace trailed off, an uncharacteristic hint of fear crossing her face. Hayden caught her tone immediately and raised a hand to place on her back, drawing her attention. He shot her a look I couldn't quite read before she blew out a deep breath and shook her head.

'All right. I think we need to do it,' Hayden said resolvedly.

'I think so, too, mate,' I agreed sincerely.

Hayden ran his tongue along his lip before nodding to himself, eyes unfocused and distracted. He let out a short breath and broke the huddle to stride back towards Renley and the others, who were waiting patiently.

'Well?' he asked calmly.

'When can we get our food?' Hayden asked, studying him closely.

'As soon as tomorrow, if you like,' Ari answered.

'And how often can we get more?'

'As often as you need it. Within reason, of course,' Ari replied. 'We have to feed our own camp, as well.'

Hayden nodded and shot one last look at Grace, who gave him an encouraging look. With a reluctant sigh, Hayden stepped forward and extended his hand, Renley doing the same as they met in the middle and shook.

'You've got a deal, Renley. Don't make me regret it.'

Eleven: Camaraderie

Grace

It had been about fifteen minutes since those from Whetland had left, but Hayden, Dax, Leutie, and I had yet to move from our position. An obvious air of unease hung around us as we cast anxious glances at each other. Leutie remained silent as she hovered behind Dax, and I hadn't missed their obvious connection. It seemed they were getting along very well indeed.

'So tomorrow, then?' Dax asked, breaking the silence. Before Renley and the two women had left, we'd made arrangements to bring weapons to Whetland in exchange for our first portion of food. Hayden, who stood beside me, let out a deep sigh.

'Yeah, I guess so. We should tell Kit about all this so he's on board, as well.'

'He'll be pissed he missed this,' Dax said with a cheeky grin. I let out a small chuckle of agreement.

'Have you guys seen him lately?' I asked. I hadn't seen or heard from him or Malin since I'd been taking care of Hayden. I'd barely left our hut, but today was the first day that Hayden seemed completely back to his normal health.

'Only briefly, why?' Dax answered.

'Just wondering,' I replied. I was curious to see how

things had gone with him and Malin but wanted to hear from one of them.

'When will you leave tomorrow?' Leutie asked, redirecting the conversation.

'In the morning, I suppose,' Hayden answered with a shrug.

Leutie nodded in response, shifting her hair off her neck and drawing my eye to a dark, discoloured spot on her skin. I grinned immediately as I recognised what I was certain was a hickey. Leutie saw my smile and looked confused, following my gaze to her throat before raising a hand to press her fingertips to her skin. She seemed to realise what I'd seen just as I spoke.

'Hey, Leutie—'

'Grace—'

Panic flashed across her face as she realised what I was doing.

'What's on your neck?' I asked, grinning widely as I teased her. Hayden shifted beside me to get a clearer look, but he was denied the opportunity as Leutie flattened her hand over her neck.

'Grace, oh my god,' Leutie mumbled in embarrassment, unable to keep her guilty smile off her face.

Hayden snorted a laugh beside me, causing me to let out an uncharacteristic giggle as I watched Leutie blush furiously.

'Jesus, Dax,' Hayden chuckled.

'What?' Dax asked obliviously. It took him a few moments to fully catch on before he turned to Leutie and tugged on her hand, revealing the hickey. 'Ahh, my bad.'

He didn't look the least bit apologetic. On the contrary, he seemed almost pleased with himself as he inspected the spot on her skin.

'Okay, you can all get a good look now,' Leutie said

exasperatedly, giving up trying to hide it. She scooped her hair off her neck and moved it to the other side, exposing her skin. 'Happy?'

'Thrilled,' I laughed, shooting Hayden an amused look out of the corner of my eye. He caught it and gave a good-natured shake of his head.

'You should own it,' Dax said brightly. 'Many a lady would love to have such a mark from me.'

'Oh, god,' I muttered, rolling my eyes playfully. 'You're the worst.'

'Best,' he corrected, shooting me a wink.

'Right,' I indulged him. Then I turned my focus to my friend. 'Hey, Leutie, I need to do something. Want to come with me?'

'What do you have to do?' Hayden interrupted, shooting me a confused look.

'Just something,' I said quietly, shrugging. 'It won't take long.'

Hayden frowned, unhappy with being out of the loop. 'Okay.'

'So, Leutie?'

'Yeah, of course,' she answered easily. Her cheeks were still bright red from her embarrassment. Dax shot her an endearing look before they whispered a few words of parting to each other. I turned to Hayden.

'I'll find you later,' I told him with a smile.

'All right,' he replied simply. He took a few steps forward and stopped to reach up and tuck his finger gently under my chin, then he pressed a soft, chaste kiss to my lips. It only lasted a second or two but it was enough to send a small wave of butterflies through me.

'See you,' he concluded with a small nod of his head.

'I love you.' I fulfilled the promise, as always.

'And I love you.' With that, he dropped his touch and turned to Dax. 'Dax, shall we go and fill in Kit?'

'Yeah, sounds good,' Dax replied.

Hayden and Dax started off in the direction of Kit's hut, leaving Leutie and I alone.

'Thanks for pointing that out in front of everyone,' Leutie said, her voice playful and sarcastic. I laughed.

'Sorry, I had to,' I replied lightly.

'Mmhmm,' she hummed sceptically, raising her brows. 'So, what's up?'

'Well, I just had a thought after seeing that,' I started, pointing to her neck. Her hand flew up automatically to press to the spot again. 'Do you, um, need anything?'

I felt somewhat awkward even though she was my best friend. Though we were the same age, she felt much younger simply because of her innocent outlook, like the younger sister I never had.

'Need anything?' she repeated in confusion. 'Like what?'

'Like, uh, protection?' I said, feeling more and more awkward by the second.

'Oh, no,' Leutie answered, shaking her head. 'I've no idea how to use a weapon so it's probably best if I don't carry one.'

My jaw opened to reply before snapping shut again as a confused frown pulled at my lips. Her smile remained calm and peaceful as she watched me.

'That's not what I meant,' I finally said.

Her head tilted to the side as she tried to understand. I sighed, accepting that I needed to be blunt.

'Leutie, are you and Dax having sex?'

Her jaw dropped open and the blush that had started to fade across her cheeks returned in full force.

'What?! Oh my god, *no,*' she replied adamantly. She was

obviously flustered because her hands seemed incapable of remaining by her sides. She fidgeted with her shirt, her hair, anything she could reach as she dropped my gaze.

'It's okay if you are,' I said quickly. 'I'm just saying that if you are, we can go and see Docc to get you on the birth control shot he has.'

'We're not!' she denied sharply, eyes wide as she shook her head.

'Okay, okay,' I replied, raising my hands in surrender. 'I just didn't know since you have that hickey and all . . .'

Again, I was unable to stop the grin from crossing my face.

'That, um, that just happened,' Leutie replied. 'We haven't . . .We don't do anything besides kiss.'

I felt a weird sense of déjà vu with this conversation. I was reminded of when Malin had approached me with the exact same subject. Then, I had been the one in denial rather than Leutie.

'Okay, but I know how that goes, so if it changes . . . just know you have that choice, all right?'

'I doubt that'll change, but okay,' Leutie said. She blushed and looked anywhere but at me.

'Never know,' I said with a shrug. 'I just offered because I have to go and get mine again today and it would be a good chance to get yours as well.'

'You get it?' Leutie asked, eyes snapping to me. I blinked at her.

'Yes.'

'Wait, so . . . You and Hayden have . . . You guys sleep together?' Her eyes were wider than ever as she spoke, mouth hanging open in surprise. I was torn between amusement and confusion.

'Yes,' I repeated simply.

'Wow,' Leutie said, blinking a few times as she absorbed my words. 'I guess that makes sense, I just never really thought about it.'

'You mean you haven't thought about my sex life?' I joked, grinning once more.

'No,' Leutie said with a sheepish laugh. 'It's just I've never done anything, so I never really thought about it.'

'Nothing?' I asked curiously. She shook her head and pinched her lips together.

'No, nothing. Dax was my first kiss,' she admitted, blushing again.

'No way. You're twenty-one years old!'

She shrugged and shook her head. 'I'm serious. I mean, a few tried, I guess, I just never let anyone until now.'

'Wow,' I said, impressed. 'Don't tell him that or he'll get an even bigger head.'

She let out a soft laugh and dropped my gaze, glancing at the ground in thought.

'Thank you, though,' she said sincerely. Her eyes reconnected with mine. 'I really don't think I'll need that anytime soon, but if I ever do . . . I'll let you know.'

'Deal.' I grinned at her. 'Want to come with me anyway?'

'Yeah, sure,' she replied with a shrug.

We turned and started walking towards the infirmary. It was a nice day with only a few clouds in the sky. The sun continued to rise in the sky, bringing heat even though it wasn't even noon yet. As we walked through camp, we passed many people going about their business. Near the garden, we saw Perdita, humming to herself as always as she tinkered with some plants. Barrow appeared to be back to his rounds, because he moved with a gun and gave me a respectful nod. Maisie was outside the kitchen, emptying a pot of water before giving us each a small wave and a grin.

'She let me help the other day,' Leutie told me as we passed Maisie. 'Had me work on that soup we all had.'

'Really?' I asked in surprise. Maisie usually handled most of the food herself. 'That's great.'

'Yeah, I enjoyed it. I figured if she lets me, that could be my "job" here, you know?'

I nodded in agreement. Everyone in Blackwing had some sort of responsibility and if Leutie had found a place to help Maisie in the kitchen, all the better for everyone. 'Yes, seems more suited for you than raids.'

Leutie let out a soft ghost of a laugh. 'Indeed.'

We chatted casually on our way to the infirmary. I kept my eyes searching those we passed for Kit or Malin, eager to find out what had happened with them, but neither appeared.

As always, it took a few moments for my eyes to adjust to the dim lighting inside. Murmured voices came from within, and it didn't take long to distinguish them as Docc and Shaw's.

'. . . I expect you'll be up in a week or so,' Docc was saying to Shaw.

Shaw looked disgruntled and impatient but nodded in acceptance. Both of their gazes turned to Leutie and I as we entered.

'Hello, ladies,' Docc said calmly. 'How are we today?'

'Fine, you?'

'I'm well,' Docc said, giving a solemn nod. 'I was just telling Shaw here that he should be healed up enough to leave the infirmary in a week or two.'

I frowned. We hadn't really discussed plans for Shaw after he healed. Would we force him to stay? Let him go back to Greystone? I didn't know, and I wasn't sure if Hayden knew either.

'Interesting,' I settled for saying.

'Suppose I get no say in how things go from there, huh?' Shaw asked coldly, arching a brow at me.

'You would suppose correctly,' I shot back, not in the mood to get into a fight with him. 'Docc, can I speak with you?'

'Certainly,' he replied.

With that, he turned away from Shaw and moved to the other side of the infirmary, where we would have more privacy. Leutie hovered for a moment, unsure of what to do, before deciding she did not want to be alone with Shaw and followed after me.

'What can I do for you, Grace?' Docc asked, studying me with his dark brown eyes.

'I need to get my next shot,' I told him, trying not to feel awkward.

'Ah, yes,' he said, nodding. 'Time has flown by, hasn't it?'

'A little bit, yeah,' I said with a sigh. So much had happened that it seemed like a lifetime ago.

'I'll get that prepared for you. Give me a moment.'

I nodded and he turned to get whatever materials he needed. Leutie looked curiously into a cabinet on the wall.

'Sure you don't want it?' I offered one last time. She turned and shook her head, eyes wide.

'I'm sure. Even if . . . anything happens, *that* won't be for a very long time.'

'Okay,' I resigned, tone light.

It wasn't long before Docc returned with his supplies, prepping my skin with alcohol before giving me the injection. As always, a slight burn ran through my veins before it dissipated.

'You're all set,' Docc said, disposing of the needle. 'Anything else?'

He cast a seemingly innocent look in Leutie's direction. She blushed again.

'No, we're all good,' she answered.

'Okay. Grace, if you wouldn't mind passing that along to Hayden about Shaw, I'd appreciate it. We'll need to figure out a plan of action for him.'

'Yep, that's fine, talk about me like I'm not even here,' Shaw called bitterly from across the room. His arms were folded over his chest like a large, unhappy child. I rolled my eyes and ignored him.

'I'll tell him,' I told Docc.

'Thank you.'

'Yeah, and thank you,' I returned, lifting my arm to indicate the shot. 'We'll see you later.'

He gave one final nod before Leutie and I left, heading back outside and through camp once more. Just as before, we saw no sign of Malin or Kit, adding to my small sense of disappointment. I was surprised to see Hayden and Dax, chatting casually in front of our hut. As we approached, they both turned to greet us.

'Hey,' Hayden greeted, giving me a soft smile as I came to stand next to him. Leutie did the same beside Dax.

'Hello,' I returned lightly. 'Did you guys tell Kit?'

'Yeah,' Hayden replied. 'He's in but he thinks we're mad for doing it.'

'He might be right,' I laughed lightly before growing more serious. 'But we really don't have a choice, like they said.'

'I know,' Hayden murmured reluctantly.

'Was Malin there?' I asked, trying to sound casual.

'No, why?' Hayden questioned.

'Just curious,' I said, shrugging.

Hayden didn't look like he believed me but accepted my answer.

'Okay, well, we're going to leave tomorrow morning, all right?' he said, directing his words at Dax.

'Sounds good, Bossman,' Dax agreed. He turned to Leutie. 'Shall we?'

He offered no further explanation but tipped his head backward, away from Hayden and I. Leutie let out a soft giggle and grinned at him.

'We shall.'

I smiled at seeing how giddy he made her. They waved goodbye to us before turning and heading back into camp.

'What did you have to do?' Hayden asked, once we were alone.

I raised my hand to point at my upper arm where Docc had given me the shot.

'Birth control,' I said simply.

'Ah, okay,' he replied. 'That's good.'

'Mmhmm, very,' I laughed. He flashed me a somewhat guilty grin before speaking again.

'Want to help me get stuff ready for tomorrow?'

'Sure,' I replied lightly. Again, he grinned at me before ticking his head to the side and starting to walk towards the centre of camp.

The rest of our day passed quickly as we prepared for the trip to Whetland. A lot of the time was spent going through the weapons and trying to decide which we could spare. It was difficult to choose and even more difficult to pack up the ammunition, but after painstaking debate, we'd finally packed what we thought were the most dispensable. We also loaded up the jeep with as many containers as we could find, unsure of what they'd give us to carry the food in, and basic supply kits should things take a turn for the worse.

When we went to dinner that night, I was pleased to see Leutie helping Maisie in the kitchen. I was also relieved yet confused when I saw Kit and Malin eating together, their expressions impossible to read. They sat at the edge of the room and looked like they did not want to be disturbed. I spent most of my meal studying them and trying to understand their dynamic, but Hayden and Dax kept interrupting, making it impossible to figure anything out.

Later that night, after a quick shower, Hayden and I finally crawled into bed. We exchanged a few casual words before Hayden passed out, apparently still recovering from being sick more than I realised. His arm curled around my waist as he hauled me to him, my hands resting on his bare chest. The skin was warm and soothing, and his steady heartbeat lulled me to sleep. It was with a content sigh and a gentle kiss to Hayden's throat that I finally fell asleep.

The next morning, I was awoken by a light kiss behind my ear that was followed by a rough, raspy whisper of my name as he tried to wake me. It felt so nice that I pretended to be asleep longer to encourage him to continue.

'I know you're awake, come on,' he teased lightly, grin evident in his tone. I felt his teeth nip lightly at my neck. 'You're shit at that, remember?'

'No,' I whined, but smiled too. I remembered the very first time he'd said that to me way back when I first arrived. Even then, he'd known when I was pretending to be asleep. I was so warm and comfortable wrapped in his arms and curled against his chest that the last thing I wanted to do was get up and go to Whetland.

'Sorry, Bear,' he rasped, sounding like he genuinely meant it. 'We've got to go.'

I let out an unhappy moan as Hayden untangled himself from me and rose from beneath the covers. I was much less tempted to stay in bed if Hayden wasn't there, so it made it easier for me to admit defeat and crawl out after him.

Hayden cast me a sleepy smile as he dressed. I did the same, feeling slow and lethargic as I forced myself to move. After heading to the bathroom and splashing a little water on my face and getting ready for the day, I could feel myself waking up a little more. I knew the inevitable adrenaline would kick in as soon as we started heading to Whetland.

Just as I moved back into the main room, a sharp knock sounded at our door, followed immediately by a boisterous call from the other side.

'Rise and shine!'

Hayden groaned and moved to answer the door, revealing a very energised Dax and an impossible-to-read Kit.

'Ready to go?' Dax asked brightly.

'Always, Dax,' Hayden muttered exasperatedly.

'That's the spirit,' Dax replied, clapping his hands together loudly to make me jump.

Hayden shook his head. I followed, pleased to see Kit and Dax had already brought the jeep, which was rumbling just outside our hut. Dax moved to take the passenger seat while Kit climbed in the back, waiting for Hayden and me as we paused outside the door.

Hayden didn't hesitate to pull me into a hug, winding his arm around my shoulders while his lips pressed into my temple. My arms roped around his waist as I hugged him back.

'Be careful, as always,' Hayden murmured just loud enough for me to hear. 'I love you.'

'I love you,' I returned easily. 'Be careful, too, yeah?'

'I will,' he replied softly. He gave one last tight squeeze before releasing me and opening the door behind the driver.

I smiled at him as he shut the door and climbed into the driver's seat.

'You guys and that thing,' Dax said sarcastically, shaking his head. 'Saps.'

'Shut up, Dax,' Hayden muttered drily as a wry smile crossed his face.

I smiled as well while Dax let out a boisterous laugh. Hayden shifted the engine into drive and took off, weaving carefully down the path until we reached the edge of Blackwing. As he drove, I took a few deep breaths to prepare for this trip. I wanted to trust Whetland and knew that this was the logical thing to do, but that didn't stop the hint of nervous tension that lingered in my stomach. The sooner this was over with, the better.

Twelve: Covetous

Hayden

A heavy unease settled in my stomach as I drove, closing in on Whetland more and more by the second. My eyes flashed up to the rearview mirror to connect with Grace's beautiful green ones. As always, her smile managed to calm some of the jittery nerves bouncing through my system. I had no idea how this was going to go and had to agree somewhat with Kit that we were mad for accepting the deal, but we had no choice; too many people depended on me to play it safe.

No one spoke as we approached the outside of Whetland's camp. Dax leaned forward beside me as he studied the outer edges, scanning for any presence. I did the same, and it wasn't long before I spotted four people waiting for us. I tried to remain calm as I aimed the jeep towards them, slowing before stopping about ten feet away. I recognised Renley, Ari, and Kenna. Another man roughly my age stood with them, though I did not know who he was.

'Everyone be careful,' I murmured under my breath. My eyes flicked to Grace's again when I felt her hand land on my shoulder and squeeze lightly.

I was acutely aware of the metal of the gun pressing against my lower back as I turned off the engine and climbed reluctantly out of the jeep. Grace, Kit, and Dax did the same, the four of us approaching those waiting for us with cautious eyes. We stopped a short distance away, Grace right at my side.

'Renley,' I greeted steadily, holding his eye contact.

'Hayden,' he returned. His eyes then moved to each member of Blackwing, giving respectful nods at each of them. 'You all know my friends Ari and Kenna.'

Everyone remained silent in acknowledgement, so he gestured to the man near him. His short, black hair was sharply offset by a pair of piercing grey eyes which stared at us. He was relatively tall, about my height.

'And this is Prett,' Renley continued. 'He'll be helping us out today.'

Prett flashed a smile at everyone and I noticed his gaze linger on Grace a little too long. Immediately, I decided I didn't like him and a scowl crossed my face.

'Great,' I said flatly. Grace shot me a confused look that I chose to ignore.

'Indeed,' Renley replied, unfazed. 'If you'd like to follow us in your vehicle, we'll take you to our food holding.'

'All right,' I said, giving a curt nod.

With that, we all turned to pile back into the jeep.

'They're an interesting lot,' Dax mumbled from beside me.

'Interesting' was probably not the word I would have chosen, but I said nothing as I started the jeep. Renley and his small crew set off at a brisk pace and I followed.

'Keep a good lookout for anything suspicious,' I instructed, my voice low even though there was no way they'd hear us.

Nerves started to creep up, battling with the adrenaline, as we drove deeper and deeper into their camp. Curious bystanders appeared and watched, though no one made any moves to attack. I saw women, children, frail elderly people, and a few that looked young, strong, and healthy. I could see Dax, Kit, and Grace shifting anxiously as they tried to stay alert to everything, but it was nearly impossible. I was practically waiting for some sort of trap to appear.

Nothing happened. Everyone seemed transfixed by our strange caravan as we followed after Renley and the three others, but no one followed. As soon as we passed, they resumed whatever they'd been doing before, as if they were already bored with us.

It wasn't long until we reached a large building in the middle of their camp. Immediately, I was impressed with how sturdy it looked. The walls were made of solid brick. They were mismatched and not very cohesive, as if they'd taken whatever brick they could scavenge from the city to construct it, but it looked solid and firm all the same. The size was also impressive, stretching at least a hundred and sixty feet in length and about two stories high. It was a stark contrast to the buildings we had at Blackwing, the largest of which was *maybe* sixty feet in length, and all only a single storey high.

'Wow,' Grace muttered, studying the structure in awe.

'Why hasn't Malin drawn up something like this for us, eh Kit?' Dax asked jokingly. Malin was one of those in charge of building in Blackwing and while she designed strong, sturdy structures, this made ours look like children's toys in comparison.

'Shut up,' Kit murmured, ignoring Dax's attempts to lighten things.

Renley had stopped and turned to wave us forward. I continued to scan the area as I parked the vehicle, but there were only a few other people around now besides Renley,

Prett, Kenna, and Ari. As we climbed out of the vehicle, I felt the reassuring pressure of my gun at my back in case I should need it. Grace walked beside me and I resisted the urge to reach out and nudge her, knowing she wouldn't like that.

'This is where we store most of our supplies,' Renley explained as my group joined his. I couldn't stop my eyes from darting to Prett, where I was displeased to see him smiling at Grace again. My fist clenched in anger before I forced myself to relax.

'Food, supplies, what little we have for weapons, it's all here,' Renley continued. 'I'm telling you this in the hope of keeping your trust. Full disclosure.'

Renley tried to smile but ended up grimacing as he looked from me to everyone else.

'Good to know,' I finally said, unsure of how I was supposed to respond. 'Now, how is this going to work, exactly?'

'Well, we figure we can show you the food we've gathered for you just to prove it's all there, then you can give us the weapons to clear the space in your truck, and you can take your items and leave,' Prett said calmly, his pleasant smile still on his face.

Or what was meant to be pleasant, anyway, and was actually incredibly irritating.

'Peachy,' Dax replied, answering for me. My jaw seemed clenched shut as I glared at Prett.

'This way, then,' Ari said, ticking her head back so we'd follow.

They turned and headed into the building, leaving us to follow. Kit and Dax went first, leaving Grace and I to bring up the rear.

'I don't like this,' I muttered, keeping my voice low so only she would hear.

'What? Why?' she asked, confused. She glanced up at me and frowned.

'I don't know,' I admitted bitterly. 'I just don't.'

'They seem nice,' Grace said honestly, shaking her head.

'Hmmph,' I grumbled.

As we entered the building, my jaw dropped open in shock. I had been expecting a large, dark room, but it was brightly illuminated from above. Giant bins that held what looked like some sort of grain lined the sides, and the middle was filled with shelves stacked full of all kinds of foods. Canned goods, bottled water, fresh fruits and vegetables, breads, and so much more that I couldn't even see. There were other things, too – clothes and basic necessities – but it was the food that held my attention.

'How do you have the power for this?' Kit asked, reading my mind.

'We've figured out how to refurbish some generators and engines using the force of the river,' Renley explained as he looked around the building with pride. It seemed it was more of a warehouse now that we were inside. 'Took a while to get it right, mind you, but it's been the key to our success.'

'I see that,' Dax murmured. His mouth was open as he gaped around the area, shocked by the vast amounts of everything. 'Impressive.'

'Thank you,' Renley answered genuinely. 'Over here we've got our first group of rations set aside. Prett can help you three load them into your jeep if you want to come and talk weapons with me, Hayden.'

A red flag flashed in my mind at the prospect of being split up. The last thing I wanted to do was leave Grace's side, especially with the ever-smiling Prett lurking around. She flashed me a small smile and nodded, silently giving her okay. Dax and Kit had already started walking towards the bags of food. Grace turned and jogged after them, all following Prett, Ari, and Kenna.

I let out a deep sigh as I turned reluctantly to Renley. 'All right, let's go.'

He nodded and allowed me to lead the way back outside and to the jeep.

'It's really nice of you guys to agree to this,' Renley said casually. 'Even if you're benefiting from the arrangement as well.'

'Yeah,' I replied gruffly, hardly in the mood to make small talk with him. I could practically see Grace sending me a scolding glare in my head, so I continued. 'It was a good offer.'

'We have to do what's necessary,' he said with a shrug. 'We have only a few guns and very little ammunition. Other than that, we have to rely on knives and such, so we really appreciate this.'

'Sure,' I answered. 'How often have the Brutes been attacking?'

'It used to be only every few months, but lately it's been much more frequent. At least every week, if not more often. Every time, we lose people, and it's never a quick thing, either. It's been very difficult.'

We had arrived at the jeep now, and I popped open the back to reveal the weapons and ammunition. Renley's eyes widened at the sight, and he reached forward slowly to pick up a handgun to examine it.

'Wow,' he murmured quietly, voice laced with awe. 'These will definitely help. Thank you.'

'You're welcome,' I replied. I was still on the fence about if I trusted him or not, but if what he said was true, he had my sympathy. He was losing people left and right with no power to stop it; I knew exactly how that felt.

'You haven't had any trouble with the Brutes?' Renley asked as he returned the gun to the others. He leaned casually against the bumper of the jeep as he studied me.

'Some, yeah,' I admitted. 'But they don't come to Blackwing. We always seem to run into them in the city.'

Renley gave a nod of understanding. 'I see. We haven't been to the city in probably a year.'

'A *year*?' I repeated, stunned.

'Yeah, roughly,' Renley said with a shrug. 'That's why we were so surprised when the Brutes started coming after us. Seems odd, doesn't it?'

'Very,' I agreed. My mind was racing a hundred miles a minute as I mulled it over. The Brutes had plenty of supplies in their storage, so I couldn't understand why they'd be branching out of their usual confines in the city.

Our conversation was interrupted by a loud laugh as everyone started to file out of the storage building. I turned to see Grace, Dax, and Prett walking towards us, laden with baskets and bags of items. All three of them were grinning at something I hadn't heard, and I immediately felt a flash of jealously when I saw Grace smile at Prett as he said something else to her.

I was forced to break my glare in Prett's direction when they approached the trunk and I realised Renley and I had yet to move the weapons. Quickly, he and I loaded our arms with as much as we could carry to move them out of the way. Prett set his basket of food down and appeared at my side.

'Here, let me lend a hand,' he offered smoothly.

'I got it,' I replied sharply. More sharply than I'd intended, and I was sure Grace noticed my tone, judging from the way her brows furrowed in confusion. I ignored her and cleared all I could carry before turning to follow Renley, who led me back inside the building. Voices sounded from behind me, though I couldn't make out what they were saying. I let out a sharp huff and shook my head, silently scolding myself for the irrational feelings.

'Just over here,' Renley said as he glanced over his shoulder.

He led me down a sort of hall created by the shelves, and before long he stopped and deposited all he carried. I did the same and was surprised to see Kenna and Ari appear behind me, carrying the rest of the weapons and ammunition we'd brought.

'Is that all of it?' Renley asked them.

'It is. There are just a few more baskets of food if you want to grab them on the way out.'

'Sure thing,' Renley said with a respectful nod towards Ari. She smiled, and we all manoeuvred to the dwindling pile of supplies across the building.

Again, a twinge of jealousy flashed inside me when I heard another round of laughter coming from outside. My pace quickened, rushing to grab a basket and get back outside. Renley, Ari, and Kenna did the same. Once outside, I scanned the area as I approached the jeep.

Grace, Dax, Kit, and Prett were standing near the back, all of them grinning or laughing. Even Kit, who had been in a very odd mood ever since we'd picked him up, had a smile on his face. Confusion, annoyance, and jealousy all fought for attention as I approached and practically threw my basket into the back of the jeep.

A loud *thud* sounded as I dropped it, drawing Grace's attention. She looked to me, a grin still on her face, and cast me a small wave. I did not return it and seemed unable to remove the scowl from my face. My scowl only deepened when my gaze shifted to Prett to see him studying Grace far too closely for my liking, the annoying smile still plastered on his face.

My hand twitched by my side as I resisted the urge to hit his stupid grin right off his face. I settled for standing much closer to Grace than was probably necessary. It was all I could do to stop myself from kissing her on the spot to claim her as mine, but I knew she wouldn't like being claimed.

'Are we set, then?' I asked, eyeing the group, Prett suspiciously. Renley joined us as well.

'I believe so. If it suits you, you can come back whenever the supplies run out. Within reason, like we said. Don't go eating all this in a day or two because then we won't have a deal any longer.'

'Fair enough,' Dax said.

'All right,' I agreed, clenching my jaw as I tried not to glare at Prett any longer.

'You know the way out?' Prett asked, making me unable to ignore him.

'Yeah, we should be good,' Grace replied, giving a friendly smile.

'Excellent. Well I look forward to seeing you all again. Especially you, Grace.'

My head snapped to the side to shoot a blazing scowl at Prett while my hands balled to fists. I felt the familiar tic in my jaw as the muscle clenched, barely managing to restrain myself from spitting out some sort of insult. If Grace noticed my reaction, I would have had no way of knowing because I couldn't tear my eyes from Prett's stupid face.

'Um . . . yeah, right,' Grace replied somewhat awkwardly. 'See you guys.'

Renley and Prett stood side by side to wave us off as Kit and Dax climbed back in the jeep, slamming the trunk shut along the way after everyone had loaded their items. I turned over my shoulder to glance back at Renley and Prett, irritated to see Prett was *still* smiling at Grace as she walked away, oblivious to his eyes on her. Just like that, I lost the semblance of sense I'd been clinging to as I marched towards her.

Her back was to me as she prepared to climb into her seat, but when I reached forward and grabbed her arm, she spun to face me. A startled look appeared on her face before both of my hands landed on her cheeks to haul her to me, pressing my lips into her own firmly. She was obviously surprised, but after a moment, she relaxed slightly and returned my kiss.

I was unable to resist letting my eyes dart back to Prett, where I was pleased to see the grin had finally fallen from his face. My brow ticked upward in satisfaction as I gave them a curt nod, leaving no time for reply before I jumped into the driver's seat. Without a second glance, I started the engine and took off, propelling us forward. We'd barely driven ten feet when Dax spoke.

'Well, they're a nice lot,' he said happily as he relaxed back into the seat.

I scoffed but didn't say anything, still irritated with Prett's overly nice attitude with Grace.

'I can't believe that power system they have set up,' Grace replied. 'Prett said they have it over half of their camp.'

'Oh, did he?' I snapped, unable to hold back. My eyes flashed to the mirror just in time to see Grace roll her eyes.

'Oh, Hayden,' she muttered under her breath as she shook her head gently, shrugging off my comment and glancing out of the window calmly.

'Awkward,' Dax said, grimacing as he dragged out the

sound. Kit snorted a laugh from the back seat but still didn't speak.

I frowned unhappily as I drove. We passed the last few buildings in Whetland, then drove through the empty expanse that separated their camp from the city. Every time I glanced in the mirror at Grace, she continued to look out of the window. I knew I was being irrational but I couldn't help feeling annoyed.

I tried to focus on keeping a lookout to distract myself from how I was feeling, but there was nothing to draw my eye. We skirted around the city without incident and were driving through the barren area that preceded the trees that hid Blackwing. It wasn't until we were about halfway back that something finally caught my attention in the distance, jerking my gaze in that direction.

'What is it?' Grace asked, immediately noting my reaction. So she *had* been paying attention. She leaned forward between the seats, squinting towards the place I'd seen movement.

'I don't know,' I muttered, looking as much as I could while continuing to drive.

Dax rolled down his window to get a clearer look, raising a hand over his brow to block the sun. 'Oh, shit,' he murmured.

'Brutes,' Kit said gruffly from the backseat. I glanced in the mirror to see him looking through the scope of a rifle he carried. 'Three of them.'

'What are they doing?' I asked quickly, slowing the jeep to stall.

'Looks like they're heading to Blackwing,' he admitted bitterly. My stomach clenched painfully. The second group of Brutes heading to our camp in two days was not a good sign.

'Shit,' Grace swore. She was still leaning through the seats and I caught the concerned glance she shot in my direction.

'Kit, can you take them out from here?' I asked.

'No,' he admitted. 'Can you get us a little closer?'

'Yeah,' I replied, redirecting the jeep towards them. They grew closer and closer by the second, about three hundred feet away now.

Adrenaline started pumping through my system as I drove, staring them down. It didn't take long for them to notice us, and they halted their progress to face us. They seemed to be trying to figure out who we were, and it wasn't until we were about fifty feet away that they seemed to realise.

'Shoot when you can,' I instructed, gritting my teeth as we zoomed forward. I felt Grace's hand land on my arm, giving a reassuring squeeze before she leaned back and reached for her weapon.

Kit, Dax, and Grace all leaned out of their respective windows, guns raised and ready to fire. We were so close now that I could make out the tattered details of their clothes, the scars that marred their skin, the missing teeth in their mouths as they glowered at us and prepared to shoot back.

'That's her!'

My blood practically ran cold when one of them shouted, raising a hand to point at Grace. The air in my lungs ripped harshly from my chest, confused and fearful of what they meant. All three of the Brutes seemed momentarily distracted as they gaped at Grace, studying her face before snarling viciously at her.

'You little bi—'

A loud *bang* cut off the Brute that had been speaking as a gun fired, dropping him to the ground after one shot to the head. The other Brutes scrambled to try to fire at us, but it was only a fraction of a second later that two more *bangs* rang out, each striking their target as Kit and Dax fired on them. Within seconds, all three of the Brutes had dropped to the dirt, dead.

'Good shooting, bro,' Dax said, high-fiving Kit before they both pulled themselves back into the jeep. Grace, I noticed, hadn't fired.

She retreated into her seat slowly, eyes wide and blank with her mouth slightly open in shock. Her eyes fixed on the back of my seat, and it was easy to see how distracted she was.

That's her.

It seemed they had recognised her. Not only recognised her, but held great animosity towards her. A chill ran down my spine as I realised how dangerous this situation could be. Something must have happened that Grace hadn't told me, because the stunned and admittedly fearful look on her face right now told me there was a reason they'd known who she was.

If the Brutes were after Grace, we were going to have a whole new problem on our hands.

Thirteen: Avowal

Grace

My body seemed at war with itself, torn between being chilled to the bone and burning with apprehension as we drove away from the three dead Brutes. Even though I could feel Hayden's eyes on me in the rearview mirror, I couldn't force myself to look at him. I stared, unfocused and unseeing, at the back of his seat.

That's her.

My stomach churned anxiously and I could feel my palms sweating against my gun, unused thanks to the way I'd frozen on the spot. Flashbacks of every second I'd spent in the Armoury ripped through my mind, intensified by the gruesome images I'd seen in my nightmares. It was getting to the point now that I couldn't tell fact from fiction, reality from dream. Everything cascaded together in an indistinguishable blur of horrors until it rendered me useless, a pitiful girl frozen in the backseat of the jeep.

'Grace!'

Hayden's voice finally snapped me out of my trance, his tone making it clear he'd repeated my name several times.

'Are you okay?' he asked, voice laden with concern.

'Mmhmm,' I lied unconvincingly. The jerky nod I gave did little to back up my attempt at deception. 'I'm fine.'

But I wasn't fine.

I was far from fine.

I was terrified.

Terrified, and ashamed to admit it.

I could see Hayden didn't believe me for a second, but he didn't question me further. His lips pursed into a displeased expression and his brows furrowed over his blazing green eyes. Kit and Dax were silent as we drove into camp, but I had the feeling that they, too, were casting questioning looks in my direction. I ignored them all, unable to focus on anything other than the paralysing fear ripping through me.

My body jerked forward suddenly as Hayden slammed on the brakes, probably more sharply than he intended to. Without a word, he threw open his door and exited the jeep, opening my door before I had even managed to look around and see we were outside of our hut.

Hayden leaned into the doorframe. 'Come on, Grace,' he murmured, voice gentler than it had been all day. He took my hand and tugged, ignoring my sweaty palms as he guided me out of the backseat. His free hand took my gun out of my grasp and stowed it behind his jeans before running it down my side comfortingly.

'Dax, Kit, put the stuff away, will you?' he asked.

'Of course,' Dax replied. I barely absorbed their words as I let Hayden start to steer me back to our home.

'Hey, Grace,' Kit called, surprising me by appearing a few feet away from me. 'I, um, I know what happened in the Armoury was tough, but we've got you, all right? Not just Hayden.'

My throat tightened at his words and I felt a surge of emotion roll through me. Kit knew perhaps better than anyone right now what I was feeling because he'd been there with me the second time.

'Thank you, Kit,' I replied as firmly as I could. Hayden

didn't say anything but squeezed my hand lightly.

'Yeah, include me in this whole Grace-protection-programme thing,' Dax said flippantly from the front seat. He flashed me a grin that I couldn't quite manage to return. I mustered a soft smile.

'Thanks, guys. Really.'

Hayden was quiet but clearly tense as he opened the door and led me to the bed, tugging me down gently. His hand sustained its claim over mine, and soon his other hand joined as well. I watched as his long fingers traced over my skin, feathering over mine before squeezing my palm.

'Grace, what happened in there?' he finally asked. I could feel him watching me again but I was too mesmerised by the gentle way his hands played with my own to look at him. I knew he was holding off impatience when I finally drew a deep breath and spoke.

'I told you everything, Hayden,' I said softly, still unable to look at him.

'Are you sure?' he questioned.

I squeezed my eyes shut and blew out a slow, deep breath.

'Grace, come on. They recognised you,' he urged. He squeezed my hand in both of his.

'I told you the truth,' I pleaded, shaking my head as I finally looked at him.

'You went to the Armoury, got caught, Kit shot some Brutes, and you got away, right?' Hayden questioned. 'That's it?'

'That's it,' I repeated, drawing my shoulders up in an exasperated shrug.

Hayden frowned with concern, eyes peering into mine.

'Why would they be coming after you then?' he asked. He grimaced at the thought.

'I don't know,' I admitted. 'Maybe they weren't coming

after me? Maybe they were just . . . I don't know, trying to sneak up on us for some other reason and they happened to recognise me?'

'Maybe . . .' Hayden murmured. His tone made it clear that he was just appeasing me. I couldn't blame him; I didn't believe my words, either.

I racked my brain to try to remember something that could have spurred such a reaction. Kit had been there as well, but they hadn't so much as looked at him. If anything, they had more reason to go after Kit than they did me, seeing as he'd shot the ones who had caught us that night. Anything I'd done, Kit had done as well, yet they'd seemed focused on me. There were no differences that made me stand out more than him.

Except . . .

I felt myself pale as I sucked in a shaky breath, fighting off the shudder that ran down my spine. Hayden noticed immediately and leaned forward, ducking into my line of vision as his hand reached up to tuck gently under my chin.

'What is it, Grace?'

I suddenly felt like I was going to be sick. I should have realised right away given their history, but it was like my mind had blacked it out.

'I forgot to tell you about one thing,' I admitted, my voice burning my throat as I spoke.

'Tell me, please,' Hayden begged gently. His face looked more intense than I'd seen it in a long time, including earlier when he'd been writhing with jealousy.

'I-I can't think of the exact words, but you remember how they spoke about . . . women? And getting what they want from them?' I started, unsure if I'd be able to speak the words without throwing up.

Hayden's face mirrored mine now as he visibly paled. He

cleared his throat roughly as he studied me, never looking away from my face. 'Yes.'

'Let's just say they said something to that effect directly to me,' I explained. 'About my hands and my . . . my mouth.'

'Oh, god, stop,' Hayden pleaded, shaking his head quickly. 'You don't have to say it. I'm sorry, Grace.'

He didn't even speak again before reaching for me to haul me into his chest. I let him as I crashed into him, roping my arms around his neck as I clung to him. He held me tightly and let me bury my face in his neck, desperately trying to suppress the fear that was ripping me apart.

'Why didn't you tell me, Grace?' he asked weakly, words muffled by my shoulder as he held me.

I gave a weak shrug and a pathetic sort of whimper. I blew out yet another deep breath and tried again, pulling back just enough to look at him.

'I didn't think it would matter,' I said truthfully. 'And you were sick . . . That was all I was worried about. Getting you better.'

Hayden gave a minute shake of his head. His hand snaked between us to rest his palm gently against my cheek, fingers winding into my hair.

'I didn't want to think about it, or worry you, or anything. I'm sorry, I should have told you. I should have—'

I was cut off by a choking gasp that ripped through my throat, my last attempt to hold down the tears that had started to creep up.

I was growing weaker and weaker by the second.

'Hey, shh,' Hayden soothed gently. He held my face tenderly between his hands while his gaze burned into mine. 'It's going to be okay,' he promised softly.

'I'm afraid, Hayden,' I admitted, voice shaky and thick with fear.

'You don't have to be afraid,' he coaxed.

'But I am,' I replied tightly, shaking my head as I swallowed harshly. 'You love me because I'm strong, but I'm falling apart . . .'

'Grace, no,' Hayden rebutted quickly. 'I love you for so many things, okay? And even now, you're the strongest girl I've ever met.'

My eyes squeezed shut, causing a few more tears to slip down my cheeks. Hayden's thumbs brushed them gently away from my skin.

'No one is going to touch you, Grace, do you hear me? I'm going to keep you safe. I'd give my life up to keep you safe.'

Instead of feeling reassured, all I felt was more fear. My stomach flipped over and my heart pounded painfully against my ribs.

'I don't want that, Hayden. I don't want you to even think about dying for me,' I contended quickly, voice tight.

'Too bad,' Hayden said with a tick of his head. 'If it came down to it, I'd take that deal. Your life for mine? Any day.'

'You're crazy,' I murmured.

'Am I? Look me in the eye and tell me you wouldn't do the same,' he challenged knowingly.

I instantly knew I couldn't deny that.

There was no debate to be had.

If given the choice, I'd die to save Hayden's life.

'You're right,' I admitted with a reluctant sigh.

'So it's only fair, yeah? It all comes down to the same thing: you protect me, I protect you. This is just an extension of that,' he said with a shrug.

My heart gave a heavy thud, and I let out a deep sigh that felt like it deflated my entire body. I slumped forward and rested my forehead against his shoulder. Instantly, he wrapped his arms around me and let his hand trail soothingly across my back.

'I love you,' I murmured softly.

I felt drained in every aspect, empty of what strength I usually carried and weak from desperately trying to hold onto it. The only thing keeping me afloat in the tumultuous sea of fear and uncertainty threatening to drown me was Hayden.

'And I love you, Grace. I meant what I said earlier. I'm going to keep you safe.'

I felt a sudden surge of determination. Hayden undoubtedly meant every single word he said – I could feel that truth and the weight behind it down to my bones – but I would do everything in my power to keep him from needing to act on his promises.

'I know you will,' I whispered. 'As I'll do for you.'

He still looked concerned, but some of the uncertainty was gone. I had no tears as I studied the beautiful man who loved me so much more than I deserved, still stunned that he was mine to give my heart to.

As if he could hear my emotion-laden thoughts, he leaned forward, drawing me gently towards him with his hand on the back of my neck. The gentle kiss he pressed to my lips sealed every promise we'd made to each other, spoken or unspoken. He remained for a few moments, letting me soak in the warmth his kiss provided and the comfort that always came as well.

'We'll figure this out, okay?' Hayden murmured. 'We're not going to sit by any longer. We'll end this once and for all.'

I felt an odd mixture of relief, fear, and trepidation at his words. We all knew that the time of ignoring the Brutes and hoping they'd go away would eventually come to an end.

We'd reached that time now, and it was time to take action.

'Okay,' I sighed, nodding. Hayden gave me a small smile that didn't quite reach his eyes.

'Don't worry,' he reassured me.

I let out a strange ghost of a laugh and felt my eyes widen momentarily. 'I'll try.'

Hayden nodded, satisfied for the time being.

'Are you all right? Be honest.'

'Yes, I'm all right,' I replied truthfully. I was still scared of a lot of things – the Brutes, their dark desires for women, their search for me in particular, what could possibly happen to Hayden because of all this – but talking with him had helped. While I was terrified he'd risk hurting himself to help me, I tried to be confident in my own strength to avoid such a situation.

We would make a plan, as we always did, and we would be okay.

'Good,' Hayden said gently, voice deep and low as it rumbled from his chest. After a quiet pause as we simply sat together, he spoke again.

'Shall we go and see what Whetland gave us?'

'Yeah, good idea,' I said, perking up a little. Hayden gave my hand one last squeeze before climbing off the bed, tugging me up with him before we both headed to the door.

It was warm out as we walked through camp, enjoying the feel of the sun on our faces and the breeze at our backs, Hayden's hand in mine. Then I remembered his behaviour from earlier in Whetland.

'Hey, Hayden?' I started, keeping my voice casual.

'Hmm?' he smiled.

'What was all that earlier? At Whetland?'

Immediately, his smile faltered and a scowl replaced it. 'You know exactly what that was.'

'You were jealous,' I said with a light eye-roll.

The tight clench in his jaw was answer enough to confirm my words.

'You know you have nothing to be jealous of,' I said when he didn't speak. His hand had grown stiff in mine as we walked.

'I know,' he replied gruffly.

'You know I'm yours,' I continued. I kept my voice gentle even though it seemed like something I shouldn't even have to explain.

Hayden let out a heavy huff and finally looked at me again. 'I know, I just can't help it.'

'Did I do something to make you doubt that?'

'No, not at all,' he replied quickly, shaking his head. 'It's just . . . I don't know, I don't like other guys looking at you or thinking they can have you.'

'Is that why you "claimed" me?' I asked, arching a brow. I was torn between being flattered and offended that he'd kissed me in front of everyone, because I knew his intention had been to rub Prett's nose in it, rather than something purer.

'Hmm?' I pressed, watching him as closely as I could while still looking where I was going.

'Yes,' he finally admitted reluctantly.

'You didn't need to do that,' I told him.

'Yeah, I get you,' Hayden muttered in defeat. 'I'm sorry.'

He looked relieved when he saw I wasn't mad. I truthfully wasn't mad, but I also wasn't thrilled that Prett might get the impression that the only reason he couldn't have me was because of Hayden. I wouldn't have *wanted* Prett. I sighed, accepting there was nothing I could do about it now.

'It's all right,' I said with a shrug. 'Maybe he was just being nice and wasn't even interested.'

Hayden let out a derisive scoff. 'Oh, trust me, he was interested.'

'Hmm,' I hummed sceptically. 'Apparently I'm popular today.'

'It's not a shock that everyone wants you, Grace,' Hayden said slowly, as if it were obvious. 'You're beautiful, strong, brave, selfless, smart . . . I could go on forever but I'll stop to spare you from denying it like I know you will.'

He said them so casually, but they were some of the kindest things anyone had ever said to me. I found it difficult to respond without rebuffing him.

'Thank you, Hayden.'

'Mmhmm,' he murmured in reply.

We'd arrived at the mess hall now, and already an excited buzz was audible as we opened the door. There were so many people that the building looked like it was about to overflow. Cheerful chatter, laughter, and general excitement flooded the room as people crowded around the serving area.

After gently pushing our way to the front, we saw that Maisie, Kit, Dax, and Leutie were going through the boxes. Every time they'd pull something out, the crowd would buzz with excitement as they brandished a loaf of bread, a can of beans, or a bag of some sort of dried meat. They'd formed a sort of assembly line, ending with Maisie, who closely studied each item before putting it away in her storage area. All around me, I could hear glimpses of conversation, all of which revolved around how delicious our meals would be or how we *finally* would have enough food to feed everyone a proper meal.

I absorbed the delight, and it only spread further when I glanced at Hayden to see him smiling as well. Even though it had hurt his pride to do it, it was obvious that he'd made the right decision. Blackwing needed food desperately and now we had enough not only to sustain people physically, but mentally as well.

'You made the right choice, Hayden,' I told him, my voice loaded with pride. He glanced down at me and smiled.

'I think so, too.'

We beamed at each other for a few more moments before we were interrupted by Dax calling our names.

'Hayden, Grace! Look at all this! We'll be set for a month, at least,' he said happily.

'That's great, Dax,' Hayden said lightly. 'How much do you have left to unpack?'

'This is the last of it, so we're pretty much done.'

'All right, good. There's one more thing we need to do today,' Hayden said, piquing my interest. I waited, brows lowered anxiously.

'What's that?' Kit questioned, joining our conversation as he handed Maisie the last item out of his box.

'We need to go check out those Brutes we just ran into. See if we can get any clues off them.'

Kit and Dax both nodded, as if they'd expected this.

'All right, done!' Dax said.

He handed the last item, which looked to be a bag of apples, to a beaming Leutie. He whispered something to her that brought a look of concern to her face. A few more words from Dax changed her frown to a smile, and I saw him pinch her side lightly before retreating from behind the serving area. Kit followed, but I saw no sign of Malin.

'Let's go,' Hayden said lightly, ticking his head towards the door.

Together, we manoeuvred through the exultant crowd back outside. The jeep was waiting with all the windows rolled down. Even though it couldn't have been more than an hour since we'd arrived back home, Kit, Dax, and I piled back into our regular seats.

Instead of climbing in the front, Hayden gripped the window edge with both of his hands, leaning through the frame towards me.

'Come here,' he murmured deeply, voice low and raspy.

Without control or hesitation, I obeyed. Leaning forward, I pressed my lips to his, revelling in the flutter that erupted in my stomach as he kissed me. The kiss lasted a few seconds before he broke off to climb into the driver's seat. I felt a slight heat in my cheeks as I noticed Dax smirking at me, which I ignored.

We spent the time driving from Blackwing to where we'd encountered the Brutes readying our weapons just in case of trouble. I was torn between determination to figure something out and resistance to fully examine their bodies up close.

'Wasn't it over there?' Dax asked from the front seat, pointing through the windshield.

'I thought it was here . . .' Hayden murmured distractedly.

He squinted out of the window, glancing in all directions as he tried to find the exact location of the bodies. It was difficult to see much across the flat expanse from the way the sun beat down on the dirt and patchy grass.

I joined the search as Hayden manoeuvred the jeep in a different direction. Again and again, Hayden turned the jeep around, muttering under his breath as he frowned. Kit and Dax diligently searched their side of the jeep while I looked out of mine, but there was nothing that caught my eye.

'What the hell,' Hayden muttered in frustration. 'Was it further west?'

'I don't know . . .' I trailed off.

He drove a little longer, circling over areas we'd clearly

already been as I noticed our tyre tracks in the dirt. My eyes scanned the land, suddenly praying I'd see the three bodies, but it was something else that caught my eye as the jeep zoomed past a little patch of dirt different than all the others. For the second time that day, I felt the blood drain from my face, taking the warmth with it as a chill ran down my spine.

'Stop,' I choked out, twisting in my seat to try to get a better look. I felt like I had a lump the side of my fist lodged in my throat as I tried to swallow, but my uneven breathing and flash of fear was making it difficult.

Hayden obeyed immediately, slamming on the brakes before turning anxiously over his shoulder.

'What is it? What did you see?' he asked sharply, alternating between studying me and trying to see what I had.

'I'm not sure,' I admitted.

With an unsteady hand, I reached for the door handle and forced it open. I mustered my strength before jumping out of the jeep, landing in the dirt seconds before the others. As I turned, my eyes focused on what I'd seen immediately – a flash of red spreading in the dirt.

Hayden quickly fell into stride with me while Kit and Dax followed. It was as if the world had fallen away and I'd landed in a tunnel as my vision became solely focused on what was ahead of me. I heard buzzing, blocking out Hayden's voice. It was almost impossible to sense anything other than nervous fear, and soon the distance had depleted enough to see more details. The large accumulation of red was formed by a pool of blood so enormous that it reached out to within yards of my foot before I finally stopped.

There was no mistaking now that this was where Kit and Dax had shot the three Brutes. A pool of blood so large could only come from three deaths, bled dry to create such a vast expanse of gore and horror. It was patchy in areas, as if it had sunk into the ground or been smeared away by unnatural causes.

My stomach twisted violently as I took in the next detail. In the centre of the pool of blood, starkly pale and revoltingly mottled, was a memory that had haunted me. A hand, severed from its arm and long having lost the colour of life, lay staked to the ground by a knife at least six inches long that pierced straight through the palm.

All of this was enough to cause anyone to jump back in fear, but what horrified me was something else entirely.

There were no bodies.

No dead Brutes.

Just a pool of blood.

A severed hand with a knife through the palm.

And a single word, scrawled in the very same blood that littered the dirt, bold and written so clearly it could not be ignored.

Thieves.

Fourteen: Distraction

Grace

My blood seemed frozen in my veins as my eyes stayed locked on the grisly sight in front of me. I would have fallen to the ground if it hadn't been for Hayden's quick action, catching me as I staggered clumsily backward. All I could focus on was the bloody word scrawled into the dirt, a message left for us to find by those who had been here.

Thieves.

I didn't know exactly what had happened or how, but I knew exactly who had done this: the Brutes.

Fear ripped through me and I tried to shove off whoever was touching me before Hayden's concerned face came into focus before me.

'Grace,' he murmured.

His voice sounded muffled, as if he were speaking with a pile of blankets pressed over his mouth, or perhaps as if he were across a crowded room instead of inches away. My words seemed anchored down in my throat as I opened my mouth to speak, because nothing more than a petrified gasp managed to escape. I was all the more aware of the shake of my body by Hayden's steady hands running up and down my arms.

'Hey, come on,' Hayden coaxed gently, ducking down so he was just a few inches away. 'Breathe.'

I tried to obey and blew out a long, shaky breath. His voice still sounded stifled and I was having trouble focusing on him with the grotesque scene behind me, but I mustered all of my strength and channelled it into listening to him.

'That's it,' he continued. 'You're okay.'

He gave me a reassuring nod, but I could see the quiet hint of fear in his own eyes. Even as I stared at him, I couldn't stop the gruesome images from flashing through my mind over and over again, joined by things I'd seen in the past and things I'd conjured up in my dreams.

'Remember what I told you earlier,' Hayden continued, keeping his voice low. 'I'm never going to let anyone hurt you. You'll be safe with me.'

His words calmed me a little, and I was able to control my shaking.

'Yes,' I managed to say, voice quiet and weak. I cleared my throat and spoke more firmly. 'Yes, I remember.'

'Good,' Hayden replied. He looked relieved when my breathing evened out more and all but my hands stopped shaking.

'What a mess,' Kit muttered from beside us, making me jump as I jerked my gaze to him. I had completely forgotten he and Dax were there.

'This was left for us, wasn't it?' Dax asked. His voice was flat, as if he already knew he was right. 'It's like what you said was in the Armoury, yeah?'

'Yes,' Hayden murmured darkly. 'But we're not going to hang around. Let's get back and figure this out.'

Kit and Dax murmured their assent, but I didn't bother looking at them. Everything seemed to sharpen as Hayden looked at me. His hand had yet to leave its gentle position on my face as he held my body protectively close to his.

'Do you want me to have Kit drive?' he offered.

I shook my head. 'No, it's okay.'

'You sure?'

'Yeah, promise,' I said, forcing an attempt at a smile that just felt like a grimace.

Hayden frowned gently and pressed a lingering kiss to my forehead, before directing me to my usual seat in the jeep. Kit and Dax, I noticed, had already taken their spots. After making sure I was safely inside, Hayden climbed into the driver's seat and started the engine, taking off to leave the horrid sight behind.

I wished my mind would just go blank after everything, but I had no such luck as Hayden drove us quickly back to camp. Over and over again, I saw everything. Eyes clamped shut, eyes open and desperately trying to focus on Hayden, it didn't matter. My fingers twisted nervously in front of me, fidgeting with anything I could grab. My shirt, the seat, my other hand.

Unconsciously, my hand drifted upward until I felt the fine scar running over my chest, from when Jonah had tried to kill me, completely healed yet marked forever. My fingers shifted to the delicate gold chain around my neck that symbolised so much: our love, our future, those we'd lost. The reminders of my past covered my body in one way or another, leaving their mark on me.

How long ago that seemed that we had been dealing with those things. Now we had a whole new set of problems, terrible in their own haunting way.

I was ripped from my reverie when I noticed we were nearly back to camp. Everyone was pensive and quiet, and I caught Hayden's concerned glance in the mirror more than a few times as he parked the jeep outside of the raid building. I forced myself to open my door before Hayden could, knowing he would feel the need to comfort me. I felt weak, vulnerable. Gritting my teeth in determination, I decided I would put those feelings aside so we could focus and figure out a plan without my fear clouding my thoughts.

Hayden blinked in surprise when I landed beside him outside but didn't say anything before heading into the raid building. Dax followed, and Kit darted across the path to summon Docc. I could feel Hayden's eyes on me as we settled around the table. I offered him a small attempt at a smile that I knew wasn't convincing. He looked unhappy.

Nobody spoke as we waited for Kit and Docc.

'Kit's given me the details of what just happened, so we can get right down to it,' Docc said, looking serious. 'Thoughts?'

'We think the Brutes are after Grace,' Hayden began.

'We don't know for sure,' I said. I wanted to believe that, but I knew deep down that Hayden was probably right.

'We've got a pretty good idea,' Kit replied. 'We both went in there a second time and stole from them, but they didn't even notice me today.'

'Maybe they just didn't see you? We have to think rationally. We can't go starting *another* war just to protect me.'

'Why not?' Hayden asked seriously. He almost looked angry.

'Because I'm just one person,' I said simply, shrugging.

'I told you—'

Hayden was cut off, however, as Docc started speaking calmly yet loudly.

'If the Brutes are actively invading Whetland and encroaching on Blackwing, we need to take action no matter what their motivation is. If they are indeed after Grace, all the more reason to act quickly.'

'Couldn't have said it better myself, Docc,' Dax said with a shrug and a shake of his head.

'I agree,' Hayden said. 'We can't let this escalate any further like it did with Greystone.'

He sounded like he was speaking to the group, but his eyes were riveted on me, burning into me so strongly I could practically feel his gaze down to my toes.

'I just don't want anyone else to get hurt,' I said softly, giving a little shake of my head. A small face, grinning and excited as always, flashed through my mind as I remembered one life in particular that had ended too soon.

Jett.

'Nobody does, but we can't just ignore it,' Hayden said gently. His voice was somewhat strained and I knew he was thinking the same thing I was. The pain he'd managed to begin to deal with flashed behind his eyes.

'We could talk to Renley,' Kit suggested. 'If they've been having problems too, maybe they'll help somehow.'

'Yeah, maybe,' Hayden murmured. His eyes finally dropped from mine as he glanced down at the table in thought. 'Whatever we do, we're not doing it today. We all need time to calm down and think this over.'

'Good thinking, Bossman,' Dax agreed easily.

'Yes, I think taking a day or two to recalibrate and think would do everyone some good,' Docc consented. 'Besides—'

This time it was Docc who was cut off by a sudden banging as the door flew open quickly. All five of us whipped around, most of us reaching for weapons instinctively before we recognised who had entered. I felt my jaw drop open in surprise and confusion as I stared at Malin, rushing through the building before stopping right in front of Kit.

'Kit!' she shouted angrily, shoving her hands at his chest.

'Whoa,' Dax muttered in surprise, taking a step back from them.

'Where the *hell* did you go?!' Malin demanded. She tried

to shove him again, but he hardly moved as he looked down at her, eyes widened in surprise as well.

'We just went to Whetland and ran into some Brutes so—'

'*We just went to Whetland and ran into some Brutes?*' she repeated angrily, voice tight as she glared up at Kit. 'You couldn't tell me you were leaving for something that dangerous?!'

'Hey,' Kit said, reaching gingerly forward to grip either side of her arms with his hands. 'We're all back. I'm fine.'

I was surprised by how gentle his tone was. A quick glance around the room showed Hayden and Dax looking just as confused and stunned as I was. My attention was quickly drawn back to Kit and Malin, who seemed to have forgotten anyone else was around.

For the first time today, my mind wasn't focused on the Brutes.

'You should have told me,' Malin grumbled, voice softening as some of her anger melted away at his touch. A concerned and somewhat hurt expression crossed her face as she studied him closely.

'I'm sorry,' he said quietly.

'You should be,' Malin continued. She still sounded somewhat disgruntled even though her voice was softening more and more by the second. 'If you think I'm still going to marry you now—'

'Wait, *what?!*'

Dax's shocked voice mirrored my exact thoughts as my jaw dropped open even further. Had she just said what I thought she'd said?

'You guys are getting *married*?' Dax questioned. It seemed he was the only one capable of speaking at the moment, as Hayden and I were both stunned into silence. Only Docc seemed completely unsurprised and even somewhat amused at the conversation.

'Um,' Kit started. He blinked as if he had just remembered we were all there. He cleared his throat awkwardly and looped his arm around Malin's shoulder. 'Yeah, we are.'

'If you're lucky,' Malin muttered playfully, reaching up to grip his hand casually while she leaned into his side. The smirk on her face made it clear she didn't mean it, and it brought a grin to Kit's face as he glanced down at her.

'Yes, if I'm lucky.'

I was even more surprised when he ducked down to press a light kiss to her cheek, bringing a full-blown smile to Malin's face this time.

'Well, damn,' Dax said, raising his brows and shaking his head in surprise. 'I reckoned you two had broken up with how odd you were both being. Now we find out you're getting *married*? Will wonders never cease?'

I laughed, but I agreed with Dax. I had also assumed something worse had happened and certainly hadn't expected this.

'Congratulations,' I finally said, grinning widely at them both. 'When do you plan to do it?'

It occurred to me that I had no idea how 'weddings' even worked these days. Before the world had fallen apart, weddings were huge life occasions filled with family, food, dancing, and all the beautiful details only someone living in a world unlike our own could dream of having.

'Well, it was supposed to be tomorrow . . .' Kit trailed off and glanced down at Malin again. 'But I may have just screwed that up.'

A wry grin crossed his face as he waited for her response. She just let out a small laugh and rolled her eyes.

'It's tomorrow, yes. Maisie's been preparing some food and getting some other things ready. Won't tell me what, but I'm sure whatever it is will be lovely.'

'This seems sudden,' Dax said. He placed his hand on his chin and raised a single finger to tap thoughtfully along his jaw. 'What's the rush?'

Kit shrugged. 'I figured I'd wasted enough time. Time to commit or get out, right? Especially with how things are now.'

Malin nodded, beaming at him. The words sounded vaguely familiar to something I'd said to her, and it made me smile. They both truly looked the happiest I'd ever seen them.

'Taking things a bit far, mate. I think she would have settled for a title,' Dax teased, grinning at them before shooting a wink at Malin.

'Always the charmer, Dax,' she replied with a sporting grin.

'This is so great, you guys,' I said honestly. My smile was wide as I surveyed them a few more moments before glancing at Hayden, who I noticed was watching me with a soft smile on his lips.

'Well, I, for one, am all for this. Weddings mean hooch and hooch means Dax gets to have some fun,' Dax carried on happily, rubbing his hands together mischievously in front of him.

'Oh, no,' Hayden muttered, pretending to look afraid.

A happy lightness started to spread through me, chasing away some of the crippling fear I'd been feeling all day. I remembered the last party Blackwing had thrown; there had been music, dancing, food and drink. I was very much looking forward to experiencing it again after so many tense and stressful events lately. Another happy thought occurred to me when I realised that Hayden and I would be able to dance without worrying about standing too close, talk without worrying about someone overhearing.

Dax's chuckle brought my attention back to the group, and again, I caught Hayden watching me. I could tell he was still concerned about me from the way his brows furrowed. As soon as our gazes connected, he closed the distance between us to stand in front of me. Docc, who seemed very unsurprised by all this, and Dax had gone over to talk with Malin and Kit some more, leaving us alone.

'You okay?' Hayden asked quietly.

'Yeah, I am,' I answered truthfully. I had got pretty shaken up earlier, but knowing we were going to take action after some consideration made me feel better. And, I had to admit, the happy news about Kit and Malin had helped as well. 'This will be a good distraction.'

Hayden smiled at me again. 'It will be, yes. I'll make sure we have double the rounds going just in case.'

'Good,' I said, relieved. 'Thank you, Hayden.'

'It's nothing,' he said, waving away my gratitude. 'I have a question for you.'

His eyes were glowing as he watched me expectantly.

'What's that?'

'Will you be my date to the wedding?'

He let out a low chuckle.

'I would be honoured to,' I said, giving a mock bow as I ducked my head.

'I haven't got a suit, I'm afraid. Hope you'll forgive my appearance,' he continued with a grin. With every word he spoke and gentle smile he sent my way, more and more of the fear dissipated from my body.

'That's all right, I haven't got a dress,' I replied, beaming up at him. 'I can't get all prettied up for you.'

'You're always beautiful,' Hayden murmured softly. His hand reached forward to tidy a strand of hair behind my ear.

'Thank you,' I responded. His words were sweet, but I felt

like I was thanking him for so much more. 'For everything.'

Ever since we ran into the Brutes, he'd done everything in his power to make sure I felt safe, loved, cared for. He'd been gentle, devoted, protective. He'd managed to distract me even though there was still so much to think about. He made me inexplicably happy simply by being himself, and there were not enough words in the world to describe just how grateful I was.

'Just, thank you,' I repeated. It felt inadequate, but I hoped he'd understand.

'Anything for you,' he answered simply. His hand landed on my hip and he gave a gentle squeeze.

Kit and Malin's upcoming wedding was just proof that even when things seemed terrible, good still persisted in the world. It was as if my own old advice was coming back to remind me of how I used to think.

There was still so much beauty left in the world – you just had to let yourself see it.

Fifteen: Enamoured

Grace

I watched with a happy grin as Maisie fixed Malin's long, dark hair into a beautifully loose updo. The cracked mirror Malin sat in front of gave me a view of her face, which hadn't lost its smile since I'd stepped into her small hut. Leutie sat beside me, sighing happily every few minutes as she observed.

'Malin, you look so beautiful,' Leutie told her kindly. Malin's smile widened even more as she glanced at Leutie in the mirror.

'Thank you, Leutie,' she replied happily.

'I can't believe you and Kit are getting married,' I said for what felt like the hundredth time. It was so difficult for me to wrap my head around, but I was undeniably happy for the pair of them.

'I know,' Malin said with a laugh. 'Talk about fast, right?'

She let out a giddy giggle and continued to beam around at everyone.

I shrugged. 'Well, you and Kit have been together a while, right? Just not like . . . officially?'

I couldn't think of a nice way to state that they'd basically only been friends with benefits, so I just left it at that.

'Two and a half years, I think,' Malin replied with a small nod. She winced as she noticed she'd disrupted Maisie, who was trying to pin a strand of her hair in place. With a sheepish grin, she added, 'Sorry, Maisie.'

'It's all right,' she said softly. 'I'm glad you two are doing this. It's been a while since we've had something happy to celebrate.'

'I hope everyone will have a nice time,' Malin said with a contented sigh.

'What do you guys do for weddings?' I asked curiously. We didn't have weddings in Greystone, and I knew little more than the basics about how they worked before the world had fallen apart.

'We have a small ceremony. Docc officiates things, I do the food. We have those with instruments play music and have a little party to celebrate,' Maisie explained. 'It's nothing like how my wedding was back in the day. We don't have bridesmaids or groomsmen or any of that.'

I absorbed very little of what she said aside from one detail. As far as I knew, Maisie lived alone now that Jett was gone, which could only mean one thing.

'I didn't know you were married,' Malin said gently, frowning at Maisie. Her fingers worked smoothly as she nodded, finishing up her work before taking a step back to admire it. Malin's hair looked somehow effortless and intricately done all at once, making her more beautiful than ever.

'I was, yes. About a year before everything happened, I married a man named Trent.'

Everyone was silent for a few moments as they absorbed this information. My heart felt heavy because I already knew how this story must have turned out, even though no one dared ask the question we were all thinking.

'It's okay to ask,' Maisie said gently, smiling at us sadly.

'What happened to him?' I finally said. I found it difficult to look at her, so my eyes stayed trained on the floor as I waited to hear her surely sad response.

'He was killed the day the bombs fell. We had just over a year together before it was all over, but it was a wonderful marriage. Full of love and happiness, which is what I truly hope you and Kit will have,' she finished with a genuine smile at Malin, who looked sobered by Maisie's story.

'I'm so sorry, Maisie,' Malin murmured softly.

I glanced at Leutie beside me and could see her eyes looked damp with tears that had welled up. I was suddenly struck with deep admiration for Maisie. She'd first lost her husband, then her foster son in Jett, yet she remained so strong. Her outlook was overwhelmingly positive after so much heartache and loss. I didn't know what I would do if I had gone through what she had. The thought of losing Hayden absolutely destroyed me, yet she'd lost her husband and somehow carried on.

'I'm sorry, too,' I finally said, meaning it with every bit of me.

'Thank you,' Maisie replied with a nod to Malin and me. 'But I didn't mean to make this about me. This is Malin's big day and we should all be celebrating!'

She somehow managed a genuine grin as she placed her hands on Malin's shoulders and beamed at her in the mirror. She grinned again, unable to resist.

'Now, we just need a little make-up I've had saved and a dress and you'll be all set,' Maisie continued.

Malin let out a giddy, enthusiastic laugh and Leutie leaned in excitedly to examine the small bag Maisie had pulled out. Inside it were several little containers I did not recognise. I watched in silent curiosity as she applied what little make-up she had left to Malin, giving a soft glow to her cheeks and a little colour to her lips. It wasn't much, but it was enough to make her look like she was glowing.

'I'll get the dress,' Leutie said excitedly, bouncing out of her seat.

The tears that had gathered in her eyes were gone now, replaced once again by the happy grin on her face. She hurried to the other side of the room to grab the dress Malin had procured. It was a simple white dress with long sleeves and a hemline that fell roughly around the knees, certainly not a wedding dress, but it would do the trick anyway. Malin stood with a small squeak of excitement and moved to stand behind a small partition Maisie had constructed to get dressed while Leutie hovered around the edge to assist if needed.

'Maisie, you should fix Grace up!' Malin called from behind the partition.

Immediately, my stomach twisted in resistance.

'Oh, no, that's okay,' I rebutted instantly.

'That's a wonderful idea, Malin,' Maisie said with a smile.

There was a small 'oof' from Malin as she accidentally bumped into something while trying to get her dress on, followed by a quiet giggle before she spoke again.

'Oh, come on. Let her!' she coaxed happily.

'Think what Hayden will do,' Leutie added with a conspiratorial giggle.

I felt stupid as a blush crossed my cheeks.

'No, really,' I insisted. 'You don't have much of that stuff, right? Don't waste it on me.'

'It's just make-up, Grace. Hardly a necessity. Besides, we rarely get the occasion to use it, so we might as well!' Maisie said with a grin. 'Of course, you're already beautiful and don't need it, but it could be fun.'

'Come on, Grace!' Leutie encouraged excitedly. 'Do it for us.'

'Oh, for you, huh?' I laughed, grinning at her.

'And for Hayden,' she continued, winking at me.

I rolled my eyes and let out a reluctant sigh. 'Fine. He probably won't even notice though, honestly.'

'Hmm. We'll see,' Maisie murmured calmly. 'Have a seat, dear.'

She gestured at the chair Malin had previously occupied. I felt a bit like a science experiment as I let Maisie do whatever she wanted, refusing to look in the mirror for fear of what I'd see. It seemed like hours passed as she put stuff on my face, brushed and styled my hair, and forced me into a dress that had come seemingly out of nowhere. Malin and Leutie continued to get themselves ready but did a lot of watching and excited squealing as Maisie continued her work on me.

'This was my dress from when Trent purposed,' Maisie told me as she gently zipped up the back. I sucked in a breath as I realised it must be very special to her.

'Maisie, really, I don't have to wear this,' I protested, shaking my head.

'Hush,' she rebutted gently. 'I've kept it all these years but haven't been able to bring myself to wear it. Someone ought to, and you'll look stunning in it.'

'Maisie—'

'No more arguing, Grace,' Leutie said, cutting me off with a wide grin. 'Look at yourself first, will ya?'

Maisie placed her hands on my shoulders and turned me towards the mirror, which I'd successfully avoided until now. A stranger stared back at me.

A light pink tinge dotted over my cheeks, a similar colour staining my lips darker than usual. Wisps of blonde hair fell to frame my face while the rest fell over my shoulders in loose waves that seemed so much softer than before. I hardly ever wore my hair down because it tended to get in the way, but now it looked so beautiful as the long, light strands cascaded gently down my back.

The dress was perhaps the most significant change. It was made of a soft silver, almost cream in colour, with thick straps and a fitted top before coming away from my waist and ending a few inches above my knee. The colour highlighted my features even more than the make-up Maisie had applied. My lips parted in stunned surprise as I took in my appearance, unable to really register that it was me I was looking at.

'You're magnificent, Grace,' Maisie said softly as she observed my reaction.

I frowned, trying to focus my thoughts. There was no denying the girl standing in front of me in the mirror was beautiful, but she didn't look like me. I felt the sudden urge to take off the dress and wash my face to transform back into my regular self.

'Grace, you're going to look better than me at my own wedding,' Malin teased, finally having emerged from behind the partition. Leutie had assisted her to zip up her dress and she now stood before us, fully ready for her big moment. She looked absolutely stunning.

'Not possible,' I said with a smile, finally finding words now that I could focus on someone other than myself. 'You'll outdo us all, as you should.'

Malin beamed at me and looked like she wanted to argue but dropped it with a playful shake of her head. 'Thank you, Grace.'

'Leutie and I will get dressed quickly and then I think we're all set. Malin, are you ready for this?' Maisie asked with a grin.

Even though I still felt somewhat uncomfortable, I decided to push it down. Today was about Malin and if she wanted me to wear the dress, I'd wear the dress.

'I'm ready,' Malin confirmed, beaming once more. 'Time to get married!'

Hayden

I stood with my hands on my hips as I looked around the area that had been set up for Kit and Malin's wedding. Excited people buzzed about, putting last-minute touches on things here and there. It was in the same area of camp we'd had the last party, with much of the same equipment, but no one seemed to mind. Rows had been set up with an aisle down the middle, a few tables laden with food and drink lined the sides, and a large pile of wood had been assembled for use as a bonfire after the sun went down. The people who owned instruments had set up towards the back of the rows. They'd already started playing, and the soft music coming from their guitars and other instruments drifted around me as evening began to fall.

I hadn't seen Grace since this morning when she'd started helping me prepare, but our time together had been short before she was swept away by a very excited Leutie. It had taken a lot of effort not to feel worried about her absence even though I knew she wasn't far away.

'Can you believe this?' Dax asked as he appeared beside me.

A quick glance down at him had me doing a double take when I saw what I assumed to be a tie slung around his neck. The top looked completely wrong, as if he'd given up trying to figure it out and had just tied it in a knot like one would a shoe. I had to admit that I didn't know the proper way to tie it, either, so I didn't say anything.

'Not really,' I admitted. 'Can't remember the last time we even had a wedding.'

'It's been years,' he agreed. 'Who was it, George and Sierra?'

'Maybe,' I said non-committally. I knew I'd never remember who it was because I hadn't attended; I'd been on duty, just as some from Blackwing were right now.

'Good of you to dress up for the occasion,' Dax said sarcastically as he eyed my clothes. I wore a simple white T-shirt and black jeans – pretty much what I wore every day.

'This is a clean shirt,' I pointed out.

'Right, sure,' Dax said doubtfully, raising a disbelieving brow.

'At least I didn't try and fail to properly wear a tie,' I shot back lightly, changing my decision to not say anything.

'I know how to tie a tie,' Dax rebutted. 'But Leutie doesn't know that, so guess who's going to feel special when she gets to fix it for me, huh?'

I snorted a laugh and shot him an amused look. 'I don't know if you're an idiot or a genius.'

'Funny how often people seem to contemplate that . . .' Dax trailed off lightly, eyes scanning the quickly dimming camp. The sun was setting, casting a soft glow around the space. 'Anyway, I see the ladies are arriving. Best find our seats for the show, yeah?'

'Yeah, all right. Don't get too crazy with the hooch. I heard Perdita made it strong,' I suggested, half jokingly, half seriously.

Dax clicked his teeth and winked as he started to stray away. 'You got it, Bossman.'

With that, he headed off towards the edge of things, where I could see Leutie and Maisie approaching. People had started to take their seats, moving in time with the music. Docc stood at the front, a patient, serene smile on his face while Kit paced around restlessly. Someone had found some sort of suit coat to put on him, and judging by the way he fidgeted relentlessly with the sleeves, he was not particularly enjoying wearing it. His obvious nervousness amused me.

'Hayden.'

Grace's soft voice behind me caused me to turn, prepared to greet her with a smile before I felt my jaw drop open. I was unable to speak as my eyes roamed over her features, stunned by how breathtaking she looked. While I couldn't fully put my finger on exact details, there was no denying the way she appeared to be glowing as she watched me apprehensively. Her fingers fidgeted with the edge of her dress, as if trying to resist doing so but not quite managing to stop.

'I, um, I know it's different—'

'Very,' I agreed quickly.

Again, she fidgeted with her dress.

'I told them you wouldn't like it,' she said, backtracking as she tucked a strand of hair hurriedly behind her ear. 'I should have just—'

'Grace, you look so incredibly beautiful,' I told her. Now it was her turn to be speechless, but she grinned, as if reluctant to believe me.

'Thank you,' she accepted modestly.

'Just . . . wow,' I said, struggling to find words. I blew out a deep huff and felt my heart give an extra-hard thump in my chest. 'Beautiful.'

She beamed up at me, pursing her lips as she smiled. Without another word, I grabbed her hand in mine, brought it to my lips to press a light kiss into it, and tugged her gently towards the seats. I could practically feel her happy gaze as it burned into mine, and I relished the warmth. Soon, we were seated in the front row, as per Kit and Malin's request. Beside us sat Dax, Leutie, and Maisie.

I never released Grace's hand as we sat patiently, waiting for Malin to arrive. Kit now stood still at the front, though he still fidgeted with the cuffs of his jacket. Docc stood calmly beside him. I snuck a glance down at Grace to see her smiling gently as she observed everything around us, the light catching and illuminating her features beautifully. My thumb rolled over hers absent-mindedly, feeling the softness of her skin against my own.

I felt a sudden wave of adoration for her and couldn't resist leaning forward to press a light kiss onto her temple. She seemed surprised yet thrilled as she turned to beam at me after I pulled away. Any words she might have spoken were stopped as the music changed, alerting everyone to the back. Along with the whole crowd, Grace and I stood and turned around to see Malin waiting at the end of the aisle.

She stood alone, no father left in the world to walk her down the aisle and apparently no one else she wanted to do the honour. I couldn't remember what was even considered normal anymore as I watched her slowly proceed forward. She was grinning from ear to ear, focused entirely on Kit, who waited for her anxiously. Grace nudged me gently, drawing my attention away as I glanced down at her again.

'Look at Kit,' she whispered, pointing subtly.

As I watched, he reached up to wipe away what could only be a tear before sniffing once and collecting himself, unable to suppress his ecstatic grin as he watched Malin approach. Grace squeezed my hand and leaned into me, tilting her head momentarily to rest on my shoulder as we watched Malin finally arrive at the end. Kit immediately grabbed her hands as they faced each other, radiating happiness off each other.

Everyone settled down, resuming their seated positions. After waiting a few moments, Docc spoke in his low, mellow tones.

'Hello and welcome. Today, we celebrate the union of two in love – Kit and Malin . . .'

The rest of the wedding was a blur. I completely gave up on trying to pay attention to the words Kit and Malin were exchanging and devoted my full attention to carefully studying Grace. Even now, I felt a flutter when I thought of how lucky I was to have her. After a while, she noticed, and turned to glance at me fondly.

'You're missing it,' she whispered.

'No, I'm not,' I replied softly. The only thing I'd be missing would be her if I were to look away from her for even a second.

After a while, when I'd taken in every detail of her face at least twice more, I finally managed to look away when the crowd cheered suddenly. A quick glance towards the front showed Kit and Malin pressed together, Kit's hands along her cheeks as they kissed to seal their vows I hadn't heard.

I watched happily as Docc held his hands above them, dusting them in a mixture of spices Maisie had collected, as was tradition in Blackwing. Each spice represented something – love, happiness, loyalty, selflessness – and was meant to be good luck for the married couple. I wasn't sure who had started it or how, but as long as I could remember, every wedding in Blackwing had included the tradition.

Finally, they broke apart, both grinning from ear to ear as they smiled at each other. The crowd quickly erupted into cheers and applause. Again, I glanced at Grace to see her positively beaming as she watched, only this time, I didn't bother trying to resist as I ducked down to press another kiss to her temple. Immediately, she snaked her arm around my waist and hugged herself into my side as we watched Kit and Malin turn to face everyone, hands linked.

'Let's celebrate!' Malin cheered excitedly, hardly able to speak through her exhilarated grin.

As if on cue, the music changed to something much more lively, and Kit wasted no time in sweeping her into his arms for a dance. Several people rushed forward to start clearing away the chairs, positioning them to form a sort of ring that everyone gathered inside. People paired off for dancing, while others helped themselves to food or drinks. Another person ignited the bonfire, casting a warm glow around everything now that the sun was almost completely gone. The candles and lanterns that had been lit for the ceremony were now dwarfed in comparison by the giant blaze that illuminated the area.

'Come dance with me,' I requested gently. I unwound myself from Grace but kept my grip on her hand, which I held as I backed away slowly towards where people were dancing. She hesitated, grinning at me as she let me tug lightly on her arm a few times.

'All on your own this time, hmm?' she teased. I knew she was referencing that the only way she'd got me to dance with her last time was because Dax had used my jealous tendencies against me to lure me out.

'Mmhmm, how could I not?'

She laughed as I pulled her close – much closer than last time – and looped my free arm around her waist. Her arms wound around my neck, heating my body with her touch. She had to tilt her head back to look up at me, and when she did, I was rewarded with the same beaming smile she'd worn all day.

'God, you look beautiful, Grace,' I murmured again, unable to resist. It was times like this that I was grateful our relationship was no longer a secret, because I didn't think I was capable of pulling back even if I had to.

'Thank you. I'm glad you like it because I feel so . . . weird. Like I'm not myself,' she said with a soft laugh. I was disappointed when I saw her smile fade a bit.

'I do love it,' I told her, ducking my head. 'And you look so, so stunning. But I love *my* Grace more. That's the one I fell in love with and that's the one I'll always love, even if you dress yourself up once in a while.'

Her grin brightened again at my words. 'Really?'

I nodded and hummed softly in affirmation. 'Really.'

She bit down on her lip and closed her eyes, leaning forward to hug me while resting her head against my shoulder.

'I love you,' she breathed, a happy sigh pushing past her lips.

'And I love you,' I returned easily.

There was absolutely nothing I was more certain of than the fact that I loved Grace with everything I had. Our kiss lingered, and I could feel her melting into me in every way as the tingling fireworks I always felt ripped through my body.

'Ahem,' a small voice said, interrupting. I drew back in surprise, leaving my hand along Grace's face as I glanced around for the source of the voice. It took me a minute, because it was only when I looked down that I saw who it was.

'Rainey,' I said, clearing my throat as I noticed it was raspy and low. 'How can I help you?'

'Hi, Rainey,' Grace said gently, pulling back a bit.

I felt a wave of sadness roll through me as I studied the little girl, younger even than Jett had been. It was so strange to see her now as I remembered the affection Jett had carried for her and so miserably failed to hide. He was gone, but she was still here.

'Maisie has told me I'm to be the flower girl, so I'm handing out flowers,' she said with a shy smile. As she spoke, she lifted a hand that held two white daisies, offering them to Grace and me.

'I don't think that's how—'

I was cut off when Grace nudged me, stopping my words before she spoke.

'They're beautiful, thank you,' she said kindly, smiling at her.

'You're welcome. You can get back to kissing now,' Rainey said with a cheeky grin. She let out a little giggle before prancing away, giving us no chance to respond. Grace laughed and watched her run away, almost managing to hide the bit of sadness that flitted across her face.

'She makes me think of . . .' Grace trailed off softly, finally returning her gaze to mine.

'Me, too,' I admitted. We didn't need to say his name to understand.

As happy as I was, I couldn't help but feel the pang of hurt that always came with such thoughts. He would have loved this. I could practically see him running around in the crowd, dancing and eating as many sweets as he could manage before Maisie finally shut him down. He thrived in crowds, spreading his unrivalled cheer to anyone around him.

I hadn't realised, but we'd stopped dancing. Grace and I simply stood, arms linked around each other while deep in thought. Her mood had been so light before and I wanted her to feel that way again. What surprised me, though, was when she spoke first, as if she'd just realised the same thing.

'Hey,' she said. 'Let's just try to enjoy this, yeah? Like he would have.'

A small, sad smile pulled at my lips. 'You're right.'

'I know,' she said lightly, flitting her eyes upward and giving an exaggerated grin.

'And you're cute,' I told her, grinning wider now.

'Oh, yeah?' she questioned playfully with a raised eyebrow.

'Mmhmm,' I hummed, nodding.

Only for Grace would I try to do what she asked.

Only with Grace was it possible.

Sixteen: Reflection

Grace

Everything felt wonderfully surreal as I revelled in the beauty of the evening. It was getting late, and the only light came from the candles, the large bonfire, and the millions of stars shining from the clear sky above. All around, people danced, conversed, and generally enjoyed each other's company.

The barrel of hooch Perdita had prepared was nearly empty, and the evidence was clear in more than a few people. Dax, for one, was more drunk than I'd ever seen him. I watched and stifled a laugh as he whipped Leutie around the dance area, very similar to the way he'd danced with Perdita at the last celebration. Leutie, also quite drunk, giggled happily as she barely managed to stay on her feet.

My eyes roamed over everyone as I sat next to Hayden, leaning into his side without even realising as we took a little break from dancing. I grasped a cup of Perdita's hooch in my hand, but I couldn't really bring myself to drink much of it because it was strong. Hayden hadn't even bothered getting any, more than content to enjoy the night as it was.

I sighed contentedly as my eyes fell on Kit and Malin, who hadn't been able to look away from each other all evening. They danced together in the crowd, beaming into each other's eyes as they moved. I'd been wanting the chance to congratulate them but couldn't bring myself to interrupt them when they were so obviously captivated by one another.

'They look so happy,' I sighed wistfully, smiling softly as I watched.

'I hope they are,' Hayden replied. He'd grown somewhat quiet ever since our interaction with Rainey, as if he'd retreated in his head a bit, but his touch had never left my skin despite his distraction.

I continued to look around, feeling peaceful and happy even though I still felt like I was wearing some sort of costume rather than a dress and simple make-up. The only thing holding me back from pure bliss was the fact that Hayden was clearly thinking of other things, even though he'd said he'd try to enjoy the evening. I spoke again in the hope of distracting him from his thoughts.

'Have you had fun so far?' I asked gently.

'I have indeed,' he answered, turning to connect our eyes.

'Good,' I replied simply, grinning at him. I ducked forward and pressed a light kiss into his shoulder as I let my fingers trail absent-mindedly over his forearm.

'Hey, you two!'

Our quiet moment was abruptly interrupted by Dax's overly loud voice. Both of us turned away from each other to find him standing, or rather swaying, in front of us. A giddy Leutie stood next to him, trying to keep her balance as she held onto his arm. The stench of hooch seemed to be leaking off the pair of them, causing my brows to raise in surprise.

'Hey,' I returned with a grin. Dax looked very unsteady with his tie hanging loosely. Leutie, who had started the wedding with her hair in a soft bun done by Maisie, also looked fairly dishevelled thanks to Dax's style of dancing.

'Jesus,' Hayden muttered before giving a low chuckle. 'Haven't fixed your tie, I see.'

Dax frowned in confusion before glancing down and grinning, as if he'd just noticed. 'Turns out Leutie can't tie a tie, mate.'

Leutie giggled and grinned at Dax. My brows lowered in confusion but my smile stayed on my face while Hayden let out another low laugh. 'You tried.'

'Mmhmm, sure did,' Dax slurred, giving an overenthusiastic nod. 'Anyway. We just came to inform you guys that this is a wedding and that sitting in the corner is unacceptable behaviour at such a fine event.'

'Oh, really?' I laughed, amused at the overly serious expression he tried and failed to maintain as he grinned at us.

'Really,' he said as he gave a formal nod.

'It's so *fun* here,' Leutie said to me, beaming. 'We never did this stuff in Greystone!'

I smiled. 'Fun' seemed like such an odd word to describe anything in our world, but compared to the bleak and dreary lifestyle of Greystone, Blackwing certainly was much more fun. Hayden squeezed my thigh as if reading my thoughts, making me think it had more to do with the company than anything.

'It is,' I agreed simply, smiling at her.

My eyes darted behind Dax and Leutie as Dax continued to tease Hayden about sitting out. I was surprised when I saw Kit and Malin part for what I thought was the first time all evening. Malin was quickly accosted by several people who eagerly rushed forward to congratulate her, leaving Kit to meander off to the side of the crowd.

'Hey, I'll be right back,' I said, turning to Hayden. 'I just want to congratulate Kit.'

Hayden nodded and leaned forward, pressing a kiss into

my cheek before untangling himself from me. 'All right, see you in a bit.'

I smiled at him and stood, brushing past Dax and Leutie with a small wave.

'Don't tease him too much, Dax,' I said, winking at him as I left.

He returned a sloppy, uncoordinated wink that caused his entire body to duck forward and nearly lose his balance. 'No promises.'

I laughed and rolled my eyes playfully before leaving them behind, weaving through the crowd until I reached Kit, who was standing and observing things with a contented smile. It was the happiest I'd ever seen him, and it made me happy to see.

'Hey,' I greeted, moving to stand next to him. 'Congratulations on the wedding!'

'Thanks,' he replied, grinning. 'Got to say it probably never would have happened if it weren't for you.'

'Really?' I questioned, surprised.

'Yeah,' he said with a nod. 'If she'd never cut things off and made me really think about stuff, I don't know if I ever would have figured it out on my own.'

'Oh, I'm sure you would have.' I shook my head.

He shrugged. 'Guess we'll never know, so just let me say thank you, yeah?'

My smile widened, pleased. 'You're welcome.'

'You guys having fun?' he asked casually. His eyes were focused on the crowd again, searching. I saw him grin again and followed his gaze to see Malin, who was chatting happily with someone from camp.

'Yeah, everything's been so beautiful,' I replied truthfully.

'How's Hayden?' Kit asked, turning to focus on me.

'He's . . .' I trailed off, unsure of what to say. He'd gone through just about every emotion in the book tonight and I was still a bit unsure of how he was currently feeling. I finally spoke again to conclude, 'I think he's okay.'

'Hmm,' Kit hummed thoughtfully. 'Just want to give you fair warning . . . he might be a bit weird this next week.'

'What?' I asked, frowning in confusion. 'Why?'

'I'm guessing he didn't tell you and I'm not really sure it's my place to say, but I feel like I owe you because of all this, so . . . it's his birthday next week.'

'Okay . . .' I trailed off, unsure why that would make him behave differently.

'He hates his birthday,' Kit told me. He glanced down at me with a frown.

'But why?' I pressed. My eyes searched for Hayden, but I couldn't see across the crowd of people that were busy dancing.

'I don't know if it's my place,' he repeated hesitantly.

'Well, you already started telling me so now you have to finish,' I coaxed. I could feel some nerves starting to creep up as I waited anxiously for his explanation.

'It's kind of a long story, but it happened a while ago, on his fifteenth birthday.'

My heart already gave a heavy thud, apprehensive about what sort of event could have affected him at such an age. I waited for Kit to continue.

'We were still training to go on raids, but we were going more and more, usually with one more experienced person so they could observe how we did things and teach us, you know?' Kit paused and took a deep breath. 'Well, it was his birthday when he went on one with Barrow and I into the city. We were looking for food and we went in this grocery store when we ran into this family.'

My stomach started to twist as I listened to Kit carry on.

'It was kind of weird to see a family, you know? But that's what it was – a mum, dad, three kids, all younger than Hayden and me. They were looking for food as well when they ran into us in that store . . . They asked us for help, for somewhere to go . . . but Barrow said no because that's just how things work, you know? Trust your own, that's it. Of course Hayden wanted to help them, but he was overruled. So we left them and carried on, ready to come back to camp.'

Kit cast a quick glance at me before continuing. I noticed my breath had picked up speed now, waiting for the bomb to drop.

'But right outside the store, we ran into some Brutes. Fought a few off and managed to escape without killing any of them, so we sprinted back to the jeep and prepared to come back to camp. But the thing is . . . after we left the Brutes behind, they went into that grocery store and found that family. There was a lot of screaming and shouting . . . So much that we could hear it from the jeep. Hayden forced Barrow to stop and jumped out, but by the time he got back inside, it was too late . . .'

I realised where this was going. Suddenly I didn't want to hear the end of this story.

'When he got to them, the father, mother, and two of the kids were dead. No Brutes in sight. All that was left was a huge pool of blood and one kid, a little girl, with a huge gash through her chest. She was bleeding out, dying slowly and painfully. By the time Barrow and I got in there, Hayden was holding her, watching her die. But it was taking so long and there was nothing he could do . . . She was crying, begging him to stop the pain, to help her, to do anything. Finally he couldn't take it anymore and . . . he put her out of her misery. A quick shot to the head, no more pain. But it ruined him to do it.'

My throat felt tight as I listened, suddenly feeling sick to my stomach at the thought of barely fifteen-year-old Hayden having to see and do such a thing.

'Wow,' I finally managed to say. 'That happened on his birthday?'

Kit nodded slowly, flicking his eyes to mine. 'Yeah. And you know how he is, so you can bet he blamed himself even though he was probably the least at fault.'

'Of course he did,' I murmured sadly. Again, I glanced around to try to locate him, but again, the dancing people obscured my view.

'So now every year, on his birthday, that's all he can think of. Seeing that dead family and having to kill that little girl. Feeling that guilt. It's horrible for him.'

'Even though it wasn't his fault,' I added softly. I felt the overwhelming urge to run to him and comfort him, but I didn't want to bring up the story.

'That's Hayden for you,' Kit replied.

I frowned at the dirt, feeling helpless to fix such a horrible thing that had happened nearly seven years ago.

'Anyway,' Kit said when I didn't speak. 'I didn't mean to bring the mood down or anything. I just thought you should know why he's behaving differently because I doubt he'll talk about it, you know?'

'Yeah, thank you for telling me,' I said distractedly. I truly was grateful to Kit for telling me and saving me the confusion, but now all I felt was sad for Hayden. 'I didn't mean to get all serious either. I just wanted to congratulate you on getting married.'

Kit gave me a small smile. 'Thank you, Grace.'

'Of course,' I said, returning his smile that still felt sad on my face. 'I'll see you later. Have a good rest of your wedding night.'

I nudged him lightly in the ribs and earned a quiet chuckle. 'Will do.'

With that, I gave a small wave and started to weave my way back through the crowd. I felt overwhelmed by the horrible thought of what Hayden had gone through. Something like that would be terrible enough to deal with once, but it was even more terrible that he was forced to relive the memories every single year on his birthday, a day which should have been spent celebrating.

A few people bumped into me as I moved through the dancers, but I hardly even noticed. It was getting to be very late, and suddenly all I felt like doing was going home with Hayden to retreat to the quiet of our hut. I hoped he'd feel the same as I approached where we'd been sitting. Dax and Leutie stood with their backs to me, and I noticed Dax's arm slung around Leutie's waist. His fingers fiddled with the fabric of her clothes covering her hip, causing her to squirm and giggle every so often as if it tickled.

When I finally reached them, I moved around to reclaim my seat next to Hayden. The only problem was, Hayden was gone. In his place sat Perdita and Docc, both of whom greeted me with a smile as I approached.

'Where's Hayden?' I asked, interrupting whatever they'd been talking about and ignoring their greetings.

'He just nipped away to the loo, don't you worry,' Dax slurred, raising a cup of Perdita's hooch at me.

'The whispers called,' Perdita said, nodding wisely at me. I frowned, choosing to ignore her statement.

'How long has he been gone?'

'About ten minutes, I'd say,' Docc replied calmly. 'I'm sure he's fine, girl.'

I frowned, unconvinced and probably overly sensitive after hearing Kit's story.

'Here, have some of this to loosen you up,' Leutie said with a giggle that turned to a hiccup as she offered me her cup.

'That's okay,' I muttered distractedly, waving away her offer.

I turned on the spot to search the crowd, hoping I'd see his messy dark hair or wide shoulders among them, but I had no such luck. Despite everyone's reassurance, I still felt on edge not knowing where exactly he was.

Dax, Leutie, Docc, and Perdita carried on their conversation from before, though I couldn't pay attention. I shifted to stand next to Perdita so I could survey the entire area and look for Hayden. Every so often, bursts of laughter from the group I stood with would make me flinch in my inattentiveness.

I noticed that people were starting to leave the area, stumbling home to their huts for a good night's sleep. I wanted nothing more than to do the same, but I couldn't without Hayden. Restlessly, I fidgeted with the hem of my dress and felt my leg bounce quickly up and down, growing more and more anxious the longer time went on.

After about forty-five minutes of waiting and no return of Hayden, I couldn't take it anymore.

'Are you sure he just went to the bathroom?' I asked, interrupting again.

'That's what he said,' Dax replied. He'd given up trying to stand and had fallen into a chair, where he'd pulled Leutie down with him. She now sat on his lap, unable to squeeze in beside him.

'He's been gone nearly an hour,' I muttered bitterly, frustrated that almost everyone appeared drunk or senile aside from Docc.

'The whispers, my dear, the whispers . . .' Perdita said, nodding. 'Boom.'

I blinked, completely unsure of how to respond. I finally settled for a flat, 'Right.'

'Is no one else concerned?' I said, a little more harshly than I intended.

'He's a big boy, Grace. Don't worry,' Dax said with a sloppy wave of his hand. His head lolled backward before he whipped it upright again, a drunken grin on his face as Leutie giggled again.

'Dax, you—'

'Grace, might I speak with you a moment?' Docc interrupted gently. I snapped my head in his direction to see him watching me.

'Yeah,' I replied, eager to get away from Dax before I snapped at him for no reason.

Docc nodded and stood, walking a few yards away from the crowd before turning to face me. He was a very tall man and he towered over me even more than Hayden did.

'Now, Grace,' he started, voice somewhat stern. 'I know you're concerned about Hayden, but I really don't think there's any reason to be.'

'How do you know?' I questioned with a sigh.

'Just trust me,' Docc said pensively.

A small wave of frustration rolled through me before I forced it down. Docc gave me a small, indulgent smile before he spoke again.

'Look, I know he said he was going to the bathroom, but he headed out to that side of camp.' He gestured over his shoulder towards the woods. 'Now, I know there's only one thing out in that direction, and it's not a bathroom.'

I frowned, completely and utterly confused. 'What's out there?'

Docc studied me closely and remained quiet for a few long moments. 'I trust you'll find out.'

I blinked and frowned. Docc just gave me a soft smile and a short nod before leaving to head back to the group. My eyes drifted from where he'd been standing to where he'd pointed, noting the thin trail that led through the trees. A glance over my shoulder showed Docc rejoining the group and taking no notice of me. Had he meant for me to go that way, too?

With no idea what to expect, I started off towards the trail. I felt oddly vulnerable in my dress with no weapon, but I trusted Docc enough to know he wouldn't send me into a dangerous situation unprepared. The light from the bonfire started to fade as I got closer, and by the time I stepped beyond the treeline, it was all but gone. It was eerily quiet now, as if the trees buffered the noise of the party. All I could hear was the quiet buzzing of nature around me, only the faintest hints of music managing to break through the thick foliage.

My steps were nearly silent as I followed the path. Any worry I might have had about steering off-path was irrelevant, because it didn't branch off at all. The longer I walked, the darker and quieter it grew. It was odd to think that just a few hundred yards away, an entire camp was celebrating, but it was impossible to tell from where I was.

After what felt like ages of walking, I finally saw a soft glow from ahead. My heart gave a heavy thump as I approached quietly, unsure of what to expect. Silent steps carried me closer, the glow of the candle getting brighter to illuminate more of what was in front of me. It wasn't until I passed by a thick tree trunk that I saw it was a small clearing, and it wasn't until I took another few steps that I saw him.

Hayden was sitting on the ground, legs folded beneath him as he sat near the candle he must have brought. His back was to me, and while I couldn't see what he was looking at, it didn't take long for me to figure out. As I glanced around the small clearing, I noticed countless rocks placed strategically into the ground, each with words carved into them. I sucked in a quiet gasp as I realised where we were. Such a place could only be one thing.

A graveyard.

Hayden heard my breath and turned around, looking unsurprised when he saw me. I gave him a soft, guilty smile that only felt sad on my face as he observed me, ticking his head lightly to draw me forward. My steps were cautious, careful to avoid stepping on a grave, before I finally arrived next to him. I lowered myself to the ground, sitting beside him as my eyes fell on the headstone. I was not surprised to see whose it was. All the stone said was his name, but it was enough.

Jett.

'You found me,' he said quietly, glancing sideways at me.

'I had some help,' I admitted, keeping my voice soft.

'Hmm,' he nodded. 'Sorry, I didn't mean to disappear or anything. I just went to go for a walk and ended up here . . .'

'You don't need to apologise,' I told him. He swallowed and gave a small nod, reaching for my hand to link it with his own. He pulled our hands into his lap, where he proceeded to fiddle with my fingers gently.

'Okay,' he said simply. His eyes flashed to mine for a moment before returning to study Jett's grave.

It was the first time I'd been to this place. I knew others had come to pay their respects, but the days following his death had been so chaotic that I'd never had the chance. I suddenly felt guilty for not making time to come.

'This was you, right?' I asked gently. 'You buried him and made the headstone?'

'Yes,' Hayden admitted, his voice low and rough. 'It looks horrible.'

'No, Hayden,' I consoled immediately, shaking my head. 'It looks perfect. It's so fitting for Jett, you know?'

Hayden cleared his throat once and nodded, reluctant to speak.

'How are you feeling?' I asked cautiously. It was so difficult to read his mood.

'I'm not sure,' he replied. 'Sad, I guess. But less sad than I thought I would have the first time coming back. It's almost . . . peaceful.'

I squeezed his hand and leaned forward to press a kiss into his shoulder. 'That's good, Hayden. That's really good.'

Hayden nodded again and let out a deep sigh before turning to look at me. 'Thank you for finding me.'

'Of course. I'm glad you wanted to be found,' I said with a soft smile, resting my chin on his shoulder. He leaned into me and pressed a kiss to my forehead.

I let out a sigh as he turned back to Jett's grave, tilting my head to rest it on his shoulder. I felt my heart give a painful thump when Hayden spoke in a soft, hushed voice.

'We miss you, little man.'

Again, I squeezed Hayden's hand, this time for my own comfort as the pain of losing Jett hit again like a ton of bricks. It was my turn to speak, and my voice was thick with emotion as I did.

'And we love you.'

Hayden drew a deep breath and reached forward to trail his fingertips lightly across the name carved into the rock. We sat in silence for a little while, drawing comfort from each other and thinking of all the memories of Jett. Finally, after a while, Hayden squeezed my hand one last time before standing up, pulling me with him. He hugged me to his chest, his arms wrapped around my shoulders. I melted into him as I let my head rest on his chest.

He held me for a long time, not speaking or moving. It seemed as if, finally, Hayden was getting some closure on Jett's death.

After a while, he pulled back and slid his hand into mine. Hayden bent to pick up the candle, illuminating our faces as he spoke.

'Ready?'

'Ready,' I repeated, giving him a soft smile.

Even though not much had been said, I could practically feel the shift in things. He seemed lighter again, as he had at the start of the evening. I was relieved that the heavy burden seemed to have lifted after his visit to Jett's grave.

When we reached camp, we found that most of the people had gone home. Dax and Leutie were nowhere to be found, nor were Docc, Maisie, and Perdita. Malin and Kit were across the way, holding hands and speaking to the small crowd that remained. Hayden and I hesitated.

'Do you want to say anything to them?' I asked. He shook his head.

'No, that's okay. I'll congratulate him tomorrow when he's not so busy,' Hayden said with a shrug. 'Let's just go home.'

I smiled, loving the way 'home' sounded as it fell off his lips. My words were quiet and content.

'Home sounds perfect.'

Seventeen: Anticipation

Grace

It seemed that nearly everyone who had been at the wedding had turned in for the night, leaving only those on duty to roam through camp. We passed someone on guard on the way, a man of maybe fifty, who looked quite disgruntled at having missed the celebration. He gave a respectful nod to Hayden anyway.

My hand was still claimed in Hayden's as we walked. He was in a strange mood: not quite sad, not quite happy. Not quite anything, it seemed, as we remained in comfortable silence as he pushed the door to our hut, holding it open for me, before following inside. He kissed me briefly before moving deftly through the dark to light a single candle on the desk.

I moved to sit on the couch, attempting to remove the flimsy shoes that Malin had forced me to wear. There were far too many straps and they would be useless if I ever had to actually do anything physical. I made a mental note to return them to her as soon as I could, certain they'd go to waste in my possession.

Hayden leaned against the desk, arms crossed loosely over his chest while he wore an amused grin that lit up his eyes. Seeing me struggle clearly entertained him.

'Something funny?' I questioned, arching a brow at him.

'Oh, no. Carry on,' he replied lightly.

'Mmhmm, shut it, you.'

After a few more seconds of struggling, I successfully removed the first shoe. I put it down triumphantly before moving to the second. My fingers fidgeted with the buckle, but it was placed awkwardly and I couldn't seem to get ahold of it.

'You're doing so great,' Hayden commented sarcastically. I didn't need to look at him to know he was grinning his head off.

'I almost – ah,' I grimaced, twisting my arm as I felt around blindly. 'Almost—'

'Here,' Hayden interrupted, clearly unable to watch me struggle any longer. 'Let me.'

'No, you stay over there,' I commanded, unable to hold back a laugh as I glanced up at him.

Just as I predicted, his face was lit up in a beaming grin as he moved towards me, crouching down as he let his hands slide smoothly down the sides of my leg. A chill ran over my skin, raising goosebumps.

His fingers taunted me more than necessary before he finally released the clasp much quicker than I ever could have managed and removed the shoe. I could feel his breath on my leg just before his lips pushed into the skin above my knee, gravitating towards the inside of my thigh.

Without a word, he held out a hand to me, pulling me to stand in front of him.

'Turn around,' he said softly, voice gentle and deep.

I obeyed, turning on the spot as my breath hitched yet again.

'I'm guessing that if you couldn't overcome the shoes, the dress will be a struggle as well,' he lulled.

I let out a soft laugh, though it was quickly cut off when

I felt his hands on my hips. He moved slowly, as if trying to feel every curve of my body. I felt the heat of his breath at my neck as he gathered my hair and brushed it out of the way. He pressed another warm kiss between my neck and my shoulder.

I could feel his fingers tickling along my shoulder blades before they finally reached the zipper. He tugged gently, undoing it inch by inch to expose my skin. He kissed his way down my back, each touch melting me into submission.

He placed one final kiss at the base of my spine before he stood, trailing his fingers along my exposed skin. It wasn't long before his fingers dug loosely under the straps covering my shoulders, easing them down until the dress fell, pooling on the floor around me.

'Better,' he commented deeply, voice low and heavy.

My lips curled into an 'O' as I blew out a breath, before I ducked to grab the dress, reluctant to let such a special garment crumple on the floor. I could feel Hayden's eyes on me as I straightened it out on the couch so it wouldn't get dirty.

A wave of butterflies rushed through me when I turned around, watching his face as his eyes travelled slowly up my body, clad in only my underwear. He did not rush or avert his gaze, taking in details that I wanted only him to see. When he finally met my gaze, I was surprised to see it was similar to the one he'd worn at the wedding rather than pure lust.

Again, for what felt like the hundredth time that night, I felt beautiful.

Once I reached him, my hands moved to his hips, where my fingers toyed with the hem of his shirt. My eyes flicked up to meet his, which were watching me with such a burning intensity that I could feel it down to my toes. Slowly, I tugged the fabric upward, revealing the skin of his flat, firm stomach. Inch by inch, more of him was freed until he had to lift his arms to pull it over his head.

He was much less careful with his shirt as he cast it aside. I indulged in letting my hands run down his chest, feeling the few hairs that speckled his skin, then the smooth ridges of his abs. The coarse hairs that trailed down from his navel were the last thing my fingertips passed over before reaching the buckle of his jeans. Now it was Hayden's turn to suck in a breath as I started to undo them, much more successfully than when I'd tried to undo my shoes.

He stepped out of them and lifted his hands to cradle either side of my face, giving me a small smile and burning gaze as he hovered a few inches away.

'I love you so much, Grace,' he murmured.

'I love you, Hayden.'

He ducked forward again, reconnecting our lips and deepening the kiss by sliding his tongue slowly along my own.

'Let me show you how much I love you.'

'Okay.'

Slowly, he took a step forward, guiding me backward while keeping his hand on my hip and his lips on mine. He manoeuvred me carefully, pushing me backward until I felt my legs connect with the end of the bed.

His hands moved reverently over my body, brushing my skin here and there before he slipped his hand behind my back, undoing the clasp of my bra. Again, his lips followed wherever he removed the fabric as he pulled gently on it to rid me of the garment.

'You're so beautiful, Grace,' Hayden murmured, voice muffled by my skin as he hovered over me.

All of his slow, sensual actions and his unhurried manner were practically driving me crazy.

I reached for him, unable to withstand any more of this

beautiful torture. His hips, clad in just his boxers, landed between my legs before he rolled his body slowly, digging into me to draw a low moan.

His fingers dug under the fabric covering my hip before tugging down, shifting my weight in the process to pull my underwear down before his body got in the way. Reluctantly, he lifted his hips before managing to remove them completely.

I gasped into the kiss when I felt his fingers drag up the inside of my thigh, his actions tantalisingly slow before he finally reached where I ached for him. His movements were almost delicate as he dragged his fingers up my centre, his touch feather-light and gentle as he circled the pads of his fingers around my sensitive bundle of nerves.

My breathing was quickly becoming ragged under his careful, deliberate touch, and I was practically buzzing with need to feel all of him. As best as I could with slightly shaky hands, I ran them down his sides, feeling the scars and divots in his skin caused by years of fighting. Each one was different, just as each told a different story in the life of this man I loved so much.

Finally, I reached the hem of his boxers, linking my fingers beneath the band to push them down. My actions were slightly uncoordinated thanks to the way his hand moved between my legs, but I finally managed to push them down enough for him to kick them on to the floor, leaving us both naked for each other.

Hayden's fingers circled over me, pushing me closer and closer to the edge that I so desperately craved. When my hips began shifting uncontrollably and my back arched off the bed, Hayden pulled his lips from mine. With a final circle of his fingers, I felt my orgasm rip through me, making my body practically vibrate. I felt a light, wet kiss against my throat as Hayden dropped his lips. Then I felt his body shift as he pulled his hand from between my legs and let his hips move in.

'You good?' he breathed into my ear, teeth tugging lightly on the lobe.

'Yes,' I gasped, still unable to open my eyes as the blissfully amazing feeling rolled through me.

'Okay,' he replied softly.

I was still enjoying the end of my first orgasm when I felt him push into me, stretching me beautifully for the first time today. My jaw dropped open and my head fell back on the pillow, hands grasping blindly at whatever I could reach of him. His lips tended to my neck again as I tried to calm my shaky limbs, somehow managing to wrap my legs around his hips as they rolled into me again. Scars and jagged edges in Hayden's skin passed beneath my fingertips as they raked up his sides and over his shoulders before tangling into his hair to haul his lips back to mine, desperate to kiss him again.

His actions were slow, unrushed, and deliberately designed to show me just how much he loved me. Each roll of his hips was devastatingly patient, each kiss was sensual. His hands caressed my body gently wherever he touched me: my ribs, my hips, my thighs. Every move he made radiated the heat that always burned between us, backed up by such emotion like I'd never felt before.

'God, Grace,' Hayden groaned, his voice raspy and low as he pushed into me again. His hand lifted my hips, pulling me against him as he drove himself deeper.

I could feel sweat pricking at his skin, and I could taste it on his neck when I lifted my head to press a few kisses there. The pressure was starting to build, with each and every action. Quiet moans and strained whimpers pulled from my throat as he moved, and my body started to grow restless beneath him as the tingling crept up from my toes.

With every roll of his hips, I felt his muscles expand and contract in time with the rhythm he'd set. I thought I couldn't hold out for a second longer.

'Ha-Hayden,' I gasped, back arching off the mattress as the pressure grew stronger and stronger.

He was everywhere, overwhelming me in every way possible. His hand gripped mine, holding on tightly as he moved. His other hand cradled my face, holding his body up on his elbow. Our bare chests were pressed together, separating only for a moment when his hips rocked back before he pushed deeply into me again. Over and over, his hips rolled against mine in a steady rhythm that somehow maintained his slow yet devastating pace. I grasped at his side, digging my nails into his hot skin as he pushed into me once more, deep enough to push me over the edge for the second time.

Just as before, my orgasm ripped through me, sending a sizzling wave of heat through my entire body. My back lifted off the mattress as my body convulsed forward, all control lost.

'Oh, god,' I gasped, still feeling the orgasm buzz through my veins.

Hayden's lips puckered at the base of my throat, where I could feel my pulse pounding. His smooth and languid actions continued as he pushed me through my high, my thighs tightening around his hips as he did so. A few more rolls of his body forward into me brought him to his end. His jaw fell open, and my teeth tugged lightly on his lower lip as he let out a strangled moan that sent a jolt through me.

I released his lip and relaxed back into the mattress, panting and covered in my own sweat as I watched the beauty unfold above me.

'I love you,' he breathed, chest rising and falling heavily as he tried to catch his breath.

'And I love you,' I returned, still breathless and worn out from how we'd come together.

He lowered himself one last time, hovering an inch away from my lips as if breathing in that beautiful moment while we both revelled in the aftermath of our climaxes.

Hayden loved me as I loved him, and that was all I needed.

A sharp knock on the front door jolted me from sleep, my body jerking instinctively. I didn't go far, however, as my head lay on Hayden's shoulder. I could feel his arm tense around me as he drew me close.

After a quick shower, we'd both fallen asleep last night within minutes. Our bodies were spent from a long day and how we'd come together, making sleep blissfully peaceful once we'd cuddled beneath the blanket.

Now, however, a second round of knocking sounded at the door, breaking up our serenely wonderful sleep. Hayden groaned and pulled me tighter against him, burying his face into my hair as he snuggled against me.

'Morning,' he rumbled, voice impossibly low in the early hour. I could feel his chest vibrate as he spoke.

'Morning,' I returned. I squeezed my eyes shut as yet another knock sounded, desperately wishing they'd go away even though I knew they wouldn't. This time, a voice accompanied the knocking.

'Guys, come on. I'm hungover, don't make me wait out here all day.'

It was Dax's voice, and despite my reluctance to get up, I smiled.

'What, Dax?' Hayden called as loudly as his raspy voice would allow. He, too, seemed very disinclined to move. I let out a small laugh and snuggled closer into his side.

'We've got a problem,' he called. 'You're seriously going to make me yell through the door? Lazy ass . . .'

His voice trailed off as he mumbled disgruntledly. Hayden let out a deep sigh, rolled his eyes, then pressed a light kiss to the top of my head. I drew the blankets up around me, robbed of his warmth. I watched the muscles flex in his back as he moved to the door.

Hayden, who was wearing nothing more than a pair of shorts, cast one look at me over his shoulder, grinned indulgently, and opened the door before slipping outside rather than letting Dax in. I almost wished he had so I could hear, too. Straining my ears, I sat perfectly still to try to catch their words.

'. . . here and want to talk . . .'

I frowned, turning my head towards the door as if that would help me hear better. Dax's voice was muffled and hard to decipher.

'. . . I don't know . . . to talk to you . . .'

I let out a huff of frustration and gave up, whipping the blankets down before rushing to dress quickly. I strained to catch fragments of their conversation as I tugged on my clothes but gathered no more than a few bits and pieces that made no sense. Finally, I rushed to the door and snatched it open, causing both Hayden and Dax to stop mid-sentence and look at me.

'Hey,' I said somewhat flatly. They both blinked before they seemed to recover from my sudden appearance. When they didn't speak, I continued. 'Carry on.'

'Erm, right, sorry,' Dax said, shaking his head. 'That hooch has me feeling a bit slow, you know?'

'I'm not surprised,' I said with a smirk.

'Grace,' Hayden said. I noticed his hair was very messed

up from the night before; I hoped Dax hadn't noticed.

'What's going on?' I asked, catching his serious expression.

'Renley's here. We need to go and talk to him.'

I was certain his unexpected visit could not be a good thing. I swallowed and nodded, clearing my head to prepare to focus.

'Okay,' I replied. 'Dax, do you know why?'

He looked like he was still half asleep. Dark circles hung under his eyes, his dark hair was plastered flat on one side and wildly dishevelled on the other. I was also pretty sure his shirt was on backwards judging by the tag sticking out near the front of his neck.

'He wouldn't say. He asked for Hayden.'

Hayden slipped past me, gliding back inside through the open door to pull on a shirt and some shoes. While he moved, he questioned Dax.

'How'd you know he's here?'

'I was supposed to do rounds this morning but wasn't quite feeling on my A-game so I went to find someone to take over when Renley showed up.'

'Is he alone?' Hayden asked.

'No, that Prett guy is with him.'

Hayden let out a derisive scoff as he hunched over to tie his shoe, shaking his head as he did so. Hayden had absolutely no reason to worry or feel jealous, but I knew he would no matter what I said, so I refrained from acknowledging anything.

'Great,' Hayden muttered unhappily. 'Well, let's go, then. Where are they?'

'Raid building with Docc.'

'No Kit?' I questioned.

'Yeah. Figured we'd give the newly-wed the morning off,' Dax said with a lopsided grin.

'He deserves it,' I agreed, returning his grin despite the trepidation I now felt.

'Come on,' Hayden said, crossing the room to rejoin Dax and I at the door.

After slipping my feet into my boots, the three of us took off down the path towards the raid building. Dax grumbled about how much his head hurt and received absolutely zero sympathy from Hayden, who chided him for doing the harm to himself. Their words were casual, but it was impossible to miss the ominous air that hung around us. I knew they had to be just as worried as I was about what we were walking in to.

After letting Dax inside the building, Hayden paused outside the door, gripping my wrist gently to hold me back. He opened his mouth to speak before I cut him off.

'Try to remember that I love you and only you, yeah? Whatever this is about, please don't get distracted because of Prett or something else that doesn't matter.'

Hayden's green eyes studied mine. He opened and closed his mouth as if to speak before pausing. He let out a deep sigh and nodded in acceptance.

'Just for you, Bear.'

I beamed at him, pleased with his response.

'Thank you, Herc. Now, what were you going to say?' I asked lightly.

'I was just going to tell you that you look really pretty today,' he said with a quick wink.

My jaw fell open in amused surprised, unsure if I believed him or not but unwilling to press him.

I followed him closely and soon saw the gathering around our table. Docc, Dax, Renley, and Prett all stood waiting for us, allowing Hayden and I to stand side by side to complete the circle. A thick tension settled over the room, as if everyone was somewhat unsure of how to proceed. Hayden cleared his throat and spoke first.

'Renley, Prett,' he said stiffly in greeting. 'What's going on?'

Renley looked at me with a serious, sombre expression before he returned his gaze to Hayden.

'I'm afraid it's bad news, so I won't waste time. We were attacked by Brutes again last night. We lost several buildings and more than a few people.'

'Shit,' Dax muttered, voicing my exact reaction.

I felt an odd sense of déjà vu, except now instead of Blackwing being attacked by Greystone, it was Whetland being attacked by Brutes. What made this odd, however, was the fact that up until very recently, the Brutes had never bothered to leave the confines of the city.

'Do you know why?' Hayden asked, his tone gravely serious. Prett stood silently beside Renley, looking equally solemn.

'No. It's impossible to say what they're trying to accomplish. We can't afford to lose any more people or supplies. If it keeps happening, eventually we won't be able to recover. Since both of our camps are pretty dependent upon our food, I think you know what that means.'

Reality was starting to sink in as I absorbed his words. The fact that it wasn't our camp being attacked had made it easy to ignore, easy to put off until another day, but there would be no more of that. Renley was right in saying that we were largely dependent on them for food. Without food, neither camp could survive.

Hayden let out a deep sigh beside me, as if he, too, had just gone through this thought process in his head.

'I know what it means,' he repeated grimly.

Judging by the serious looks on Docc, Dax, Renley,

Prett, and Hayden's faces, everyone had reached the same conclusion.

'We need to take them out,' Renley said, his voice flat and unhappy. 'And we need you to help.'

My stomach twisted tightly and I frowned.

'That was our deal. You take our food, you help us when we need it. We're cashing in that deal,' Renley continued when no one spoke.

'Is there nothing else we can do?' Hayden pressed, stalling. His hand shoved through his haphazard hair, making it even more unruly.

'No,' Prett said, speaking for the first time. Hayden's jaw clenched and he stiffened beside me. 'You made the deal. We held up our end, now you hold up yours.'

'I never said we wouldn't,' Hayden snapped, glaring at Prett. 'I'm just trying to figure this out the best way possible.'

'What are the options?' Docc queried, surveying us each in turn.

'Option one: do nothing. This results in Whetland continually being attacked by the Brutes, most likely losing our food source and causing a lot of innocent deaths. From *both* of our camps,' Renley said slowly. He sounded as if he were trying very hard to remain level-headed.

'Not the greatest option, that,' Dax said sarcastically. 'What's the second option?'

'We start *another* war, which will *also* result in a lot of innocent deaths,' Hayden replied, voice low and heavy as he, too, tried to stay calm.

'Also not a great option,' Dax muttered. He frowned. 'What to do, what to do. Innocent death by starvation or innocent death by Brute.'

'Or a combination,' Prett added, matching Dax's sarcastically flat tone.

My mind seemed to be buzzing with all the sudden developments. None of this should have been surprising, but it had always seemed like a problem for another day. Something we could put off for another month or two before finally dealing with it. But our blissful ignorance had come to an end, something that was abundantly clear.

Everything that had happened in the last twenty-four hours had been so amazing and surreal that I'd almost forgotten most of our days weren't like that. Our days weren't allowed to be that happy, that carefree. We didn't have time to celebrate often, didn't have the luxury of letting loose and relaxing. Our time to enjoy dancing, friendship, freedom, *life,* was so small that it felt almost unnatural to indulge in such things. I thought about everything.

Kit and Malin's wedding.

Dancing with Hayden without a care in the world.

Visiting Jett's grave for the first time.

Perdita's hooch and her strange, senile way of communicating.

Wearing things like dresses and make-up for no practical reason at all.

Wait.

My mind practically screeched to a halt as my jaw dropped open, inspiration striking like a lightning bolt. All the sound I had tuned out came rushing back in and thc room returned to focus.

'Guys,' I said sharply, trying to draw their attention.

Everyone ignored me as they continued to bicker, angry glares and frustrated body language ample in the room.

'Guys!'

I was louder this time, but again, everyone ignored me. I gave an irritated huff before I slammed my hand down on the table, making a loud *slapping* sound that jerked everyone's attention towards me. I nodded in satisfaction, relieved they'd finally listened.

'There is one more option,' I said slowly, glancing around at every single one of them before landing on Hayden. I had a strong suspicion he would not be too fond of my idea.

'What's that, Grace?' Docc questioned calmly.

I took a deep breath, grimacing and wondering if it made me a terrible person for even suggesting it.

'There's one thing we haven't considered that will solve this problem in one shot, but it's going to be very . . . destructive.'

'Enough with the suspense, get on with it,' Dax urged, physically leaning forward in anticipation.

Hayden frowned, and I could already imagine the disappointment that would appear in his eyes after I spoke. As I drew one final breath, I had to look away, unable to watch his reaction. I hoped Hayden wouldn't think any less of me.

'There's one way to end this quickly . . .' I started. 'We have to go to the Armoury while all the Brutes are in there . . . And we have to bomb it.'

It was the only way I could think of.

We had to bomb it all.

Bomb it to hell.

As Perdita had said, *boom*.

Eighteen: Adjudicate

Grace

'. . . And we have to bomb it.'

As soon as I spoke, it was as if a bomb had actually been dropped. Everyone stopped talking, stunned by my bold declaration. The seconds seemed to stretch on for an eternity, allowing my nerves to gnaw away at my stomach as I waited for a reaction. Then, just as quickly as everyone had fallen silent, they started talking. It was impossible to distinguish any one voice, though the one voice I truly needed to hear was the one not speaking.

My stomach started to twist inward on itself the longer Hayden went without speaking. The background noise of everyone else's voices was drowned out as I focused on him, but a sudden *slamming* of a hand on the table managed to jerk my attention away from him. After snapping my head towards the sound, I saw, much to my surprise, that it was Docc who had caused it.

'We're never going to accomplish anything if we're all talking over each other,' Docc said calmly, giving each of us a stern look. 'We must speak one at a time like civilised humans.'

A sheepish silence fell over us after the light scolding.

'Right you are, Docc,' Dax finally said after clearing his throat. 'Grace, since it was your idea, care to explain?'

I felt the sudden heat of everyone's gazes as they turned to me. My eyes flashed to Hayden to see him watching me, but I diverted my gaze to focus on explaining my thoughts.

'Well . . . I know it sounds really extreme but . . . it's the only way I can think of taking care of the problem without bringing harm to both of our camps,' I said slowly.

Again, everyone was silent as they thought this over.

'It is a bit extreme,' Renley agreed, nodding. 'But it may be necessary. We've already lost more people than we should have and I have no reason to believe they'll just stop attacking.'

'And it's a good bet that once they finish off you lot, they'll be coming for us,' Dax said. Renley shot him a glare, causing Dax to shrug before continuing, 'No offence.'

'You're talking about killing *hundreds* of people,' Hayden said, speaking for the first time. My heart sank when it finally became clear that Hayden was not on my side of this. 'Hundreds.'

I opened my mouth to reply but fell short, unable to justify it when he put it like that. To kill hundreds of people in one fell swoop was something truly malevolent.

'If we do that, we're no better than the Brutes,' Hayden continued, driving a cold stake into my heart. I suddenly felt ashamed for suggesting it.

'But think about it,' Prett said. 'If we do nothing, they're just going to keep going. Attacking, killing, other things . . .'

The way he trailed off made it clear that those from Whetland also knew about the Brutes' desire for women, and the evil things they did to them. It was a good point in my favour, but I wished that Prett hadn't been the one to make it as Hayden would surely be reluctant to listen to anything he said.

'Look, we all know the Brutes are a bunch of smarmy bastards,' Dax said quickly. 'So while, yes, we'd be killing hundreds of people, do they really count? Don't they kind of deserve to die for the things they've done?'

It was another good point, and while the backup from the others helped a little, what I really wanted was for Hayden to agree. Not appease me or give in to me, but to really agree.

No one seemed to want to answer, as if reluctant to be the voice of condemnation. After a while, Renley spoke again.

'Look, I can't speak for you all, because the truth is, I don't know your history with the Brutes. But I can say from my experience, the world will be a better place without them.'

'Agreed,' Prett said, nodding. While I was still having trouble deciding if I fully trusted Renley and Prett or not, they seemed like decent people. Their actions seemed motivated by their desire to protect their own camp, for which I respected them. My mind flashed to Jonah who, instead of protecting his camp at all costs like Hayden and Renley did, had almost single-handedly destroyed it.

Not all leaders were fit to lead, just as not all humans were inherently good.

Humans like the Brutes, who enjoyed attacking, killing, and worse. Humans who were a danger to others, and thus a danger to the future. With people like the Brutes around, there was no guarantee the world would even have another generation of humans to inhabit it.

I let out a deep breath and nodded to myself, cementing my belief that they needed to be dealt with, even if Hayden didn't like it.

'There is another issue to consider,' Docc said, redirecting everyone's attention. 'The Armoury is perhaps the most well-stocked area left. By destroying the Brutes, you'd be destroying the supplies as well.'

'That's true,' Hayden said seriously. 'Food, medicine, weapons . . .'

Everyone frowned, considering this.

'But do we really want them in control of all that? Maybe it would be best just to blow it all up and get it out of anyone's control,' Dax mused.

'But if we blow it up, there's no chance we'll get it,' Hayden argued. 'We've already taken stuff from there a few times. Who's to say we can't do it again?'

'I don't know, but I have a feeling those times were limited. Odds are, they'll be ready for another attempt to raid them again,' reasoned Renley.

'Plus, if the Brutes are gone, Greystone is pretty much gone, and we have this truce thing going on, do we really need more weapons than what we already have?' Dax questioned.

My head was spinning. They all made good points. While it seemed foolish to destroy such an impressive stockpile, it could be better than leaving them in the Brutes' possession. I opened my mouth to say just that.

'I think Renley is right. I don't think we'd be able to get in there and get out with supplies again. They're going to be ready for it now. Wouldn't it be better to destroy the supplies completely and take away our chance of getting them than to let the Brutes keep them to potentially use them against us?'

'That seems to be the most logical thought, yes,' Docc agreed solemnly.

'Destroy the Brutes, sacrifice the supplies,' Dax murmured, thinking aloud. 'We may have to do it.'

'We have food now that you've figured out how to grow it,' I said to Prett and Renley. 'And the weapons . . . I mean, I guess we'll never know if something else could come up in the future where we'd need them, but if the Brutes are gone, we wouldn't need weapons anytime soon. The medicine is the only thing we'd really be sacrificing . . .'

I trailed off, thinking. Even though it had been my idea, I didn't like the thought of destroying the medicine so readily. The food and weapons we could do without, but destroying the medicine could be insane.

'You all seem to be forgetting that we'd be killing hundreds of people.'

Hayden's harsh voice snapped everyone's attention to him. His jaw was set sharply and his eyes were narrowed intensely beneath his furrowed brow.

'Hayden, think about it,' I pleaded gently. 'We could finally have . . . peace. This could be the end of fighting for a long, long time.'

It seemed odd to think about, and it hadn't really even occurred to me until I'd spoken, but it was true. With the Brutes gone, Greystone reduced to those with no interest in fighting, and this truce with Whetland, this truly could be our chance to start over with a new way of life.

For the first time ever, things could potentially be what was once considered normal.

'Hayden,' Dax said slowly, his voice low and oddly serious. 'They came after Grace.'

A pained look crossed Hayden's face, and his eyes darted to me. The fear from that moment returned, chilling me down to the bone.

'Okay,' he sighed, voice strained. 'We need to do it. We need to bomb the Brutes.'

Rather than relief or excitement, his statement was met

with a heavy silence. People nodded in agreement, their moods solemn and serious. I was glad that even though everyone had finally agreed, no one had celebrated or cheered. I felt a sense of pride for how everyone reacted.

'It's decided, then,' Docc stated softly.

I couldn't seem to tear my eyes away from Hayden, and it was impossible to miss the heavy sadness in his eyes, but the look of determination and strength was there as well. I knew why he'd agreed: to protect me. He was going to sacrifice so much of what he believed in to keep me safe. I felt the sudden urge to rush forward and hug him, to find some sort of other option, to take back everything I'd said, but I didn't.

'How are we going to do this?' Renley asked.

Hayden finally broke the blazing eye contact he'd maintained with me. He placed his hands flat on the table. I could practically see the stress radiating off his body and felt horribly guilty for putting it on him.

It took me a moment to realise that everyone was looking at me expectantly, as it had been my idea in the first place.

'Perdita,' I said, clearing my throat. 'She makes bombs. She could make us whatever we need and show us how to do it.'

Everyone nodded in thought.

'We'll come with you when it's time to place the bombs. How long will she need to get them ready?' Renley asked.

'I don't know,' I answered uncertainly, glancing at Hayden. He frowned.

'A day or two, I'd guess,' he replied.

'So . . . meet back here in two days? Then we do this?' I asked, glancing around the group. It felt odd to be the one making decisions when that job usually fell to Hayden.

'We can be ready whenever you are,' Renley said calmly. Prett nodded in agreement.

'Be here in two days. Early,' Hayden said firmly. 'We'll be ready.'

'Okay. We'll go and do what we can to prepare, then,' Renley said. Everyone began to shift as the meeting concluded. Renley and Prett moved towards the door, nodding silent goodbyes to those they passed. They had pulled open the door and were nearly out when Renley paused and glanced back at us.

'Thank you for upholding your end of the deal.'

Hayden ducked his head, pulling his lower lip into his mouth before releasing it. 'You're welcome.'

With that, Renley and Prett left. I noticed Prett's eyes flit to me for a fraction of a second before the door closed behind them. I hoped Hayden hadn't noticed.

Now that only Hayden, Dax, Docc, and I remained in the room, I suddenly felt even more nervous. Hayden had agreed, but he hadn't fully spoken his mind because of Renley and Prett's presence. I glanced at him, hoping I wouldn't find him glowering at me. A sigh of relief pushed past my lips when I was met with no such gaze, but what I saw was perhaps worse. He looked as he did before: stressed, tense, and sad.

'Hayden—'

'Don't, Grace,' he said quickly, cutting me off. 'I know it's what we need to do.'

A somewhat awkward tension fell over the room as Hayden and I watched each other, unsure of what to say.

'Well,' said Dax with a shrug. 'Guess I'll go and tell Kit the plan. I'm sure he'll want to join.'

'Okay,' I said when Hayden didn't reply. 'See you later.'

He gave us a somewhat lopsided grimace, raising his

brows as if unsure of what to say before he left. Docc started to shift towards the door as well.

'If you need anything, let me know,' he said. Again, Hayden didn't reply, so Docc continued. 'I know this goes against everything you've ever thought, Hayden, but I think it's the right thing to do. To let the Brutes carry on and to let them maintain control of those supplies would be a grave mistake. This is what's best. I firmly believe that.'

I felt a sudden rush of gratitude for Docc and his calming words. If he truly did believe that, it made me feel better about the situation as well. I only hoped it would have the same effect on Hayden's thoughts.

He nodded, eyes distracted and focused on the table. 'Thanks, Docc.'

He left, leaving Hayden and I completely alone. When I saw his chest expand slowly with a deep breath and the way he tilted his neck to the side with stress, I couldn't resist moving forward. My hand landed on his lower back, feeling the tight muscles there and the heat of his body through the thin material of his shirt. He didn't react to my touch, merely stayed leaning over the table, hands splayed wide as he propped himself up.

'Hayden,' I said softly, weighed down by his stress as if it were my own. Slowly, I ran my fingertips along his back, attempting to soothe away some of the tightness in his muscles. He moved suddenly, surprising me as he straightened up. His arms roped around me quickly, hauling me against his chest in a tight hug. I felt the heat of his breath on my neck as he ducked down to tuck his face in the space between my shoulder and throat. My arms wound around his waist to hold him, confused and comforted at the same time by his sudden movement.

'I told you I'm going to keep you safe, Bear,' he murmured. 'This will keep you safe.'

Guilt raged inside of me. I had a strong suspicion that he never would have agreed if it hadn't been for Dax's final point: that the Brutes had come for me.

'I don't want you to go back on everything you believe in,' I murmured, words stifled by his shoulder as I hugged him. 'Especially not for me.'

He didn't reply right away, and I felt the hot breath he exhaled on my neck as he let out a deep sigh.

'I'm not,' he finally replied. He pulled back, but we didn't lose contact. 'I believe in keeping my camp safe. I believe in keeping *you* safe. If this is the only way . . . if we have to kill people to do it . . . it's what we need to do.'

I searched his eyes for signs of deception but only found honesty. 'Are you sure?'

'Yes,' he said earnestly, nodding. He leaned forward and pressed a light kiss to my forehead. 'It was your idea, why are you questioning it now?'

'I don't want to . . . to ruin you or something.'

My mind flashed to what Kit had told me about his birthday. He'd already done so many things he didn't want to do, so many things that had ripped him apart bit by bit. I didn't want to add another dark mark to his history, and I certainly didn't want to push him to the point where he could lose the beautiful humanity he still maintained.

'I'll be fine,' Hayden murmured. 'It'll be hard, but losing you would be harder. Losing more innocent people would be harder. Please don't think that way, okay?'

Hayden's eyes peered intently into mine, silenty begging for me to agree. I let out a heavy sigh and nodded.

'Okay.'

He gave me a soft smile, though it didn't completely

placate the tumultuous feelings wrestling in my stomach.

'Well, Mastermind, want to go and see Perdita about some bombs?' he said with a crooked grin, taking a step back. It felt good when a small laugh escaped my lips.

'Yeah, that sounds good.'

He flashed me a smile before leading me out of the raid building. We walked along the path in a contented silence, staying in the centre of Blackwing, where all the major buildings were located. It occurred to me that I had no idea where Perdita spent her time. She was quite the enigma and always seemed to turn up out of nowhere.

'Where does she live?' I asked Hayden curiously.

'Round the corner, there,' he said, gesturing ahead. 'She lives in her shop. Wait until you see it.'

I thought I caught a hint of amusement. He didn't elaborate further and continued to lead me down the path. As soon as we turned the corner, I noticed we were heading to a small cluster of huts I had never really taken notice of before. However, as soon as my eyes fell on the building that could only belong to someone like Perdita, I began to question how I'd ever possibly missed it.

Unlike most of the huts in Blackwing, which were constructed of wood and resembled small cabins, this building was made completely of varying types of metal. Seemingly useless pieces of metal stuck out in odd places, with wires draped off and poking out in all directions. One large window, stretching from the ground to the ceiling, gave a glimpse of the mess of materials inside. It was a little larger than the homes surrounding it, but the way the sun glinted off the metal and the space taken up by the protruding pieces made it seem massive in comparison.

'Wow,' was all I could think of saying. Hayden let out a

low chuckle as he reached up to knock on the door, which was made out of metal bars that had been welded together to form a rectangular shape. Instead of the usual hollow sound that came from knocking on our door, the sharp *ting* of his knuckles against the metal sounded out.

'Come in, come in,' called a voice. I recognised Perdita's wispy tones.

'Does she live alone?' I asked quietly as Hayden pushed open the door.

'Yeah,' he answered before directing his attention inside. 'Hello, Perdita.'

I couldn't seem to form a greeting of any kind as my eyes fell over the space. Everywhere I looked, scraps of metal, wires, explosives, and other things I couldn't even identify littered the space. Little pathways wove between the piles of materials, just wide enough to fit Perdita's tiny body. A bed occupied one corner of the room. In another, I saw a chair and a surprisingly organised cabinet full of buckets. Hayden nudged me to explain.

'Her tattoo stuff,' he murmured.

I imagined Hayden sitting in that chair, letting this woman, who I was growing more and more certain was insane, ink his skin forever.

'Hayden, hello,' Perdita greeted with a wide grin. She was missing several teeth, and I saw dark gaps in the smile that she aimed at me. 'Hello, dear.'

'Grace,' I offered, unsure if she remembered my name.

'Oh yes, I know,' she replied, nodding. 'Whispers.'

I cleared my throat somewhat awkwardly. 'Erm, right.'

'Perdita, we need your help,' Hayden said, cutting to the chase. Her eyes, framed by wrinkles all around, turned to Hayden once more.

'Oh?'

'Yeah. We need you to make us some bombs. Whatever you think would bring down a substantially sized underground fortress.'

'How delightful!' she exclaimed, clapping her frail hands together. She gave an odd sort of laugh that made me doubt her sanity even more. 'I'd love to. Might I ask why?'

It was the most I'd ever heard her talk, and while she seemed to be grasping the conversation, the slightly off look in her eye made me feel somewhat concerned.

'We're going to destroy the Brutes,' Hayden said, his voice firm and steady. 'For good.'

Perdita nodded wisely and accepted this with no further questions. 'I shall get to work straight away.'

'Brilliant, thank you,' Hayden said. 'We can check back in a bit to see how it's coming along. You'll have to show us how to set them up and such, if that's all right.'

Perdita nodded again, shooting him another spotty grin.

'I'd like the girl to stay,' she said. She completely ignored me, speaking as if I wasn't there. My lips parted in surprise before I recovered.

'Why?' Hayden asked, frowning.

'Whispers,' was all Perdita offered.

Hayden glanced at me, raising his brows in a silent question. I just shrugged, unsure of what she could possibly want with me. While I felt somewhat awkward and uneasy around her, I certainly wasn't afraid.

'Okay,' I finally said, drawing her attention.

'I can stay too if you—'

'No,' Perdita said sharply. 'Just the girl.'

Hayden frowned again but nodded before turning to me.

'I guess I'll see you later, then?' he said, as if asking a question.

'Yeah, I'll find you,' I promised with a smile. He tried to return it but mostly just looked confused. He squeezed my hand gently once and retreated.

'So, what do you—' I began once he'd gone.

'You remind me of my daughter,' Perdita said, cutting me off again.

'Um, I do?' I asked, trying to catch up with her abrupt conversation change. She nodded and hummed.

'Mmhmm. Her name was Isla.'

'I see,' I said stupidly, unsure of what else to say. It was relatively clear that Isla was no longer around and I couldn't think of any other way to reply.

'Come now,' she said, dropping the topic as quickly as it had started. 'Let's get to work.'

With that, she turned as quickly as her old body would allow, weaving cautiously through the piles of supplies and scraps. I followed, careful not to bump into anything or knock anything over in the process. She led me to the back of her home, where a small table sat with a large lantern atop it. Numerous tools were laid out on the surface, like wire cutters, scissors, tape, and countless other things I couldn't identify.

'Sit,' she instructed, pointing at one of two stools perched beneath the table. I obeyed and didn't speak.

As I watched, Perdita began to move around, picking up various items here and there before depositing them on the table. She did not speak as she collected her things, and I was silent for fear of distracting her. Before long, the table was piled high with what I could only assume were bomb-making materials. With a soft hum and contented smile, she somehow heaved her tiny body up onto the second stool and began to tinker.

'I remember when Isla was just a young thing,' she said,

glancing up at me with a strange stern look. 'She'd ride this bicycle around the neighbourhood. Clumsy thing, she was. Always falling off and scraping her knees. And when she was older, oh how the boys loved her. They'd always come to call, bringing chocolates or flowers or other little trinkets.'

I frowned, trying to imagine a world like that. It all seemed so foreign to me.

'And she loved the boys back. She'd laugh and smile and accept their trinkets. She was a happy thing all her life.'

Perdita's wizened fingers worked smoothly, manipulating the materials with an ease that surprised me. She had very steady hands by anyone's standards, much less for a person of her age. The bomb began to take shape before my very eyes, much quicker than I had anticipated.

'She sounds lovely,' I finally said when she didn't continue.

'I'll make you four bombs,' she said, switching conversation again. 'Three of the same and one much larger one.'

I felt like I was getting whiplash from her constant change of direction. 'That sounds good.'

Perdita nodded and started to hum, apparently no longer interested in sharing with me. I let my eyes drift around her home at all her equipment. Upon closer investigation, I noticed a few odd things I did not expect. On one of her many shelves was a small rose, twisted together from thin wires to form an intricately beautiful design. Hanging from a wall was a circle of flat metal with what looked like a picture of a tree etched into the surface, with fine detail for such a small piece. One nail in the wall held several slender chains, each link a slightly different size, indicating it was made by hand rather than found somewhere. Everywhere I looked, I noticed tiny objects made with exquisite detail and a steady hand.

'Perdita,' I began.

'Hmm?' she hummed, eyes staying focused on her work. She tinkered with a tool to position something inside the mess of metal.

'Did you make all those? The little pieces of art?'

I didn't know what else to call them, but art seemed the only proper title.

'Art?' she questioned. 'Whispers, shhh!'

I blinked in surprise as I watched her swat her hand around her ear as if waving off an invisible fly. I chose to ignore it and continued.

'Yeah, like those little chains? The rose?' I pointed to the items I'd seen, causing her to twist in her seat to look.

'Oh, my trinkets,' she said, nodding. 'Yes. I made them.'

An idea sparked in my mind and my heart gave a little thump.

'Do you think you could help me with something?' I asked gently. She did not look at me as she went back to her work.

'Of course, darling. What is it?'

I grinned, thrilled. I explained my idea as best I could, hoping it would make sense to her. She nodded calmly when I finished speaking.

'Oh, yes, I can do that.'

'Thank you so much,' I gushed, grinning again.

'Of course, Isla my love. Of course.'

My chest caved in and my heart gave a painful throb, taken aback by her words.

'Yes, Isla, my darling daughter . . .'

Perdita trailed off again, still focused on her work as she put the final touches on the first bomb.

'Thank you,' was all I said. I didn't have the heart to

correct her. I also didn't know if she'd actually absorbed any of what I'd just said, but I chose to let it be.

She was quiet again for some time. I watched as she spooled up what looked like a long fuse, the final piece to her bomb. I jumped about a foot in the air when she suddenly clapped her hands together.

'Okay, Grace, here's what you'll do,' she said, pointing at the bomb. I blinked in surprise as she suddenly seemed to remember who I was. 'You'll place this near whatever you want to collapse. It *must* be near the supports, not from the top, or it won't work. Unravel the fuse as long as you can, then light it and run. You should have enough time to light all four of them and get out of there.'

I nodded, focusing on remembering all this information. 'Okay, I've got it.'

She nodded. 'You may leave now. I'll finish these on my own. Whispers call, you know,' she continued with another strange, slightly empty smile.

'Okay,' I replied uncertainly, frowning slightly as I stood from the stool. 'Thank you again. For everything.'

Perdita nodded easily as she began to pick up more materials for her second bomb. 'Goodbye for now, my dear.'

'Bye,' I murmured. Carefully, I began to weave my way back through the strange collection. I was nearly to the door when Perdita's voice stopped me.

'Oh, Grace,' she called. I paused and turned back to face her. 'I'll have what you asked for by tomorrow.'

I grinned, surprised and pleased she'd remembered after all. 'Perfect. Thank you, Perdita.'

With a contented yet bemused grin, I left her peculiar contraption of a home. She was a strange woman in a strange situation, but if I really thought about it, we all were. It was still so hard to wrap my head around what we were about to do. We had to destroy the Brutes; it was the one massive obstacle that remained between us and a potentially normal life. Such a concept was so foreign to me, but that didn't stop me from daring to hope for it.

Nineteen: Expedient

Grace

In the two days since our initial meeting, Hayden and I had met with Dax and Kit several times to try to iron out the details. We had our plan, but not knowing exactly what we were walking into made it difficult to count on much. A tension hung around the camp, as word must have spread of our daunting mission.

Perdita had finished our bombs only a day later and had shown each of us in detail how to work them, though there really wasn't much to it: place it near a supporting structure, light it, and run. Once she'd dismissed the boys from our lesson, she pulled me aside and presented me with a small item. It had turned out just how I had hoped it would.

The memory brought a small smile to my face as Hayden loaded the last of the supplies up into the jeep. It was very early, so early the sun wasn't even up yet, and we were preparing to depart on our mission into the city. Renley and Prett were there, strapping down extra ammunition to the four-wheeler they would drive. I still felt an irrational bitterness towards the inanimate object from the time, so long ago, when Dax had fooled me into thinking Hayden was dead.

Kit was standing chest to chest with Malin, who looked

to be a mess of emotions as he prepared to leave. They exchanged a few more words before he ducked down to kiss her, which was when I stopped watching because it felt like I was intruding on a private moment.

My eyes then fell to Dax, who stood with Leutie. They were not quite as intimate as Kit and Malin, though they were speaking quietly to one another as Dax checked his weapon one last time. Leutie reached out to brush her fingers along his, making no note of the missing digits. I smiled as I saw her lean forward and press a kiss to his cheek, which brought a wide grin to his face. It seemed that Dax had made her braver and more likely to act on her feelings. She was still as soft and kind as ever, but now she held an air of confidence.

'Spying on people?' Hayden's low voice drawled. He strolled up beside me, glancing out over the other couples.

I shrugged. 'Kind of.'

Hayden laughed.

'I'm glad she's here,' he said, nodding at Leutie. 'It's good for Dax to take something seriously again.'

I watched him say something to her that brought a beaming smile to her face, which made me smile. 'They're good for each other.'

Everyone said their goodbyes as we prepared to leave. I looked back at Hayden and was surprised to see his gaze fixed on me. When he pulled back from the kiss that followed, his voice was low and deep.

'Be careful, Grace. I love you so much.'

As it did every time he fulfilled that promise, my heart gave a heavy thump.

'You be careful, too. Don't do anything stupid to protect me, okay? I love you.'

'That's not part of the deal,' he said with a light grin. 'I'm going to protect you whether you like it or not, even if you don't need it.'

I shook my head, resigned to the fact that I'd never be able to convince him otherwise. He looked satisfied before he leaned forward again to kiss me one last time.

The sharp slam of a door brought us out of our bubble as Kit and Dax climbed into their respective seats in the jeep. Malin and Leutie stood together, both looking very nervous as they waved goodbye. Renley and Prett started the four-wheeler, indicating they were also ready. As Hayden opened my door and allowed me to climb into the seat behind him, I took a deep breath to focus myself. Just as with every raid we went on, Hayden filled the driver's seat. I felt jittery as he started the car and began to drive, weaving out of Blackwing to leave Malin, Leutie, and everyone else behind.

'So what's it like to be a husband, eh?' Dax asked, twisting in his seat to grin at Kit.

I let out a small chuckle but didn't contribute to the conversation as they carried on around us. I felt ready to take on this challenge, and the adrenaline I always felt was already coursing through my veins as Hayden drove us closer and closer to the city. The quiet rumble of the four-wheeler behind us reminded me of Renley and Prett's presence, the only indication they were there because of how we all drove with our lights off to be more inconspicuous.

My fingers ran over the small grooves and edges of my gun, feeling the familiar and reassuring weight of it in my hand. A knife hung from the side of my belt that held up my jeans, and more ammunition was tucked into the pockets of the jacket I wore. Each of us were loaded down with similar weapons, with even more stowed into the jeep along with the bombs.

In the darkness, it was difficult to see around the jeep as

we started to enter the suburbs that surrounded the city. As my eyes flashed to the rearview mirror, I could barely make out the striking eyes that were so familiar to me, but the wave of comfort I got from them was the same as ever as Hayden glanced at me. My hand reached forward to land on his warm shoulder, where I gave a gentle squeeze of reassurance.

As we drove further into the city, I began to feel more conscious of the noise the four-wheeler was making. Now that we were surrounded by broken buildings and destroyed ruins, the sound seemed to echo off every surface. I cringed as they hit what sounded like a piece of metal, sending a loud *clang* resonating out around us. I twisted in my seat and glared at Renley and Prett even though they wouldn't see.

'Almost there,' Hayden murmured. 'Keep a sharp eye out.'

Our plan was to park a few blocks away and advance closer until we could see the guards, similar to before but hopefully without the added surprise of another attack. A sigh of relief pushed past my lips when we arrived at the spot and silenced the noise of the engines. Things seemed oppressively quiet in contrast as we all climbed slowly from the vehicle.

Without a word, we opened the trunk and distributed the four bombs Perdita had made. Hayden, Dax, Renley, and I each carried one in a small backpack that strapped over our shoulders. Perdita had said we'd be safe to run and move around with them, but I couldn't deny that the thought of running around with an explosive strapped to my back made me more than a little nervous.

As soon as the trunk was shut, I immediately felt Hayden's hand press to my waist as he guided me forward to meet in a huddle with Kit, Dax, Renley, and Prett. Each and every one of us had our guns drawn, ready for action.

'All right,' Hayden whispered. 'We're not splitting up until it's time to place the bombs. We'll wait here until we see the guards do two rounds, so we know how often they do them. Then, on the next guard round, we take them out and go in. Anyone we encounter has to be taken out, and quietly. We can't risk them knowing we're on our way in before we even get there.'

Everyone nodded, already familiar with the plan as Hayden reviewed it. Our goal was to be as stealthy and silent as possible, like shadows slipping through the night. If even one Brute we tried to kill escaped and managed to warn the others, we'd all be in grave danger. It was imperative that we killed anyone we encountered.

'Try not to use your guns unless you have to. Stick with your knives or hands, got it?' Hayden continued.

'Got it,' everyone murmured in reply, nodding.

I was excited, afraid, and anxious all at once.

'All right, let's go,' Hayden said sharply.

Everyone broke apart and crept towards the side of the building, where a crumbling wall gave an excellent view of the entrance of the Armoury about three hundred feet away. Hayden surprised me by reaching for me, hooking his fingers under my chin to pull me to him and press a rushed kiss to my lips. It lasted only a second, but it was long enough to send a wave of determination through me. We had to do this for so many reasons, but doing it to protect each other was one of the most important ones.

With that, he crept forward to join everyone else. I followed and crouched down between Hayden and Kit, with Dax on one side and Renley and Prett on the other. Everyone was silent as we waited, eyes focused intently on the door of the auto body shop that hid the entrance to the Armoury. It was still dark, but the sun was beginning to rise in the early morning, casting a somewhat eerie glow over the shattered remains of the city. With every trip I made here, things grew even more decrepit.

We didn't have to wait long for the first guards to appear. I felt the heat of Hayden's arm as it pressed to mine and felt his muscles tense at the sight. Unlike last time, when there had been only one guard, there were now three. They walked along the path as expected before disappearing around the corner of the building. My heart thumped heavily in my chest, anxious for them to reappear. My eyes stayed fixed on the spot, silently praying they hadn't changed their route. With every second that ticked by, my body grew more and more anxious. I was about to whisper my concerns to Hayden when they finally reappeared, as predicted.

A sigh of relief pushed past my lips and I felt Hayden physically relax next to me. Apparently he'd been having similar thoughts. Our group watched silently, unseen by the guards, as they walked away and re-entered the building. We were quiet for a few moments longer before Hayden broke the silence, keeping his voice so low it was almost hard to hear.

'Now we wait for the next round to see how often they come out,' he murmured.

I nodded before I realised he probably wouldn't see, but no one else voiced their response, so I stayed silent. My gun rested in my left hand while my right held my knife, both gripped tightly in my slightly sweaty palms. Just as Hayden had said, it was essential we didn't draw attention to ourselves, so I knew the gun would have to be a last resort. My mind was racing as I tried to focus on keeping watch, corralling my strength, and remembering exactly how to set off the bombs. The fuses were long enough for us to escape, but not long enough for the Brutes to catch on, giving us a very small time frame to get out safely.

I figured we'd have a while before the next guard, so I was surprised when only about ten minutes later, another round of guards appeared.

'Shit,' Hayden swore under his breath when he saw it too. 'How long was that?'

'About ten minutes,' I guessed dejectedly.

'Great,' Kit muttered beside me.

Everyone grew tense. Such short times between guards would not be a good thing, because it meant we'd have to face more Brutes and run the risk of them coming to find out why the previous guards hadn't returned. Things had just got even *more* difficult.

'Should we wait one more round, just to be sure?' Renley asked, his voice a soft whisper. I grimaced, reluctant to wait. The longer we waited, the lighter it got, which would mean it'd be easier for us to be spotted before we were ready.

'Probably,' Hayden agreed. 'Next round, we go, got it?'

He glanced around at everyone before focusing intently on me. He held my gaze as I nodded in agreement. My body felt strong and my mind felt clear; I felt ready.

Satisfied with our reactions, Hayden faced forward again. I was surprised when I felt his hand close around mine, folding over my hand and the gun in my grip as he squeezed gently in reassurance. I leaned into his shoulder lightly to return the silent sentiment.

The next ten minutes dragged on forever, and I was certain it had been closer to an hour than ten minutes by the time the guards finally appeared again even though I knew it hadn't been. As if on cue, everyone tensed, bodies ready to spring to action as we watched them approach the first corner that would hide them from our view.

'As soon as they turn, we go. We'll catch them before they come back onto this street,' Hayden murmured sharply. His body was crouched down into a position that could launch him to his feet in a fraction of a second, knife in one hand while the other splayed out on the ground. I copied his position, ready. 'Remember, be quiet.'

My eyes squinted through the dim light, feet bouncing against the cracked pavement anxiously. Finally, the three guards took the last steps that carried them around the corner and out of sight.

'Go,' Hayden commanded quietly.

He sprang to his feet, leaping over the crumbling wall we had been hiding behind as we all jumped to action and followed. We flew silently across the cracked ground, avoiding debris and divots as we sprinted for the alley the Brutes always appeared out of after their rounds. We had to make it into the alley and down to the corner before they did, or else they'd see us before we got the chance to attack.

My body felt strong as I pushed myself after Hayden, keeping my breathing even and footsteps light. We all skidded around the first corner, leading us into a narrow alleyway that was crowded with rubbish, broken bits of the building next to it, and countless other obstacles. Hayden's body glided effortlessly around the items, so I was careful to follow his exact path. Dax ran behind me, while Kit, Renley, and Prett followed him. I watched Hayden's shirt billow out from behind as he ran, closing in on the final corner of the alley. I knew the Brutes had to be just around the corner, just as I knew they'd appear in front of us at any second.

Finally, Hayden slowed, his feet just as silent as ever as he came to a stop and pressed his back into the wall only a few feet away from the corner of the building. I copied him, followed by Dax and the others. We all waited silently, pressed flat against the wall. My ears pricked when I heard low, grumbling voices. From what I could tell, they were maybe twenty yards away from the edge we hid behind. Adrenaline pumped through my system as I gripped my knife tightly, ready.

'. . . bloody early for this,' one grumbled. Heavy footsteps could be heard before a loud, dull thud sounded, as if one of them had kicked something.

'I don't know why we always get stuck on this stupid shift,' another said. 'No frigging idiots are going to attack us now . . .'

My heart jumped at the irony as their steps brought them closer. I could practically feel their proximity, and I swore I could hear their ragged breathing before they turned the corner. The three of them looked dirty, as if they hadn't bathed in years, and each carried heavy guns in their arms. They didn't even seem to see us at first, because their unsuspecting faces took a few seconds to react and take in the sight of us as we sprang to action.

Several things happened at once as we attacked. Hayden jumped at the first Brute, locking his arm around his head, then dragging the blade of his knife across his throat, spilling his blood along the dirt-packed pavement before the other two even realised what was happening. I lunged for the next, wasting no time in plunging the long blade of my knife into his jugular, severing the major artery in one quick attack before withdrawing my weapon. His hands dropped his weapon as he clutched at his throat, then fell to his knees. He gasped and desperately clawed at the now gaping hole in his neck, but it was only a few seconds before he, too, fell to the ground. The third was abruptly halted by Dax, who drove his knife into his chest with a sickening, wet *crunch* as he pierced flesh, muscle, and bone before finally slicing his blade into the man's heart.

Just like that, in a matter of seconds, all three of the Brutes were dead with no more than a quiet gasp left in the air.

Immediately, the group of us stilled and listened intently, searching for signs that someone had heard our attack. There were no sounds of alarm or warning, and after a few moments of uninterrupted silence, we all breathed a sigh of relief. Without a word, we stepped forward to take the now dead Brutes' weapons. Hayden, Dax, and Kit each slung one of the guns over their shoulders, letting them hang by their sides in case they were needed.

'Let's go,' Hayden whispered, ticking his head down the alley. 'We have to hurry.'

His gaze lingered on me long enough to allow me to send him a reassuring nod before we took off the way we came, with Hayden leading. Once we reached the main street again, he paused to look around. Apparently no enemies could be seen, because he bolted out of the alley and sprinted down the cracked sidewalk, leading the way for us to follow. Again, our hurried steps were silent as we sprinted towards the door to the auto body shop.

We were closing in quickly, and it didn't take long for Hayden to skid to a stop just outside the door. He held up a hand, commanding us all silently to fall into line behind him. He leaned forward slowly, glancing into the broken windowpane. One hand held his gun while the other signalled us to remain behind him. His raised hand held up two fingers. I instantly knew what he meant: there were two Brutes inside.

He cast a wary glance over his shoulder before mouthing the words, *one, two, three*.

On three, he whipped the door open and dashed inside,

surprising the two men who must have been on guard. Hayden tackled one to the ground while I charged towards the other, but Dax beat me to him, repeating his deadly assault from before. All he had to do was duck the shocked punch the Brute threw his way before stabbing his knife into his chest, killing him. My eyes flashed to Hayden as my body reacted, stepping towards him and the man on the ground, but I quickly saw my assistance wasn't necessary.

A thin, severe line weeping trails of red crossed the man's neck as he lay dead on the ground, surrounded by a quickly growing pool of his own blood. Hayden sniffed once and shoved his hand roughly through his hair before climbing off the man. He wiped his other hand, which was tainted with streaks of blood that did not belong to him, across his shirt to clean it, leaving a trail across the fabric. Again, his eyes flashed to me, making sure I was okay before he nodded in silent thanks to Dax.

Guilt twisted at my stomach as I realised that Hayden had already had to kill two people in a very up-close and personal manner. I felt terrible for him for having to experience it, even if I knew it was what needed to be done.

My thoughts of guilt were cut short, however, as Hayden waved his hands to gather us close. He cast a quick look over his shoulder before we huddled together. Renley, Prett, Kit, Dax, and I all waited for him to speak.

'It's going to be almost impossible to see, so listen carefully. We don't know if they'll be on guard in the tunnel or not,' Hayden murmured. 'Everyone be careful.'

While he spoke to the group, his eyes were on me. It was impossible to miss the vast array of emotions his face held, the dominant one being determination.

'You, too,' I reminded him, cocking a brow. He gave a small nod and held my gaze for a fraction of a second before we broke apart, falling into line again: me behind Hayden, Dax behind me, and so on down the line.

Even though I'd only been to the Armoury a few times, this trip felt hauntingly familiar. All the nightmares and terrors I'd experienced made my heart pound. I could feel the quickened pace of my heart, feel the way my pulse thudded in my veins, and practically hear my own stomach churning as I followed Hayden to the stairs that led into the dark depths. He moved cautiously yet quickly, reluctant to be caught at the top if another round of Brutes were to appear. I took one deep breath before I took my first step on the staircase, determined to hold it together in spite of what haunted my reality and dreams.

My ears pricked in the near silence, hearing nothing more than our hushed breathing and soft padding of feet on the old, wooden stairs. It felt like we descended forever, and I was beginning to think we'd never reach the bottom when I felt my feet land on the damp dirt. It was completely dark, heightening my senses. Even now, so close to the entrance, it already smelled musty. My stomach churned in anticipation of the horrific smell I knew we would encounter as we drew closer to the Armoury: the smell of rotting bodies.

I jumped when I felt someone touch my arm, but relaxed when the fingers tickled gently across my skin. I could feel the warmth of Hayden's breath on my face, and I recognised the distinct smell that I'd come to know so well. His words were no more than a soft breath as they escaped his lips, but they gave me strength.

'Be careful, Bear.'

This time when my heart thudded, it was with good reason.

'Be careful, Herc.'

Because of the dark, I could not see his response, but I

knew him well enough to picture the soft smile that would pull at his lips, the gentle glow that would emit from his eyes. I didn't need to physically see him to see the reaction. Without another word, I felt him pull away and start down the tunnel. I followed, and heard the soft footsteps behind me as everyone else did the same.

As we walked, I kept my knife in one hand and my gun in the other. We were at the point of no return, and our discovery was inevitable as we drew closer and closer to the main entrance to the Armoury. The smell I knew would come but could never prepare for started to creep into my nostrils. The sounds of hundreds of rough human beings began to drift down the hallway. Even light, non-existent at the start of our journey, began to appear as the torches inside the Armoury filtered down the seemingly endless hallway.

Finally, when my heart felt like it was going to pound out of my chest, we arrived just outside the door. The noise from the Brutes was so loud that we probably could have spoken at our regular volume without being heard, but that wasn't what was so overwhelming. The most potent and unimaginably horrific part of this was the rotten, decrepit smell wafting from the room. I almost gagged and had to tug my shirt up over my nose as the stench of decaying flesh hit my nostrils.

It seemed that things had grown even more drastic since the last time I'd been to this place.

Just as before, we all paused outside, pressed into the wall as Hayden leaned carefully around before whipping back. He held up one finger and pointed. There must have been a guard in the exact opposite spot from where we stood.

'Let me,' Renley whispered, stepping forward.

Immediately, red flags flared in my mind. While I did not want Hayden to have to kill the guard, I also was not completely sure if I trusted Renley to do it. What if this whole plan was some sort of trap to ambush us? Had we just willingly walked into disaster?

But my fears hardly had time to develop before Renley darted forward, moving so quickly that he had the man on guard caught and dragged back around the corner. I watched in slight shock as Renley locked his muscled arms around the man's throat, giving one sharp twist that caused a sickening *crack* to echo briefly through the small space. In less than a second, the man crumpled to the ground, dead.

I could hardly make out anyone's faces, but I had a strong suspicion that they reflected mine as I watched Renley drag the man against the wall in surprise. A loud, boisterous laugh from inside the Armoury brought me back to my focus, and I felt the reassuring weight of the bomb in the bag over my shoulders. I watched anxiously as Hayden leaned around the corner again, scanning the area closely.

'We've got to go *now,*' he whispered over his shoulder. 'It could be our only chance. Remember the plan.'

I swallowed harshly and looked at his face, but his green eyes didn't meet mine as he peered intently into the Armoury. I watched as his body reacted, darting forward with no warning as he slipped through the entrance and slinked along the wall before crouching behind a pile of boxes. I copied him and it was then that I could feel his gaze on my face, but I didn't return it as I focused on watching for my chance. When a nearby group of Brutes got distracted in some kind of argument, I darted inside, heading in the opposite direction of Hayden.

It was almost like I was watching myself as I streaked through the dim room. I could feel the fear of the last time I'd been here, but I pushed it down. The bombs had to be spread out to be effective, and I had to do this on my own.

It was with a silent sigh of relief that I reached the nearest hiding space undetected. Crouching down, I turned to face the entrance. Within moments, I watched as the rest of my group sprinted inside, spreading out to place the bombs. Since only Hayden, Dax, Renley, and I carried bombs, Kit and Prett darted to places between the four of us to give us cover if necessary.

Now that everyone was successfully in position, I could no longer see them. It was down to trust now as I crept forward, staying low to the ground and skulking along the wall. I was supposed to place my bomb in the right quadrant nearest to the door. Dax mirrored me on the other side, while Renley and Hayden were supposed to go the furthest in to place their bombs. We had to light them and get out within minutes of each other or we would all go down in flames with the Armoury and the Brutes.

Silently, I crept on. Every few feet, I paused, listening and glancing around. It seemed that, in the early morning, most of the Brutes were asleep, which was what we had hoped for. While it was still loud in the Armoury, there was very little movement, as most seemed to be lazing about unconcernedly. I'd crawled about a hundred and sixty feet into the Armoury before I decided I'd found a good spot for my bomb. I was hiding behind a large pile of boxes, stacked high enough to allow me to sit down and pull off my backpack. The wall here already seemed weak, as large cracks showed in the surface as if waiting to be blown apart. It would be perfect.

With miraculously steady hands, I stuffed my gun in my waistband and pulled out the bomb. Even though my heart felt like it was about to shatter in my chest and like the adrenaline flooding through my veins would never cease, I somehow managed to set everything up exactly as Perdita had showed me. Last, I took out the small swatch of matches I'd been given and drew myself into a crouching position. I waited, wishing we had some sort of signal to light the fuse that would set off the bomb.

My leg bounced anxiously as I waited, trying to decide exactly how long I'd been in the Armoury. The anxiety, the stench, and the obvious threat of hundreds of Brutes made it seem like it had been an eternity. After glancing around uneasily, I decided it had been long enough for Hayden and the others to set their bombs. I held my breath and steadied my hands before dragging the match along the rough stone that made up the wall, bringing to life a tiny flame that would end in so much destruction.

A few seconds passed as I hesitated, transfixed by the bright point of light in front of me. I was surprised the Brutes hadn't heard my heartbeat and found me, because nerves like I'd never felt before were ripping through me. The timing had to be perfect or we would all die. I drew a deep, shaky breath, drawing courage from all the horrific things I was determined to conquer, and brought the flame to the fuse. It sparked to life, making a small *sizzling* sound that gave voice to our short window of escape.

Without hesitating any longer, I snuffed the match in the dirt and turned around, retreating the way I had come. With every move I made, I was certain I would hear the voice of a Brute or feel the hands of an enemy as I was found, but it never came. Despite my increasing tension and mounting fear, my path back to the entrance was unhindered. When I arrived at my first hiding place, the last real location to conceal myself before darting to the door, I paused. I could not see a single one of the people I'd come with, hiding or moving. I glanced around anxiously, my body growing jittery as I saw the fuse getting shorter and shorter in my mind. Time was running out, and the longer we took to reconvene, the higher the chance we had of getting blown to bits.

'Hayden, come on,' I muttered urgently, gritting my teeth and squinting around the dark Armoury. Everywhere I looked, I could see Brutes. Some sleeping, some supposedly on guard, others just sitting around. All Brutes, none of my friends.

Just as I was about to abandon the plan and go searching for them, I saw two shadows streak through the darkness towards the door. A small patch of light from a lantern briefly illuminated them, showing Kit and Prett's faces. I breathed a small sigh of relief, but it didn't distil my quickly mounting despair.

Where were the rest of them?

My hands clenched to fists over my knife as I felt the seconds tick by. I had no idea when the others had lit their bombs or if they'd even managed to at all. All I knew was that mine was lit, and that every second I wasted frozen on the ground brought me closer to a fiery end.

My heart leaped when two more shadows appeared, silent and unnoticed just as the ones before. This time, it was Dax and Renley, which meant only one person remained to be seen. The one person I cared about more than anyone in the world: Hayden.

'Hayden, come on . . .' I urged quietly, my voice harsh and bitter.

As much as I knew I should dart out the door like the others, I couldn't move. I couldn't willingly leave without knowing Hayden was right behind me. I sprang abruptly to my feet, determined to find Hayden and get out before the bombs went off.

At the exact same time, a loud shout followed by the *bang*

of a gun echoed through the Armoury, dropping my heart to the ground.

'Hayden,' I gasped, drowned out by the immediate sound of more shouting and gunfire. Flashes of light exploded from deeper within the Armoury as people fired their weapons at what I could only assume was Hayden. Without my control or consent, my feet started moving, carrying me towards the sounds rather than away to safety. Brutes, both sleeping and awake, flashed past me as I sprinted by. I couldn't spare a look to see if they'd noticed me as I darted over piles of supplies, boxes, and more Brutes along the way.

The shouting and gunfire grew louder and louder, and it didn't take long for it to sound like they were right on top of me as I sprinted further into the Armoury than I ever had before.

'Hayden!' I shouted, abandoning all sense of secrecy now that it was obvious we'd been discovered. I was certain there could only be moments left before the bombs went off. 'Hayden!'

Miraculously, he appeared. My chest caved in with a momentary gasp of relief when he leaped out from between some piles of boxes, eyes narrowed intensely and body strong as he ran towards me.

'Run!' he shouted.

He looked stunned and angry to see me but didn't have time to say anything else as he moved. I skidded to a stop, relieved now that I was with him again, and turned as sharply as I could before running back the way I'd come. He ran behind me, pushing me faster than ever before as we navigated the depths of the Armoury together. Judging by the sound of angry men and gunfire, there were Brutes right behind us.

My breath was ripped from my chest as I ran, dodging

fists that swung towards me as Brutes ahead of us tried to attack. Because of all the supplies obscuring their view, it was difficult for anyone to see us coming until we were already past them, which worked in our favour.

'Keep going, Grace,' Hayden urged. Surely he could have passed me, but he remained a step behind me the entire way as we ran.

I was aware of nothing other than running, dodging attackers, and the exit. Finally, mercifully, I spotted the door. I pushed myself harder, darting around a Brute who lunged at me with a large knife. Hayden was still right there, following me and shouting words I could barely make out over the deafening noise as the first bomb exploded. It sounded like it came from the back, meaning it was either Hayden's or Renley's. A blast of hot air blew past me, nearly knocking me from my feet as I felt the residual power of the explosive. Thunderous *cracks* sounded throughout the Armoury as the ceiling started to crumble, and booming *thuds* could be heard as bits of the place caved in at the back, starting the process of what we hoped to achieve.

'Go, Grace!' Hayden encouraged.

My feet practically flew over the remaining ground as I finally reached the door and nearly slammed into the wall outside before I managed to turn, sprinting down the impossibly dark hallway.

'Go, go, go,' Hayden continued, reassuring me of his presence.

His voice was instantly followed by the savage tones of men who pursued us, their words indistinguishable but undeniably threatening as they echoed in the narrow hallway. They were right behind us, and somehow the bullets they fired at us continued to miss as they tried to run and shoot at the same time in a pitch-black hallway. Each time they fired, the flash would briefly illuminate the space, burning hauntingly terrifying images into my mind.

I felt a sudden sharp pain as my shins slammed into the steps, unable to see them coming because of the darkness and blinding flashes of light. I swore under my breath and scrambled to my feet, climbing the stairs as quickly as I could. A second shattering *bang* sounded as the next bomb went off behind us, shaking the ground and causing dust to rain down on us as the building over the stairs rattled. More yelling and shouts of anger could be heard from behind us as we ran, somehow making it to the top of the stairs. Hayden's hands pushed lightly on my back as he urged me forward, and I wasted no time in sprinting through the empty auto body shop.

The door was wide open, and I hoped it was because our friends had already made it out. I was almost at the door when I felt a white hot burning sensation at my arm, causing me to hiss in pain just as I heard the simultaneous bang of a gun. I glanced at my arm to see blood streaming down, my flesh ripped from a bullet that had grazed over me. I kept running, grateful it seemed to have missed the more important parts of my body.

Hayden and I had just made it through the door outside, where the sun had now risen to completely illuminate the street, when a heavy body collided with mine, pushing me to the ground, the wind knocked from my lungs. I felt the weight of a heavy man holding me down and causing rockets of pain to shoot through my body as my injured arm was pressed against the unforgiving concrete. I completely lost sight of Hayden as I struggled against the weight of the man, unable to do much because of my difficult catching my breath.

Somehow, I'd managed to hold onto my knife, which I

stabbed at whatever I could reach of the man as he manoeuvred to pin me down. His knees pressed into my shoulders as he pushed me onto my back, and his hands tried to get hold of my face as I thrashed beneath him.

'Sit still, bitch,' he growled menacingly. His rough hand grabbed at my jaw as he tried to make me face him, and his other hand tugged on my hair to hold me still. Rage, fear, and so many other emotions ripped through me as I struggled to free myself. I managed to sink the blade of my knife into his thigh, earning a growl of pain before his fist swung forward multiple times, connecting sharply with my jaw and stunning me into a submissive stupor.

'It's her,' I heard him say. His voice sounded fuzzy in my head, and there seemed to be two or three versions of his face swimming in front of me as I desperately tried to regain control of my limbs.

'Hayden . . .'

His name slipped from my lips, but it was no more than a breath that got lost in the swelling sound of angry Brutes. I could hardly keep my eyes open as the man hauled me off the ground, arms locked tightly around my body as he forced me to stand. Almost immediately, my knees buckled as I struggled to cling to consciousness. The sudden *slap* of a hand across my face forced me to blink, bringing things back into focus. As soon as they did, however, I suddenly wished they hadn't, for what I saw was the stuff of nightmares.

I was surrounded by more Brutes than I could count. There were men of all ages, but they had one thing in common: burning, angry hatred that was being directed solely at me. The man who had hold of me was at least twice my size, and his grip so strong that it made it difficult to breathe, much less stand up.

'Well, well, well,' he slurred, voice low and rough as he

pressed his jaw against my temple. I cringed as I felt his cracked lips over my ear. 'Look what we have here, boys.'

The world swooped in front of me as my body threatened to shut down again. My stomach dropped as I heard the sickening sound of depraved laughter, darker and more disturbing than anything I'd ever heard before. The man's grip tightened on me further, his arms locked around my shoulders and his chest pressed to my back as he sneered into my ear.

'Looks like your boyfriend is gone,' he continued, sending a chill down my spine.

'No,' I muttered automatically, somehow still conscious.

'He left you,' he growled gleefully. 'Ran off and left you for us. How thoughtful of him.'

'No . . .' I repeated, eyes fluttering shut as I felt my legs start to give out again. The man yanked me back up, rousing me once more as my eyes popped open.

'Ah, ah, ah,' he protested lightly. 'There's something you need to see before you pass out on us.'

'Grace!'

My heart leaped and fell all at once as I recognised Hayden's voice. My eyes widened as I searched for the source, scanning frantically before I finally saw him sprinting towards me. But my momentary relief turned to fear as I noticed he was so far away, at least three hundred feet, and he was alone. He didn't seem to notice or care about the massive crowd of Brutes he was running into, because his eyes were focused on me.

'No,' I gasped, shaking my head and bringing a pounding pain at the same time. 'Stop . . .'

'Grace!' he shouted again, continuing towards me.

'Ohh, what's this?' the Brute cooed in my ear. 'He's making our job easy.'

'Hayden . . .' My eyes fluttered shut again as I whispered his name. The man's hand slapped at my face again, waking me.

'Just wait until he gets here . . .' the man continued. My eyes stayed trained on Hayden, silently pleading with him to stop. 'Think of the show we'll give him . . . You'll be the star, of course.'

I would have thrown up on the spot had I been able to as I realised what he was saying. My mind felt so woozy yet clear all at once. My body was weakened because of the hits to the head, and while I seemed to struggle to think clearly, I understood.

Snickers and mutters sounded around me as the Brutes enjoyed this thought. From what I could tell, there were at least fifty men surrounding me. Hayden shouted my name again as he ran, half as far away as he had been. Everything moved in slow motion.

'First we'll give him a show . . .' the man continued. 'Then we'll kill him. Slowly. Painfully. You both must pay for what you've done.'

My chest heaved up and down now as I regained the ability to breathe, and my mind was growing clearer by the second. As the man pressed me tightly to his chest, I felt the sharp edges of the gun I still had stowed in my waistband behind my back.

'Grace!' Hayden called again. He was even closer now, elevating the panic in my quickly clearing mind.

'Hayden, stop!' I shouted.

He didn't listen, however, as he continued to race towards me and the huge crowd of Brutes.

'He's almost here,' the Brute murmured, touching my ear with his cold lips again. 'Then the fun will start.'

He let out a terrifyingly chilling laugh. Several others

echoed his warped pleasure and turned to watch Hayden like hyenas awaiting their prey.

'Stop, Hayden!' I begged, desperately trying to ignore the Brutes. But again, he didn't listen. He would not stop, no matter how much I begged.

'He touches you, it's over,' the man whispered, tightening his arms around my body so his hands brushed over my breasts. A shudder ran down my spine as I squeezed my eyes shut, clinging to any sense and strength I had left. When I opened my eyes and locked them on Hayden's, I knew what I had to do.

With a deep breath, I mustered all the strength I had left as I thrust my elbow backward into the man's stomach, drawing a surprised huff of pain as he released me and doubled over. In the split second I had of separation, I reached behind me and grabbed my gun. The metal was warm and heavy in my hand as I lifted the gun, aimed, and pulled the trigger.

There was a bang.

A kickback.

A fraction of a second that seemed to last for an eternity.

And finally, the dull thud that sounded as the bullet hit its target, sending Hayden's body sprawling into the dirt.

Twenty: Fate

Grace

I felt like the breath in my lungs had turned to fire as I watched Hayden's body fall flat to the ground, unmoving, as my bullet ripped through him. It was like the world imploded around me as I stared, wide-eyed and frozen, unable to think clearly. Sound disappeared, and the weight of the air around me seemed to press inward, suffocating me until I was unable to breathe at all. My body was limp as I collapsed, unable to hold myself up any longer after witnessing what I'd done to the only man I'd ever loved.

Just as quickly as all sense disappeared, everything came rushing back. I felt hands pulling at my body, tugging roughly with no concern for my well-being. I heard rumbling voices, some jeering derisively, others growling insults in my direction. All I could do was stare at Hayden's stilled body, lips parted as rattling breaths ripped in and out of my lungs. Two unfamiliar hands held me up, their grip too tight and unforgiving. If I had been able to feel my heart, it would have been pounding so hard it would have practically been vibrating, but the shredded fragments felt no more substantial than dust in the wind.

'Way to ruin our fun, you stupid bitch,' growled the Brute who'd been speaking to me earlier.

I was unable and unwilling to reply. I tried to stand up

again, but the rough way they were holding me and the lack of strength in my body made it difficult.

'Now you're going to have it even worse,' a second man said. My eyes darted to him to see him leering darkly at me, the unsettling sneer upon his face making my stomach twist.

'Let's go,' commanded the first man.

He jerked my body roughly as he started to drag me backwards, hauling me along with him as he pulled me over cracks in the pavement and scattered debris. I did not struggle, because I feared any attempt to fight back or escape would draw them back to Hayden, and I did not know if he was dead or alive.

Hayden hadn't moved since I'd shot him. I was torn between utter agony and relief. To actually shoot him had been the most difficult thing I'd ever done. It was the only way to stop him, the only way to spare him from the horrible fate I was surely about to suffer. His love for me would have driven him straight into the pack of Brutes, who would have tortured him and killed him any way they pleased.

Better for him to die quickly than to see whatever they did to me, be tortured, and finally killed.

But that hadn't been my intention.

I hadn't shot to kill him.

I had hoped to injure him, shoot him somewhere that wasn't vital just to slow him down long enough to stop him from coming after me. I had aimed at his right shoulder, but under the pressure of the situation, I had no idea how accurate my shot had been. Judging by the way he went down and the lack of movement now, I'd missed my target.

If my shot had been off by even a few inches, that would be it.

That was the chance I had taken by shooting.

I had possibly killed Hayden.

My chest caved in painfully as I gasped in a breath of air, feeling pain both real and imagined in every cell of my body as the man dragged me back through the door. Hayden's body was cut off from my sight, and he had yet to move. Instead of kicking and fighting, I gave up. I went limp, allowing the Brute to drag me wherever he wanted.

If Hayden was truly dead, what did I have left to fight for?

Maybe if I didn't fight or struggle, they'd get bored and kill me quickly.

I squeezed my eyes shut and hoped for a quick, painless death as the man dragged me to the stairs that led down to the Armoury. My feet bumped recklessly down the steps, causing me to wince in pain every now and then, but still, I did nothing to stop it. The darkness pressed in on me as we dived deeper beneath the earth, and it wasn't long until we reached the lengthy, constricted hallway. I had no idea what shape the Armoury would be in, but I couldn't seem to think straight enough to figure anything out. All I could see was Hayden.

Hayden running towards me.

Hayden trying to save me.

Hayden ignoring me as I pleaded with him to stop.

Hayden falling to the ground, wounded by my bullet.

Hayden lying lifeless in the dirt, unmoving.

Hayden potentially dead.

My throat felt like it was burning as I tried to hold back tears, but I failed as they spilled over. I stayed silent but was unable to stop the vigorous shake that ripped through my body. The Brute who dragged me sniggered, clearly amused by my reaction, though it had nothing to do with this place. The horrors I'd experienced here were nothing compared to the horror of losing Hayden.

It seemed like only minutes before the Brutes and I reached the doors that led inside the Armoury. Unlike before, when it had been dark and dimly lit, now it was bright as fires from the two bombs that had gone off successfully burned inside the area. Smoke billowed out the doorway and down the hall, unnoticed earlier because of the way my throat had already burned with tears. As the Brute hauled me around the corner, chaos unfolded before me.

I watched with a blank, lifeless expression as Brutes ran around, trying to put out fires and ushering smoke into what looked like some sort of ventilation system that had been built into the bunker probably years before they inhabited the space. Half of the vast room had collapsed, leaving huge chunks of stone and smashed supplies piled high. From what I could tell, it looked like it had been my bomb and Renley's that had gone off. The other half, which was meant to be destroyed by Dax's and Hayden's bombs, looked untouched.

Now, mixed with the putrid stench of decaying bodies and human waste was the smell of acrid smoke as the fires blazed on. It was enough to choke a person, and I began to hope the smoke would suffocate me before the Brutes could get to me.

'This is all your fault,' the man hissed into my ear. 'You are going to pay for this.'

He snickered malevolently before taking off again, forcing me to my feet so I had to stumble alongside him. The rest of the Brutes that had come down with us branched off to try to clean up their bunker, aside from a few who followed us. As hard as I tried to look around and observe whatever might be potentially beneficial, I could not. My eyes were glazed over, blank, flat, and lifeless, as I forced my feet to move.

'Where are you going to take her, Jenks?' one of the other Brutes behind us asked.

'The Pit.'

The term sent a shiver down my spine, even though I had no idea for sure what it was. I'd already seen so many gruesome things in this place, and one image in particular came to mind at the mention of something called 'the Pit'.

It could have been my mind playing tricks on me, but I thought the stench was getting worse. My body felt numb, my heart all but gone from my chest, but that didn't stop the overwhelming fear from creeping up. Each step I took further into the Armoury only added to it. I had no hope of leaving this place.

After walking a few more minutes, I knew it was not in my head; there was no denying that the horrific stench of rotting bodies was growing stronger. When my body was yanked around a corner of a wall built up from boxes of supplies, my eyes landed on the sight that had inspired so many nightmares from ages ago.

Bodies piled on top of countless other bodies lined a deep pit, all in varying stages of decay. Some were so rotten that their features were indistinguishable, while others seemed to have been dead only hours. Limbs were missing hands or feet, torsos were without legs or arms. Much to my horror, I thought I saw a severed head before my eyes darted away, unable to take the sea of rotting greys and decaying blues that coloured the skin of the abandoned bodies.

Just as before, I saw the hands that had been nailed to the wall. Hands of all sizes that had belonged to men, women, children. Hands separated from their limbs as a symbol of what happened to those who took from this place. Those who stole.

Thieves.

Thieves, like the warning painted in what could only be blood, starkly red against the grey wall as if it had been freshly reapplied.

My eyes squeezed shut and I felt like I was about to vomit on the spot. I braced myself, preparing to be thrown into the pit or to have some part of me sliced off. My eyes stayed shut and I stood on quivering legs, unable to be strong and brave when faced with such brutality of humankind.

But moments passed and nothing happened.

The man who held me, Jenks they'd called him, gave a gruff snicker before yanking me sideways.

'Not yet, little peach,' he cooed darkly. My stomach turned at the nickname. 'We have some use for you before you join those poor souls.'

My breath was forced out in a huff as he tugged me roughly again, forcing my feet to move from where they'd grown rooted to the spot. Jenks took me to a small area about sixty feet away from the Pit, where a pole about ten feet tall stood in the middle of groups of chairs. To my horror, I saw that the ground around the base of the pole was stained a dark, muddy red. It didn't take much to figure out that it was blood, left over from who knew how many victims before me.

I felt a sharp pang as he finally released me, nudging the gash along my arm from where the bullet had ripped through the flesh. He shoved me sharply, sending me sprawling into the dirt at the base of the pole. The few men who had followed us sniggered while Jenks came forward, gripping my arms before dragging me so my back was against the cold metal. He raised my hands above my head and tied them to the pole using a thick rope one of the men handed him.

The rope was fastened so tightly that I could feel it cutting off the circulation in my hands. I drew my legs as tightly to my chest as I could, barricading myself from the men as they circled around me. Jenks tugged on the rope, digging it even further into my wrists before he was satisfied. As he took a step back and leered at me, I focused on keeping my features blank, reluctant to give away all the pain and fear I was feeling. I may have been sitting on the ground, back against a pole with my hands tied above my head, but I was determined not to complain. Even if I had resigned myself to this, I wasn't going to give them the satisfaction of letting them see me cry.

'Pretty one, isn't she, boys?' Jenks finally said, flashing a bone-chilling sneer. I noticed that half of his teeth had rotted away.

'What a nice change of pace,' said another man. His hair was shorn close to his head, much shorter than the scraggly beard that adorned his face.

'She's young, too,' said another. 'Can't be more than twenty-one. You know what that means.'

He sent suggestive looks around at the other Brutes. A quick glance allowed me to count six in total, all staring at me like hungry dogs who had just found their supper.

'Some of those older broads have no strength left down there,' hissed a man. 'Judging from the fight she put up earlier, that won't be a problem with her.'

I felt my blood curdle in my veins as I listened to the disgusting things they were saying. It was as if their vulgar words were reigniting the fight in me that had been extinguished. I knew that this sort of thing happened in this place, but to hear them discuss it so openly made me sick.

I wanted to kill every single one of them.

'We can't touch her yet, boys,' Jenks said, disappointment obvious in his voice. 'Venn will want to see her, first.'

Grumbles sounded around the small group. One man

rubbed his hands together before dropping his palm over his crotch, adjusting himself while he stared at me greedily. My lip curled into a sneer and bile rose in the back of my throat as I looked away in disgust.

'Blindfold her and tie her legs,' Jenks commanded.

I sucked breath back into my lungs as I recoiled, trying to curl into as small a ball as possible. It did nothing to stop them, however, as two men stepped forward. They moved to one of the chairs that surrounded the pole I was tied to and retrieved a blindfold and another rope from a pile before stepping to me. I said nothing, merely clenched my jaw and tried to keep my breathing even as one man draped the cloth over my eyes and tied it roughly behind my head.

The other tied my legs together, taking little care to keep his fingers to himself. I shivered in disgust as I felt his hands brush deliberately along my thigh, creeping upward before I instinctively kicked out my leg. My initial decision to not fight back was already difficult to maintain. Somehow, I knew that no matter how much I wanted to give up and hope for as quick an ending as possible, I wouldn't be able to do it.

I wouldn't be able to just give in.

'Feisty one, she is,' said the man as he finished tying up my legs. He seemed somewhat amused rather than angry, which only caused my stomach to twist even more. Now, I had no control over my hands or legs, and I couldn't see. I was beyond vulnerable and completely in the dark, putting me at a massive disadvantage in literally every situation imaginable.

I could feel the man move away from me and even though no one spoke, I knew they all still surrounded me. It was like their eyes were giving off vibes that settled on my skin, making it crawl unpleasantly. A pounding headache throbbed through my brain, my arm stung from where I'd been shot, and the rest of my body felt like jelly waiting to melt into a puddle.

'Get Venn,' Jenks commanded, addressing one of the men.

I heard some light grumbling as the remaining men argued about who would go before a dull thud sounded, as if one had hit the other. There was a little more grumbling before Jenks interjected sharply.

'I said, get Venn!'

'All right, all right,' one of the men muttered.

I listened carefully as his footsteps carried him away. Now that my sight had been taken away my remaining senses felt sharper than usual, and my ears pricked at the slightest sound. I could hear the remaining men talking quietly, though I couldn't make out what they were saying. Behind me, I heard a repetitive dripping sound as something plopped into the dirt every few seconds. All around me, voices shouted, fires crackled, and loud crashes sounded as Brutes tried to put out the fires caused by the bombs. It seemed that my wish for the smoke to take me out before the Brutes did was not going to come true, because there was little smoke to be detected. The ventilation system must have been working.

'Well, well, well.'

I jumped as a new voice joined the area. The footsteps that carried it were silent, giving me no warning. This voice was velvety smooth and calm, unlike the rough voices of the other Brutes. I froze, my muscles clenched tightly in anticipation.

'This is the one responsible for this, hmm?' the new voice continued. He sounded intrigued.

'Yeah, it's her,' replied Jenks. 'Same one that was here a while ago, too.'

'Ahh,' said the new voice, which must have been Venn. 'Slippery one.'

I couldn't conceal the cringe that contorted my face.

'What are we going to do with her? The usual?' Jenks continued. It was obvious how eager he was to reach a conclusion, which made my stomach churn.

'Oh, no,' Venn replied. 'I think this one deserves a little *special* treatment, don't you?'

I flinched when I felt a hand run up my leg, jerking away as much as I could in the tight bindings. There was nothing I could do to stop the hand from trailing up my leg, over my hips, and up my side before unfamiliar fingertips brushed over my chest. Even though I was blindfolded, my eyes clamped shut as harsh huffs of air forced from my nostrils. The hand lingered on my chest for a few moments before trailing up to my face, where I felt the rough pads of fingers across my cheek. I resisted the temptation to turn and bite the hand.

'Determination,' Venn whispered as he noted my reaction, voice still icily smooth and vile. 'You shall be fun.'

He retracted his touch and stood, letting out a low, malevolent snicker as he pulled away from me.

'Don't touch her yet,' Venn commanded. 'Let her sit like that a few hours.'

I was torn between relief and fear at this decision. While I would have at least a few hours, it sounded like the reprieve would be short-lived.

'And take off her blindfold for now. Let her see what her fate shall be.'

A round of dark laughter sounded around me, and I was surprised to hear what seemed like many more people than

I'd previously thought. It seemed more Brutes had come to witness the welcome of their newest victim. A few hurried footsteps were all the warning I got before a pair of rough hands ripped the blindfold from my eyes. I blinked, adjusting to the light once more, before I saw that I was, once again, surrounded by Brutes. At least thirty had come to gather around me, each and every one of them watching me with the same hungry, expectant expression.

I felt the warmth drain out of me as I realised what those expressions meant. For a few hours, I was safe. But after that, whenever Venn decided it was the right time, I would be handed over to these men.

These men, who were so starved for female attention that they surely had lost all touch with how things were supposed to work.

These men, who looked like they wanted nothing more than to use me and be done with me.

These men, who would no doubt be the reason for my death, only after I had served my purpose.

I stared at my fate, just as Venn had wanted, and fate stared back.

Blank.

Bleak.

Hopeless.

Hayden

I awoke with a gasp, bringing a sharp stinging sensation to my right shoulder instantly. My face contorted in pain as my hand shot to the area, feeling the soft padding of a bandage. I opened my eyes in confusion and was immediately blinded by the bright light above me. After blinking a few times, my eyes adjusted and I managed to look down.

Pristine white bandages were looped countless times over my shoulder, covering the source of the pain but doing little to dull it. Each breath I took felt like someone was spearing a white-hot rod through my shoulder, and every muscle in my body felt like it had been put through a shredder. It took my mind a few seconds to catch up as I became more alert, trying and failing to block out the pain.

'Grace,' I murmured, voice so low and raspy it was hardly distinguishable. Even my throat felt like it was burning.

I tried to sit up and look around, but the attempt caused pain to ricochet through me again. I made a second attempt, but I met resistance when a hand pushed gently on my other shoulder, forcing me back down.

'Easy, son.'

I recognised the voice immediately as Docc's, which meant we were back at Blackwing. My stomach practically dropped out of my body as my confusion started to lift.

'Grace,' I tried again, voice still thick.

'Just stay calm,' Docc said smoothly. 'You're lucky to be alive.'

'Where is she?' I demanded as sharply as I could, ignoring his words. My throat burned and I had to sputter out a cough, which sent an unbearable amount of pain ripping through my shoulder as my chest expanded and contracted. I took a gasping breath and clenched my hands into fists as I gritted my teeth. 'Grace!'

My voice grew stronger and more frantic as I shouted her name, sitting up again, despite Docc's instructions. I was in the infirmary, and my quick scan of the place showed her to be nowhere in sight. Panic started to rise in my body.

'No, no, no . . .'

I tried to sit up and swing my legs around, but I was

pushed back again more firmly by Docc. My back slammed onto the mattress and I winced again in pain, but the panic and anger I felt overwhelmed it.

'Where is Grace?' I shouted. I sat up yet again, earning a disapproving look from Docc that I ignored.

'Hayden,' Docc said slowly. My heart felt like it was trying to beat its way up my throat, trying to escape what I knew he was going to say. A constant string of panicked thoughts threaded through my mind, making my eyes unfocused and jittery as they darted around the space, searching for what I knew I would not see.

'*No!*' I shouted again. 'Where the fuck is she?'

'You need to stay calm, Hayden. You were shot inches away from your heart. If you keep moving around like that, you could rupture something and bleed out.'

'I don't care,' I muttered distractedly. 'Where is Grace?'

I tried again to get up and was yet again pushed back down. Normally, I would have been much stronger than Docc, but things seemed so hazy as I looked around I wondered if he had given me something. The excruciating pain in my shoulder indicated otherwise.

'Hayden.'

This voice jerked my head towards the door, for it wasn't Docc who spoke. Dax stood in the dim lighting, his face solemn and flecked with dirt and blood.

'Where is she?' I questioned, voice dropping to a dangerously low whisper. I felt my jaw quiver tensely as my chest heaved up and down with uneven breaths.

'Hayden, I'm so sorry,' Dax said, shaking his head slowly. His features tightened and wetness gathered in his eyes as he watched me, transfixed and filled with pain.

'Dax,' I breathed, giving a minute, disbelieving shake of my head.

'I'm so sorry,' he repeated. A single tear streaked down his cheek. He sucked in a rattling breath and shook his head again.

'No.'

The words forced their way from my lips as my eyes glazed over, causing the world to swoop around me.

'No, no, no . . .'

My breathing was so quick that I was starting to get light-headed now, and the pain from my shoulder spread to every cell in my body. Everything came rushing back as I relived the last few moments I remembered.

Grace surrounded by Brutes.

Sprinting towards her in determination to save her.

Grace fighting off the Brute that held her.

Grace raising her gun.

Grace firing.

At me.

Falling to the ground.

That was it. That was the last thing I remembered. Whatever happened after that was a mystery to me, though it wasn't hard to work out.

She'd shot me to stop me.

It had worked.

And now she was gone.

'Dax,' I repeated, blinking furiously to try to refocus on him. I tried to find words but couldn't seem to. My mind was unable to string more than a few thoughts together at once as panic overtook my body.

'I'm sorry, Hayden,' he said simply. His face was wet with tears now and it was clear to see he was falling apart.

'You didn't . . . tell me you didn't . . .' I begged, voice cracking as reality started to set in.

'I'm sorry.'

It seemed it was all he could say.

'You . . . Why . . . You left her there,' I finally said, eyes flashing. Agony was clear in his features and I felt the same emotion stretch across mine. Tears, hot, angry, panicked tears, gathered in my own eyes as I stared at him in disbelief. 'How could you leave her there?!' I roared, finding strength in my voice again. 'Why did you take me back?'

Dax shrugged tightly and opened his mouth but nothing came out besides a staggering breath. His hands rose slightly beside him as if unable to explain.

'*Why did you leave her?*'

My chest heaved more than ever now, but the pain in my shoulder felt like nothing compared to the complete and utter pulverisation of my heart.

'How could you leave her . . .'

My voice was harsh and accusing as I glared at Dax. He made no attempt to explain, simply looked at me with wet eyes and a broken spirit.

'You should have left me there,' I gasped. 'You should have left me with her.'

On my last word, my voice shattered completely as tears spilled down my face, hot and angry as they streaked across my skin. Gasping sobs ripped through me, wrenching out my insides and twisting them around my heart. Docc murmured to me, but I couldn't make anything out as I collapsed in on myself, breaking down into destructive tears.

'You let me leave her . . .'

I drew a shaky, gasping breath and choked out a sob.

'I promised I'd keep her safe—'

Another sharp sob ripped from my throat.

'You should have left me—'

Gasp.

'No, no, no . . .'

My throat burned as I muttered out unintelligible words, losing all sense of things as my agony destroyed me. Dax moved closer, barely visible through the tears that blurred at my eyes. Grace, the woman I was completely in love with and needed more than anyone, was trapped in the place that haunted her, and it was because I couldn't save her.

Trapped, or worse.

My blood ran cold at the thought. Choking sobs ripped through my body, burning my throat and shredding my lungs. Each thump of my heart ached, as if it were tearing itself apart and punishing me for what I'd failed to do. My promise to keep her safe was broken now, just like my body as I imploded into dizzying panic and petrifying agony, shattered in every sense of the word.

Tears leaked down my face, stinging at cuts in my skin. I brushed them away in frustration as I tried to calm my shaking body, indulging in the cathartic tears for a few moments before trying to catch my breath.

'We have to go back,' I said, sniffing heartily and wincing in pain. Yet again, I tried to stand up, and yet again, I was forced back down.

'No,' Doçc commanded. Dax stood by my bed, still crying silent tears as he watched but didn't speak.

'What do you mean, "no"?' I bit back spitefully. 'I'm going to get her. I can't leave her there.'

'Hayden, you'll die,' Docc explained sternly. 'If you get up, you'll die. Trust me. I was barely able to stop the bleeding the first time.'

'I don't care,' I dismissed quickly, shaking my head.

It was the absolute truth. I would rather die than leave Grace in that place. I'd told her I would give up my life for hers. If it came down to it, I would do just that. Whatever it took, I didn't care.

I just knew one thing, and one thing only: I had to save Grace.

Twenty-One: Loathsome

Hayden

Countless tumultuous emotions seared through me, competing for attention in my shattered heart and hazy mind. All I could seem to focus on was Grace, and doing whatever I could to save her. I could feel the eyes of Docc and Dax focused on me as I sat on the edge of the bed, stewing in my agony. There was no way I could sit here and do nothing while Grace endured that place of torture. With a silent nod to myself, I started to stand again.

'Hayden, no,' Docc repeated, again trying to push me back down.

A sudden rage burned inside me as I shoved his touch away, bringing an agonising pain to my shoulder. My hand shot automatically to the bandage, but the touch did nothing to dull the heavy ache.

'I'm going. You can't stop me,' I hissed, glaring angrily at Docc. He stood a few feet back now, which allowed me to stand. Almost immediately, the world swooped in front of me and I felt light-headed, but I stood determinedly in place.

'You're right, I can't stop you,' Docc said calmly. 'But you are no use to Grace if you're dead, which is what will almost certainly happen if you insist on this suicide mission.'

'I don't care,' I snapped again, emotion making me irrational.

Dax stepped forward, close enough to stand between me and any possible exits.

'Hayden, look—'

'No!' I shouted, raising my voice. 'You don't talk to me, Dax.'

A flicker of hurt crossed his features as his brows knit together.

'I'm sorry—'

'Shut up!' I hissed, shoving him in the chest. 'She *never* would have left you behind. *Never*. And you left her to die.'

'I didn't have a choice, Hayden!' Dax replied quickly, voice raising in stress. 'You don't know what happened . . .'

'It doesn't matter, she never would have left you to die,' I seethed, glaring at him.

He took another tentative step forward, which was met and rebuffed by another firm shove to his chest from my hands. He stumbled backward a few steps and stared at me, clearly upset. I felt no remorse for him.

'I can't believe you,' I muttered bitterly, dropping my voice and shaking my head in stunned disbelief.

'Hayden, you were dying!' Dax retorted, frustration clear in his voice. 'You were shot and bleeding and I couldn't get you to respond at all. I just – I didn't think! All I knew was to get you back here to save you.'

'Oh, yeah?' I whispered, voice suddenly deadly calm. 'Do you know why I got shot?'

My voice teetered on the edge of enraged shouting, holding back as I shook irately. Dax gave a minute shake of his head and a feeble shrug.

'Grace shot me,' I told him, glaring straight into his dark brown eyes. 'She shot me so I couldn't save her. So *she* could save me.'

Dax's lips parted in surprise and renewed tears pricked at

his eyes. He couldn't seem to find words to speak.

'She saved my life, and you left her behind to die,' my voice was shaky now as I glared accusingly at him. I had no doubt in my mind Grace never would have left him behind the way he had left her, whatever the situation.

Unless it was to save you.

The tiny voice nagged in the back of my mind. Despite what I was saying, I knew there was one situation in which Grace would sacrifice anything or anyone, including herself. She'd already proved it.

To save me.

Pain ripped through me again as my chest expanded, and I finally managed to drop my eyes from glaring into Dax's. It was only then that I noticed a bright red spot on the previously white bandage. Docc seemed to notice it as well, because he rushed forward suddenly.

'You're bleeding,' he said quickly, forcing me to sit down once again. 'What did I tell you? Haven't even walked ten feet . . .'

Docc muttered quietly to himself and shook his head disdainfully at me as he forced me to lie down again.

'Don't move,' he commanded sharply, his usual calm demeanour replaced with something more intense. I got no warning as he leaned forward, pressing his palms firmly into the wound over my shoulder. I hissed, eyes squeezed shut against the pain renewed tenfold of anything I'd felt previously. My legs shook as I gritted my teeth and tried to hold back, but the pain was almost unbearable.

After a few minutes of agonising torture, he relented, removing his hands gingerly to peek at the wound. The stain was bright red and about the size of my hand, but it didn't appear to be getting larger. Docc let out a sigh and stepped back, frowning as he observed further.

'You can't go,' Docc said, eyes flicking to meet mine. I opened my mouth to protest, but he raised a hand to cut me off. 'No, Hayden. You'll die before you even get to the city.'

Frustration so strong ripped through me that I felt like punching something, but I remained still. Dax still hovered back a short distance, watching.

'If I can't go, someone else has to,' I finally said, my voice sharp and angry. 'Where's Kit?'

My eyes darted expectantly to Dax.

'He's home with Malin,' he said slowly. 'But he's badly injured and can't walk . . . He took a pretty heavy beating with a knife.'

'Renley and Prett?' I pressed.

'Renley is back at Whetland, also injured badly,' Dax explained. He paused a second before continuing. 'Prett is dead.'

Given my dislike for Prett previously, I wasn't sure what I expected to feel at this news. My response was disappointment that a potential saviour for Grace was off the list. My petty jealousy no longer seemed important.

I huffed in frustration and clenched my jaw. I racked my brain for any potential help that would be up to the task and stood any chance of survival, but I could think of no one. My mind flashed briefly to Shaw, who was almost completely healed, but I didn't trust him to even leave camp, much less go on a mission to save the girl I loved. Barrow was too old and had a bad leg. Malin wasn't strong enough. There was only one person I could think to send, and he was standing right in front of me.

'What about you?' I asked, eyes darting back to Dax. His facial expression didn't change, as if he'd been expecting this conclusion.

'I could go, yes,' Dax said solemnly.

Despite how angry I was with him, it didn't stop me from feeling the pang of apprehension at the thought of Dax going alone. It would be incredibly dangerous, and the chances of him getting killed were very high. He seemed to realise this, too, because his face displayed a tortured mixture of sadness, guilt, and fear.

'Hayden,' Docc said slowly, his voice trailing off lightly. 'One person alone cannot complete this task and make it out alive. You know that.'

'Yeah, I know that,' I snapped harshly, shaking my head and dropping my gaze. I ran my hand down my face, pinching my lip momentarily before sighing heavily. I couldn't send Dax into almost certain death all on his own. 'How long?' I asked, training my gaze on Docc again.

'How long until what?'

'How long until I can go?' I snapped impatiently. Docc hesitated, thinking deeply.

'Two days.'

'*Two days?!*' I hissed, shaking my head. 'She could be dead by then!'

'She could already be dead,' Docc replied fairly. My stomach twisted anxiously and my heart screamed in protest.

'Don't,' I warned, squeezing my eyes shut momentarily.

'It's an outcome we need to consider, I'm afraid,' Docc continued diplomatically. 'If she's not already dead, chances are she'll still be alive in two days.'

'What makes you say that?' I snapped harshly.

'Well . . .' Docc's eyes flitted to Dax quickly before refocusing on mine. 'I see two possibilities. One, they kill her right away. If this is the case, we're already too late and there's nothing that can be done. Or two, they keep her alive for some time, using her in their deplorable ways. In which case, I doubt they'll kill her before two days is up.'

'Let me get this straight,' I snarled through gritted teeth. 'You think she's either already dead, or they're going to – to—'

I grimaced and shook my head, unable to verbalise his implication. The thought of anyone even touching her made me want to throw up on the spot. I swallowed and started again.

'Or you think they're going to do *that* and you suggest we just wait around and let them?' My voice was shaking again.

'I don't see what other choice we have, I'm afraid,' Docc replied solemnly. 'The only way to save her is to wait two days for you to heal and attempt a rescue mission. If it's too late . . . it's a blessing that she didn't suffer.'

'Unless she's suffering right now, huh?' I growled. 'What happens if while we're just waiting around, they're hurting her?'

A heavy silence fell over us as everyone let the reality of the situation sink in. I was starting to question which would be the best possible outcome. Would I rather Grace die quickly and avoid the pain and suffering, or get her back only after having been tortured mentally, physically, and emotionally?

I couldn't seem to answer.

'I guess we'll just have to see,' Docc finally said in resignation.

'There's *no one* else who can go?' I asked doubtfully.

'No,' Dax said, shaking his head. 'No one that would survive it.'

I frowned, frustrated, angry, and heartbroken. With a heavy huff of defeat, I nodded.

'Fine. We'll wait two days. But after that, you can't stop me. I don't care if I'm bleeding out. In two days, Dax and I are going.'

Grace

My body ached from being tied to the pole. It was impossible to tell how long it had been, but it felt like an eternity as I tried to twist around and get more comfortable. The blood from the gunshot wound on my arm had long ago dried, leaving a crusty trail of scarlet down my skin. My legs had fallen asleep from the tight ropes binding them and my position on the ground, and my shoulders ached unrelentingly from the way my arms were tied above my head.

The menacing crowd that had surrounded me earlier had dissipated, as if they were unable to withstand the temptation of having me right in front of them without being able to act on it. Venn, who was clearly in charge, remained behind with two other men, who hadn't taken their eyes off me yet. The way they watched me was as if they were trying to see through my clothes; I got the sick sense that they were eagerly anticipating the time whenever Venn decided I'd been tied up long enough.

'It'll make her weaker,' he'd said earlier. *'The longer she's tied up, the less she'll be able to resist.'*

It had made my stomach churn the moment he said it and it did so now as I let out a deep sigh, desperately trying to remain alert and strong despite the deterioration of my body. I needed to get up and move around or I knew what he said would be the absolute truth. If I couldn't even feel my limbs, how was I supposed to defend myself?

Against my earlier decision, I knew there was no way I'd be able to resist fighting. It was so strange to know the inevitable end to this and not be able to do anything about it. The most I could do was muster my strength to fight as long as possible before I was eventually overcome. It was a grim reality that didn't seem to set in.

I closed my eyes and tilted my head to the side, trying to stretch the stiff muscles there. Even now, I could feel the eyes of the men on me, watching my every move. Venn, a man of maybe thirty-five or forty, had jet-black hair, wide, piercing grey eyes, and a very pale complexion that made him look like he'd never set foot in the sun. All of the Brutes had this strange, blanched look to them. No matter what colour their skin was or what part of the world they originally came from, they all looked oddly washed out. I suspected this was because they lived underground and spent very little time out in the daylight.

'Comfortable?' Venn asked, a knowing glint in his eye.

I refused to answer, sending him a sharp glare before diverting my gaze. My body ached from sitting in the same awkward position for hours. A sudden idea struck me that could maybe allow me to move around and regain a little strength.

'I have to go to the bathroom,' I said flatly, still avoiding looking at Venn or the other two men. I wasn't surprised when they let out childish snickers. I didn't actually have to go, but if it allowed me to be untied for even a few minutes, it was worth a shot.

'No one's stopping you,' Venn said in an oddly calm, sickeningly sweet voice. I couldn't stop the look of disgust that crossed my face as I realised what he meant.

'You won't let me get up to go to the bathroom?' I asked, arching a brow as I finally looked back at Venn. He stared at me with strange eyes, the pupils blown wide in the dim lighting.

'Trying to give us a preview of your goods or what?'

My stomach churned in disgust. I forced my features to remain blank.

'Never mind.'

'On second thoughts,' Venn continued, tapping his chin as if considering something. 'That sounds good. Let's get you up.'

'I'm fine,' I replied sharply, suddenly changing my mind. Maybe it wasn't such a good idea.

'Oh, no,' Venn said with a shake of his head.

He stepped forward, motioning for the other two to join him as he approached. I flinched away when I felt his hands on my skin, undoing the ties around my wrist. My arms practically fell onto my lap, causing me to hiss in pain after hours of being stuck in the same position. The deep ache multiplied tenfold as they moved, but it wasn't enough to stop me from feeling the hand that was creeping up the inside of my leg. I jerked away, eyes flashing to the second man, who sniggered darkly, amused at my actions, before he moved to untie the binds around my ankles.

Before I had a chance to adjust, the two men appeared at my side and hauled me upward, setting me on my feet before my legs promptly gave out. I crashed back downward, landing in a heap in the dirt. It took a few seconds for the feeling to return to my legs, and I managed to stand up when they jerked me to my feet a second time. Again, it amused them that I could barely feel my body.

'Let's make a little detour, shall we, boys?' Venn said, addressing the men.

He had a menacing look on his face as he cocked his head to the side, leading them down a small path. Anxiously I noticed we were walking directly towards the Pit. Quickly, I averted my gaze towards the ground, reluctant to look at the horrific sight ever again. Their grip on my arms was stiflingly tight as they steered me straight towards the one area I did not want to be, and I gave a sharp gasp when my eyes reached the edge of the Pit. I squeezed my eyes shut as we came to a halt, pausing just a foot or two away from the edge.

'Look at it,' Venn said silkily, appearing behind me as the men held me steady. I could feel the heat of his body just inches away from mine, but I had nowhere to go to escape his proximity.

I ignored him and kept my eyes shut, refusing to obey.

'I said, look at it!' Venn snarled, losing his strange sense of calm as he snapped at me. He shoved one of the other men out of the way, replacing him by my side as one hand roughly gripped my upper arm and the other clamped around my jaw, jerking my face forward and opening my eyes. His hand was rough as he held me still.

Immediately, I felt bile rise in the back of my throat. The horrific images I'd seen from afar were right in front of me, and now that my eyes had landed on them, they couldn't look away. I felt my body start to shake as my eyes pored over the dismembered bodies, the lifeless bits of people, and the seemingly never-ending brutal gore that sprawled out before me.

'You'll join them soon,' Venn whispered darkly in my ear. His grip tightened momentarily on my jaw, squeezing tightly before he dropped his hand with a small shove.

I shivered when I felt the rough texture of his lips on my skin. My body automatically tried to get away from him, but his tight grip on my arm only pulled me closer while the man on my other side pushed me back. My eyes were wide, unable to stop the gruesome exploration of the sight before me. They passed over a rotted leg before landing on the body of a woman, which was surprisingly whole. I sucked in a harsh gasp that I regretted immediately, because the stench nearly made me throw up on the spot.

I had seen this woman before. The last time I'd spoken to her, she'd taken over Greystone and was hoping to rebuild it peacefully. She'd known my father, and she'd known who I was.

It was Marie, the last leader of Greystone, and she was dead.

My legs nearly buckled again at the realisation. My panic-stricken eyes darted away from her body, desperate to unsee, only to fall on another shocking sight. This time I did actually gag as I saw another face I recognised, his body devoid of his hands and feet. He was young. So young that I'd spared him and settled for crippling him instead, but now I began to think it would have been better if I had killed him, for Nell, another boy from Greystone, lay dead in a pile of rotting bodies.

When my eyes darted away from his, I saw yet more faces I knew from Greystone, confirming what I'd begun to suspect.

It seemed that, finally, Greystone was truly finished, for the last remaining people from the place I grew up lay rotting in this dismal pile inside the Armoury.

'Seen enough?' Venn asked lightly, drawing my focus enough to allow me to clamp my eyes shut again. I didn't want to see any more.

I didn't reply as I tried to slow down my breathing, but it was nearly impossible as shock stalled my body and thoughts.

'Like I said, you'll join them soon. How quickly and in what manner is up to you. Maybe we'll add you piece by piece like we did with this one. She thought it was a good idea to struggle,' he murmured.

I sneered in disgust as he reached out to nudge a body that was severely dismembered with his boot.

'You'd be surprised how long you can live without limbs,' he added thoughtfully. I flinched away when he leaned in again, running the tip of his nose along my throat and inhaling deeply. He let out a chilling sigh of satisfaction. 'Come on, then.'

My body was jerked away from the Pit as they started marching me back down the path. Despite the horror that surely awaited me, I was relieved to be away from the sickening sight. My senses were too overwhelmed to take in any details as they tugged me roughly along, and we walked for a few moments before I was briskly shoved into a corner.

'There you go,' Venn said with a disgusting sneer. 'Do your business.'

I frowned and tried not to glare at him as he watched me expectantly, the other two men falling in behind him with equally revolting stares. It was the first time I'd been free from any sort of constraints, but they had me backed into a corner with no way out.

'Could you turn around?' I requested as calmly as I could manage. Venn chuckled deeply.

'I don't think so.'

The other two copied him, glancing at each other and sharing grotesquely amused looks.

'Then I'll hold it,' I said flatly, crossing my arms over my chest.

'What for? No sense in preserving your modesty since that'll be gone soon anyway,' said one of the men as he leered at me over Venn's shoulder. My stomach twisted again when Venn and the other man nodded in agreement.

'I'll hold it,' I repeated, glaring at them. My eyes darted around again, searching for a gap, but there was none. There was no way I'd be able to escape when I could still barely feel my legs.

'Suit yourself,' Venn said with a shrug before he stepped forward again, gripping my arm tightly while the other man copied him on my other side.

We retraced our steps back to the pole, thankfully this time without the detour to the Pit. My glimmer of hope for escape was quickly destroyed when they shoved me back into the dirt and hauled my arms over my head again, tying them around the uncomfortable pole as I resumed my previous position, and soon I found myself in the exact situation I'd just tried to avoid.

I huffed in annoyance as I tried to think of another plan, but my thoughts were disturbed when my head snapped backward, banging painfully against the pole before a dark cloth covered my eyes. A frightened breath rushed through my lips as someone tied the blindfold around my eyes again, blocking off my sight and leaving me more vulnerable than I'd been since the first time they'd done it.

'I think it's been long enough, don't you, boys?'

My insides convulsed as Venn's repulsive words settled into my mind. I automatically drew my legs up into my chest and clamped my jaw shut, determined not to show fear despite the utter panic ripping through me. My breathing grew quick and sharp, and I could feel frightened sweat pricking at my forehead as I flinched away from any sound that reached my ears. Tears of fear stung my eyes behind the blindfold, and despite everything I'd done to avoid thinking about it, I desperately wished I was safely back at Blackwing, with Hayden, where I belonged.

But I wasn't.

I was in the place of nightmares, which was quickly becoming even worse than I ever imagined it could.

And my grace period was up.

Venn's voice cut through the air again, slicing through me like knives as his words pierced my body in every possible way. My blood ran cold as he spoke.

'Oh yes, it's definitely time for some fun.'

Twenty-Two: Desolation
Hayden

It had been nearly twenty-four hours since I'd woken up back in Blackwing.

Twenty-four agonising hours of the most painful moments of my life.

It took every ounce of self-control and discipline to keep me still, and several times I almost cracked and made a break for it before Docc read my mind and shot me a harsh glare. I felt like I was going crazy being stuck in the infirmary under his constant watchful eyes. Every move I made was observed closely, and more than once he'd said my name calmly, as if to remind me of the necessary wait when my mind started to run away from me.

The ache in my shoulder never seemed to subside, and I'd resisted any medications that would cloud my mind or diminish my strength. It was all I could do to accept the simple antibiotics.

Worse, though, than the physical ache in my shoulder was the gut-wrenching pain that lingered in my heart. With nothing to do but stare at the ceiling, there was no way to avoid the dark thoughts that constantly bombarded me.

Over and over again, I saw horrific images that tortured me. No matter how tightly I clamped my eyes shut, I couldn't stop images that flashed through my mind.

Grace being touched.

Grace being hurt.

Grace being tortured.

I grimaced and shook my head, desperately trying to think of anything else, but it was impossible. I let out a harsh huff of air as I tried to calm down for what felt like the thousandth time. A low chuckle from across the room managed to draw my attention. My eyes snapped open, immediately narrowing in a punitive glare as I stared hatefully at Shaw.

Now that he was growing healthier and stronger, we'd taken to tying him to his bed. We still seemed to struggle to find a solution for what to do with him, although after the last twenty-four hours, I was leaning towards just killing him because of all the snide remarks I'd endured.

'Thinking about your girlfriend again?' Shaw taunted. I clenched my jaw, refusing to reply as I looked away.

We'd already got into several spats that Docc had intervened in. Each time, I grew closer and closer to jumping out of bed to strangle him.

'Thinking about how you left her?' he continued. I knew he was just trying to get a rise out of me and that I should ignore him, but I couldn't. Anger seared inside me.

'Shut up,' I hissed. I drew my breath between my teeth as I bit down sharply, trying to hold my tongue.

'Can't even deny it, can you?'

'Shaw,' Docc warned. He sat at his desk in the corner and didn't even bother looking up from the book he was reading when he scolded him.

'What?' Shaw asked in mock innocence. I could feel his eyes on me but I didn't look at him. 'It's true.'

'I didn't leave her!' I snapped, unable to hold back any longer. 'I would never leave her.'

'But your mates did,' Shaw conceded. 'Guess you're not all as tight as I thought.'

'Shut the fuck up, Shaw,' I muttered. My head tilted back against my pillow and I forced a deep breath through my nose.

'I don't need to say any more,' Shaw replied lightly, clearly pleased to see he had got to me yet again.

'Screw this,' I muttered, sitting up sharply from the bed and throwing the blankets off my lap. A sharp sting ripped through my shoulder at the movement, but I held back a grimace.

'Hayden—'

'I'm not going,' I snapped, frustrated and irritated beyond belief. 'I'm just going home.'

'That's not a good idea,' Docc advised, watching me as I stood as quickly as I could manage. I took a few shaky steps, ignoring the way the world blurred momentarily in and out of focus. It had been a while since I'd stood up and I could feel the blood rushing to my head. After a few moments, it cleared and I started walking again.

'I can't rest here with that sack of shit,' I muttered, throwing my hand in Shaw's direction. 'I'm going home until time is up.'

Docc let out a heavy sigh and regarded me closely, frowning. I rolled my eyes derisively and continued towards the door.

'I'll come and check on you in a bit. Remember what I said, Hayden. You're no use to her if you're dead.'

'Yeah, I got it,' I snapped harshly. My irritation with Docc's rationality was impossible to put aside.

I shoved the door open and exited the infirmary. It was dark outside and there were very few people around. My steps were loud and not at all my usual smooth, silent actions. Despite my best efforts to ignore it, I couldn't miss the way my breathing quickly grew laboured and the way the pain intensified with every movement. It was all I could do to make it back to my hut, but the physical toll was nothing compared to the mental assault I took as soon as I arrived at our home.

Just the sight of the small building hit me like a ton of bricks, as if every emotion I'd been trying to ignore was hurled straight at my chest with the force of a cannon, my pain renewed as I noticed Grace's obvious absence. Every inch of our home reminded me of her, and I knew it would be agonisingly painful to go inside, but the masochist in me persisted as I opened the door and stepped through.

With methodical actions, I crossed the space and moved to light a candle that stood on the small bedside table. I winced when I saw a hair tie of Grace's next to it, such a simple reminder of her, yet still incredibly painful. I moved to sit on the edge of the bed, hunching over so my elbows rested on my knees and my forehead fell into my hands.

I closed my eyes and felt the muscles in my arms clench tightly, unable to relax no matter what I did. This position put strain on my injury, but I couldn't find it in me to care. I hoped that maybe the physical pain would distract me from the mental agony, but it didn't.

It took hardly any effort at all to imagine her here. Like I'd seen so many times before, I pictured her on the other side of the bed. I pictured her at the desk. I pictured her coming out of the bathroom as she ran a towel over her damp hair. I pictured her ducking down to pull clothes out of the drawer she'd claimed in our dresser. So many simple things that I had been taking for granted without even realising.

I missed her desperately.

Her laugh. Her smile. Her gentle, reassuring touches at my hand or side that I now longed for more than anything. Even the air felt different in here, as if her scent was missing, thus making it seem less like home. There was no comfort, no familiarity, only a blank building that felt no more like a home without her than the infirmary had.

With a deep sigh, I pushed my hand through my hair and stood, desperate for some source of comfort. I was going to go mad sitting around and waiting. Even if what I was about to do would hurt, at least I'd be doing something. Slowly, I stood, careful not to let the wave of dizziness overcome me. My eyes fixed on the bottom drawer of our dresser as I walked forward, ducking slowly to pull it out.

Again, pain ripped through me. The mere sight of her clothes brought on another wave of images that made me feel even more despicable than I already did for leaving her alone in such a place. My hand, which had been clenched tightly into a fist by my side without my knowledge, relaxed enough to reach forward and pull out a T-shirt she often wore.

I let the fabric run through my fingers, feeling the familiar texture. It was soft, worn, and had a few holes here and there. It was nothing special, just a T-shirt, but that was what I loved about it. Grace looked absolutely stunning in anything, and I doubted she'd ever spent a second thinking about what she wore. In her mind, it made absolutely no difference, which only made me admire her even more.

I sniffed once, ignoring the sting of a burn that started to creep up my throat. I was careful to put it back neatly, tucking the edges in so it was even with the other shirts piled there. I had just pushed it back when I felt something unexpected brush along my fingers. I pushed aside the shirt and felt around. When my fingers closed around a small package wrapped in some strangely fine paper, I sucked in a small breath and extracted it from the drawer.

I stood, object in my hand as I backed onto the edge of our bed. It was small, no larger than the size of my fist, and it was wrapped neatly in a thin, blue paper that I'd never seen before. It was light, too, with almost no weight to it. A fine string was tied around it, and a small piece of paper hung off it that had a few words scrawled across in hasty handwriting. My heart thumped heavily as I recognised Grace's handwriting, which was messy and rushed as always.

Herc – Happy birthday. Love, Bear.

As soon as I read the words, my heart broke all over again. Seeing her handwriting and the simple, sweet message felt like enough to destroy me. I was fighting off the tears as I hunched forward, cradling the small gift in my hands. I hadn't even opened it yet and it was already allowing guilt, regret, and pain to rip me apart.

I sat like that for a while, my fingers fiddling with the tag Grace had written, tracing over the small indent caused by the pen. It was almost like I could see her writing it in my mind. How she knew about my birthday was a complete mystery to me, but she'd found out. Not only found out, but got me something. My birthday wasn't for three days yet, and I knew I shouldn't open it, but the tantalising allure of her gift was too overwhelming to dismiss.

My fingers twitched in mild hesitation, eyes poring over the details one last time before I sighed in resignation. Slowly, I unravelled the string from around the package, setting it aside carefully to keep it safe. I lifted each corner of the paper gently, cautious not to rip or wrinkle it. When

I lifted the final flap, a gasp so strong ripped from my lungs that I winced in pain because of the movement in my shoulder. The pain was quickly forgotten, however, when my eyes settled on what Grace had got me.

There was a fine silver chain, each link slightly different than the one before it as if someone had put in the time and effort of handcrafting each and every one. There was no denying it was beautiful, but what took my breath away was the tiny pendant that hung off the chain. It was no larger than my thumbnail, round yet not perfectly so, again hinting at handcrafting. In the circle were tiny, fine etchings. I picked it up gingerly and held it close to read what I now saw were tiny words carved into the small circle of metal.

Be careful, Herc. I love you.

Again, for what felt like the hundredth time that day, my eyes squeezed shut in pain. My hand closed gently around the necklace and brought it to my lips, where my knuckles pressed into my mouth as I tried to stifle the weak whimpers that accompanied my tears. Grace was absolutely the best thing to ever happen to me, and I loved her more than I could even fathom.

The thought of potentially losing her was excruciating.

With sudden clarity, I straightened up, sniffing harshly as I roughly wiped away the tears that had fallen down my cheeks. My hands shook slightly as I looped the necklace around my neck. The cool metal landed on my chest, and my hand moved to touch it reverently before I blew out a deep breath.

I had tried to wait.

I really, really had.

But there was no way I could wait any longer. I desperately needed to rescue the woman I loved more than anything, the woman I did not deserve but could never give up, and I needed to do it now.

Gritting my teeth in determination, I nodded once to myself and stood. My actions were as slow as I could force them to be. Despite my full intention to ignore Docc's previous warning, I knew he was right: I was no good to her dead. If I forced myself to move slowly, maybe things would be okay. My stomach turned over and my heart thumped painfully at the thought of being too late, which only propelled my determination to save her even further.

I had just reached the door when a sharp knock sounded, making me flinch.

'Shit,' I muttered, like a child caught sneaking out of bed.

'Hayden?'

I had assumed it would be Docc checking up on me, but it wasn't. Dax's voice sounded again as he repeated his words.

'Hayden, you there?'

I opened the door quickly, causing him to blink in shock before he adjusted.

'Hey, what are you—'

'I'm going,' I told him. 'I can't wait any longer.'

I expected him to protest, to try to stop me. I expected him to tell me I was being crazy and that I should go and lie down. But all he did was nod understandingly, pulling his lips between his teeth in thought before releasing them.

'Yeah, all right,' he said calmly. 'Let's go.'

Grace

My body felt numb as I lay in the dirt, exhausted and broken in every sense. Every nightmare I'd ever suffered through had come to life, only a hundred times worse. It had happened just as they said it would, and there had been nothing I could do to stop it. Every inch of my skin felt tender and damaged. Bruises covered my body. The bruises, however, were nothing compared to the mental damage I had endured.

I'd fought the first one. Even with both my hands bound, I'd kicked, screamed, thrashed about. I cursed, yelled, fought, even spat at my attacker, but no matter what I did, it wasn't enough. It didn't stop the hands from touching my body or the unwelcomed lips from touching my skin. It didn't stop what came after that, too gruesome and inhuman to even think about.

I'd fought the second one, too, but I paid for it dearly. More than a few blows were landed on my face, dulling my senses and lessening my ability to fight back.

By the third, my attempts to retaliate were weak, with only meagre efforts to kick and throw off whichever disgusting man was taking his turn.

The fourth man got hardly any fight out of me at all, with no more than a groan of agony in rebuttal. My body was spent, exhausted from my constant fighting and the torture it had endured. There was nothing more I could do but try to escape my mind to a better place where such crimes against human nature didn't exist.

After that, I stopped counting.

I lay now as they'd left me: legs untied, one hand slipped free from the restraint. My hair sprawled across the dirt, spattered with blood that had leaked from my mouth when they'd hit me. I'd managed to tug my jeans back up, and while my shirt was severely torn and fragmented, I miraculously remained covered.

My eyes drifted in and out of focus as I fought consciousness, torn between wanting to wake up and wanting to never wake up again. It ached to even breathe, much less try to move. Blood still ran down my one arm that was still tied, evidence of the gash that had cut into my wrist from the rope and the wound from being shot earlier.

I could feel eyes on me even now, when I was broken and shattered, weaker than I had ever been. One man sat watch: Venn, the very first man who had assaulted me. The one I'd fought the hardest. He had a book in his lap, and he watched me now with a smug look that churned my stomach with terror, pain, and anger.

Despite how defeated I was, I couldn't ignore my simmering anger. I so desperately wished I had the strength to get up, to kill each and every one of the men who had touched me, but I didn't. I swallowed harshly, my throat dry from all the screaming I'd done.

When I stirred, Venn's voice floated silkily through the air, low and quiet in comparison to how loud it had been earlier.

'Coming around again?' he questioned smoothly, observing me. My stomach twisted as I realised that must have meant I actually had been unconscious for some of the time.

'Good,' Venn continued when I did not reply. 'Very good.'

I let out a short huff as I shifted, straining every single bruised muscle as I tried to push myself up out of the dirt. My arm shook under the weight of my body and dropped, sending me crashing back into the ground. I could feel the rough texture against my cheek as I drew shallow, shaky breaths. Venn snickered as he watched me. Trying again, I mustered all the strength I had to push myself back into a semi-sitting position. My left arm, which was still tied to the pole above my head, felt a rush of pins and needles as the blood rushed after being numb for so long.

It was then, as I shifted and tried to find a decently comfortable position, that I felt something sharp jab into my back. I grimaced and tried to disguise the pain as Venn watched me. He didn't seem to notice, because his eyes were studying my lower body. I sneered in disgust. Luckily, after a few minutes, Venn returned his attention to his book. Slowly, I felt along behind me until I came across something hard. My fingers moved along the object until I felt a sharp blade.

A knife.

I sucked in a small gasp that sent a sting of pain through my body, and my eyes quickly darted to Venn to see if he'd noticed, but he hadn't. My fingers traced along the knife to discover it was fairly small with a blade no longer than my index finger, but it still seemed like a miracle that it had appeared there.

A brief memory flashed through my mind, horrific and terrifying. I vaguely remembered feeling it land on my body as an unknown man moved over me, as if it had fallen out of his pocket without him noticing. Somehow I'd managed to move it beneath me, where it must have stayed until this very moment. It was amazing that no one had found it.

My heart picked up speed. Suddenly my desire to kill every man in here, Venn specifically, was a possibility.

But my brief hopes of seeking revenge were dashed when another minute movement caused me to hiss in pain. Right now, my body was too broken, too weak, too fragile. I had no strength left; even moving myself into a sitting position had taken every bit of strength I had. Worst of all, perhaps, was the damage done to my mind. I couldn't stop feeling their hands, their lips, everything. I could not escape what had happened.

I felt my head dip forward as the world swooped in front of me again. The last thing I wanted to do was pass out again, for fear of what had happened being repeated. My eyes fluttered open again when Venn spoke.

'Perking up a little, yeah?'

His voice was slimy and promised more pain. My fingers closed around the knife handle to try to cling to reality. A sudden idea struck me, though I wasn't sure how realistic it was because of the way my mind seemed to struggle to stay focused.

'Feeling up for another round?' Venn pressed archly.

'No,' I replied. I tried to keep my voice calm and devoid of emotion.

'Well, hate to tell you, sweet peach, but you don't have a choice in the matter,' Venn said with an unconcerned shrug.

I swallowed and felt my stomach twist at the thought of what I was about to do, but I was determined.

'We're alone now,' I told him, locking my gaze on his.

'How observant of you,' he replied flippantly.

I shifted to sit up even more and was careful to keep the knife out of sight behind my back.

'What I mean is . . . maybe the next round, could be just the two of us.'

I felt like I wanted to punch myself for even saying the words, but I hoped it would work. I tried to ignore the uncomfortable knotting of my stomach as I waited with bated breath.

'Nice try. You fought me the first time.' His voice didn't sound completely confident, however, as he watched me with intrigue now rather than amusement.

'That's because there were so many others around,' I lied, shaking my head. I resisted the urge to vomit. 'Now that we're alone, it could be different.'

Venn watched me and stayed silent for a few moments, frowning in thought.

'You want to be with me?' he questioned, clearly confused.

'Yes,' I replied as convincingly as I could. 'You're a real man and I've never known I wanted that until now.'

I pulled my shoulders back to push my chest out slightly. I tilted my head to the side as I managed to smile at him. I watched his eyes drop to my body before he swallowed. It seemed that he was used to taking what he wanted, but not to women actually offering it.

He shifted on the chair he sat on and put his book down, pausing as if unsure of if he believed me.

'You coming over or not?' I asked quietly, doing my best to be seductive as I raised a brow at him. A smirk crossed his face and he stood before starting to walk towards me. It seemed his arrogance led him to believe I could ever actually want such a thing.

Heavy breaths ripped through my lungs as my chest rose and fell quickly, but I hoped he'd put it down to excitement rather than adrenaline. I could feel my palm sweating in my deathly tight grip on the knife, and the deep ache in my muscles as they tightened, preparing for action as best I could.

He stopped just in front of me, looking down at me curiously with obvious lust in his eyes. I ticked my head backward, drawing him down. He smirked again and dropped to a hunched position in front of me, hands snaking up my legs just as before. I had to physically hold myself back from flinching away from him, and I was afraid he'd catch the flicker of panic that ripped through me, but his eyes were focused on my body again, sparing me from his careful observance.

I sucked in a panicked breath when his hands automatically reached for the top of my jeans, starting to tug before I could exact my plan.

'Wait,' I gasped, voice thin and hurried. He paused, and I was relieved that he hadn't succeeded in moving my jeans yet. 'Aren't you going to kiss me, first?'

He leered at me as he licked his lips disgustingly, making my stomach churn. He displayed a self-satisfied grin as he removed his hands and shifted forward, bringing his body over mine. The stench of him was almost unbearable as he drew closer, and I endured it for as long as possible. My muscles quivered as I waited, and fear was quickly surging through me, but somehow I managed to force my body to cooperate.

Venn's lips were just an inch from mine, his hot, rancid breath washing over my face the final straw before I snapped. As quickly as my aching, injured body would allow, I whipped the knife out from behind my back. Venn, whose eyes had closed as he brought his face next to mine, never saw the blade coming before I plunged it straight into his neck, severing the major arteries I knew lurked beneath the skin.

He let out a choking gasp as soon as the knife made contact, and I watched as blood spurted from beneath the blade and dripped onto my body. He collapsed almost instantly, hands reaching up to his neck as he landed on his back in the dirt beside me. Choking sputters and gasps of panic sounded as he clawed at his throat, but I already knew there was nothing he could do. Using all my strength, I yanked the knife from his throat, letting loose yet another surge of the blood that was quickly pooling around him. His eyes widened, shocked by my sudden action and filled with fear of his imminent death.

I hissed in pain as I reached above to cut the rope that bound my other wrist. I bit down on my cheek to stifle the groan when my arm fell, the pain almost causing me to pass out again as the bloody mess beside me swooped in front of my eyes.

Once my eyes refocused, I could see Venn quickly slipping away. His skin was pale and blanched of colour as the blood left his body, and his breaths were quick and laboured as he tried to hang on to life. Even now, his eyes were focused on me as they practically bulged out of his skull. Suddenly, I leaned forward, bringing my lips next to his ear.

'I could *never* want you. You are a disgusting, despicable pig, and I can't wait to see you die.'

His lips moved as if trying to speak, but no sound came out. Jerky breaths ripped from him now, each more ragged than the last as his life started to end.

'Oh, and one more thing . . .' I trailed off.

I raised my knife one last time before plunging it down straight over his groin. His face contorted in pain as I pulled my knife out and sank it down again. Over and over and over, my knife left his flesh only to re-enter until blood was flying around us in all directions. My body ached and my chest heaved with the effort as I put all my strength into hurting him as much as he had hurt me.

I wanted to scream, to writhe in agony, but I had to stay quiet, so I would have to settle for this one, small victory.

'I hope you rot in hell,' I seethed, glaring at him.

His eyes were wider than ever, and I watched as his chest rose one last time before falling and stilling, his last breath as he finally died. Despite what I thought, I felt no relief. Killing and hurting him had done nothing to soothe the agonising ache in my mind.

Finally, I tore my eyes away from Venn's face to see I was kneeling in a massive puddle of blood. I wiped the blade on the leg of my jeans. I was still exhausted and unsure if I'd even be able to stand, but I knew I had to move. The Brutes had been stupid enough to leave me alone with one guard, but odds were there would be another coming to replace him soon, which meant my time was quickly dwindling.

I used the pole I'd been tied to as leverage, and finally, I was able to stand. I paused a few moments to catch my breath and let the room stop spinning before I took a few steps back to Venn's body. Quickly, I knelt down to search his pockets, where I was rewarded with another knife, this one much larger than the one I already had. With a knife in each hand, I crept towards the alley that had been created between the countless piles of boxes. It was the only way out of this corner I'd been kept in.

As I moved, I was certain the other Brutes would be able to hear me. My hands were shaky and sweaty, but I gripped the knives as tightly as I could as I crept along. I crouched low, staying in the shadows. It wasn't long before I heard the first sign of life, so I rushed forward until there was a gap amongst the boxes, giving me a place to hide. Footsteps approached, and from what I could tell, it was only one person.

I waited until I saw the soft flicker of light creeping towards me, holding my breath until they turned around the corner and came into my line of vision. As quickly and silently as I could, I darted forward. The man dropped the candle he was holding as I crashed into him, stunned into silence by my sudden surprise attack. Before he could shout for help or really understand what was happening, I'd dragged my knife across his throat, spilling his blood even faster than I had Venn's.

It only took a few seconds for him to die, though I took no satisfaction in his death like I had hoped. I waited until he drew his last breath before moving on, bracing myself for the inevitable next encounter.

It took about ten minutes for me to run into the next enemy. I had made it to the point where Hayden's bomb was supposed to go off – although I didn't realise it until I almost tripped over it. When I heard voices, I grabbed it without thinking, and darted into a small corner that I hoped would hide me from sight. I had hardly settled into place when three Brutes appeared, their voices loud. They took absolutely no notice of me before carrying on their way.

As soon as they were gone, I stepped out of the small alcove and set Hayden's bomb down. I searched the area, silently praying for a match to appear. I had all but given up when my eyes fell on a small, wooden stick that was red on the end.

Just what I had hoped for.

'*Yes,*' I hissed quietly, picking it up quickly.

A quick examination of Hayden's bomb showed it to be completely intact, as if the Brutes had never found it after our attack. I searched the ground for another match, but I couldn't see one. My heart thumped in disappointment before something else caught my eye: a small scrap of wood that lay on the ground a few feet away. I rushed forward and picked it up, disappointed when it was damp to the touch. It might not light, but I had to try.

Quickly, listening for any sounds of incoming enemies, I dragged the match along the ground. Nothing happened at first. Every movement caused great pain, making it difficult to stay clearly focused. Finally, mercifully, a small flash appeared as the match lit. I almost dropped it in relief but managed to hang on as I brought the small flame to the fuse, where it immediately lit.

My shaking hands reached for the small scrap of wood before holding it next to the fuse, desperately trying to get it to catch fire.

'*Come on, come on,*' I breathed. My legs jittered anxiously up and down and I was about to give up and make a run for it when the piece of wood started to smoke, glowing briefly before a small flame burned to life. I let out a huge sigh of relief and cupped my hand around it before standing, grabbing one knife in one hand and tucking the other into my pocket.

Then, I started to run. I was much less cautious, because I knew my time was practically non-existent if I wanted to accomplish what I had planned. Suddenly, a Brute appeared, just as stunned to see me as I was to see him. His jaw dropped open and his eyes widened as he recognised me, sending a flicker of panic through me. He opened his mouth to call out to someone.

I darted forward, wood in one hand and knife in the other, as I aimed my blade at his throat. He dodged it easily and swung his fist forward, connecting it straight to my temple to send me sprawling into the dirt. Dizzying images swam before my eyes as I tried to get up, but I fell back a few times as my arms scrambled to push me up. I'd somehow managed to hang onto my knife, but the piece of wood had fallen into the dirt.

The man stood a few feet away, watching me before a sound caught his attention. He turned away and opened his mouth again to shout. As quickly as I could, I finally managed to push myself out of the dirt and rush forward. Just before he spoke, I plunged my knife straight into his back, causing him to hiss in pain as he dropped to his knees. Quickly, I yanked my blade out and brought it around to his neck, where it sliced through the sensitive skin. He let out a sputtering cough, a flustered movement of panic, and a final breath before he fell to the ground, dead.

Without sparing a second to look at his body, I jerked backward, where I was relieved to see the scrap of wood still had a small flame on the end. I grabbed it and took off at a full-on sprint now, giving little thought to any more enemies I might encounter. I was lucky, however, to make it to the next point without any further interaction. It took me a few moments to find it, but it was hidden among a huge pile of supplies just as I hoped it would be: Dax's bomb.

I brought the small flame that burned on the scrap of wood to the fuse, where it lit instantly. I let out a huge sigh of relief just as an ear-shattering *bang* ripped through the Armoury. An overwhelming blast of heat ripped through the air, its sheer force knocking me flat on the ground. Flames roared up from behind me and angry shouts echoed throughout the massive room as the first bomb I'd lit went off.

I felt dizzier than ever and my limbs felt like noodles, but I somehow staggered to my feet. My steps were shaky, and I could feel blood trickling down my face. No matter how hard I tried to focus, the room continued to swoop and swirl in front of me. It took me a long time, therefore, to notice the door about fifteen yards in front of me.

Finally, I sucked in a gasp as I recognised it, and my hope that I could maybe escape this place started to grow stronger. With stumbling footsteps and several veers to the left and right, I staggered towards the door. I was just a few steps away when the second bomb went off, this one much closer than the first. It knocked me to the ground with a heavy huff. Dust and smoke clouded the air, making it almost impossible to see or breathe, and my hope that I would escape started to slip away. All the good in my life that I was striving to get back to flashed through my mind, as if somehow my body was trying to motivate me.

I saw Blackwing, and all the people there: Dax, Kit, Docc, Maisie, Malin, Leutie.

Hayden.

The thought of Hayden sent a searing shot of pain through me, for I still did not know if he was even alive. The small chance that he was, however, was what gave me the strength to push myself off the ground. I could barely see and I felt moments away from falling unconscious, but somehow I managed to move my feet. The distance between the door and myself shrank until I finally passed through the arch, practically falling into the darkness of the hallway. I stumbled into obscurity, moving blindly away from the terror behind me.

If I had been more aware, I would have heard the quickly approaching footsteps. If I had been more alert, I would have hidden from sight as the man sprinted towards me. If I had more strength, I would have been able to muster more than a weak swipe of my knife at the body that suddenly appeared in front of me.

My wrist was caught by a hand as I tried weakly to shove them away, but my mind was failing as much as my body now, and I could feel my knees about to give out at any second.

'Get off me,' I mumbled, words slurred as I gave another weak shove.

The hands that had gripped my wrists paused, stilling the moment I spoke. My heart gave a weak thump, certain this was finally the end of my great attempt at escape. At least I had tried. I could be at peace after I had tried. I squeezed my eyes shut, preparing for the final blow.

'Grace?'

The sound of the voice caused my eyes to pop open and a painful breath to suck into my lungs.

It was impossible.

'Grace.'

The voice repeated my name in obvious shock and awe. I

heard both in my own, but no more than a breath of a whisper before I finally succumbed to everything I'd endured and drifted off into unconsciousness.

'Hayden.'

Twenty-Three: Contrition

Hayden

After hearing two ear-shattering bangs from within the Armoury, I had all but given up hope that she would still be alive. When her shadowy figure had emerged from the blazing room, I had frozen in place, shocked and relieved. The warmth of her skin beneath my palms as I gripped her wrists felt too impossible to be real.

I had a strong suspicion the bombs that had gone off were her doing. If that were true – if she had endured the most inhuman form of torture, set off the bombs, and managed to escape all on her own – then she was truly the most incredible human being I had ever met.

I was in absolute awe of her.

My moment of relief was cut short, however, when her eyes fluttered and her body collapsed before I caught her at the last second. A sharp sting of pain ripped through my shoulder as I supported her weight, but I ignored it as fear took over once again. I had no idea what she'd just gone through, or what had happened to result in such chaos, but even in the dim, flickering light I could see that she was covered in blood; whether it was her own or not, I did not know.

Without pausing to think, I ducked and scooped her up, like a bride, supporting most of her weight on my non-injured side. I'd lost my weapon a while ago, not that I'd have been able to use it with her in my arms. I took one quick, pained look at her unconscious form and felt a sharp spike of fear and panic, but that was all I allowed myself before I took off as fast as I could.

'It's going to be okay, Grace,' I murmured. I doubted she could hear me, but it didn't matter. I had to reassure myself just as much as I did her.

She did not stir in my arms as I jogged through the corridor, which was brighter than usual thanks to the blazing fires. The light flickered enough to allow me to see, and I did not encounter anyone as I ran towards the stairs. My heart pounded with fear, adrenaline, and exertion, determined to get her out of this horrific place once and for all.

I cringed and ducked my head instinctively as yet another deafening bang sounded from behind me, followed by others. These sounds were different than before, somehow less extreme. Earlier, when Dax and I had been trying to sneak our way in, we'd heard the first bang. It was then that I abandoned all reason and took off, sprinting down the hall, leaving Dax behind. That was the last time I'd seen him.

Finally, I reached the stairs. At this point, I felt like my entire arm was being ripped off given how much pain I felt, but still I ignored it as I began the ascent. I could feel a warm stickiness at my shoulder and knew I'd started to bleed, but still I carried on.

I would get Grace out of this place even if it killed me.

My ears pricked when I heard muted grunts and restless shuffling from the top of the stairs, which I was about ten steps from reaching. It was hard to decipher what was going on, because of the roar of the fires and the continuous small explosions behind me. When I heard a muffled groan, I finally recognised what it was: a fight.

If possible, my heart pounded even more. The light from the doorway started to blur in and out of focus as I climbed, Grace's body secure and protected in my arms despite how wobbly I was becoming. Finally, after climbing what felt like a mountain, I reached the top of the stairs. My chest rose and fell quickly as sharp, heavy pants escaped my lips. Even now, I felt oddly hazy, as if I were looking through some sort of warped glass rather than my own eyes.

'It's okay, Grace,' I breathed, no more than a whisper as my eyes fluttered and I staggered to the side.

Finally, my eyes landed on the source of the noise as I saw two men fighting with nothing more than their bare fists. One was on top of the other, and his hands were closed around the other's throat as he pressed down tightly. The other scratched and clawed, trying to free himself, but it was too late. I watched through dizzy eyes as the man on the bottom kicked feebly a few times, giving one more half-hearted attempt to throw the other off before he succumbed and went still.

Shallow breaths rattled from my throat as I took another step forward, feeling the trickle of blood that leaked from my shoulder, down my arm, and to the floor. I couldn't focus on the man's face, but I saw him stand and turn to face me before stepping forward. His face swooped in front of me and it wasn't until he was about a foot away that I was able to make it out.

Dax.

'Jesus, she's alive,' he murmured in awe, staring down at Grace's unconscious face. He panted heavily, as if exhausted from his fight, but that was all I noticed about him as the world swooped in front of me again.

'Dax,' I croaked, throat dry because of all the smoke I'd

inhaled. His eyes snapped to my face before quickly darting to my bleeding shoulder.

'Shit,' he cursed, rushing forward immediately to press his hands over the wound, one on either side of my shoulder. I hissed in pain and almost collapsed, but managed to stay standing as my grip tightened around Grace.

'We have to go,' I slurred, taking a step forward. 'Keep . . . keep pressure on that.'

'Okay, let's go,' Dax said hurriedly. He did his best to walk beside me as we made our way through the auto body shop that housed the entrance to the Armoury.

I didn't think about the pain in my shoulder, or the potential to be attacked as we fled. I didn't think about what could have possibly happened to her in the time she spent in the Armoury, or what had happened to cause all the destruction we'd stumbled upon. All I could think about was the fact that Grace was alive, and I had to get her home.

We made for an awkward, clumsy trio as we stumbled through the street, tripping over debris and cracks in the pavement as we made our way back to the jeep. Miraculously, we did not encounter any Brutes to fight; it seemed there were none left. The world continued to swoop and blur in front of me, and I was all but certain I was going to collapse and pass out from loss of blood when the jeep appeared in front of us. Dax's pressure over my wound seemed to have stopped the bleeding for now, something I was grateful for as he darted away to throw the back door open.

'Here, give her to me then get in,' Dax instructed, keeping his voice clear and in control. I was finding it difficult to speak.

'No—'

'Hayden!' he shouted sternly. 'Get your ass in the jeep!'

My eyes fluttered once as I drew a rattled breath,

reluctantly allowing Dax to gently shift Grace's body from my arms to his own. As soon as her weight was gone, my arms crashed to my sides, burning from the exertion of carrying her for so long. Clumsily, I climbed into the backseat and shifted around, shaking my head to try to clear my vision.

'Okay, Dax,' I called. I watched Dax lean through the door, to make sure he didn't injure Grace further as he shifted her into the backseat. I reached for her, grabbing her gently and pulling so her head rested in my lap.

As soon as my eyes landed on her face, the world seemed to disappear. Now that we were in the light and I could clearly see her without holding her in my arms, I could really get a good look. I vaguely heard Dax close the door and jump into the driver's seat before starting the vehicle and pulling away, but it didn't fully register because of the way my heart all but stopped.

'Oh my god,' I choked out, studying her with stunned eyes and a shaky jaw. 'Grace . . .'

My fingers shook as they feathered gently over her skin, taking in the details that caused my heart to break all over again. Bruises of every colour covered her skin: blue, purple, green, yellow. So many colours that didn't belong on her beautiful face. There were cuts, too. Some deep enough to potentially scar, others faint and shallow, but too many for me to count. I hardly dared touch her as the tips of my fingers brushed along the side of her cheek, feeling the damage my eyes had trouble comprehending. Her lip was swollen and cut on one side as my thumb passed carefully over it, and I could feel the slow, thin breaths that pushed past her slightly parted lips.

'I'm so sorry, Bear,' I murmured. The rumbling of the jeep almost completely drowned out my voice, but it didn't matter because she was still completely unconscious.

I could already feel the warm sting of tears at the backs of my eyes as I blinked a few times to try to hold them off. Seeing her now, with such obvious damage done, made me feel like the most inferior and unworthy man that ever existed. She had endured all this just to save me, and it was probably only a tiny fraction of the damage actually done.

Trees started to flash by the window, telling me we were finally closing in on the safety of camp. If Dax tried to speak to me, I didn't hear it, for my heartbreak over Grace's condition had smothered my capacity to think or feel anything other than guilt and pain.

My stomach twisted anxiously as I let my eyes finally stray from her face, where they had been transfixed since the moment we got in the car. Bile rose in the back of my throat as I saw the bruises and cuts in the skin that peeked through the gaping tears in her blood-stained shirt, making it obvious her body had suffered a great deal.

With my free hand I searched for her hand, gripping it tightly as I ducked forward, folding myself over her in an attempt to protect her from the world, but it was too late.

I was too late.

I hadn't protected her from anything.

Finally, I felt the jeep slow before coming to a stop altogether as Dax killed the engine. Again, I seemed vaguely aware of him as he jumped out and opened my door, calling for me a few times before I managed to process it.

'Hayden, come on,' he called. He was trying to be gentle, but there was also urgency in his voice that registered with me. 'Let's get her to Docc. And you, too.'

I sat up, reluctantly releasing her hand and brushing my fingers across her battered cheek one last time before nodding at Dax. He stepped in quickly, helping me shift her as gently as he could out of the jeep. I followed and had to blink a few times as dizziness swept through me when I stood, but I managed to wave it away.

'Give her to me,' I requested, my voice a low monotone.

Dax obliged and shifted her weight back into my arms. Even in those few seconds, I'd missed the warmth of her body against my own. Dax then darted forward, opening the door to the infirmary while calling for Docc. I hurried to carry Grace inside, placing her on a bed on the far side of the room. As gently as I could, I laid her down, careful not to bump or jostle her any further as I slowly withdrew my arms from beneath her.

My eyes never left her face as I sat down beside her, taking her hand in both of mine. I was hardly aware of Docc's arrival until his voice was right next to me.

'. . . can't believe you went when I said not to,' he scolded sharply. 'Could have got yourself killed . . .'

I ignored him as he trailed off, muttering to himself while he hurried to gather whatever it was he needed.

'And you, Dax,' Docc continued angrily. His voice seemed to fade in and out as I studied Grace's bruised face. 'You're an *idiot* for letting him go.'

'Yeah, yeah, Docc, we're idiots, now get to work before they both die,' Dax replied sharply, clearly in no mood for a scolding.

Docc moved faster than I'd ever seen him as he darted in and out of my peripheral vision. In a matter of moments, he had a range of medical equipment placed next to Grace's bed.

'Dax, some privacy,' Docc requested quickly.

'Yeah, of course.' That was the last I heard before he crossed the room. He lingered, as if reluctant to leave.

Docc's hands moved quickly as he picked up the hem of

her shirt and began to cut it away with scissors, much like I'd seen him do when she'd broken her rib.

'What about you, son? You bleeding?' he asked sharply, eyes focused on his hands.

'Not anymore,' I muttered.

I sucked in a sharp breath as he cleared away the remaining fabric of Grace's shirt, leaving her bra and jeans. What I had seen earlier had been just a tiny glimpse of what was done, it seemed, because the bruises that covered her skin were so numerous that they started to blend together across her abdomen. What induced such agony were the distinctive shapes of the bruises, horrific and unmistakable.

Hands.

Handprints so clear it was as if someone had painted them on her sides, her arms, and what I could see of her hips. I fought the urge to throw up as I realised what that could mean. Shaky, quivering breaths rattled through my lips as my jaw fell open in shocked horror.

'Hayden, maybe you should leave for this,' Docc said solemnly. His words sent a chill down my spine, confirming what I desperately hoped wasn't true.

'No,' I choked out. 'I'm not leaving.'

Docc paused and looked up at me, his actions less urgent now that he'd discovered no massive, bleeding wounds to stifle.

'Hayden,' he said slowly. He ducked forward, trying to make eye contact with me. It seemed impossible because things kept blurring in and out of focus as the thoughts came together.

No, no, no . . .

'Hayden.'

Docc repeated my name, finally managing to snap my eyes to his.

'If this is what I suspect, I need to know you'll be okay to remain here.'

'I said I'm not leaving,' I snapped. My anger was misplaced, but I couldn't control it as a flood of devastating emotions started to rip through me.

Docc studied me for a few long moments with his dark brown eyes before nodding and pursing his lips in acceptance.

I tried to brace myself as Docc picked up his scissors again, this time cutting each leg of her jeans. It wasn't until he managed to pull away the tattered fabric that I sucked in a harsh breath, more painful than any so far because of what was revealed now that she was just in her undergarments.

Black started to blur the edges of my vision as my eyes pored over the deep purple and blue bruises that covered her thighs. Unlike the distinct hand-shaped marks on her sides, there was simply a wall of blue bruising.

'Oh my god,' I gasped, voice cracking.

Hot tears leaked instantly from my eyes and streaked down my cheeks as my stomach churned in my abdomen. What was left of my heart seemed to shatter into dust before being swept away in the tumultuous tornado that seemed intent on destroying my insides. My mind could hardly process anything, but somehow I knew what it meant.

Grace, my beautiful, strong Grace, had endured the worst kind of torture. The most barbaric, inhuman, disgusting form of torture known to man. They had defiled her.

'Oh, Grace,' Docc murmured softly. It was clear from his tone that he was heartbroken to discover such a malevolent thing. 'You poor girl . . .'

My face contorted in pain as I leaned forward, covering her body with my own as my hands cradled her face gently, hugging her to me as much as her limp body would allow.

Tears continued to leak from my eyes as I squeezed them shut, not even bothering to fight them off any longer. My lips fumbled at her ear as I murmured things she couldn't hear, unable to find a way to soothe the agonising pain for her that ripped through me.

'I'm so sorry, Grace,' I whispered. 'I love you so much.'

The ghost of her breath on my neck was all I felt in return.

'Hayden,' Docc said gently. I flinched when I felt his hand on my shoulder, sitting up slowly while ducking my head to wipe my cheek on the sleeve of my shirt.

'What do you need to do?' I asked. My voice was hollow and flat, and my eyes were once again trained on Grace's face. Her chest rose and fell slowly, breaths much more even than mine as my chest heaved chaotically with each shaky breath I drew.

'She's got a pretty good tear in her arm, from a bullet by the looks of it. And some cuts that should be cleaned and sutured.'

My eyes managed to flick to meet his. I was surprised to see tears gathered there, reflecting my own as a single tear streaked down his cheek.

'She was . . . They . . .'

I couldn't force myself to say the word. It got stuck in my throat and tried to choke me on the way out.

It didn't matter. Docc understood.

'Yes, Hayden.'

To have Docc finally confirm it was enough to rip me in half. I couldn't imagine what terror she had endured, and I felt certain I'd never be able to comprehend just exactly what a traumatic toll it would take on her.

'Now,' Docc continued, sniffing once and clearing his throat. 'I'm going to get to work fixing what I can, but I'm afraid the majority of the damage won't be anything I can heal. I can only fix physical damage, not mental.'

I nodded slowly. As desperate as I was for her to wake up and talk to me, I was grateful now for her momentary reprieve. I hoped she wouldn't feel any pain as Docc worked to fix what he could. I hoped she would sleep long enough for this to all become a distant nightmare, but I knew that would never be possible.

She would be scarred by this in every way possible for the rest of her life, just like I would be for her.

Hours seemed to pass as Docc worked carefully, but I never moved from her side. My fingers constantly smoothed over her own, and my lips never stopped murmuring soft, comforting words I doubted she could hear. I told her that I loved her, that she was safe now, that I was sorry. Over and over again, I told her I was sorry, but it didn't help. Her eyes stayed closed, and her breath remained as slow and even as ever.

Finally, after more time than I cared to count, Docc was finished. He'd stitched the cut along her arm, washed and bandaged the gash on her wrist, and cleaned every single cut and speck of blood from her skin. A few other places on her body had required a few stitches, like a particularly jagged cut along her lower back and a few on her face. She looked a little better, but no amount of cleaning or suturing could hide the massive purple and blue blotches that inked her skin.

Worse, no amount of anything could erase the pain that surely lingered in her mind.

Docc gathered his remaining supplies and started to put them away. For the first time in hours, I stood from the edge of her bed. My body screamed in protest, stiff from my lack of movement and the trauma it had endured. I ignored it as I gathered the blanket at the foot of her bed and gently tucked her in. Then, I resumed my position by her side, sitting so I could let my fingers trail lightly down the sides of her face once more. I gently smoothed her hair back, never letting my gaze leave her face as I waited patiently for her to wake up.

'I need to look at you, yet, son.'

Docc's voice sounded as he appeared beside me, pausing as he studied me curiously.

'Go ahead,' I murmured. I didn't move or divert my attention from Grace. Her skin was warm beneath my fingertips as I touched her cheek gently.

Docc didn't speak again, and I was vaguely aware of him prodding at my shoulder. He let out a heavy sigh and moved to gather more equipment, but I couldn't be bothered to spare a thought. Even now, with a bruised and cut-up face, she was still so beautiful.

Docc returned by my side and manoeuvred my shirt to free my arm before cutting away the old bandage, which was still damp with blood from earlier. I hardly flinched as he cleaned the wound once more and re-bandaged it. I knew that, despite his disapproval of my recklessness, he was beyond relieved to have Grace back where she belonged. He finished by replacing my shirt before stepping back.

'I'll leave you with her. When she wakes up, please let me know.'

Docc crossed the room to leave us alone. I could hear him murmuring words to Dax but couldn't find it in me to care what they were saying. All I cared about at that moment was Grace.

Time passed, though I wasn't sure if it was quickly or if it dragged. I had no awareness of it at all, only that it happened. As my fingers traced down her neck, I was surprised and pleased to discover the necklace I'd given her settled there. I rolled the chain gently beneath my fingers and took in the two, small gold circles that linked together. It seemed like a small miracle that she'd made it out of there with it still intact.

Gently, I placed the necklace back over her chest as it had been. My face hovered just inches from hers, and it was then that I noticed the first shift in her breath as it caught in her throat.

'Grace,' I murmured softly. My hands continued their gentle action of smoothing her hair back from her face.

My heart skipped a beat when her breath quickened again, this time accompanied by a slight twitch of her features. Her eyes squeezed more tightly shut and she gave the tiniest of movements.

'Grace, it's okay,' I soothed quietly.

This time when my fingers ran along her cheek, she flinched away from me, eyes squeezing even tighter shut as she started to breathe more quickly. It seemed that my touch frightened her rather than soothed her, causing my heart to break even more.

'Grace, wake up,' I coaxed gently, retracting my hands from her face. 'Please wake up.'

My hands drifted uselessly in front of me, desperate to comfort her but unable to for fear of scaring her. She continued to flinch, and a low groan left her throat as her body became restless. Surely she could feel my body next to hers, as I sat beside her and leaned over her in my attempts to take care of her. It had all backfired.

'It's okay, Bear, you're safe,' I tried, desperate for her to wake up now as torment twisted at my stomach.

Finally, mercifully, her eyes popped open as she sucked in a breath, waking like she often did from her nightmares. She blinked a few times and looked around in bewilderment before her eyes landed on mine. I watched as her jaw quivered in disbelief, unable to speak as she stared at me with wide eyes.

'Grace,' I murmured, anxiously awaiting some sort of response.

She drew a few more shaky breaths and her eyes were wide beneath lowered brows, as if confused.

'Grace, you're here with me. In Blackwing,' I tried again.

'Hayden,' she breathed in disbelief. Slowly, she raised a hand and brought her fingertips to my face, where she let them trail gently along my jaw.

'Yes, babe,' I replied.

'You're alive,' she murmured.

'Yes, and so are you.'

It was as if the entire world had fallen away to leave us together, locked in a moment filled with every emotion a person was capable of feeling.

'We're alive,' she said slowly. 'In Blackwing.'

'Yes, we're safe.'

I nodded reassuringly at her and sniffed as tears threatened once more. Relief like I'd never felt crashed through me, momentarily stunning all the other emotions fighting for attention.

'You saved me?' she questioned, eyes intently focused on mine. I shook my head and held her gaze.

'No, Grace. You saved yourself.'

Her eyes fluttered in confusion and she frowned. 'But how . . . how did I get here? The last thing I remember is going through that doorway and running into . . .'

Her eyes widened and she sucked in a breath.

'You,' she concluded. 'You *did* save me.'

Again, I shook my head adamantly.

'I was just lucky to be there at the end. To take you home.'

Grace's jaw quivered as she drew in a stunned breath, eyes drifting out of focus for a moment before snapping back to mine.

'I'm home,' she said slowly, as if it were finally sinking in.

'You're home,' I confirmed.

'With you.'

I let out a breath of relief and felt a sad smile tug at my lips, more of a stunned reaction than anything.

'With me. I love you so, so much, Grace.'

I tentatively raised one hand to cradle the side of her face. She closed her eyes instinctively and flinched, briefly, but gathered herself, then she opened her eyes and focused on me.

'And I love you, Hayden.'

Twenty-Four: Sullied

Grace

I desperately wanted to sleep, to escape the endless string of torment that ran through my mind, but I couldn't. Despite Hayden's constant presence, complete with reassuring whispers and gentle touches, I couldn't seem to truly believe I was safe. No matter what I did, I couldn't stop the shadow of fear from creeping in to darken my spirits. It felt like any second, the Brutes would burst through the door and take me away again, even though I knew they were most likely dead.

Dead, but this gave me no satisfaction. No justice. Knowing they were dead did nothing to ease my fear or take away the pain they'd caused.

Hayden was alive. My fears that I had accidentally killed the man I loved were now placated. Never had I felt such relief, and I still seemed to be having a difficult time processing it, but I could cling to that tiny spark of light in my endless stream of dark terrors. It was the only thing keeping me going, and I couldn't find words to express to him what that meant to me.

I couldn't seem to find words for anything at all.

It was dark out now, though I had no idea what time it was. Hayden sat in a chair beside my bed, leaning over to rest on his elbows. His hands held one of mine, and his fingers brushed along my own continuously as he moved absent-mindedly. He hadn't spoken for a while and neither had I.

So desperately did I want things to just go back to normal, to go back in time to when I could let him hold me, touch me, kiss me, but I couldn't. Contrary to before, when his touch would only bring warmth and comfort, it now brought fear and anxiety. While I knew there was no way Hayden would ever harm me, I couldn't stop the haunting images from flashing painfully through my mind at even the slightest touch. It was all I could do to let him hold my hand as he did so now.

Docc sat on the other side of the room, where Shaw's bed was. Shaw hadn't said a word, much to my surprise. Docc came over every so often to check on me, but since my wounds were mostly superficial, there wasn't much for him to do.

The physical wounds, that is.

The mental wounds ran deep, so deep that they'd caused me to fear touches from the man I loved more than anything in the world.

I hated the Brutes for what they'd done to me, and for what they still did to me even though they were now gone.

'How are you?' Hayden asked quietly. I blinked, refocusing my mind after it had drifted, as I looked at him.

'I don't know,' I said honestly. To say I was fine would be a lie, and he would know it.

A pained expression crossed Hayden's face. 'Is there anything I can do?'

He'd been asking me this several times an hour, and each time, I turned him down. I truthfully didn't know what would help if the way he usually comforted me by holding me close caused such emotional turmoil. I felt dirty, like I was unworthy of his attention.

'I want to go home,' I said weakly, feeling defeated. It had taken all the strength I possessed to get as far as I had, and now that I was back in Blackwing, my strength had yet to return.

'Okay,' Hayden replied quickly. He ducked his head to press a kiss to the back of my hand. It was the only place I'd allowed him to touch me so far. 'I'll go and talk to Docc quickly and I'll take you home.'

I nodded and tried to smile at him, but it ended up looking like a sad excuse as my lips barely twitched.

He got up from his seat and crossed the room quickly, finding Docc as they exchanged hushed words I could not hear. I watched but didn't really see as my mind started to drift again. Maybe if I got to go home, I would feel a little better.

Hayden had only been gone for a matter of seconds when he turned and crossed the room once more. He paused by my bedside and started to reach out for me before he caught himself and lowered his hands reluctantly.

'Docc said we can go,' he told me softly. 'Do you, um, want help getting up?'

'No, I'm okay,' I said. I grimaced as I pushed myself into a sitting position and swung my legs off the edge of the bed. I had yet to really examine the physical damage done, but I didn't need to see it to feel it. I ached everywhere, hurt everywhere, and worst of all, I felt contaminated everywhere. I wanted to shower and scrub my skin until there was nothing left.

Hayden stood a few feet away, fidgeting with his hands to stop himself from reaching out to me, constantly at war with himself over what to do; I felt guilty for putting him through that.

'Okay, let's go,' I said as I took a slow step. My trouser

legs dragged on the ground, too big for my body. After my clothes had been cut up and removed, Hayden had given me some of the spare clothes he'd found in the infirmary. They were far too large, but I preferred them that way because they weren't tight on my aching body. My boots lay beside the bed, and I carefully stepped into them without bothering to tie them.

Hayden hovered beside me as I walked, moving slowly through the infirmary until I reached the front door. Then, he held it open for me as he allowed me to go outside into the darkness of night. I was grateful it was late, because there was nobody around as I made my slow progression through camp. Several times, Hayden would start to speak to offer assistance, but every time, I insisted I was fine. It took much longer than usual, but finally we made it to our hut.

I breathed my first sigh of relief when my eyes landed on it, comforted by the familiar sight. This was the place I had fallen in love with Hayden and come to know him in every sense; maybe this would be the place I could learn to let him comfort me again.

Hayden continued to be the perfect gentleman as he held the door to our hut open, allowing me to pass through before rushing around the hut to light candles. The warm glow that was cast around the place was comforting, but it didn't stop me from jumping when Hayden spoke from behind me.

'What can I do, Grace?' he asked lowly, voice laden with a sad helplessness that broke my heart. 'Sorry,' he added when he saw me jump.

'I'd like to shower,' I said softly, turning to face him. My eyes locked on his and I could see the thoughts racing behind his eyes.

'Would you like me to help?' he offered kindly.

I felt a strange mix of emotions at his words. I didn't like feeling so helpless, so weak. I wanted to be able to do things on my own, but I also wanted to give in completely and just let Hayden take care of me how he wished. My decision was made when a memory of hands on my body flashed through my mind. I flinched instinctively, squeezing my eyes closed for a few seconds before I opened them to see Hayden watching me with concern.

'No,' I said gently, clearing my throat. 'I can manage.'

Hayden nodded slowly and pulled in a slow, deep breath.

'Okay,' he replied. 'I'll be right out here if you need me.'

I nodded and tried to smile at him, but again, it fell short. I could feel his eyes on me still as I turned and went into the bathroom. After shutting the door, I leaned back against it. My head tipped back and I blew a deep breath between my lips, hating myself for shutting down in such a way.

After a few moments, I managed to push myself off the door to start to undress. Just as before, my muscles screamed in agony. It wasn't until I'd peeled off the last piece of clothing, started the shower, and stepped beneath the spray that I managed to finally look down. Instantly, I sucked in a gasp so large that my body ached.

Bruises covered almost every inch of my skin. Dark browns, blues, purples, greens, every colour imaginable inked my flesh. My stomach churned at the sight and I was once again bombarded with mental images of the faces that haunted me: faces of the men who had ruined me. I sucked in a gasping breath and squeezed my eyes shut, desperate to fight off the memories.

With shaky hands, I managed to grab a rag and some soap. I pulled rattling breaths through my lips as I brought the cloth to my skin. Docc had done his best to clean my wounds, but still I felt dirty. As soon as the rag touched the surface, I winced in pain. There were too many bruises to avoid, so I stopped trying. In frustration I repeated my actions, pressing harder this time even though it hurt.

I let out a shaky whimper and gritted my teeth, angry with the world. This time, I scrubbed as hard as I could. I felt the slight sting as soap settled into the small cuts I already had and the new ones I created with the rough texture of the rag, but still I didn't stop. My breath was coming out in uneven pants now, and my actions were quickly growing sloppier and less coordinated as my heart picked up speed and my fear started to come back.

Each time I pressed the rag to my skin, I saw flashbacks of what had happened.

It wasn't enough to wash away the evidence.

No matter how hard I scrubbed, I couldn't wash away the filth.

I threw the rag down in frustration. My breath became even shakier and the world started to blur around me as I felt the horrors coming back to me. One more look at my marred skin was all it took for me to be thrown right back into the fearful mindset I'd endured for too long.

It was like I was right back in that terrible place. I could feel hands on my body, smell the stench of dirty humans and decaying bodies, feel the cold chill that hung in the air. I could feel the shivers creeping down my spinc as I remembered what it felt like when they touched me, when they hurt me. The gentle trickle of water washing over me felt like knives rather than a mere shower, as if each drop that pelted my skin drove straight through it down to the bone.

My breathing became quicker and quicker until I could only gasp, my body shaking uncontrollably as my legs gave out beneath me. They were all around me, touching me, hurting me, forcing me to do things I did not want to do. My mind was running wild with fearful thoughts, no longer under my control as I choked out a gasping sob. I collapsed into a ball on the ground, frozen beneath the spray of the shower as my arms locked around my legs in an attempt to escape the constant stream of horrors.

Even in my waking hours, my nightmares haunted me.

'Grace!'

Hayden's concerned voice sounded through the door, and I had the distinct impression it wasn't the first time he'd shouted it because of his frantic tone. I dropped my head into my arms, curling tighter into a ball as the water washed over me. My hair was plastered over my face and arms, muffling the sound of Hayden's voice as he called for me again.

'Grace, please . . .'

My already shattered heart seemed to break even more when I heard him pleading through the door. I gasped again and sniffed, not even bothering to wipe away the tears that streamed from my eyes. The water from thc shower would wash them down the drain, if not the torturous memories.

When another shaky whimper escaped my lips and echoed through the small room, it seemed Hayden could no longer resist. I heard the door open, felt his eyes on me, but I didn't move. I stayed curled into a ball on the floor, head down as I cried against my arm.

'Oh, Grace . . .' Hayden soothed softly, heartbreak clear in his tone.

I heard a shuffling and footsteps before he turned off the water and placed a towel around me. I recoiled before I realised it was him.

'I'm going to help you up, okay?' Hayden's voice was as gentle as ever, soft so as not to frighten me. I nodded against my arm, bracing myself.

I flinched when I felt his hands grip my arms gently, tugging me upward to stand. Hayden's actions were tender as he shifted the towel around me, covering me completely. I found it difficult to look at his face, so I focused on his chest. He grabbed another towel to wring out my hair enough so it wasn't sopping wet.

'Come on, Bear,' he murmured.

He gingerly placed a hand on my lower back to guide me into the main room, though he removed it when I involuntarily twitched away. Every time my body reacted without my control, a little more of my heart broke. Again, guilt flooded through me.

Once in the main room, I could see he'd laid out clothes for me on our bed. A small flicker of warmth washed through me at his thoughtfulness. Even now, when I was a complete mess, I felt so incredibly lucky to have him. Even now, when I could barely manage to let him touch me, I loved him so completely.

'Thank you, Hayden,' I murmured as he gathered the clothes and came to stand before me. He shot me a small, sad smile and nodded.

'Here,' he said quietly, holding out the shirt. 'Arms up.'

Dark bruises covered both of my shoulders from the way my arms had been tied above my head for so long, and it hurt to raise them. Some of the ache was soothed, however, when Hayden's gentle touch feathered over my skin while he slipped the shirt over my head. It was the first time he'd touched me and I hadn't struggled.

Hayden let the shirt fall over me, where it bunched up around my towel. He then stooped in front of me, holding out a pair of underwear. Trying not to feel embarrassed, I stepped into them and allowed him to pull them up. I breathed in deeply before I released the towel and handed it to him, reluctant to bare my battered body to him.

'I'm so sorry, Grace,' Hayden whispered.

My eyes held his gaze for a few moments before dropping to his chest again, where I saw a hint of white bandage peeking out from beneath his shirt. The bandage was over his shoulder, where I'd shot him to stop him from coming after me.

'I'm sorry, too,' I said, nodding at his shoulder. His hand flashed briefly to the wound as if he'd completely forgotten about it. 'I did it to—'

'I know why,' he said gently, cutting me off with a shake of his head. 'You don't need to explain anything to me.'

I nodded, suddenly feeling exhausted. We had so much to discuss, so much to share with each other, but I couldn't find the energy to do it. I had to tell him what happened in the Armoury. How I'd escaped. I had to thank him for coming after me, for getting me out of there. I had to learn how to deal with this new paralysing fear. I had to find out what had happened with everyone else from our crew. Most of all, I had to tell him how much I loved him.

But those things would have to wait, because exhaustion was sweeping through me so quickly it threatened to take me down.

'Can we go to bed?' I asked softly.

'Of course,' he replied quickly, nodding. His eyes darted to the bed before finding mine once more. 'Will you . . . Will you be able to have me that close?'

It looked like it pained him greatly to even ask. It pained me as well.

'We have to try,' I replied. I took a slow, deep breath and gave a determined nod.

'Okay,' he answered gently.

Hesitantly, he reached out to grab my hand, and I managed to grasp his. He looked relieved when I didn't pull away from him before he led me to the bed. With my hand still claimed in his, he used his other to pull back the blankets. After spending so much time on the dirty ground, I'd never seen something so inviting.

'Here you go,' he murmured, tugging lightly to let me crawl into bed.

I shifted around and struggled to find a position that didn't put too much pressure on my bruises. Finally, I settled for lying on my side, facing the direction Hayden usually slept. He moved around the room quickly, blowing out all the candles but the one on the small table next to the bed. He then sat on the edge of the bed.

'You sure this is okay? I can sleep on the couch if it's going to be too . . . difficult,' he offered. He was so selfless that it made my heart warm.

'I want you here,' I told him honestly. Again, he looked relieved as he nodded.

He was careful not to touch me as he lay down beside me. About a foot of space existed between us, and I shifted closer to him, although I was scared for what would happen. I wanted to be able to let him comfort me, to let him touch me without flinching away in irrational fear. It wasn't until I was about an inch away that he responded. He lifted an arm and reached out as if to loop it around me before he paused, letting it hover over my body.

'Is this okay?' he whispered, watching me closely for my reaction. I closed my eyes for a moment and took a deep breath.

'Yes.'

He lowered his arm and gently secured it around me, drawing me closer to him. Immediately, flashes of unwanted hands and bodies connected with mine swarmed over my mind, blinding me momentarily in fear. There was something else, though, too.

Something good.

It was like the first time he'd ever done that, ages ago when we'd had to spend the night in the city and slept on the floor in an office. He had moved similarly then: hesitantly, uncertain if I would allow or reject his action. Then, I'd felt nothing but warmth and happiness. Now, I felt conflicted, but that one happy memory was enough to allow me to push away the haunting images. I felt my body relax as soon as I accepted this, and I tried to settle into him. I could feel some of the tension lift in him when I didn't shift away.

'Don't let me go, Hayden,' I murmured, closing my eyes as I snuggled into him.

It wasn't the same as before. The complete ease and effortlessness of our previous moments in this position were nowhere to be found, but at least I was able to let him touch me without being crippled in fear. It was a small step, a baby step, but it was something.

'Never, Grace. Never.'

Twenty-Five: Progression

Grace

It had been two weeks since I'd arrived back at Blackwing.

Two weeks of terrifying flashbacks that crippled me at the most unexpected of times.

Two weeks of hardly being able to let Hayden touch me without twitching away instinctively.

Two weeks of the worst kind of torture: to be safe, but not feel like it.

My bruises had almost faded completely now, leaving only faint traces of light yellows and greens. The sharp outlines of hands were gone, with only patchy, indistinguishable blotches remaining. Most of my cuts had healed, and the deep ones were no longer hidden behind bandages as they were sufficiently healed to be exposed to the air. Only the gash across my arm from where I'd been shot remained fairly fresh, though Docc's care had done wonders for that as well. Though my body was healing physically, my mind only seemed to deteriorate.

In that time, I had never left the safety of our hut. I stayed inside every single day, shutting out the world and anyone who tried to come and see me. Only Hayden was allowed near me, and even then, it was difficult.

Night was the only time I could let him touch me, though it never lasted long. No matter how comfortably we settled in together, it always ended the same way: badly. I still hadn't been able to explain what had happened or how I'd escaped. Every time I tried, the haunting images rushed back and shut me down. It was like the memories were meant to stay locked in my head forever, no matter how badly I wanted them to leave.

That had happened every single night since then.

Each time, it broke a little more of my heart.

It broke a little of his, too.

Hayden had been reluctant to leave me alone at first. For the first week and a half, he stayed with me every moment of the day. Every potential need I had was anticipated by his careful and thoughtful actions; even though I could hardly show it, I was so grateful for him. He had food brought in by Maisie, which I noticed was much more substantial lately thanks to our assistance from Whetland. I tried to eat, but I didn't have even the slightest hint of an appetite. I could feel my body growing thinner and weaker, but it didn't help my motivation, or lack thereof.

A few days ago, Hayden reluctantly had to resume the responsibilities that came with leading the camp. He never left me for very long and always offered to let me come, but I always declined.

Now, a soft knock at the door jerked my attention. I had been sitting on the edge of our bed, staring blankly at the floor. Hayden was off somewhere, though I couldn't remember exactly where. I felt like a shell of a person, like everything that was said to me went in one ear, echoed around a bit, and drifted out the other before I could process it.

The knock sounded again. I took a few tentative steps towards the door and paused, uncertain if I wanted to see anyone. I breathed in, and nodded to myself in determination, deciding it was time to really put some effort into leaving the grotesque horrors behind.

I opened the door to reveal a surprised-looking Leutie. She blinked and gathered herself before smiling gently.

'Grace,' she greeted calmly. 'I didn't think you'd answer.'

I knew she'd come to see me before, but each time, she'd either been ignored or gently turned away by Hayden.

'I didn't either,' I replied blandly. It was like the life had been drained out of me.

'Can I come in?' she asked gently.

I paused uncertainly. 'No, let's go somewhere,' I resolved. Leutie brightened and flashed another smile.

'Okay.'

I ducked back inside to put on my boots. Even wearing shoes felt odd again. Leutie waited patiently by the door as I scrawled a note to Hayden saying I'd gone with Leutie, in case he returned before I did.

'Where do you want to go?' she asked, as we made our way outside.

Blackwing was set in a warm glow of light as the sun started to set. Part of me feared being outside after dark, but I pushed it away. I was getting tired of fearing things.

'I don't care,' I said honestly. It was just nice to be outside for once.

'Have you seen the crops since you got back? The ones Whetland gave us?'

'No, I haven't.'

'Let's have a look,' Leutie said lightly. She reached out as if to link her arm with mine, causing me to flinch away at the movement. She withdrew quickly and a guilty look crossed her face.

'I'm so sorry,' she gushed. 'I totally forgot . . . Hayden told us not to – to – I'm so stupid.'

'No, it's okay,' I insisted. 'You're not stupid.'

'No, really, I should have known—'

'I can't go my whole life without letting people touch me,' I said. 'I have to get over it eventually, right?'

'Oh, Grace, no,' she rebutted gently, shaking her head. 'What you went through was absolutely terrible. No one expects you to just forget it and be completely fine, just like that.'

I didn't reply right away. I knew she was right, but it didn't help. *I* wanted to forget it and be okay again.

'Do you want to talk about it?' she asked cautiously, keeping her voice low as we passed a pair of people. They gave us small waves and sad smiles as they continued on.

'No,' I replied quickly. Too quickly. I cleared my throat and spoke again. 'No, but thank you.'

'Okay. I'm here for you, you know?'

'I know,' I answered quietly.

'Dax, too,' she continued. We were almost to the area the crops had been planted now. 'I know you haven't seen him, but he wanted me to tell you. He feels absolutely terrible about everything.'

I shook my head. 'It wasn't his fault.'

Now Leutie was the quiet one for a few moments. We stopped when we reached the edge of an area of about five hundred square feet. I felt my jaw drop in surprise, stunned that they'd been able to seed such a large area. A variety of little green plants were rising, some higher than others and with different-shaped leaves. It was a major improvement over the poor excuse for a crop field we'd had before.

'Wow,' I breathed, surprised.

'They're not big yet, but they'll grow,' Leutie said proudly. She was beaming around at the tiny crops.

'This is amazing,' I said honestly. If we could manage

to grow our own crops, the impact would be absolutely huge.

'There's still some good left, yeah?' Leutie mused. The smile on her face faded to a more serious look as her eyes met mine. 'Look, Grace . . . I can't even begin to imagine what you've gone through so I won't pretend like I do. I won't tell you to just forget it and move on because I know you can't . . . but I just want you to know I'll always be here. And Dax. And Kit, Malin, Docc, Maisie . . . Everyone loves you so much and we all just want you to be okay. And I know that you have Hayden and that he'll probably be the one to get you through this but . . . let us help, too. We want to.'

The back of my throat suddenly felt tight as I held her gaze, where I noticed tears welling up in her bright eyes. When she continued speaking, her voice was somewhat shaky with emotion.

'I hope you know how strong you are,' she said softly. 'You're my best friend and I'm so proud of you. You inspire me to be stronger in my own way.'

'You think too highly of me,' I managed to say, shaking my head in disagreement.

'No, Grace. You don't think highly enough of yourself.'

I sniffed once and blinked back the tears that had started to prick at my eyes, refusing to let them fall. 'Thank you, Leutie. For everything.'

'Of course,' she said, satisfied I had stopped arguing. 'I won't hug you because, you know, but just know that I'm hugging you mentally.'

A ghost of a laugh pushed past my lips and for the first time in what felt like forever, I felt a smile tug at my mouth. 'That's just fine.'

As Leutie returned my smile, I felt the strongest I had in a long time. Maybe this could finally be the time I could talk to Hayden about what had happened. Maybe if I told him just a little, I'd stop seeing it so vividly in my mind. Leutie's offer to help was appreciated, and I would be sure to take her up on it soon, but I knew the only one I'd be able to talk to about what I'd gone through would be Hayden. Leutie could help in other ways.

Just not with that.

'Grace?'

The sound of my name drew my attention, and I turned to see Dax heading towards us. He squinted as he approached as if unsure if it was really me.

'Hey, Dax.'

I hadn't seen him since arriving back. I hadn't seen anyone, really.

'Good to see you out and about,' he said. His voice was serious, and there was a hint of something hidden beneath his tone that I couldn't quite catch.

'You, too,' I replied honestly. It truly was good to see him.

'Hey, listen . . .' he trailed off and twisted his fingers into the hem of his shirt nervously. It was odd to see him act in such a way when he was usually so bright and full of life. 'I'm . . . I know you probably don't want to talk about it, but I'm so sorry for – for leaving you behind. I shouldn't have done that.'

I blinked in surprise. I opened my mouth to speak but was cut off by another rush of words from Dax.

'I just didn't think and I saw Hayden lying there bleeding all over the place and I panicked and brought him back instead of going after you and I—'

'Dax,' I said, cutting him off and raising my hand. He sucked in a breath and looked at me guiltily. 'It's okay.'

He breathed a sigh of relief and seemed to shrink as some of the nervous tension left his body. 'Really?'

'Yeah,' I said honestly. 'You saved his life. That's exactly what I would have wanted you to do.'

Dax was, for the first time possibly ever, silent. I continued.

'If you had let him die to come after me . . . I never would have forgiven you.'

Dax let out a gasp of a laugh.

'You two are scarily alike,' he told me. 'He basically said the same thing, except I kind of failed him by saving him and not you.'

'Can't win them all,' I said with a hint of a smile.

'Clearly,' he muttered with a small grin.

'Is he still angry?' I asked. It felt like so long since I'd absorbed any information that I felt stupid for not knowing. If Hayden had said anything, I couldn't remember.

'I don't know,' he said honestly with a shrug. 'I've hardly seen him since we got back. But he was furious with me before we went after you.'

'I'll talk to him,' I promised, pinching my lips together in a flat smile. 'Don't worry.'

Dax let out another sigh of relief and nodded. 'Thanks, Grace. If you need anything—'

'Leutie already covered it,' I said with a soft smile. Dax's eyes flitted to hers, and I saw the moment they shared. I suddenly felt like I was intruding. 'Thank you, though.'

His eyes flitted back to mine after blinking once.

'Sure thing.'

I nodded. 'I think I'm going to get back, but I'll see you guys later, yeah? Hopefully Kit and Malin, too.'

'We'll all be here whenever you're ready,' Leutie said. I was pleased to see Dax step closer to her and sling his arm around her shoulders, hauling her into his side.

'What m'lady said,' Dax quipped with another grin.

'Thanks again. See you guys later.'

We waved goodbye as I turned and headed towards our hut. I doubted Hayden would be back yet, but I wanted to be home when he returned. With this new-found strength, I wanted to use it to talk to him. It was like facing any other fear: you could avoid it for your entire life and live in constant apprehension, or you could flood yourself with what terrified you the most and desensitise yourself to it once and for all.

Just as I predicted, our hut was still empty. I felt as if my senses had been sharpened by the brief trip outdoors, and I found myself studying the few sentimental objects we possessed. All throughout our home, there were reminders of our previous lives and how we'd changed. I hoped that someday I would look back at this time as myself again rather than this off-kilter shell of a person.

I stood in front of the painting Jett had made of himself, Hayden, and me so long ago. I felt the expected pang of sadness in my heart as I looked at the careful lines he'd created with his own fingers. There was no denying that he'd brought light to our dark world, and even though he was gone, I was glad to have the happy reminder.

Next, my eyes landed on the small silver frame that housed the single photo I had of my family. It was the frame I'd taken from my dad's office, and it now sat on top of Hayden's desk. It seemed like a lifetime ago that I'd lost my father, and just as long ago that I'd been forced to lose my brother. The way my life had changed since then seemed unimaginable.

After that, I gently pulled open the bottom drawer to reveal Hayden's journal and his family's photo album. They lay nestled in their usual space, rarely brought out but not forgotten.

The last sentimental reminder hung around my neck; the fine gold chain was warm beneath my fingertips as I reached up to touch it gently. It still brought me comfort to wear it, the meaning behind it so pure. The contact with the necklace brought around another thought – something I had completely forgotten about in my ordeal.

Quickly, I moved to the dresser. I crouched down and opened my drawer, sifting through the contents quickly as I searched for the small package I'd hidden there. Confusion and then worry started to creep up when I couldn't find it, and my actions grew more haphazard as I shoved my clothes aside. I started to feel overly emotional when I couldn't find it, leaning back on my heels with a huff as I frowned at the drawer.

'Looking for this?'

I jumped, nearly falling backwards onto the floor. My breath quickened and eyes widened before I turned and realised it was only Hayden, who I hadn't heard come in. It took me a moment to calm down, and when I did, I saw his fingers closed lightly around the necklace he wore. I swallowed and stood, pushing my drawer closed once more.

'Yes,' I replied softly.

He regarded me for a few seconds before taking a few steps closer.

'I didn't mean to scare you,' he said gently, guilt clear in his eyes.

'It's okay,' I said, brushing it off. 'How did . . . Have you been wearing that this entire time?'

Hayden was quiet for a moment before answering. 'Yes.'

I felt a flash of embarrassment. Had I really been that closed off to the world that I hadn't even noticed? I was saved from thinking of something to say when he continued.

'I know I shouldn't have opened it but . . . I found it the day I came back for you. I couldn't ignore it.'

Slowly, I reached up to touch it, feeling the warm metal between my fingers before I let them fall once more.

'It was for your birthday,' I told him softly.

'I know,' he replied. I saw his hands shift by his sides as if he wanted to reach out for me, but he caught himself and pulled back.

'I missed it,' I said, voice barely a whisper now. My eyes flitted up to find his staring intently down at me.

'It doesn't matter,' he assured, shaking his head slowly. My heart panged.

'I'm sorry.'

A pained expression crossed Hayden's face as he caught the obvious sadness in my voice. Again, the Brutes had ruined what was supposed to be something special. In my dazed state, I had missed Hayden's birthday without even a thought. I felt terrible.

'No, Grace, don't be,' he urged. Again, his hands twitched by his sides. This time they curled into fists momentarily before relaxing. 'It really doesn't matter. Besides, I already opened my present early.'

He gave me a small, sad smile as he tried to get me to lighten up.

'Do you like it?' A flutter of nerves ran through my stomach.

'I absolutely love it,' he replied quickly, lips pulling up gently. 'It's perfect. Thank you.'

My soft smile widened a bit. 'You're welcome.'

Hayden's gaze held mine for a few more seconds before dropping to the floor. Thoughts seemed to be racing through his mind, but he didn't verbalise any of them. I was trying to think of something to say when he spoke again.

'How are you now?' he asked, eyes flitting back up towards mine. 'Honestly.'

'I'm . . .' I trailed off. The truth was that I would probably never feel the same. That much I knew. But today was a first for a lot of things, and I felt good about what I'd accomplished so far. 'I'm not sure, honestly, but I left our hut just now.'

Hayden's eyes widened in surprise. 'You did? What did you do?'

I drew another deep breath and took a few steps back to sit on the edge of our bed. Hayden copied me, sitting just a few inches away, though still careful not to touch me.

'Leutie came by, so I walked with her a bit. We went to see the crops and just talked. Not about anything that happened, really, but it was nice. I saw Dax, too.'

I could see the cautiously happy surprise in his expression. 'That's amazing, Grace. I'm so proud of you.'

'It got me thinking . . .' I trailed off. My fingers picked at the blanket beneath me, suddenly too preoccupied with twisting a stray thread to look at him.

'Yeah?' he nudged gently.

'I think I need to tell you what happened . . .'

Still, I couldn't look at him, even though I could practically feel his gaze burning into me.

'Only if you want to,' Hayden said softly.

'I do,' I said, nodding resolutely at the blanket. I steeled myself and managed to look up once more, meeting his intense eyes beneath heavily furrowed brows. I nodded and mentally prepared myself to relive the nightmare.

The next hour was spent telling him everything. I spoke in a hollow, flat tone as I recounted the things that haunted me. I told him about being dragged down into the Armoury after shooting him. I told him about seeing all the bodies, including those belonging to the last people of Greystone. I told him about being tied up, about being tortured. I told him about the men – the seemingly endless stream of men, though I couldn't seem to give details on that part. I didn't have to; he knew.

I told him how I'd found the knife, how I'd tricked Venn to lure him in only to kill him. I even told him of my rage when I'd mercilessly stabbed at his groin over and over again. I told him about those I killed on the way out, the bombs, finding a match to light them, feeling the explosions. Finally, I told him how I had all but given up hope and prepared to accept my fate when he appeared, pulling me from that cavern of terror just in time.

Throughout my entire recollection, he was silent. He watched me with obvious pain in his eyes, and somewhere in the middle, his hand had snaked out to grasp mine. Still, I had flinched, but not as badly as before, and I managed to hang onto it. His hand held mine now, his thumb running along the skin on my hand as he held my gaze intently.

'Wow, Grace,' he murmured softly when I finished speaking. It was clear hearing the story had hurt him very much, but he also seemed relieved that I'd finally spoken about it. He shook his head in gentle bewilderment. 'You are . . . incredible.'

I felt my chest sink slightly as I sucked in a breath, uncertain about how he would react. 'Not really.'

'You are,' Hayden rebuffed. 'Do you even know how strong you are? Do you know how many people would have given up after one of those things, much less all of them? And you did it all by yourself . . .'

I had grown so used to feeling numb that it felt odd to feel something again.

Odd, but good.

'You saved everyone by doing that – setting off those bombs. I'm so *proud* of you, Grace.'

Again, I didn't know what to say, so I just gave him a soft, sad smile.

'You're the strongest person I've ever met. I have no doubt about that. And I know you're dealing with a lot and you probably don't need me, but I'm *always* going to be here for you. I will do anything in my power to help you heal.'

'You're wrong,' I told him gently, frowning as I shook my head.

His eyes narrowed slightly in confusion.

'Hayden, I do need you,' I said honestly. 'Of course I want to be strong . . . but I know there will never come a day when I don't need you.'

'You'll always have me,' he reassured me. He squeezed my hand gently in his. I'd missed that feeling so desperately. 'You already know how much I need you, too, right?'

He ducked his head down to hold our eye contact.

'I know,' I replied softly. 'We need each other.'

'Exactly,' Hayden said with a soft smile. 'I'll do anything I any can to help you, okay?'

'Anything?' I asked, raising one brow. I'd been playing with an idea for a while, but I couldn't deny I was terrified to try. His hand felt nice in mine, and while I desperately wanted things to go back to how they were in a flash, I knew I couldn't. I had to take baby steps.

'Anything,' he repeated solemnly.

'I need you do something for me, Hayden,' I said slowly. I found it difficult to draw a full breath as my heart pounded in my chest.

'What's that, love?'

His voice was gentle as ever as he spoke, and his gaze had softened as he studied me.

'I need you to kiss me.'

Hayden's lips parted in surprise, and his thumb briefly froze over my skin before he collected himself and resumed his actions.

'Are you sure?' he breathed. Very little space remained between us, though we were still barely touching. I was reminded of way back when I first arrived in Blackwing, when the air would sizzle with tension between us at the slightest of touches. Even now, he had such a strong effect on me.

'I'm sure,' I replied as firmly as I could. My breath hitched in my throat nervously. Already, I could feel hints of flash-backs coming, but I was determined to try this.

'I don't want to scare you,' Hayden murmured, concern lacing his features.

'I need this, Hayden,' I pleaded softly. 'Please.'

Hayden frowned, clearly reluctant to do something that would almost certainly cause me pain, but the soft nod he gave showed he would obey my wishes. Gingerly, he raised his free hand, making sure I saw it before inching it towards my face. When the tips of his fingers brushed along my jaw, I sucked in a harsh breath and clamped my eyes shut. Immediately, I was flooded with the feeling of hands all over my body, the exact opposite of Hayden's gentle touch now.

'Grace, stay with me,' he breathed. 'It's just me.'

My legs jittered anxiously as I desperately tried to push off the memories, eyes squeezed tightly shut for a few moments before I managed to blow out a deep breath and open my eyes. Hayden's beautifully concerned face hovered in front of me, just a few inches away. Then his hand slid gently along my skin until his fingers hooked beneath my earlobe, cradling my face as gently as ever.

'I love you, Grace,' he whispered.

I could feel my body shaking as I waited, torn between anticipation and terror.

'I love you, Hayden.'

He gave the tiniest of nods and closed his eyes for a moment. Slowly, ever so slowly, he advanced, eliminating the tiny amount of distance between us. I managed to suck in one last stuttering breath before his lips pressed to mine, warm and gentle and tender.

Several things happened at once. The moment his lips touched mine, images of the dark Armoury, lips tugging at my skin, hands holding me down, and other traumas flashed through my mind. I flinched, but managed not to break the kiss as my eyes squeezed shut. I was frozen, as if accepting a kiss from a stranger rather than the man I loved.

Hayden surprised me by pulling back a fraction of an inch, where his lips fumbled against mine as he spoke softly once more.

'I love you, Bear. I'm here with you.'

He paused, his hand on my face and lips so close to my own I could practically still feel them.

'It's just me,' he continued, obviously noticing my fear and reaction. 'It's just you and me.'

I closed my eyes and felt my jaw quiver beneath his hand. Somehow, I had managed to stay in such close proximity. Somehow, I had let him kiss me.

'Kiss me again,' I pleaded softly, desperate to feel only the warmth of his kiss this time.

The air sizzled between us as Hayden paused for a few moments, building up the tension once more. This time when he pressed his lips to mine, the images came back, but they seemed weaker, fuzzier. Though I could still feel the nightmarish reminders, Hayden was there, too. Hayden's lips were on mine, warm and familiar and careful. Hayden's hand was on my face, holding me to him, while his other hand held mine.

Hayden, who loved me more than anything, was fighting off the images in my mind, pressing them down but not defeating them completely. It was enough, however, for me to finally react. My lips moulded gently against his for the first time, returning his gentle kiss. He felt my actions immediately, and I could practically feel the relief that flooded through him as if it carried over through our kiss.

It flooded through me, too.

It wasn't much. The terrors were still there, dark and demanding and horrifying as ever, but the fact that I was able to kiss Hayden without shutting down completely was a start. It seemed that maybe, just maybe, I could start to heal from the terrible wounds inflicted on my mind, body, and soul.

Twenty-Six: Hope

Hayden

The sun was warm on my face as I walked through camp, but it was nothing compared to the warmth I felt inside. Grace's hand was linked safely in mine, the innocent touch comforting on a much deeper level than it outwardly seemed. It had been two weeks since she'd asked me to kiss her, making it nearly a month since she'd escaped that terrible place. In that time, she continued to struggle against the demons that haunted her. Each day was a challenge, and simple things like holding my hand or kissing me still caused her to resist me at first, but she insisted.

'*I'm never going to get better if you refuse to touch me,*' she'd said after noting my reluctance. I had begun to train myself not to touch her at all. After that first kiss, she'd demanded I stop restraining myself. Even though I hated seeing her flinch away, I did as she requested, though I was always careful never to surprise her.

Slowly, she got better at fighting off the images. If she saw the touch coming, she hardly resisted at all anymore. She grew stronger by the day, and I continued to be in awe of her fortitude. To be able to simply hold her hand and kiss her again was one of the most incredible feelings I'd felt so far in our entire relationship. We hadn't tried anything else, although I suspected that would take a long, long time; I was absolutely content to move at whatever pace she wanted.

Though she was determined during the day, she remained haunted by nightmares almost every single night, and there was nothing I could do to help her. I'd hardly slept, anticipating the moment her breath would hitch and her limbs would start to fight so I could wake her as quickly as possible. I didn't mind; I'd give up sleep forever if it meant I could keep her from that. But it didn't always work, and no matter how little I slept or how tightly I held her, the nightmares still came.

Relentlessly, they came.

I'd wake her up, and her face would be flushed with a panicked sheen of sweat. Her lips would part as she gasped in shaky breaths, and her eyes would widen wildly until she found my face in the dark. I'd whisper quiet words of comfort and reassurance, careful not to make any sudden moves. Only then, with the familiar touch of my hand on her face, would she calm down.

Then, we would talk. Sometimes about her dream, sometimes about what we had for dinner, sometimes something completely random, like what we would do if we had lived fifty years ago. Anything, really, that would calm her down. Eventually her breathing would slow and her eyes would get heavy. She'd allow me to press a gentle kiss to her temple or cheek and murmur soft words of love before falling back to sleep.

That was my favourite moment, because she was the closest to peace since before she'd been taken to the Armoury. She'd sleep the rest of the night uninterrupted, and it was only then that I could sleep as well with that thought to comfort me.

She was healing, very slowly, very carefully, but she was

healing. These were my thoughts, as they so often were, as we walked together towards the infirmary.

'Hayden?'

Grace's voice drew my attention. I blinked and turned to her. I got the impression she'd called me a few times before I really heard it.

'Sorry, what did you say?'

She gave me a soft smile that sent a ripple through my stomach. Her smiles, though rarely the full-blown smiles from before, were also growing more frequent. I'd missed seeing her happy.

'I asked if you want to eat after this,' she said patiently.

'Oh, sure,' I replied with a casual shrug.

'Okay,' she said with a contented look.

I thought I saw a hint of something else in her features, but it was gone before I could decipher it as we arrived at the infirmary. Pulling open the door, I held it for her before following her inside. Her hand stayed connected with mine as we made our way to the back where Docc worked. His back was to us as he sorted through one of his cabinets, but he seemed to hear our footsteps and he turned to greet us.

'Grace, Hayden,' he said with a calm smile. 'Good to see you both.'

'Hi, Docc,' Grace greeted.

The infirmary seemed strangely empty now. Shaw, its long-time resident, had finally been allowed to leave after making a full recovery. Since Greystone was now gone – something I had learned from Grace – he had nowhere left to go. We'd decided, after much debate and opposition on my part, to allow him to assimilate into Blackwing. He was constantly supervised and never allowed anywhere dangerous, but in the few weeks since he'd left the infirmary, he'd caused no trouble. Despite how much I hated him and how despicable I thought he was, there was no denying our common goal made us part of the same team. Now that the threats were gone, he was left to live in Blackwing as part of our camp whether I liked him or not.

'What can I do for you?' Docc asked, redirecting my thoughts once more.

'You said to come back in a few weeks,' I said. I lifted my injured shoulder and tipped my head towards it, reluctant to release Grace's hand to indicate.

'Ah, yes, let's have a look,' Docc replied.

Then, I was forced to drop her hand to reach behind me and tug at the nape of my neck to remove my shirt. The gunshot wound in my shoulder was still there, but after over a month of healing, the damage was much less significant. It hardly hurt anymore, and needed only a small, square bandage on either side.

Docc moved forward and removed the bandages carefully, ducking down to get a good look at things. He prodded gently at the skin, while Grace observed curiously. She'd taken to tending the wound when we were not with Docc; he'd given us a small stash of treatments to keep in our hut. Grace seemed to enjoy taking care of me, which was good to see because it reminded me of her instincts from before her ordeal.

'Have you finished your antibiotics?' Docc asked. He shuffled around behind me to inspect the other wound.

'Yeah, last week,' I told him.

'Good, good.'

He prodded around a little more before returning to his cupboard to get some supplies. He applied a dab of cream to the wounds before putting another small dressing over each one.

'It looks to be healing nicely. As long as you keep changing your dressing every day and keep it clean, I don't foresee any problems.'

'Excellent, thank you.' Grace handed me my shirt and I pulled it back over my head.

Docc gave a small nod and a gentle smile. I was about to say goodbye when Grace spoke.

'Hey, Docc?'

He gave her the same admiring look he always adopted when addressing her. 'Yes?'

'I, um, it's time for my next birth control shot, right?'

I felt my lips part in surprise as she spoke. It hadn't even crossed my mind that she would be due, because I hadn't thought of anything of that nature in ages.

'Yes,' Docc said evenly with a serene nod. 'If you wish to continue your regimen, you should get it sometime this week.'

'Would now be okay?' she asked. My eyes searched her face, but she did not look at me.

'Certainly,' replied Docc. Again, he turned to his cabinet to get his supplies. I lowered my voice to murmur to her.

'Grace, you don't—'

She cut me off with a dismissive shake of her head. Docc returned with a few items. I watched as he ran an alcohol swab over the skin on her arm before counting down softly for her.

'Three, two, one . . .'

He pushed the needle into her skin, and I was relieved she didn't twitch. After a few seconds, he took it out and threw it away.

'Okay, you're all set,' he told her with a pensive look. 'Anything else I can do for either of you?'

'No, thank you,' Grace replied. She gave him a small smile and wave. 'See you later.'

He nodded in acknowledgement and went back to whatever he'd been doing before we arrived. I was surprised when Grace took my hand of her own accord as she started towards the door. It wasn't until we were outside and walking through camp that she spoke without looking at me.

'I know I just got the shot but that doesn't mean . . . I'm not ready yet, I just want to be prepared for whenever I am.'

She spoke quickly, as if trying to get the words out without really feeling them. I frowned and stopped walking, tugging on her hand so she stopped, too. She flashed me a confused look as she turned to face me. We stood in the middle of a path in the middle of camp.

'I'm sorry,' she continued, slightly flustered. 'I'm trying my best but—'

'Grace, I don't care about that,' I said seriously. It was hard to keep some of the bewilderment out of my voice. She blinked.

'I know,' she replied, nodding earnestly. 'But—'

'No, seriously,' I said. I shook my head adamantly and stared intently into her eyes. 'There's no rush. I can wait forever. Hell, we could never be together again if you didn't feel comfortable and that would be perfectly fine.'

My words were meant to console her, but her frown only deepened.

'You don't want to be with me?'

She had completely misunderstood.

'Grace, *no,* that's not it at all. I love you and of course I want to be with you but . . . the last thing I want to do is hurt or scare you. Whenever you're ready, I'll be here, but not a day sooner. If that day never comes, then that's fine, too. I'll always love you no matter what.'

Slowly, I raised my hand and let my fingertips brush gently across her cheek before dipping below her ear to cradle her chin; she didn't flinch as she held my gaze. I felt the warm heat of her hands as she let them rest there.

'I love you so much,' she whispered. I could feel the emotion radiating off her, feel it vibrate through the small space that separated us, and feel it sink into my skin and settle into my bones.

'You have no idea how much I love you.'

I was surprised when she stood on her toes to press a light kiss to my lips. It was one of the few kisses she'd initiated since coming back.

An excited squeal broke us apart, shattering our bubble. My gaze was torn from Grace's to see Leutie standing a short distance away, a wide grin hidden behind two hands clamped excitedly over her mouth. I was surprised by what looked like tears in her eyes. It was only then that I realised the odd location of our sudden intimate talk.

'I'm sorry,' she gushed quickly, wiping at her eyes. 'I was just on my way to eat and I didn't mean to interrupt, but I just couldn't help myself.'

Grace's hands lingered on my chest as my hand fell from her face, looping lightly around her back instead. My heart flipped as she flinched slightly, but it only took a moment for her to relax once more.

'It's okay,' Grace replied lightly. She leaned into me comfortingly.

'It's so nice to see you two like this,' Leutie said sincerely. Her honestly was reflected clearly in her adoring eyes.

'Did you say you were heading to eat?' Grace asked.

'Yes, I was going to meet—' She cut herself off, snapping her mouth shut as her eyes widened guiltily. They darted to me quickly before going back to Grace. 'I mean, I was hoping you'd be there!'

I frowned in confusion at her strange behaviour. I was

even more puzzled when she shot a very obvious wink at Grace. I glanced down at Grace to see her roll her eyes and shake her head in exasperation before giving a gasp of a laugh.

'Wonderful, let's go,' she said lightly.

'Yes, let's!' Leutie said a little overenthusiastically.

'What—'

'Come on, Hayden!' Leutie encouraged, cutting me off.

There was something clearly off about this conversation and I felt very suspicious but obliged Grace as we walked with Leutie towards the mess hall. My arm fell from around her waist to claim her hand once more. We hardly ever used to hold hands while walking through camp, but she liked it now. I suspected it was because it was one of the few things she could handle, so she wanted as much of it as she could.

Grace and Leutie chatted lightly, although Leutie made several other overly enthusiastic and confusing statements as if trying too hard to seem natural. When we entered the hall and made for a table, the reason for the strange behaviour became clear.

At the table, seated with their backs to me, were Kit and Dax. I'd hardly spoken to either of them since Grace had been taken by the Brutes. What little conversation we had maintained had been tense and formal, very unlike our normal interactions. I couldn't seem to let go of the resentment that they had both allowed Grace to be taken by the Brutes, choosing to save me over her. Though Dax had helped me get her back, things still weren't really normal again.

'I've been set up,' I mumbled in Grace's ear as we approached.

Leutie, now an obvious conspirator, shot me a guilty grin and darted forward, sitting next to Dax to leave the other side of the table for Grace and me. That was when Kit and Dax noticed us, both taken aback at my appearance. Grace sat down and released my hand to fold hers patiently in front of her, but I remained standing.

'Hayden, please sit,' she requested, glancing up at me.

My eyes, which had been fixed somewhat awkwardly on Kit and Dax, darted to hers to see her smiling at me. It was now clear what had happened: she and Leutie had set this up so that only one half of each couple knew the others would be present. I sighed and sat down next to her, meaning Kit and Dax were directly across the table.

'Brilliant, thank you,' Grace said smoothly. 'Now, I think we all know why we're here.'

'I was told there would be food,' Dax started. All he earned was a gentle slap on the arm from Leutie and a stern look.

'Only if you cooperate,' Grace replied. 'Look, I know it's not really my place to say this, but this has to stop.'

I scoffed and tried not to shoot everyone a derisive look. 'What does?'

'This whole not talking to each other thing,' she continued. 'You're like brothers and you hardly even speak anymore.'

I clenched my jaw tightly. While she was addressing the group, I felt like she was scolding me; everyone here knew that *I* was the one not speaking to them, not the other way around.

'What is this, an intervention?' I quipped. My eyes darted accusingly to Kit and Dax. Kit raised his hands in surrender and shook his head.

'Don't look at me. I had no idea about this until you showed up,' he said.

'We set this up,' Leutie interjected. She appeared torn

between apprehension and giddiness; it clearly pleased her we were at least all in the same place for once. 'Because . . . Grace, maybe you should explain.'

Grace sighed. 'We set this up because you need to forgive them, Hayden. They didn't do anything wrong.'

'They let you get taken by the Brutes!' I grumbled, forcing my voice to stay low even though I felt my muscles tensing up.

'They saved your life, Hayden,' she replied gently. 'And I'm still alive. It's not fair to blame them for things that were out of their control.'

My jaw clenched even tighter and I resisted the urge to cross my arms over my chest in defiance.

'I really am sorry, Hayden,' Kit said. It was the softest I'd ever heard his voice. He shrugged. 'Really, but we just acted quickly, you know?'

'Trust me, mate, I've felt like hell this last month and I'm sorry, too, but I'm not sorry that we saved you, either,' Dax replied. There was sadness on his usually happy face.

'I don't blame them and neither should you,' Grace murmured gently to me. I turned to look at her. She leaned into me so she was just a few inches away, as if speaking only to me now. 'I'm so grateful for what they did. And I know you miss them.'

I held her gaze for a few moments, thinking over her words before letting out a deep sigh. If she, who had suffered the most out of anyone, wasn't angry with them, then I shouldn't be either. And, she was right: I missed my best friends.

I gave her a small smile and a sigh of defeat before turning to look at them again.

'It's all right, guys. And I'm sorry for being an ass.'

A small 'eek' sound burst from Leutie's lips as she

observed our exchange. Kit and Dax both smiled in relief.

'No worries, Bossman. We all know how wrecked she's got you,' Dax said with a grin, pointing at Grace. She laughed and grinned widely, pleased her ambush had worked.

I felt the warmth of her shoulder against my arm as she leaned into me. 'You're right about that.'

'So how are you doing, Grace?' Kit asked.

Grace beamed at me for a moment longer before turning to address Kit. It was good to see her interacting with them again, and I had to admit I was grateful for her surprise intervention.

'I'm all right,' she answered honestly. 'This helps.' She continued, 'How are you, Kit? Healing up okay?'

'Yeah, I suppose. Took a pretty good chunk out of my leg with a knife and messed up a few of my tendons in my knee, but Docc thinks it'll be okay. At least I can walk again,' he finished with a chuckle.

'And at least you still have all your fingers,' Dax chided, lifting his left hand and wiggling his mutilated digits in the air. They had healed since he'd lost his pinkie and ring finger, making the little stumps clearly visible now. Laughter, led by Dax, rang around the table.

'We're a pretty rough-looking bunch,' Grace said with a self-deprecating laugh. I couldn't laugh as easily because I knew that even though she was trying to be casual, it was difficult for her. My wounds, and Kit's, and Dax's were superficial. Hers went deep, so deep that she would probably never fully leave them behind.

'I hardly fit in,' Leutie said with a soft smile.

'That's all right,' Dax said, reaching for her to pick up her hand. He pressed a light kiss to her knuckles. 'Keep your pretty fingers.'

Again, I glanced to Grace, where I was pleased to see her

watching the interaction with a smile on her face. She observed them for a few more seconds before her eyes went quickly to Kit.

'Hey, Kit, where's Malin?' she asked, as if just realising she was missing.

'Um.' Kit cleared his throat and let his eyes flit around between the group. He was clearly thinking something over as he hesitated to speak. Everyone waited in slightly confused but patient silence. He cleared his throat again and continued. 'She's not really feeling well, so she's at home.'

'That's a shame,' Leutie said sincerely, frowning on Malin's account.

Kit let out a somewhat awkward laugh and nodded before dropping our eyes. His finger tapped anxiously on the table before he took a deep breath.

'Well, the thing is . . .'

My brows lowered curiously as I watched him, clearly extremely nervous as he stalled.

'Yes . . .?' Grace urged. She wore a quickly widening grin as if she already knew what he was going to say.

'She's not feeling well because . . .'

He paused again and looked up at everyone. A swelling, anxious silence buzzed between as we waited.

'Because Malin is pregnant.'

'I knew it!' Grace exclaimed quickly. My jaw fell open in surprise. I looked across the table to see Dax wiping a similar expression off his face and replacing it with a wide, conspiratorial grin. Leutie let out another excited squeal and folded her hands together in front of her.

'Is it yours?' Dax asked, wearing a shit-eating grin. Kit scoffed and shoved Dax's shoulder in a roughly playful way.

'Of course it's mine, you idiot,' he replied, shaking his

head. He appeared torn between amusement and indignation.

'This is so lovely, congratulations, Kit!' Leutie exclaimed. She leaned around Dax with her elbow on the table to beam at Kit. 'How far along is she?'

'Docc reckons about three months.' He looked relieved now that he'd finally told us.

'Is that why you got married?' I asked curiously.

'No,' he replied, shaking his head. 'We didn't plan it, mind you. She missed one of her birth control shots and . . . Well, you know how that works. We just found out about three weeks ago but . . . it didn't seem like the right time to tell everyone. With all that had happened.'

Everyone nodded understandingly.

'Congratulations, Kit,' Grace said sincerely. 'Tell Malin for us, will you? Hopefully we can see her soon.'

'Thank you, and I will,' he replied with a grin.

'You're going to be a freaking *dad*!' Dax said loudly. He nudged him in the shoulder. 'That's awesome, man. Congrats.'

It was such a strange thing to be discussing, and Kit was about the last one I figured to have a child first, but he seemed to be happy about it, so I was happy for him.

'I'm really excited,' he admitted with a shy grin.

'That's saying a lot, coming from you,' I laughed. Grace leaned into me again, so I slipped my arm loosely around her waist to let her settle casually into my side.

'Tell me about it,' he chuckled. 'Luckily we have quite a bit of time left. I'm not quite healed up enough to take care of a baby just yet.'

'We'll help you, I love babies,' Leutie offered instantly. 'Grace and I, won't we?'

'Of course,' Grace replied lightly. 'I don't know the first thing about babies, but I'll see what I can do.'

'Thanks, everyone,' Kit said with a sincere smile. 'Seriously.'

The chatter carried on, the mood the lightest it had been in a long time, and I hoped it would be a sign of good things to come. Maybe we could all move on from the tragedies of our past and start a new phase of life. Maybe we could learn from what we'd gone through but not completely forget. Maybe our world could slowly, ever so slowly, start to become a better place.

It was a strange and surreal feeling, something I wasn't quite used to, but it was there all the same: hope.

Twenty-Seven: Impatience

Grace

The sun was just starting to peek through the grimy windows of our hut when I awoke, unable to sleep much longer thanks to my restlessness the night before. My body felt warm because of the way Hayden was wrapped comfortingly around me. I was curled into his chest, facing him with my arms tucked between us while he held me securely, as if protecting me from the dark. The soft tickle of his breath grazed over my temple, and I could feel the quiet patter of his heart beneath his bare chest. He was still asleep, and though I felt wide awake, I was more than content to let him rest.

It had been three weeks since we'd learned of Malin's pregnancy, and in that time, I was slowly learning to live again. I left our hut more and more frequently, started taking short shifts on duty, and most importantly, was learning to let Hayden touch me without freezing. It was still incredibly difficult, and I hadn't been able to do anything beyond cuddling or minimal kissing, but there was progress.

He could hold me throughout the night without me fighting him off in my sleep. My nightmares were no longer an every-night occurrence, though they still frequented my dreams. He could reach for my hand or gently touch my back without more than a tiny flinch. These were all good signs, and I was grateful for them, but each time I tried to push things, Hayden would hold back. On the few occasions our gentle kisses had intensified, Hayden had retreated the moment I showed any sign of fear.

I loved him for his unwillingness to scare me, but it was getting frustrating that I couldn't push myself to try to heal further. I felt like I was stuck, locked in the same place I'd been for weeks now. So desperately did I want things to just go back to normal, but they wouldn't. I wanted Hayden to be able to touch or kiss me without hesitation, without worry. I wanted him to be able to surprise me with his touch without fearing my reaction. I wanted to share that connection that was so beautiful for us. Whether it was my own mind and body rebelling against me, or Hayden's reluctance to push me, it seemed my progress was halted.

I let out a heavy sigh and snuggled closer to Hayden, trying to shake off the thoughts, but it was impossible. I took in every tiny detail of his sleeping features, noting the subtle changes that had occurred. It had been almost a year since I'd first arrived in Blackwing, in which time his features had sharpened slightly.

After studying him so closely, I felt the urge to press a kiss along his jaw. I shifted ever so slightly so I could push my lips against his skin, light and unnoticed by the sleeping man I loved so much. I moved again, dragging my lips down his jaw a little closer to his mouth, where I pressed another gentle kiss. He stirred this time, shifting slightly as his eyes fluttered for a second, yet still he did not wake up. A light giggle floated between my lips as I repeated my action one last time, placing my lips just on the corner of his.

This time, I was rewarded with a flash of green as his eyes sprang open. It took him a few seconds to realise what had awoken him, but I didn't give him the chance to speak before leaning forward and pressing my lips gently into his own.

He pulled me lightly against him, breathing in the kiss in the early morning light. My heart was pounding much harder than such a gentle kiss should have warranted, but this was what happened every time we kissed now. Some of it was good, yet it was impossible to ignore the tiny shards of fear.

'Morning.' Hayden's voice was rough and sleepy, his soft smile somewhat lazy as he held me closely.

'Morning,' I returned softly.

I felt strangely pensive and determined all at once, and before Hayden could speak any further, I closed the distance between us again. My lips met his as I drew myself as close to his body as possible. I hadn't been able to kiss him for more than a few minutes up until this point, and I was determined to push past that barrier.

Hayden seemed surprised but went along with them as he kissed me back. His actions were slow and gentle, but I could feel the heat building between us when I ran my tongue along his lower lip, attempting to push things further. A low groan rumbled from Hayden's throat when I hitched my leg over his hip, tightening our contact.

As we kissed I felt love, heat, fear, resistance, and so many other things I couldn't quite pinpoint. It felt good to kiss him, and while I wanted more, I was afraid. Even now, as his lips moved over mine and his hands held me to him, I couldn't quite ignore the chill that ran down my spine. I tried to push it down and focus on the way Hayden's jaw felt beneath my thumb as I raised my hand to his face, the way his lips moulded against mine, the way his tongue tentatively met my own, and it seemed to be working.

With new-found strength, I rolled onto my back and

dragged Hayden with me, shifting so his body covered mine. He paused his actions, breaking our kiss and pulling back to look me in the eye. I cut him off with a quick shake of my head before reaching up and pulling him back down to me.

His lips found mine again, and the warm heat of his body was restored as he rested some of his weight on me. He placed one of his elbows by my head to support him, while the hand of his other arm rose to cradle one side of my face. His actions were still slow, but there was an undeniable intensity, a burning lust, building between us. I had almost forgotten what it felt like, and I yearned to feel it again without the crippling shadows of fear.

When he broke our kiss to trail his lips lightly down my neck, I let my eyes close and enjoy the warmth. He made no attempt to touch me, but at least he hadn't stopped kissing me yet. I could feel the wet heat of his tongue as it darted against my skin, and then he reached my collarbone.

Suddenly, as if transported back in time, flashes of hands and foreign lips on my body darted through my mind. I flinched harshly away from his touch, snapping my eyes shut in fear as a shaky breath ripped from my lungs. Instantly, Hayden stopped his actions and practically jumped off me, landing on the bed beside me once again.

'Grace, oh god, I'm so sorry,' he lulled quickly, voice laden with regret and anxiety. 'I shouldn't have . . . I'm sorry—'

'It's okay,' I breathed. My eyes were still shut, but I managed to slow my breathing. I blew out a deep breath and gave myself another few seconds to recover before opening my eyes. I turned to the side to see him propped up on one elbow, hovering just out of reach with an anxious expression on his face.

'I'm sorry,' he repeated, hanging his head guiltily.

'No, it's okay,' I replied weakly, shaking my head.

'I feel terrible—'

'No, Hayden,' I repeated more sternly. I forced myself to roll back to my side so I faced him once more. 'That was my doing, not yours.'

He frowned, unconvinced. I reached out to link my fingers lightly with his.

'That's what I need to do . . . push myself,' I told him gently. 'Or I'll be stuck where I am and never move past this.'

'I don't want to scare you though,' he murmured softly, concern written across his features.

'Maybe that's what I need,' I replied. 'I don't want this to stop me from things being how they were, you know?'

'I know, love, but you don't have to rush it. You can take all the time you need.'

His fingers squeezed mine gently as I chewed on my lower lip. He was so patient and so gentle with me, but I wondered if that was hindering my healing.

'I know that but . . . I just want things to go back to normal.'

'It will be,' he said calmly. He lifted my hand and kissed the back of it. 'Eventually.'

I let out a frustrated, dejected sigh and rolled forward so I was face down on the bed, leaning my shoulder into him and pushing my head into the space between his chest and the pillow.

'It'll be okay, Grace,' he murmured gently.

'What if it's not?' I mumbled, words muffled by the pillow. I felt his hand land on my back before rubbing gently up and down.

'It will be,' he repeated.

'I need you to help me,' I said. I emerged to look back up

at him again. I rolled to my back, allowing Hayden to hover over me as he lay on his side right next to me. His hand rose to gently push a few stray hairs off my face.

'What can I do?' he asked.

'You've been so amazing with me, Hayden, and I love you for that, but . . .' I paused, gathering my thoughts. 'You have to push me. You have to keep going even if I flinch or get scared.'

Hayden frowned immediately, clearly unhappy with my plan.

'I don't like that, Grace,' he said lowly.

'I know, but I need you to,' I pleaded, although I didn't want to seem unappreciative of how amazing he'd been so far. 'I want to be able to be with you, but I never will if you stop every time I so much as flinch.'

The idea seemed to concern him greatly, because his frown was deeper than ever.

'That's really what you want?' he murmured.

'Yes, Herc,' I answered truthfully. I knew it would hurt him to push me, but it was essential if I ever wanted to have a normal life again.

Hayden sighed heavily, anguish clear in his eyes. 'Okay, Bear.'

I smiled, relieved and anxious all at once. 'Thank you.'

'You can always change your mind,' he reminded me. I nodded.

'I know, but I won't. I need this so I can move on and make everything go back to normal.'

Hayden nodded slowly, and it was obvious he still did not approve of the plan, but he'd agreed to it, and I was grateful.

'If you really want me to do this, I will,' he said, pausing. 'Just not today, okay?'

My disappointment was obvious. 'Why not?'

'Because,' he said gently, ducking down to kiss me once more. I received his kiss with a mixture of confusion, rejection, and dismay. 'I already scared you once today and I don't want to do that again.'

'But Hayden—'

I was cut off by another kiss pressed to my lips. He spoke as he pulled away. 'Not today, Bear.'

I sighed heavily. 'If not today, when?'

It was such a strange thing to argue about, when to finally be together again, but my impatience was driven by a desperate desire to have things back to normal.

'When would you like?' he asked softly. His fingers still continued their gentle tracing along my temple.

A sudden idea sparked in my mind, and I instantly knew it would be perfect.

'In five days,' I said decisively.

'Why so specific?'

'Because that's my birthday,' I told him. 'And I can't think of anything I want more.'

'It's your birthday in five days?' he asked, surprised. 'Why didn't you say anything?'

I shrugged. 'I forgot about it until right now.'

His eyes fixed on mine. 'You sure that's what you want?'

'Yes,' I replied earnestly. 'I just want you.'

'Okay,' he responded softly. 'As you wish.'

'Thank you,' I replied happily, pleased I'd finally got my way. Now, I would have a few days to really sort out my thoughts and prepare myself.

'Mmhmm,' he hummed softly. His fingers gave one last gentle brush along my temple before he ducked down to kiss my forehead, then pulled away. 'Time to get up?'

'Yes,' I replied, feeling more satisfied than I had a few minutes ago.

Hayden and I got out of bed and dressed properly. We spent the day doing a lot of wandering: we visited the mess hall for meals, checked up on the crops, checked in with those on duty, and a number of other tedious tasks that quickly bored me. My mind seemed unable to focus on much else besides our conversation from earlier. I still felt a mess of emotions, and I attempted to push the bad from my mind, but they refused to leave me alone. They lingered constantly, no matter what we did.

As the day went on, I noticed a general lack of urgency in the camp. Unlike the past, there was nothing that needed to be taken care of, nothing that needed to be investigated. It seemed that with the threats from Greystone and the Brutes gone and the tentative friendship with Whetland holding, things had finally started to settle down. I didn't dare hope that it would last, but a tiny part of me wondered if this could truly be a fresh start for what was left of civilisation.

At the end of the day, Hayden and I retired to our hut. I felt acutely aware of him as he moved around, as if my mind and body were impatiently awaiting the time five days from now. Nerves swirled in the pit of my stomach every time I thought of it, and every once in a while the cold grip of imaginary hands would clench around my heart, but after a deep breath and a glance in Hayden's direction, I was able to push them off.

When we got into bed, I was able to let Hayden pull me against him without reacting at all. He murmured some quiet words to me as I settled against him. I felt content, impatient, and somewhat scared all at once as I fell asleep, reassured by his constant presence and attentiveness. That night, no nightmares awoke me, and I managed to sleep soundly.

The next few days were more of the same. Our activities were monotonous with little to worry about; camp was practically running itself, and it seemed there was less for Hayden to do with each passing hour.

In contrast, by the day before my birthday, there was a sustained nervous tingle in my stomach. I couldn't focus on any one thing, constantly distracted by Hayden's lips as he spoke or his hand as it brushed innocently along my back. Even the way his forearm flexed when he reached for something seemed to hypnotise me. There were several occasions where my name had to be repeated before I heard it.

Finally, the day had come. The morning of my birthday, I was awoken gently by Hayden's lips mumbling at my ear. My back was pressed to his chest, and his arm was looped around my waist to hold me against him.

'Wake up, Grace,' he murmured. I let out a low groan and squeezed my eyes shut, fighting off the light filtering into our hut.

'Hmm,' I hummed. He squeezed my arm lightly, and I blindly reached for his hand. I found it near my stomach and gripped it, hugging it to my chest.

'Happy birthday,' he said lightly. I could practically hear the grin in his voice.

I smiled but let my eyes remained closed. Nerves immediately assaulted me, and quick flashes from the Armoury flitted through my mind, but Hayden's light kiss along the hinge of my jaw helped dim them. I rolled onto my back, allowing him to lay against me. When I finally opened my eyes, I saw him beaming down at me.

'Morning,' he said with a soft grin.

'Good morning,' I returned, sending him a sleepy smile.

'You slept the whole night,' he told me proudly. In the

five days since our conversation, I'd only had that one nightmare a few days ago.

'I did.'

'So it's your birthday,' he reminded me with a lopsided grin that brought out the dimple in his cheek.

'It is,' I agreed, smiling at him. He didn't respond right away, which gave me the chance to reach up and pull his lips down to mine, meeting in a gentle kiss. 'You know what that means.'

We met again and he kissed me back for a second. 'Mmhmm,' he hummed. 'But not yet. I have some things planned for you.'

I blinked in surprise. 'You do?'

'I do,' he said, somewhat smug.

'What might that be?' I asked, raising an eyebrow.

'You'll have to see,' he said with a shrug. He then shot me a wide, cheeky grin before pulling away and jumping out of bed. 'Up you get.'

I frowned. I'd waited five days for this day to finally come, and now it seemed I would have to wait a bit longer. Hayden grinned widely at me from across the room. Reluctantly, I climbed out of bed.

'All right, I'm up. Let's see what you've got planned.'

'Excellent,' he said happily. He beamed at me as he moved to get dressed. I followed him and had just started to pull my drawer open when Hayden spoke.

'Are you planning to wear socks?' he asked. I glanced at him in confusion and saw him failing miserably at holding back a wide grin.

'I was going to, why?'

'Don't bother,' he said with a forced frown and shake of his head. 'This will blow them right off.'

I snorted a laugh, grabbing the socks I had been about to

put on and throwing them at Hayden. They hit him in the chest before he caught them, his eyes crinkling mischievously in the corners.

'You and your damn sock jokes,' I laughed, shaking my head in endearment.

'You love it,' he teased, tossing my socks back to me. I caught them and pulled them onto my feet.

'I do indeed,' I admitted, beaming at him. He put on a shirt and came to stand in front of me. He reached out to cradle the side of my face as his happy, amused smile faded to a softer one.

'I want you to have a good day, Bear,' he murmured gently. 'You deserve it.'

'I can already tell I will,' I replied, smiling at him gently.

'Off we go, then,' he said lightly.

I nodded, sure that whatever he had planned would be perfect. Between the mystery that surrounded our plans and the knowledge of what we had planned for later that night, I hoped it would be the first day where I felt truly and completely happy.

With any luck, it would be the first of many.

Twenty-Eight: Sublime

Grace

'Just a little further,' he said happily

My mind raced in a thousand different directions as Hayden led me through camp. It was a beautifully warm, sunny day, as if the universe had decided to give me a break on my birthday. I felt pleasantly curious as to what he had planned. He clearly took great pleasure in denying me any details. I gave up trying to figure it out and decided to simply enjoy the day.

It was still early, so there weren't many people out in camp yet, only a few heading to the mess hall for breakfast. I was surprised when Hayden's hand tugged me in a different direction, along the side of the mess hall until we came upon a smaller structure. Hayden halted, stopping me as well.

'Do you remember this?' he asked, grin on his face.

My eyes darted to the side to take in the small well that was composed of old, crumbling bricks. It was slightly crooked, as if the ground it sat on was uneven, but it still functioned perfectly. A memory flitted through my mind of the time just shortly after my arrival in Blackwing: it had been stormy, and a heavy downpour had threatened to cave in the well, which would have cut off Blackwing's only source of water for miles around. In the mess of making sure it remained upright, Hayden and I, along with a few others, had got absolutely covered in mud. I remembered what had followed with a grin.

'I certainly do,' I finally answered, smiling up at him.

'This well,' Hayden continued, raising a hand between us to point at it, 'is the reason I got to kiss you for the first time.'

'In the shower that you said would only have enough for one,' I continued, grin widening even more.

'I might have lied about that,' Hayden admitted.

'Oh, did you?' I laughed. He bit down on his lower lip guiltily and nodded, holding back a grin.

'Can't say I regret it.'

'I can't say I do, either.'

I remembered the very first time Hayden had kissed me. It had been the first real moment of intimacy between us and I'd shoved him away after, but it wasn't long before it happened again, as if we couldn't manage to stay away from each other even though we both knew we should. There was no resistance now as he bent to kiss me.

'Was this my surprise?' I asked.

'Oh, no,' Hayden said with an amused scoff. 'Just a small part of it.'

'Pulled out the big guns, did you?' I laughed.

'Hey, I didn't warn you about the socks for no reason.'

I laughed and shook my head in amusement. Hayden beamed at me for a few more moments before pulling me down a different path. A comfortably happy silence settled over us.

We were heading towards the edge of camp, where we'd been several times before a raid or any travel. Within a few moments, we arrived at the garage. Hayden shot me a quick grin over his shoulder before pulling me inside. It was fairly dark, but the beaming sunlight from outside made it possible to see around us. Hayden tugged me past the few vehicles housed inside and along the edge.

'Okay, stay here,' he requested, dropping my hand as he walked away. My eyes drifted to the workbench along the wall as another memory came to mind. It seemed to come to Hayden's as well, because he paused and turned. 'Kissed you there, too.'

I grinned as I remembered the time we'd come back from the cliff where I'd thought he would kiss me but hadn't. But then he'd lifted me and pushed me onto the bench only to be interrupted moments later.

My lips parted in happy surprise when Hayden appeared, wheeling out the motorcycle I'd only had the chance to ride a few times.

'Fancy a go?' Hayden asked, pleased with my reaction.

'Yes!' I said eagerly. We hadn't had a chance to enjoy it for a long, long time.

'I thought you might,' he replied. He ticked his head and beckoned me before handing me a helmet. He gave me another gentle kiss before I set the helmet in place. I admired Hayden's agility as he mounted the motorcycle. He started it and held it steady as I climbed on behind him, my arms looped lightly around his narrow waist.

'Ready?' he called over the roar of the engine.

'Ready!'

I gasped as Hayden pulled on the throttle, rocketing us out of the garage and onto the path worn into the ground. He turned to the side and headed through the trees, keeping to the path. My hair whipped out from beneath the helmet, and my shirt fluttered out behind me as we drove. My body felt light, airy, and free as Hayden steered us down the path and up the hill.

I held one arm tightly around his waist and allowed my

other to drift out beside me, enjoying the feel as the wind slid past my skin. I couldn't stop the wide beaming smile from taking over my face. It was such a thrill to share this with him again, and it brought me back to the first time, just as everything else we'd done so far. It was so surreal to look back and see how much things had changed, and I knew Hayden was the absolute best thing to ever happen to me.

My elation didn't diminish as we climbed the hill, and it seemed like only minutes before Hayden slowed the motorcycle and brought it to a stop. He killed the engine and allowed me to climb off before doing the same, setting the brake easily to park it. I pulled off my helmet, ignoring the surely very tangled state of my hair because of how much fun I was having.

'How was that?' Hayden asked, with a beaming smile and eyes glowing with happiness.

'Amazing,' I replied truthfully. 'I forgot how much I love that.'

'Yeah?' he asked.

'Yeah,' I nodded. I stepped forward and looped an arm around his neck, tugging him down to press my lips to his. The adrenaline from the ride was still running through me, and it spilled over into our kiss. I felt stirrings of desire as he let his lips part to melt into my own, as if the thrill of the ride had given me strength I'd been so desperately wanting to regain.

Hayden pressed his lips against mine one last time before pulling back. I couldn't stop the small rush of disappointment, but as soon as I took in the beautifully happy grin on his face, it washed away. His hand slid from my waist to capture my hand.

'Come on,' he said.

I let him lead me through the familiar area, battling under

branches until we broke through to a view that still took my breath away.

My eyes scanned over our world as it sprawled out before us from the high vantage point of the cliff. I could see hints of Blackwing, like the tower and a few huts that managed to show through the trees. I could see the shattered remains of the city, which was mostly uninhabited now that the Brutes were gone. Very far off, I could see the river snake along and the area I knew to be Whetland. And finally, I could see what remained of my former home, Greystone. A small wave of sadness ran through me as I remembered no one was left to live there, either.

'This is the place I started to let you in,' Hayden said, regaining my attention. I turned slowly to him, meeting his intense gaze. The carefree happiness from moments ago had dwindled now to a more serious mood. 'Even if neither of us realised it yet.'

My heart gave a heavy thump at his words. It meant so much to relive these little moments. Now, more than ever, when I was struggling with getting back to normal, this was exactly what I needed: to be reminded of everything we'd gone through and how exactly we'd grown together.

My hands reached up automatically to run my thumbs lightly along either side of his jaw before hitching just beneath his ears. He gazed down at me with a heavy intensity I could practically feel occluding the air around us.

'I love you so much, Hayden.'

'Never as much as I love you.'

I gave an involuntary shake of my head and resisted a smile. We could argue until we were old and grey about that fact and never believe the other to be right. I was content to disagree upon it.

'You're crazy,' I murmured. I lured him slowly towards

me, allowing our eyes to meet. The moment sizzled between us for a few delicious seconds before we finally succumbed and kissed.

When Hayden pulled back, I caught the slightly mischievous look in his eye.

'Crazy about you,' he said before opening his mouth in an overly expectant expression. I snorted a laugh and felt a grin break onto my face.

'Cheesy.'

He shrugged, unconcerned.

'So are picnics, but I brought you one of those, too.'

I blinked in confusion and looked around. He turned and retreated to the motorcycle, disappearing into the bushes for a few seconds. I could hear some rustling before he reappeared, a duffel bag clutched in his hands.

'We were out of cutesy baskets, I'm afraid, so I hope this is okay,' he said with another grin. He patted the duffel bag as he approached me and reclaimed my hand, leading me towards the place we always sat near the edge of the cliff.

'You actually brought me a picnic,' I said, both surprised that he'd thought of such a thing and that I hadn't noticed the duffel bag hidden on the motorcycle. I'd probably been distracted by the attractive man on top of it.

'Mmhmm, I did,' he murmured.

We reached the spot and he dropped my hand, putting down the duffel before unzipping it and rummaging around inside. I watched as he pulled out a blanket, two bags of what I assumed was food, and much to my surprise, a candle. Very carefully, he spread out the blanket on the ground, shooing me away when I tried to help. Then he placed a bag of food for each of us on either side of the candle, which he lit with a match that he produced from the bag.

'For you, my darling,' he made a sweeping gesture of the

spread he'd just prepared. I could tell he was somewhat amused with himself, but I felt touched he'd gone to such trouble without me suspecting a thing.

'This is amazing, Hayden,' I said, voice soft with awe.

'You like it?' he asked. He raised his brows and seemed pleased with my reaction.

'I love it.'

'I'm glad, because you deserve it,' he said with a nod. 'Now come here.'

He surprised me again. Despite having set our food out separately, he wasted no time in pulling me close to him, so I was positioned between his thighs, as he leaned against our favourite rock.

Whatever else he had planned would surely be amazing, but at that moment, I found it difficult to believe there was anything better than sitting with the one person I loved more than anything, looking out over a devastatingly beautiful view that seemed to spell out our life together so far. Surely this was the epitome of happiness.

We might have stayed like that forever, settled into silence with nothing but gentle caresses of each other's skin, if it weren't for our stomachs rumbling loudly. I tried to ignore it at first, but after a few minutes, it became almost comical how often both our stomachs were growling. But rather than untangle ourselves, we remained wrapped up in each other as we ate our meals. It was nothing special, nothing any better or worse than what we usually ate, but at that moment, it tasted like the most delicious meal I'd ever eaten.

Time passed, though I was hardly aware of it. Only the sun slipping from the sky marked the hours that ticked by. Our conversations were few and far between, but it didn't matter. Sometimes words weren't needed to convey such emotion as was flowing between us then. Hayden's hands never stopped running over my arms. His lips never stopped peppering gentle kisses into my shoulder, my neck, my cheek. I couldn't stop my own fingers from tracing little patterns into his skin, bringing fascinating goosebumps to the surface wherever I touched him.

It was in a way the most simple afternoon, but it was undoubtedly incredible in every way fathomable.

By the time it started to get dark, Hayden breathed a heavy sigh and squeezed me around the shoulders. His voice was low and easy as he murmured into my ear. 'We should go, Bear.'

I leaned back into his chest and let my head fall to his shoulder, tilting it so I could look him in the eye. 'Okay.'

He smiled, then bent to press a lingering kiss, to which I responded at once.

Then, with contented smiles and light-hearted moods, we finally rose from the ground and gathered up the picnic supplies. Hayden packed them back into the duffel before taking my hand once more to lead me back to the motorcycle. It wasn't long before we were zooming back down the hill that led to the cliff.

It seemed much darker beneath the canopy of the trees than it had moments ago at the top of the cliff, and I knew that it would probably be completely dark by the time we got back to camp. My heart started to race as I thought of Hayden's promise, which seemed to be creeping closer and closer to its moment of fulfilment. I'd managed to avoid thinking about it during the day, but now, with the impending nightfall, the sizzling nerves in the pit of my stomach became impossible to ignore. Today had been absolutely perfect, and I hoped it would continue that way; if I ruined it by not being able to handle it, I'd never forgive myself.

My thoughts kept me from fully enjoying the remainder

of the ride, and it seemed like no time at all before we arrived back at the garage. Hayden drew inside and let me climb off before putting away the motorcycle and taking my helmet.

'Thank you for today, Hayden. Everything was perfect.'

Hayden's lips pulled to the side in a somewhat amused smile.

'Oh, it's not over yet,' he said slyly. I frowned in confusion.

As if on cue, a loud round of laughter came ringing through camp. Automatically, my body turned towards the sound, where I noticed a bright glow emitting from the centre of Blackwing. Turning back around, I narrowed my eyes suspiciously and aimed them at Hayden.

'What's that?' I asked, raising a brow. Hayden shrugged, pulling the corners of his lips down in exaggeration.

'Not sure, let's go check it out.'

He grinned mischievously and reached for my hand. My heart gave a heavy, disappointed thump when I flinched. Hayden's smile dimmed slightly as he gently reclaimed my hand, not quite managing to hide the sad look in his eyes. I took a deep breath and shook my head, fighting off the cold feeling that had started to creep up.

'Come on,' he said quietly.

As Hayden steered me back into camp, I desperately searched for that all-encompassing blissful feeling I'd had earlier. I didn't want to let one meek shadow cast a darkness over an amazing day.

Soon more laughter rang through camp, and the blazing light ahead grew brighter as we approached. After a few more steps, melodic notes reached my ears, and the delicious scent of grilling meat drifted to my nose. My senses realised what was going on before my mind caught up.

Hayden squeezed my hand. 'Happy birthday, Bear,' he murmured gently.

The spectacle amazed me. Every single member of Blackwing seemed to have gathered. A blazing bonfire commanded the centre of attention, and people milled about with plates of food and smiles on their faces. Thousands of twinkling candlelights placed throughout made it look as if stars had fallen from the sky above. Bouquets of wildflowers were placed along the tables, which were laden with food and what I recognised to be Perdita's famous hooch.

'Guys, guys, she's here!' a familiar voice called from somewhere to my left. I looked just in time to see Dax raise a hand clutching a cup in the air. '*Surprise!*'

People turned in our direction and about half shouted a weak chorus of 'surprise' while the other half looked around in confusion. I laughed at the poor coordination of the crowd.

Hayden let out a sigh of relief and an amused chuckle before running his free hand over his face.

'One job, Dax. You had one job,' Hayden laughed as he approached. His steps looked somewhat uncoordinated and his grin was a little sloppy as he came to stand in front of us.

'Yeah, well, I didn't have very clear instructions, mister. "I don't know when we'll be back" doesn't give me much to work with,' he said with an indifferent shrug. He took a long swig from his nearly empty cup. I chuckled. Clearly he'd got the party started a while ago. 'Happy—' he was interrupted by a loud hiccup, which caused him to blink in confusion. 'Happy birthday, Grace!'

'Thank you, Dax,' I said with a grin.

My grin widened even more when we were joined by Leutie, who was also carrying a cup but seemed significantly more in control of herself. She stopped in front of me and reached out slowly, making sure to note my reaction before pulling me into a hug. I was grateful when I didn't flinch and was able to hug her back.

'Happy birthday,' she said kindly, pulling back to grin at me. 'Isn't this amazing?'

'It really is,' I said honestly.

'Hayden planned everything,' Leutie continued. She beamed at Hayden before looking back at me.

'Did he?' I asked, breaking eye contact with Leutie to tip my head back up to Hayden. I found him watching me closely with a calm, adoring look on his face.

'Hey, I helped,' Dax protested, tapping his chest.

'Yeah, helped yourself to the alcohol,' Hayden laughed. 'How many in are you?'

'A fair few, not that it's any of your business,' he said haughtily, though the grin he cracked belied his indignation.

'How about you, Leutie?' I asked curiously, eyeing her drink. I wasn't sure if she'd ever drank before coming to Blackwing.

'She likes it, don't you, babe?' Dax asked excitedly.

'Oh, yeah, it's great. I've had a few,' she said unconvincingly. She took a sip and almost managed to suppress the shudder that ran through her. Her eyes darted to Dax, who grinned at her, before flicking back to mine. When Dax looked away, she took the chance to mouth a few words at me and stuck out her tongue for good measure. '*It's disgusting*.'

I suppressed a laugh and agreed with her.

'Well, that's enough chit-chat,' Dax said unceremoniously. 'Grace, Maisie brought out the big guns with the food, so make sure you eat. There's hooch over there,' he said, pointing across the way. 'And it's extra delicious this time because I got to give Perdita a few words of my own input.'

'Ahh,' I said, again holding off a laugh. That explained

why Leutie was pretending to enjoy it: Dax had helped make it.

'And, of course, dancing. Hayden, you going to man up and take your girl on your own this time or will I have to do everything again?' he continued, poking Hayden in the arm childishly.

'Ha ha,' Hayden said drily, letting a self-deprecating grin break through. 'I think I can handle it myself, thanks.'

'Good to hear, Bossman. See you two later!'

With that, he looped his arm around Leutie's neck, hauling her uncoordinatedly into his side as he steered her away. I saw him murmur into her ear, to which she responded with a burst of laughter. I grinned as they walked away happily.

'Hungry?' Hayden asked. Because of the way he stood with his arm around my shoulders, his face was only a few inches away from mine.

'Starving,' I said with a grin.

Together, we wove through the crowd of people. I was greeted with more 'Happy Birthdays' than I could respond to, and I was touched so many people spared the time for me. It took longer than it should have to finally reach the food, but when we did, it was worth the wait.

I had never seen so much food presented at once. Tables were completely covered with meats, vegetables, fruits, what even looked like bread, and a generous supply of drinks. Hayden and I roamed around the tables, piling more onto our plates than could fit until they were practically overflowing.

'This isn't all for my birthday, is it?' I asked. I felt a mixture of honour and guilt, because surely this food could have lasted the entire camp at least a week or two.

'Of course it is,' Hayden replied.

I had to let go of his hand to steady my plate, so I followed him to an area where tables and chairs had been set up beside where people were dancing to music.

'Hey,' Hayden said, noticing my expression. 'It is for you, but if it makes you feel better, everyone needed something like this. Something good. And we have more food than ever now because of the crops.'

I smiled hesitantly. Maybe it wasn't so bad when he put it like that.

'Okay,' I replied. He smiled at me before pointing his fork at my plate.

'Eat up!'

Together we ate, happily observing the party around us. I was pleased when I spotted Kit and Malin dancing across the way, and even more pleased when I noticed the slight bump in her stomach, evidence of the baby she carried. The food was absolutely delicious, and it wasn't long until my stomach was more than full, but I ate as much as I could so as not to waste anything. Despite my best efforts, I was left with a small portion, but luckily Hayden reached over and finished off my leftovers when he saw me fiddling with my plate.

Hayden pointed out a few hilariously drunk individuals, telling me stories about things they'd done at past parties. I laughed and soaked up the happiness, especially whenever someone from Blackwing stopped by to wish me a happy birthday. Hayden's hand, which had reclaimed mine after we'd finished eating, never stopped playing gently with my fingers. We observed Dax attempting to teach Leutie how to dance properly, even though it appeared like he was the one who needed lessons. Each move he pulled sent Hayden and I into fits of laughter, which added to the overall lightness of my mood.

Finally, our laughter quietened down. After a few

moments of comfortable quiet, Hayden got up and came around to stand in front of me. He extended his hand and gave a slight bow.

'Grace, may I have this dance?' he said in a feigned posh tone.

I let out an uncharacteristic giggle and nodded curtly. 'You may, sir.'

'Ooh, sir,' Hayden repeated, raising an eyebrow and grinning. I placed my hand in his and allowed him to pull me up.

'I don't know if I can dance when I'm this full,' I laughed as he steered me out into the crowd.

'I could just roll you around in the dirt if you like,' he offered in mock sincerity.

'Perfect,' I scoffed, grinning at him.

Gently, he reached for my hands, squeezing them once before trailing his fingers up to my wrist. Slowly, he pulled me closer before lifting my arms and placing them around his neck. I shivered as the moment shifted from light and playful to something more intense, the palpable sizzle appearing out of nowhere. His fingers tickled the backs of my arms, dragging gently across my skin, taking his time until he reached my back. The action continued until he'd traced his fingers down my sides and settled them on my lower back, where he was able to draw me nearer still.

Just like that, in a matter of seconds, he'd practically melted me.

He swayed us gently to the music, but I could hardly hear it for the thumping of my heart and the strange buzzing in my ears.

I felt more alive than I had in a very long time.

'Have you had a good day?' Hayden asked, eyeing me closely.

'The best day,' I replied honestly. My heart felt full of happiness.

Hayden gave me a small, close-lipped smile. 'I'm glad.'

'Thank you for everything, Hayden. It's been so amazing.'

He shook his head instantly, drawing me closer. I felt his lips press into my temple as he held me, still swaying gently in time to the music. 'Don't thank me, love.'

I smiled softly and closed my eyes happily, resting my head against his chest as he held me. I hadn't felt this happy since before everything that had happened, but there was still one thing that could potentially make this day even more incredible, or could ruin everything. I was even more determined, on this day that had been so amazing, to carry out my plan to be with Hayden again.

My words were soft, somewhat scared, yet determined as I spoke only for him.

'Take me home, Hayden.'

Twenty-Nine: Rekindle

Grace

My heart thudded so heavily that it almost drowned out the sound of my words, but I knew he heard them judging by the way his actions halted. He hesitated, the seconds dragging on between us, before he nodded slowly.

'Okay.'

An excited yet nervous rush ran through me as his hands fell from around my waist, wasting no time in grabbing my hand and squeezing it once. Without a word, I allowed Hayden to lead me through the crowd, slipping silently among the happily dancing people. No one seemed to notice as we retreated from the party, slowly putting the noise and activity behind us.

When I glanced up at him, I could see his face set in an intense expression, as if he had many thoughts racing through his mind. I knew Hayden had to be feeling nervous as well, because the last thing he wanted to do was scare or hurt me. He had been reluctant to agree to this at all, and it seemed he remained so now despite leading me home.

When we reached our hut and went inside, I couldn't take the silence much longer.

He moved around the room and lit a single candle on his desk, washing us in its warm glow. I stood tentatively near the edge of the bed while he came to stand in front of me.

Reaching for his hand, I grabbed it and pulled him closer.

'Hayden,' I said slowly.

'Hmm?' he hummed lowly.

'I know you don't want to do this but . . . I do,' I told him. I'd lost track of how many times we'd discussed it now, but I wanted to give him that one final reassurance that this was indeed what I wanted. Not only wanted, but needed.

'I know,' he said softly, raising a hand to brush lightly across my cheek.

'And no matter what happens or how I react, know that I asked for this, and that I love you,' I continued. I bit gently on my lip as anxious nerves twisted tightly at my stomach.

Hayden studied me intently for a few seconds, before sighing heavily.

'I love you, Grace.'

I could feel each gentle, minute movement as he kissed me, careful to fill the gaps of my lips with his own. His pace was slow, tender, and loving. I felt nothing but warmth, as if my body could finally accept kisses without a flashback to that horrible time.

If his kiss was this gentle, I could only imagine how the rest would turn out.

He was careful to keep his hands on my face as his lips parted mine to let his tongue run smoothly along my own – cautious not to push too fast or too far. I could feel the warmth of his body through the thin fabric of his shirt.

Our lips moved in rhythm, causing my body to feel like it was vibrating. I was grateful that no haunting images had pushed forth yet, but I didn't dare believe that they would never come back. Kissing was just the surface of the deep pool we had to plunge into.

I felt him shift us ever so slightly, guiding me so the backs of my legs pushed against our bed. Slowly, his hand left my face to trail cautiously down my neck, over my shoulder, and down my side. He gripped my hip, steadying me as he applied slight pressure. He helped me to lie down, then lay his own body beside mine.

My breath hitched when I felt his hips fall between my legs, though it wasn't in the way I would have liked. The slight pressure he put there made me clamp my eyes shut momentarily as images of unwanted, dirty men flitted through my mind. My lips halted our kiss, which Hayden noticed immediately.

'Grace,' he murmured softly. I sucked in a breath and managed to open my eyes, finding his in the dim light as he hovered over me, feathery light.

'It's just me,' he soothed, holding my gaze.

My heart gave such a heavy thud that I was certain he'd be able to feel it. Slowly, I drew a deep breath and nodded. I reached up to link my arms around his neck and lure him back down, bringing his lips back to mine. Thankfully, the warmth returned as his careful kiss chased away the cold that had started to creep in. I allowed myself to revel in the pressure of his body on mine, feel the heat of his hand as it trailed over my hip and sides. I tried to let down my guard and enjoy everything he was doing, but the tiny nagging refused to completely go away.

But still, I felt no reason to flinch, so I allowed my hands to slide beneath the fabric of Hayden's shirt, pressing them lightly against his lower back. I could feel the warm, solid muscles that flexed with even the tiniest of movements as he hovered over me, still not putting his full weight down. I slowly began to tug his shirt upward.

It was so clear to see how much he loved me just from the way he was looking at me, and that was all I needed to summon the courage to lift his shirt further. Finally, he took over and reached behind to grab the fabric and remove it before tossing it to the floor. I let my hands trail down his now bare skin, feeling every ridge and bump and scar. When my hands reached his hips, I squeezed lightly, at which point he took control once more.

He was still as slow and tender as ever as he tentatively trailed his lips down my neck, moving only a few inches before he'd pause to check for my reaction. When I didn't flinch, he continued. I let out a contented sigh as I felt his warm lips sponge lightly against my skin, accompanied every once in a while by the wet heat of his tongue. Heat was flittering through my body, making my already hazy mind swoon.

Hayden trailed a hand gently down my side before his fingers slipped beneath the hem of my shirt. He let them rest there, lightly brushing his fingertips along my stomach, all while watching for a reaction. When I didn't resist, his hand closed around the fabric, raising a questioning eyebrow at me. I nodded, silently giving him permission.

He gave the smallest of nods in response before shifting his body down so his head was level with my navel. I sucked a breath in surprise when he dipped his lips along my hipbone. What should have felt warm and comforting brought a sudden rush of fear as my eyes clamped shut and my muscles tightened. My breath rattled through my lungs as I tried to fight the feeling, and after a few tense moments, I was brought back by the sound of my name rolling off Hayden's lips.

'Grace,' he murmured softly. He ceased all actions, pausing as he hovered over me. He gave me a sad smile. 'Are you okay?'

'Yeah,' I whispered. 'Keep going.'

He dragged his lips a little higher, pushing my shirt over

my skin a few inches at a time. Over and over again.

I felt like I was on fire, anxious and excited all at once. Finally, we reached the point where I had to prop myself up on my elbows so he could slip my shirt over my head and toss it to the floor next to his.

He kissed me slowly, deeply, lovingly. It was what kept me focused in the moment rather than letting my mind lose control as I felt his fingers twist behind my back, undoing the clasp of my bra, hitching the straps before he shifted to pull them down my shoulders. Gathering my strength, I reached up to pull it away, leaving my chest just as bare as his.

Slowly, he laid me back down so I lay flat on the bed once more, with him. The heat of his naked skin against my own triggered the flash of unfamiliar bodies. My eyes clamped shut again, but somehow I managed to keep kissing him. His tongue slipped against mine one last time before he broke the kiss.

'I love you,' he breathed into my ear. I felt the wet heat as his lips closed around the lobe, tugging lightly before continuing down my throat.

'I love you,' I returned, my voice barely more than a whisper.

He repeated the process in reverse this time, sponging gentle kisses down my neck, across my chest, over the swell of my breasts, and down my stomach before he reached my hips. One last kiss melted into my skin before his eyes flickered up to meet mine, burning into me.

'You are so beautiful, Grace,' he soothed.

I sent him a soft smile that he returned as he trailed a hand up my leg. Chills ran down my spine at his touch, and it was tough to tell if it was a good thing or a bad thing. As long as I held his gaze, nothing managed to break through, even though the simmering level of unease still existed in the pit of my stomach.

When Hayden's fingers reached the band of my shorts, I swallowed nervously. Just as before, he started slowly by dragging them down an inch or so, just enough to allow him to press his lips against my body. I could feel the heat as if it radiated from that spot throughout my entire being. I caught my lip between my teeth as I enjoyed the feeling, grateful I hadn't flinched.

Hayden was ever so careful as he repeated this step, dragging the band a little lower. When his lips pressed to my skin a second time and there was no flinching, his eyes flitted up to mine, silently asking for permission, and again, I nodded. After that, his fingers tugged, slowly bringing down the band of my shorts and underwear, revealing more and more of my skin until he managed to pull them free.

Finally, I was completely bared to him, more vulnerable than I had been in a very long time. I could hardly hear for how loudly my pulse was thudding. My chest rose and fell quickly as I breathed, and my skin felt like it was on fire.

He was everywhere: hand pushing slowly up my thigh, chest resting lightly against my own, lips all over my skin as he dragged little kisses up my stomach, my chest, my neck, and finally my lips as he kissed me once more.

Every single move he made was slow, careful, tentative, but it didn't stop the cold from creeping in. It didn't stop the flash of panic that ripped through me after being so completely exposed. It didn't stop me from flinching when his body shifted to cover mine once more, his weight supported by his elbows on either side of my face.

I sucked in a gasp and broke the kiss, unable to continue as fear took over.

'Grace,' Hayden said quickly, noting my reaction. I felt his hand snake beneath my ear as he cradled my face.

My mind felt fuzzy, as if I heard him speaking from a great distance away rather than just inches. It was like I was stuck in some sort of vortex, where I'd feel his gentle touches one second, only for a cold, unfamiliar hand to fight him off a second later.

'Grace, baby, it's okay,' he murmured urgently.

The fleeting moment of panic was suddenly washed away as I saw his face, felt only his hands on me, his lips on mine. Just as quickly as it had come, it was gone.

'Hayden,' I gasped, struggling for a steady breath.

'Yes, Bear,' he replied, pulling back from our kiss. 'It's just us. No one else.'

In a sudden burst of determination, I reached up and pulled him down to me again, kissing him more steadily than I had all night. He responded and moulded his lips against mine. My hands shifted down his sides and back, feeling the warm, flexed muscles. Bracing myself, I pulled on his hips, bringing his body closer to mine. I sucked in a gasp, but there was no fear. Again, I was relieved.

Slowly, cautiously, he started to move his body. He rocked his hips forward, increasing the pressure between us in the most beautiful way. While I was completely naked, he still wore a pair of athletic shorts, which did a poor job of hiding his arousal. I could feel every bit of the nervous, fearful tension in my body, but it was coupled by something else I'd been so desperately missing: desire.

Everything Hayden had done so far had been intended to ease me into this, to relax me and calm me down in the most careful of ways, and it had worked. Even though there had been a few flinches and fearful moments, I hadn't felt the need to stop. Quite the contrary, actually, as I felt another wave of heat rush through me when his hips shifted between my legs.

I knew he could feel the passion too in the careful control he held over himself so he wouldn't push me too quickly. A soft groan left my throat as Hayden's teeth tugged lightly on my lower lip, drawing it back tantalisingly before releasing it and ducking down to kiss me again. When his hips pushed against mine once more, I couldn't take it any longer.

I sucked in a deep breath before allowing my fingers to slip beneath his shorts, pushing down until I had them lowered a few inches on his hips. His lips caught mine one last time before he paused, pulling back to look at me with slightly wild eyes. He panted, just as I did, and I could practically see the inner battle waging in his mind.

'Hayden,' I breathed, holding his gaze intensely.

'Grace,' he returned, voice low and husky in the heat of the moment.

I opened my mouth to speak but couldn't seem to find words, so I bit down on my lower lip and hesitated. I struggled to catch my breath as the moment stretched out. I could only think of one thing to say.

'Please.'

My heart gave a few heavy thuds against my ribs as I waited, stomach positively rolling with nerves.

'Okay, Bear.'

I smiled nervously; he waited a few more seconds. I felt his hips shift, where he helped me tug down his shorts the rest of the way, leaving him just as naked as I was. When he settled again on top of me, I could feel the weight of him against my centre.

'You're shaking,' Hayden noted softly, a sad expression crossing his face.

I hadn't even noticed. I clenched my hand into a fist and swallowed harshly.

'I'm okay,' I promised. The desire to be with him again outweighed everything. 'I love you.'

'Grace, I love you so much,' he returned easily, brows furrowing intensely over his eyes.

I smiled, pausing a second longer before pulling him back down to me. Our lips connected, and I trailed my hands down his sides again. Steeling every bit of courage I had, I put the slightest amount of pressure on his hips, pulling him towards me. Hayden obliged me by shifting forward. My lips parted reflexively when I felt him push into me, so slowly and gently. I felt a rush of heat as his body connected with mine.

I felt cold, too, as if the hands that had held me down and done so many other horrible things to me were suddenly on my body again. My eyes slammed shut and I sucked a harsh breath between my lips, halting Hayden's kiss immediately.

'Grace, it's okay,' he murmured. I felt his hand land lightly on my face, cradling my cheek. 'Open your eyes, love.'

I forced myself to obey, opening my eyes to see him hovering over me.

'I love you,' he whispered.

'I love you,' I breathed back, desperately clinging to his body with my still shaking hands.

He nodded while speaking, 'You okay?'

I swallowed and nodded again, closing my eyes momentarily before opening them once more. 'Yeah, I'm okay.'

He kissed me for a few seconds before he shifted his hips again, drawing out of me before pushing back in slowly. This time, no haunting flashbacks emerged; there was only the warmth and familiarity of his body with my own.

I was hit with a sudden rush of love for him. I could

feel the fluid way his body started to move, pushing in and out of me ever so slowly. There was a bit of pain, but nothing unbearable. It seemed my body had physically healed for the most part, leaving only the emotional damage behind.

I gasped as Hayden's hand left my face, trailing his fingertips feathery light along my skin, across my shoulder, and down my arm before his hand found mine. His fingers intertwined with mine, though he was careful not to press them into the mattress. All of his weight was supported on the elbow resting by my head, but he was more than strong enough to hold himself up while rolling his body gently over mine.

Hayden sustained the passionate kiss as his body continued to move, pushing slowly, carefully into me as I let my hand trail down to his hip, where I could feel the muscles flex. When I felt him push most deeply yet, I had to let out a gasp to disconnect our lips. I took the opportunity to lift my head enough to pepper light kisses to his neck, just as he had done to me.

'Grace . . .'

The sound of my name rolling off his lips in such a heated tone sent a delightful shiver down my spine, nothing at all like the chilling flashes I'd experienced before.

I could feel my body starting to be undone with things I couldn't control in my helplessness. Hayden was everywhere: his hand in mine, his chest pressed against my own, his hips rocking smoothly between my thighs as he gently showed me just how much he loved me. I could feel his hot breath as it washed over my neck, feel his lips as they puckered against my shoulder, feel the damp sheen that had started to form over his skin as my hand smoothed down his rippling back.

He overwhelmed me in the most magnificently beautiful way possible, exactly as I needed him to.

'I love you, Hayden,' I breathed.

My hands shook as I reached for his face, bringing it back in front of mine. His eyes were practically glowing, and his face was flushed. His hand squeezed mine before he brought it between us, up to his lips so he could press a delicate kiss to my knuckles. All the while, his hips continued to roll, pushing into me and pulling out in a slow, tingle-inducing rhythm. I could already feel the pressure starting to build in my lower abdomen.

'I love you,' he murmured, voice impossibly low and gravelly.

Again, I felt a pleasant shudder run through me at the sound. My back arched in response to his fluid movement, pushing my chest into his and arching my neck. Hayden took advantage and dropped his mouth to my neck, his lips parting over my skin to let his tongue dart out and wet the surface.

'I love you, I love you, I love you,' Hayden continued, words muffled as his lips continuously peppered kisses at my throat. My eyes drifted blissfully shut as I enjoyed the feeling, and I tightened my grip on his hips as I pulled him even closer, earning a low moan.

His pace, which had been tantalisingly slow and gentle before, remained so now, though it was impossible to miss the undercurrent of desire and urgency. He tightened his grip on my hand as he pushed it gently into the mattress, as if he knew now that I wouldn't be frightened by the action. His other hand, which rested somewhere near my head where his elbow supported his weight, tangled in my hair as he dragged his lips back up my neck and across my face.

I could feel every fluid undulation his body made, each

and every tiny action resonating through my skin and into my bones.

My breath quickened as I panted, fighting off the urge to let go as the pressure in my stomach built to an almost unbearable level. Every time he pushed into me, the pressure grew, until I felt like my veins were sizzling.

'Ha-Hayden,' I gasped.

'Yes, baby,' he murmured into my mouth, parting only for a second before diving in to kiss me again. 'Let go.'

My grip on his hand tightened and my back arched off the mattress, breaking our kiss as I sucked in a breath. Hayden gave one last roll of his hips into me, releasing the pressure that had been building from the very start. My high ripped through me like fire through a fuse, sizzling and searing every cell along the way until all of my limbs shook uncontrollably. My muscles tensed as the deliciously incredible feeling spread throughout my body. All the while, Hayden never stopped moving as he pushed me through my orgasm with a steady surge.

Finally, after my body was completely overwhelmed, I collapsed backward, gasping for air as my eyes drifted closed. I could feel the final ripples of my muscles as they recovered, and I could feel Hayden duck to press one last kiss at my throat before his body stilled, muscles clenched tightly and shaking slightly while a low moan pulled from his lips. I recognised the reaction and knew that he, too, had hit his high. My shaky hands lifted to run down his sides, with barely enough strength left to do so. It was all I could do to let the tips of my fingers feather over his skin as he pulled from me and lowered himself, tentatively resting his weight on me as I sighed contentedly.

We lay in silence for a few moments, accompanied only by the quiet pants of our breath and heavy thuds of our hearts.

Both of us were slick with sweat and completely exhausted, as if the devastatingly slow pace of our time together had been taxing in more ways than one. Finally, after a few moments of coming down from our highs, Hayden lifted his head from where it had fallen to my shoulder and kissed me.

When he pulled back, I was overcome with so many positive emotions that I felt certain they were seeping out of my skin. I beamed, making no effort to stop it. Hayden looked surprised at first, then relieved, then, finally, he mirrored my radiant grin as he smiled down at me endearingly. His thumb stroked gently across my cheek as he hovered over me.

'You are so incredible, Grace,' he murmured lowly. 'In every way imaginable.'

'Hayden,' I replied shyly, feeling a slight blush creep up to my cheeks. My heart felt fuller and happier than it had in as long as I could remember, and it was all because of the incredible man above me.

'I mean it,' he returned adamantly. 'You are remarkable, and I am so in love with you.'

Epilogue
Hayden

The roar of my motorcycle's engine rumbled in my ears, the sound resonating through my bones as I drove home. The sun was just beginning to dip behind the horizon at the end of what seemed like a never-ending day. It had been three years since the fighting had ended, yet I still hadn't really managed to adapt to the changes our world was going through.

Things had altered slowly. It had taken over a year before people accepted that it really was the start of a new era, that our times of war and fighting were behind us. Hope had been so sparse for most of our lives that no one fully dared believe in it. Despite our hesitant start, we'd somehow made it three years without any violence. It seemed our world had finally changed for the better, and that people were remembering what a civilisation could be when it wasn't fraught with fear and desperation to survive.

Wind whooshed past my ears as I drove on, eyeing the sprawling fields of crops on either side of me. The crops we'd planted in Blackwing and Whetland had multiplied a hundred times over, growing so large that our fields, once miles apart, had merged into one giant pasture. Food was no longer a rarity, and everyone had more than enough. Because of this, people thrived.

There were more children around in the last three years than I ever remembered seeing, because people no longer feared losing a child to starvation or something more ominous. Kit and Malin's son Xander was growing quickly. It was still so strange to me to see Kit, who was once so hard and cold, as a father. He had changed, softened by a love for his son and the absence of the need to fight. There were still times when he seemed to forget it was okay to relax, as if something from his past would cloud his mind, but the change was impossible to miss, and I was happy for him.

I rode on, enjoying the feel of the wind as it whipped over my skin. The scenery changed again. Fields of corn, wheat, and countless other things disappeared as trees took over. Sunlight flickered as it filtered through the thick branches that were heavy with leaves in the heat of the summer. The path through the trees was so familiar to me that I could have driven through with my eyes shut, as it led to the place I'd spent most of my life.

I slowed as I began to encounter the huts that had been empty for about two years now. I remembered the first day people decided to move back to the city. There had been countless discussions, arguments about the pros and cons, and much debate about whether it was the right thing to do. It took weeks before a small group decided they were going back, but it wasn't long after that before more followed.

In a six-month period, people went from living in huts in separate camps to living in the city. It had been a lot of work to find places suitable for habitation, and work was still being done to this day, but they had succeeded. Renley, Dax, and a few others had managed to fix the power in a small part of the city; each day, they worked to expand the network.

I'd spent the day with Kit, Dax, and Renley as we tried

to organise our plan to clear another block in the city. We'd fallen into a sort of pseudo-government without any actual titles or elections. The leaders from the camps before remained so now, though anyone who felt the need to step up and join us was welcome. Together, we tried to figure out how to best carry on and to improve life. It was stressful work with a lot of conflict, but there was progress. People lived together in harmony, and though things were different from before, it was an improvement over our lives in the camps.

There was no currency and few actual jobs like before, but people worked. Some helped clean up the city, others helped repair buildings. Others, like Dax, worked to maintain and restore electricity. Others still, like Leutie, formed sorts of daycares where children could go while their parents participated in making better lives for everyone. Society, it seemed, had been reborn.

I slowed even more as I approached the familiar sight of my hut, which remained our home even after so many had moved back into the city. It looked the same as it always had, nestled between the trees and shaded by their branches. The wooden walls remained sturdy, and the roof still kept out the rain. Sunlight filtered through the windows, lighting the inside. When I pulled up close enough, I killed the engine and climbed off, setting the brake before pushing my hand through my hair.

It was quiet, just the rustle of leaves in the light breeze and the occasional tweet of a bird. As I reached the door and turned the knob, I was greeted with more silence. It was darker inside the hut than outside, and it took my eyes a moment to adjust as I shut the door and moved to sit on the edge of my bed. Everything was nearly the same as it had been years ago, and the bed made the same soft 'creak' as I lay back on the mattress. I sighed as I tried to shrug off the stress of the day, but it was difficult when I was alone in the silence.

My stomach rumbled, so I pushed myself off the bed and moved to the corner of the hut, where there was a small kitchen. It was one of the few changes that had been made since everyone had moved out of Blackwing. Before, I'd had no need for it because all of my meals were taken in the mess hall. Now, with Maisie in the city, I was responsible for my own meals. I opened the cupboard and pulled out a loaf of bread, a product from our planted crops. I then took some turkey meat from a small fridge I'd found in the city, powered by one of the generators we used to have in the mess hall. With everyone gone from Blackwing, there was no need for it there.

I prepared a sandwich and ate it, leaning against one of the cupboards as I thought. My heart gave a small pang, missing the other person who usually resided in this place. It seemed like it had been forever since I'd last seen her, and I couldn't seem to remember exactly how long it had actually been.

Grace, like everyone else, had a job to do. Her predisposition to anything medical had led to her working as a doctor of sorts in the city. Docc was getting quite old now, his hair nearly completely white as he aged more and more. Grace had officially become his replacement in training, and he worked to prepare her for the day she would take over completely. She was busy and stressed much of the time, but it was clear how much she loved it. Each time she told me about someone she helped or described something she'd learned from Docc, her entire face lit up. It was clear she was doing what she was meant to do, and that made me happy.

It was difficult, though. She worked long hours, and I

would often go days without seeing her. Because jobs were different than before, there were no actual 'work hours'. She worked when people needed help, which was often as our population grew and people put stress on their bodies. It was difficult for me to sacrifice my time with her, because I craved her presence every second of the day. But I had no choice, so I let her go when I needed to and suffered quietly without her.

I had just taken the last bite of my sandwich when a distant noise caught my attention. My muscles stilled as I listened, desperately hoping I hadn't been hearing things. A few moments of silence ticked by and my heart gave a disappointed pang before I heard it again, bringing an excited grin to my lips. In the distance, the rumble of a jeep was coming through the trees. My teeth sank into my lower lip as I tried to bite back my smile, but I failed and instead rushed to the door.

The sound of the engine grew louder as it approached, and I had just pulled the front door open when it came into view. It was the same jeep we'd used on raids for years, still riddled with bullet holes and dents from our various close encounters with death. Sunlight reflected off the windshield, blocking me from seeing who was behind the wheel. My grin split wider on my face as it pulled up next to my motorcycle, and it wasn't until the engine was killed and the door was pushed open that her face finally became clear.

'Grace,' I said in a hushed, happy voice.

A wide, beaming grin spread across her face as soon as she saw me, reflecting my own as I rushed forward. She had barely placed both feet on the ground before my arms wrapped around her, hauling her tightly to my body and lifting her off her feet momentarily. She gripped me closely, winding her arms around my neck as she hugged me back.

'Hayden.'

It felt so good to hold her in my arms again, to feel the warmth of her body against my own, that I could barely separate myself enough from her to pull back and press my lips to hers. The kiss spread warmth through my body, chasing off the lingering feelings of loneliness that had crept in without her.

'I missed you, Bear,' I murmured.

'I missed you, Herc,' she returned. Her hands tangled in my hair, holding me close as she leaned back enough to beam up at me.

'You've been gone way too long,' I told her, still unable to wipe the grin from my lips. Seeing her beautiful face again was more than enough to make me feel giddy inside.

'It's been two days,' she said with a light laugh.

'Feels like longer,' I complained. My hands settled around her waist and I let my thumbs trail lightly over the small of her back as I held her.

'I know,' she agreed. 'I'm sorry—'

I shook my head, stopping her. 'You don't have to be sorry. You're just doing your part. Saving lives.'

She smiled and gave a small shake of her head. 'I don't know about that.'

'You are, Grace. Even though I miss you like crazy, I know it's what you need to do. I'm so proud of you.'

She pulled in a deep breath and gave me a tired, satisfied smile. 'I love you, Hayden.'

I felt warm all over again as her words reached my heart. There was nothing better I could hear. 'And I love you, Grace.'

She let out a soft, happy sigh before retracting her arms. She patted me once on the hip as she started towards our hut. Back inside, I closed the door behind us as I watched her head straight to the bed before falling onto it with an exhausted sigh. The heat of her arm pressed into mine as I lay beside her, both of us on our backs, as we stared up at the familiar ceiling.

'Do you think we'd see each other more if we lived in the city like everyone else?' she asked quietly, her voice pensive. I felt my chest sink.

'Grace—'

'Because I can't help but think we would,' she continued softly.

'It doesn't matter,' I told her. 'I'd rather see you every few days than have you be forced to live there.'

She let out a deep sigh and didn't respond, clearly lost in her own thoughts.

We'd tried to move into the city like everyone else. A few months after people started, we'd packed up our few belongings and found an old apartment one of the work crews had cleaned up. It was our own place, much like the one we had talked about previously and had hardly dared to dream about. It had electricity, running water, even a few of those superfluous things that had so baffled me before. It was what could have been the start of a new life for us, in a new place with new developments.

We didn't last a week in that place.

Living in the city, in the place Grace endured the worst of any nightmare, was difficult for her. She'd gone months without nightmares, months without pausing as a flashback took over her sight for a moment. That first night it all came back, and it happened every night, every day. She'd jump when I touched her, flinch when something moved too suddenly. Her sleep didn't go more than an hour without being woken up in a cold sweat. After five days of watching her suffer, I couldn't take it anymore.

She'd argued when I suggested moving back to Blackwing. She'd said she was fine, that she'd learn to deal with it. She'd said she didn't want to let it get in the way of starting new things or moving on in life. She hadn't wanted to admit defeat or let the haunting nightmares win. I begged her, pleaded with her. I tried to explain that if it wasn't for her sake, it was for mine, because I couldn't bear to see her like that. Finally, after endless arguments and discussions, she conceded. After less than a week of living in the city, we were going back to Blackwing.

Back home.

She was upset with me for a while, but when we were home, the nightmares stopped. The flashbacks stopped. She was herself again, and she could finally admit that I had been right. Blackwing was the place I came to know her, the place I'd fallen in love with her. It was the place she felt safe. It was our home, and we were meant to be there.

'I'm happy here with you. This is our home,' I told her softly. I ducked my head to press my lips lightly into her temple.

Her arm snaked across my stomach before she squeezed me gently. 'It is our home. I love it here.'

'I want to spend the rest of my life with you, Grace. It doesn't matter where we live, as long as I'm with you. It might as well be the place I fell in love with you.'

Grace's fingers tickled lightly along my side as she touched me instinctively. She shifted again, propping herself up on her elbow so she could look down at me. A strand of blonde hair fell into her face, so I reached up and tucked it behind her ear.

'You are so beautiful,' I breathed. Even now, after over four years together, I was still stunned by that.

'Hayden,' she murmured lightly, shaking her head in disbelief. She was always so humble, always so reluctant to accept a compliment.

'You are. And I meant what I said, we could live anywhere and I wouldn't care as long as I have you.'

'You'll always have me,' she told me softly.

'Good,' I replied simply. 'And you know you'll always have me.'

'I know,' she said with a gentle smile. She ducked down and put her lips lightly on mine. I reached up to cradle the side of her face, holding her to me as the warmth of her lips lingered on my own. I was hit with a rush of love for her, still baffled to this day how I had managed to be so lucky.

Our kiss was interrupted by a rumbling that sounded from her stomach. She let out a soft laugh and broke the kiss, shooting me a grin.

'You hungry?' I laughed, grinning at her.

'Starving,' she admitted.

She gave me one last kiss before pushing herself off the bed and moving to the kitchen.

I sat up and watched her with a contented smile on my face, fascinated by her every move. No matter what she did, she captivated me. The simplest of things felt like an amazing adventure with her, and there was never a single second when I didn't want to be with her. She was the greatest thing in my life, my reason for living, and I needed her to know that beyond a shadow of a doubt.

I felt my stomach flip nervously as I stood, moving quietly to one of the cupboards we'd built into the walls. Her back was to me and she didn't seem to notice as I opened a door and reached to the back, feeling behind a large bag of flour for the little box I'd hidden months ago. Finally, just as my heart felt like it was about to beat its way out of my chest, my hand closed around it. I withdrew and closed the door quietly, tucking my fist behind my back.

I had no plan, no words I hoped to say. The truth was, I would have asked her years ago, but it never seemed necessary. My heart belonged to her as hers belonged to me. Our love was so strong that we'd never needed titles, as titles never seemed to do justice to how we felt about each other. Traditional terms never really applied to us, and this was something I didn't think she'd ever expected from me. She was content with us as we were, as was I, but I wanted to give her this. She'd watched happily as her friends had married – Kit and Malin, Dax and Leutie – but never said anything about that being our future. Now, however, I was hoping would be different.

It was that fact – that she'd never brought it up – that made me feel so suddenly nervous that I thought I might pass out. She prepared her food, oblivious to me standing behind her while I tried to stop my heart from exploding. My mouth felt dry, and my hands shook behind my back. It felt like hours that I stood there watching her and trying to drum up the courage to ask, but in reality it was probably only seconds. Finally, I drew one sharp, shaking breath and got ready to ask the most important question of my life.

I stepped forward and looped my arms around her waist, drawing her into my chest as my chin rested on her shoulder. I was sure to keep my hand closed over the small box, hiding it from her as I hugged her.

'Hey, Grace?' I murmured softly.

'Yes?' she returned, completely unaware of what I was about to ask her. I had no long speech to give and nothing poetic to share. Only one burning question waited patiently on my lips.

'Will you marry me?'

She sucked in a sharp gasp as I extended my hand, releasing my grip on her waist momentarily as I flicked the box open. Her jaw quivered as she stared at the ring, a single diamond set on a gold band that had taken me weeks to find. It was clean, simple, elegant, all things I thought were appropriate for Grace.

'Hayden—' she gasped, seemingly unable to process what was happening. I felt my stomach twist anxiously as I unwrapped myself from her, spinning her gently so she faced me. 'What did you . . .'

It took every ounce of courage I possessed to drop to my knee in front of her, holding her gaze as I held the ring up.

'Grace, I asked if you'll marry me,' I repeated, desperately trying to keep my voice even.

Her face was impossible to read as a thousand emotions flittered across it. Finally, she sucked in a breath and blinked, as if she'd found some clarity.

'Yes,' she breathed. Then, a wide, beaming smile split across her face as she spoke again. 'Yes!'

I immediately felt hot tears prick at my eyes as I launched myself off the ground, gripping either side of her face as I kissed her fervently. I couldn't seem to breathe as happiness like I'd never experienced before flooded through me, nearly buckling my knees as I held her to me. I could feel wetness on my hands as tears leaked from Grace's eyes, trailing down my hands that were pressed to her cheeks. When I finally pulled back from the kiss, both of us were beaming so widely that I was certain we'd never stop.

'I love you so much, Bear,' I murmured in ecstatic disbelief.

'I love you, Herc,' she said happily, her voice laced with shocked laughter. I'd never seen her look more beautiful.

She let out a giddy laugh before speaking again. 'I wasn't expecting that.'

I chuckled, unable to control the bliss rolling through me. 'Neither was I, honestly. It just felt right.'

'How long have you had that?' she asked, pointing to the ring I'd hastily set on the counter in my rush to kiss her.

'Oh, yeah,' I murmured, reaching for it quickly to pull it out of the box. It glistened as I reached for her left hand, sliding it onto her ring finger with a shaking hand. Her other hand flew to her mouth as she tried to hide the grin on her face. 'I've had it for months now.'

'Months?!' she repeated, surprised.

'Yeah,' I replied, nodding. 'I honestly could have done this years ago. I just didn't know if it was what you wanted . . . I couldn't stand not asking you any longer though.'

'Of course I want to marry you,' she said quickly, shaking her head. 'I already knew we'd be together forever anyway but . . . I can admit, this is incredible.'

She beamed at me and pulled me to her, kissing me once again. I felt like my whole body was made of light, like she'd brought every cell to life.

'You make me so happy, Grace,' I murmured against her lips, holding her closely as my arms snaked around her waist. Her arms were looped around my neck, intertwining us together as we hovered inches from each other's lips.

'Hayden, you're the best thing to ever happen to me,' she said quietly. 'There's no doubt in my mind.'

I sighed happily, more content and fulfilled than I had ever been. This woman, this strong, courageous, beautiful, smart, amazing woman, had agreed to be my wife. She was so much more than I deserved, but I would never let her go.

'I love you, Herc. I love you so much.'

It was in that moment that I was certain I was the happiest

man to ever exist. We'd faced everything together, and so much more, and we'd made it out stronger, happier, and more in love than ever. Grace was my happiness, and there was no other way to put it.

'And I love you, Bear.'

She was my everything, my happiness, my heart. She was all I needed, and all I would ever want. She was my best friend, my true love, my life.

She was my Bear.

Enjoyed *Annihilation*?

Leave a review online

Keep up to date with all Megan DeVos's latest news at

Twitter: @MeganDcVosBooks

Facebook: facebook/megandevosbooks

Find your next read from Megan DeVos . . .

Don't miss the addictive first instalment in the *Anarchy* series . . .

The world is different now.

There are no rules, no governments, and no guarantees that you'll be saved.

Rival factions have taken over, fighting each other for survival with no loyalty to anyone but their own. At 21, Hayden has taken over Blackwing and is one of the youngest leaders in the area. In protecting his camp from starvation, raids from other factions and the threat of being kidnapped, he has enough to worry about before he finds Grace.

The daughter of the head of the rival camp Greystone, she is slow to trust anyone, much less the leader of those she has been trained to kill.

This is danger. This is chaos. This is anarchy.

Follow on with the second fast-paced chapter in Megan Devos's *Anarchy* series . . .

Don't look back. That's where the danger lies.

With Grace left reeling from choosing between Hayden and her family, she knows she needs to accept her decision.

Meanwhile as the youngest leader of Blackwing, Hayden is coping with the demands placed on him to keep the camp alive. Can he protect his friends from their violent rivals? And should he trust himself to do the right thing?

Demand loyalty. Protect your family. Trust no one.

'*The Hunger Games* meets *The Road*'
MTV

Complete the Anarchy series with the third gripping episode, *Revolution* . . .

You fight, you kill, you steal, you lie . . . or you die.

As war breaks out between Blackwing and Greystone, Grace's allegiance becomes clear. But that doesn't make her task any easier.

Hayden knows that war is coming. That these raids are just the beginning, and there is something else coming for them. But can he save his camp and free himself at the same time?

Welcome to the revolution.

'*Anarchy* is the fast-paced, addictive read we've been searching for since *The Hunger Games*.'
Kelly Anne Blount